Dorothy Grey was born in Birmingham in 1913. She has a Social Science Diploma from Birmingham University, and has since worked in a variety of jobs, from newspaper reporter to personnel assistant. She is active in left wing and feminist politics. *'A Simple Mistake'* is her first novel.

A Simple Mistake

DOROTHY GREY

 Sheba Feminist Publishers

First published in 1985 by Sheba Feminist Publishers
488 Kingsland Rd, London E8

Copyright © Dorothy Grey

British Library Cataloguing in Publication Data
Grey, Dorothy
A simple mistake
I. Title
823'.914[F]   PR6057.R45/

ISBN 0-907179-22-3

Typeset in Times Roman 10/11½ by
Lithosphere Printing Cooperative Ltd (TU)
Printed and bound in Great Britain by
A. Wheaton & Co. Ltd., Exeter

For any woman who finds a part of her own life experience in these pages.

Acknowledgements

I would like to thank Connie Ford for her interest and support – Ann Oosthuizen for her understanding and conscientious editing – the young woman at CUL 1978 who told me that my few words were 'just like my mother' and so encouraged me to create Mabel – and last but by no means least the Women's Liberation Movement, without which I would not have had the confidence even to begin.

CHAPTER ONE

STEPHEN had to cross the town square to reach the spot where Jean had agreed to meet him. The square was not large, and in clear daylight the far side could be seen with ease, but now the whirl of snowflakes concealed the stone portico of the bank where they were to wait. He strained his eyes, but could make out no figure. Illogically, he at once concluded that Jean was not coming. The sharpness of his disappointment surprised and annoyed him. While walking up the road from his home, he had tried to get at the roots of the attraction she held for him. All through Christmas and New Year, her image had kept intruding on his thoughts. He was startled at the hold she had over his imagination.

And yet he had seen her in the student canteen many times without any such impression being made on him. He knew that he was attractive to women and this made him rather choosy as to whom he asked out. He had taken out more than one girl, but towards Jean he had never felt the slightest degree of attraction, until he had come on her unexpectedly at a Festival Hall concert about a month before.

During the first interval, he had walked out onto the balcony and looked over the parapet. Beneath him, the river was faintly rippling, lights from the floodlit buildings on either shore gleaming on its still surface; it was that moment in the evening when everything shows a luminous blue, just before the sky turns dark. Concert-goers were standing about in groups, many with cups of coffee or glasses of wine in their hands; couples were walking up and down, some leaning, like Stephen, over the parapet gazing at the panorama of floodlit London. There was a cool breeze which was refreshing after the crowded concert hall.

Stephen walked until he came to an almost deserted part some way from the opening which led back into the foyer. He liked being away from the chatter. As he was turning to retrace his steps, he noticed a young woman standing alone. She too was admiring the view, resting her chin on her hand, her elbow on the stonework, her head half turned in his direction so that he could see clearly the outline of her features. He was struck by the still expression on her face. He wondered what she was thinking about so earnestly. She was pretty, with the oval curve of her

1

cheek and her brown hair waving untidily in the breeze. Then he thought he knew her. He made up his mind to speak to her. He touched her arm, gently, because she was so far away and he did not want to startle her. All the same, she gave a little jump as she turned.

'Sorry!' he apologised, 'but don't I know you? Aren't you a student at the North London Poly?'

'Yes,' she answered. He could see that she was a bit flustered.

'You were far away,' he said.

'Was I? I'm sorry,' she replied earnestly. She seemed to have taken his words as some sort of reproach. This amused him.

'Coffee?' he asked and fetched her a cup.

'I don't suppose you've noticed me,' he said, easing her into conversation. He meant at the college.

'Oh, yes!' she answered. She had noticed him from the first. Indeed she couldn't avoid it, he had such a decided style. But it had never occurred to her that he might one day notice her. Now she was surprised and embarrassed.

They talked about the music and he gathered something of her tastes, but she was very shy and conversation was halting. He could not help seeing that she was not at her ease with him; she was behaving as if the experience was a new one. He took her empty cup and she thanked him as if he had treated her to an expensive drink.

He thought, 'She's old-fashioned.' She was not at all like the other women he had gone out with. They had treated him with a self-confident frankness. He had liked that. Next to them, her shyness was almost painful.

The interval came to an end and they parted. Their seats were in different parts of the hall. They did not see each other again after the concert.

In the canteen the next day, he looked for her. She was there. He did not go up to her, but he found himself looking to see what she was doing. He noticed that she often sat on her own and although she spoke to other students, she did not appear to have any special friends. He got curious about her. She was clearly different to the women he was used to. Soon he thought of her as vulnerable. And because he himself was a very self-confident young man with a strong sense of his own worth, he felt a pity for her; a pity which gradually replaced his first sense of amusement at her shyness. But he was wrong to think, as he did, that she had

2

no interest in him. With his upright bearing, his dark hair and bright blue eyes, he had an obvious appeal, and his quiet, reserved manner spoke to her of an inward steadiness of purpose.

In her own stealthy way, Jean had long observed him when he was least likely to catch her at it. She looked to see how he behaved towards women and the result pleased her. He was clearly used to treating women courteously. Finally she had summed him up as being, as she put it to herself 'splendidly independent'. That he, in his turn, should find her interesting, or in the least desire her company, never entered her thoughts. So she accepted awkwardly his invitation to meet during the approaching winter vacation. To their mutual surprise, they discovered that they were living within a mile of each other, so it was easy to arrange a date and time. Yet Stephen went off with a sense of pique that she had received his suggestion in such a cool, almost reluctant manner.

Now, when he could not see her under the portico, he was sure that she had not come. But Jean had already seen him. If she did not step onto the pavement at once it was not because of the weather, but because she wanted to savour to its fullest extent and for as long as possible the sense of his walking towards her across the square. She wanted to go on feeling this happiness until the last moment, but when he was fairly close, her impatience got the better of her and she ran out to greet him. Then he saw her for the first time and was glad. There were swirls of snow about her slim figure and he hastened his steps.

'Hello!' she called out in a cheery voice as he came up to where she was standing. She was slightly shorter than he was. She gazed up at him with her large hazel eyes shining from under dark eyebrows, her fresh, pale complexion flushed by the cold, strands of hair which had escaped from under her waterproof cap, wet with flakes of melting snow, her cheeks wet too. In her eyes were a questioning look, as if she were searching him out. His eyes often scrutinised people, but hers were looking quite differently, in a much less detached, summing-up way. And Stephen suddenly had a kind of double vision of her which made him feel that she was far more complex than he had allowed for, and well worth his future study. It was all over in a flash, and immediately after, he thought with a slight shock of surprise, 'She's beautiful!'

He answered her greeting. Now it was his turn to feel awkward, whilst she seemed free of it, but he quickly recovered himself. 'Am I late?' he asked. He was spoiled in that way. He was used to girls accepting his lateness. But Jean did not want to admit it.

'No,' she said, 'I was early.' That at least was true. There was a new ease in her manner. This pleased him. It was because she thought he liked her. 'Are we going for a walk?' she asked, as if she did not know what was done on such occasions.

'If you won't be too cold? We can go into a café.'

'Oh, no!' she answered with an amused laugh. 'I shall be all right.' They decided to walk to the river, to a spot where it bent towards the town park. They were both well wrapped up in duffle coats, trousers, scarves and with thick shoes. They were too young to mind about the cold or the snow. As they walked, they passed an occasional couple, arm in arm, once a woman exercising a dog, but otherwise they were alone.

They walked side by side, without touching, and only now and then glancing at each other. They began to talk about their studies and what future each hoped for; he to teach physics with a Headship in eventual view, she to work her way up to a senior librarianship. They discovered that they were both mature students, having chosen to get some work experience before trying for further qualifications. He had done a variety of jobs, including hospital portering; she had worked in a shop.

'I got on rather well,' she told him. 'My mother wanted me to stay.' Then hastily, lest he should think critically of her mother, 'You see, she was very short of money.' Impulsively, she added, 'But I couldn't! I needed to find things out.'

The moment she had uttered those few words, she was amazed at her frankness. She was altogether unused to speaking of what was important to her. When Stephen had come up to her at the concert, she had taken this as no more than politeness. When he had asked her out, she had thought it might mean more. When he was walking beside her down the lane, she had felt a certainty that it did mean more. This feeling had produced in her a slight sense of intoxication, so that she spoke and acted with less inhibition than was natural to her.

When he did not press her as to what exactly she meant, she was disappointed. She even felt a little cheated. She wanted to tell him of her early desire to study, of her later longing to go to a polytechnic and of how finally she had managed it. She wanted to hear him praise her for her persistence.

4

Instead they talked about how strange it was that they had lived all their lives in the same London suburb and yet had not met until a short while ago.

'Enfield is a large place,' Stephen commented.

'But Enfield Town is small,' Jean said, 'and we both live within twenty minutes' walk.' They talked about the fact that they were the same age, twenty-one, which seemed to them both quite extraordinary.

'You really had noticed me before the concert then?' he asked.

'Yes,' she assured him. His vanity was satisfied.

'Do you know,' he went on, 'you often look pensive – a little sad.'

So he had been studying her. She was pleased. 'Do I?' she queried, in a cautious tone.

'Yes. Quite often.' He was intrigued by this quality in her and by a certain aloofness, as if she were guarding herself, which had showed just then in the sudden caution in her voice. But he did not pursue the matter – her tone had stopped him.

'You look as if you enjoy life,' she told him, breaking the short silence. This was not exactly what she was thinking. She was thinking that he looked as if he could cope successfully with any situation. She herself felt by no means capable of that.

The sky had lightened, but snowflakes were still falling slowly with occasional rapid whirls. They passed the garden of rest, its tall evergreens laden with thick snow, their branches bent downwards, the tips of some almost touching the soil. As they walked the snow underfoot crunched.

'Listen!' Jean said. A bird was singing.

'It's a yellowhammer,' Stephen remarked.

'What kind of bird is that?' she enquired, a little breathless, for they had unconsciously quickened their steps to ward off the cold. He told her that it was a bird with a long drawn out whistle which sounded like a call for bread and cheese. This amused her.

'You know a lot, don't you,' she announced, looking at him. It was his turn to be amused by how little knowledge was sufficient to impress her. Now he looked steadily at her for the first time and that tender, protective feeling which had slowly grown on him as a result of his earlier observations of her, came back. He wanted to put out a hand and touch the light brown hair with its silky sheen showing from underneath her waterproof

5

cap and with his fingers gently caress her cheek, which looked so cool and soft. She seemed to him fragile and he felt a renewed anxiety for her in the damp, the cold and the wet.

'We ought to find shelter,' he said. 'You're getting very wet.'

'Oh, I'm all right,' she answered in a light, off-hand tone.

He took her hand in his, but she did not clasp his fingers. She just let her hand rest in his. He wanted to press her fingers, but some feeling restrained him. In this way they walked on with quickened steps, talking in a desultory manner; afterwards, neither could have said what it was that they had talked about.

He began to ask her questions. He soon discovered that she had a lively mind and was a good listener. She was tremendously enthusiastic about her work. She told him that she hoped to undertake some research when she was settled in a job. Then she asked about his own work; intelligent questions, so that he found himself taking the trouble to explain all that a lay person could understand of his subject. It was clear that her interests were not limited to one area. He agreed fully with the idea that women were entitled to equal opportunities with men and in this sense at least she was very modern, wanting to get on and use her mind and trained abilities to their fullest extent. He was ambitious in exactly the same way.

Suddenly he gave her hand a slight squeeze and after an instant of hesitation spoke to her in a low, soothing tone, words which largely escaped her but to which she gave a confused response. Then he gave her hand a firmer squeeze – and she felt safe. She felt that nothing in the world could do her any harm. She knew this was very irrational, but she could not help herself. And when he let go of her hand and put his arm round her shoulders and touched her left cheek with his fingers, rubbing them gently up and down against her cold skin, she felt a yearning towards him which hurt her.

While she was feeling this, he was feeling, with a vague but powerful emotion, that he wanted to protect her from everything in life that might cause her hurt; protect her as his father had always protected his mother. At that moment he felt very proud of his ability to do this. But he would not dominate her in any way because they were two people who were equals.

He was imagining all this while his arm was around her shoulder and he was stroking the wisps of hair which had escaped from under her cap, feeling her cool, soft cheek and the sense of her body which had come close to his. He was in a kind of trance.

6

Then he woke up and thought, 'What's the matter with me? I hardly know her!' He experienced a sense of annoyance at himself because his emotions were slipping from his usual firm grasp.

At this thought, he withdrew his arm from around her shoulders. They continued walking side by side. Coming to the river and standing on the first of three bridges, they gazed downstream. On one side there was a road and houses; on the other a playing field with rough grass and clumps of small trees at the far end. Except for solitary flakes, the snow had ceased to fall. The sky still held a few patches of grey, but otherwise was a pale, misty blue; a pool of darker blue, in parts almost purple, showed near the horizon; around its edges, rays of the declining sun shone out. The field was covered in thick snow, its whiteness tinged with the blue of the sky; numerous seagulls, grouped in sitting postures, showed the same blue tinge on their white plumage. As they stood on the bridge, the pool of darker blue brightened, its purple slowly melting into a hazy glow; they felt a very faint warmth reaching out to them. The river itself was frozen, the blue light from the sky reflected along its entire surface on which tiny diamond-like slivers of ice lay scattered, their splintered edges gleaming. In the few patches of clear water, ducks were swimming round and round, as if imprisoned. Now and then seagulls would take to the air, flying across the river with a sharp flap of wings, circling back to settle again on the snow; as they passed over the patches of clear water, the shapes of their wings could be seen reflected darkly.

There was a stillness in the air. Everything was a little unreal. They stood for quite ten minutes on the bridge; they had become very silent. Then hand in hand, they continued along the river until they stood on the second bridge, higher up and verging on a small green. It was three o'clock in the afternoon and the sun was low in the sky. Here the river went in a curve till it passed under the main street. Just at that point there was a church with a tall spire. Stephen and Jean crossed the street and found the river bank again. Here the water, under a thin coating of ice, ran between the town park on the left and tall sycamore and plane trees on the right.

They walked slowly on. Many of the tree-trunks were partially covered with moss, green and moist looking; while at the base of some of the boles were large, brown mushroom growths. Pointing to the mushrooms, Stephen commented, 'Those trees are starting to rot.'

They walked on, Jean saying little. He began to wish she were not so silent, always leaving it to him to speak first. But he knew a great deal about plants and trees so he was not at a loss.

'You do know a lot,' she said, repeating her earlier remark. 'I think you like the country.'

'Yes,' he said, 'that's a bonus from my evacuee days. I spent my first five years on a Welsh farm. My mother was with me until I was three, then she went back to be with Dad. He wanted her. Dad used to spend his holidays on the farm and take me long walks.' Suddenly interested, he asked, 'Where did you go?'

'Oh, I didn't go anywhere,' Jean said. 'Mum told the social worker that we'd "all go together" – I mean, if a bomb fell,' she explained.

'Oh!' Stephen said.

They talked a little about those early days in their lives and the post-war years, but all this was far off and everything too different now, including their own feelings, for their interest to remain alive for more than a short while.

They reached the third bridge. There was an opening here, through the railings into the park. They were now at that part of the river where it turned sharply left and ran alongside the golf links, which was not level but tilted gently upward to the horizon. The sun had sunk still further so that the branches of the trees lining the far side of the golf course were standing out dark and bare against the bright background of the sky.

'I know where we can go,' Stephen said, 'It's out of the wind. We can sit there for a while. I've sat often with a book in the fine weather; it's quiet and out of the way.'

They found the seat. It was set back from the path in a small patch of well-trodden grass overhung by a half circle of thick tall bushes so that the snow had not reached it. They sat down. They could see the golf course and the horizon. It was cold, but they were out of the wind. They sat side by side for a few minutes; then he drew her to him and put his arm around her waist. After a little while she laid her head on his shoulder and he laid his head against hers; then she turned towards him and put her hand on his other shoulder and he put his other arm round her body. In this way they sat, warming each other against the cold and for a long while saying nothing.

8

She felt his fingers rub gently against her right cheek.

'How smooth your cheek is,' he said in a low, caressing voice. And everything outside the caress ceased to exist for her and she wanted the feel of his fingers to go on for ever.

At last even their youth felt the chill of an early evening and disentangling themselves with reluctance they got up and walked down the slope, back through the park towards the town entrance, their steps crunching on the hard snow, their breath faintly showing in the chill evening air.

They had not kissed. Stephen felt as though something soft, gentle, and altogether exquisite had entered his life and that he must treat it with the greatest care. He had a strong sense of what was honourable behaviour.

Beneath the trunk of a large sycamore tree, two squirrels were searching in the grass, their noses twitching, bushy tails erect. For only the second time that afternoon they heard a bird chirping.

An Alsation dog suddenly made its appearance, bounding past them. A fat black and white poodle was waddling across the snow alongside its elderly owner, a lady in tweed coat and hat. Every now and then, the poodle bent its head to sniff at the un-accustomed snow.

They reached the children's playground with its bright swings, see-saws and climbing bars. Two young boys were exercising on the bars, twisting their bodies one way and an-other, letting out sharp little cries of pleasure. Close by, a girl with a skipping rope was jumping energetically, counting in a shrill voice.

Jean experienced a strong desire to become physically active. She too wanted to use her limbs, to shout, to jump up and down, to be energetic and forceful. The best she could think of was to scoop up handfuls of snow, flinging the snow vigorously from her, sometimes at Stephen, who stood laughing, sometimes at the trunks of trees, until she became breathless and had to stop. She stood drawing in deep breaths of the keen air. She felt the air cold in her lungs. 'I'd like to go on doing this for a long time.'

'It will make you dizzy,' Stephen said.

'Why?' she asked, surprised.

'Too much oxygen.'

Jean plucked one of the white berries off a small bush at the side of the path, bit it, spat it out and said, 'It's got a floury taste.'

She noticed a few red berries lying scattered about on the snow. As they walked along, she kept noticing items of interest and pointing them out to Stephen. She had suddenly found a tongue.

She noticed a tiny blue crocus in flower, all on its own in the snow.

'You notice little things,' he said. She was pleased.

She scooped up some snow and looked at it. She liked the feel of the damp snow on the palm of her hand and licked at it. It tasted chill and a bit sharp. She worked at it with her tongue, curling it up into a ball.

'Look!' she said, with an air of triumph, holding out her hand for Stephen to see.

He took her hand by the wrist, bent down, and licked the snowball with his tongue. She felt his moist tongue touch the palm of her hand.

The sun had become an orange red and was close to the horizon. Darkness was near. They reached the Library Green. They walked past the empty bench beneath the oak tree. Long, deepening shadows were lying across the grass. The warmth from the passing traffic had melted some of the snow. It was lovely to see the grass again, so green and fresh after so much white.

The Sunday traffic was visible along the main street. They saw the traffic lights turning from red to yellow and then to green and both were thinking the same thought: how strange that ordinary everyday life was carrying on unchanged with people boarding and getting off buses, eating meals, reading news-papers, visiting, washing their cars, all the normal activities.

They both became aware that they were feeling hungry, and they crossed the main street to a Wimpy Bar. The bar was crowded with young people, eating and chatting, dressed in warm clothing, like themselves. After the quiet of the park, this sudden continuous murmur of sound struck them as strange. Young waitresses were bustling to and fro. The serving area was by the entrance and there was a long narrow passage-way between two rows of tables with sofa-like seats. They found a vacant table and sat down opposite each other. Both walls were framed with mirrors so that the bar seemed three times as large as it really was; looking in the mirror, customers could see other customers and what they were doing – talking, leaning foward, lolling, eating, drinking, peering around,

10

or simply sitting, staring ahead. Privacy had been dispensed with.

The bar felt hot and steamy after the cold air outside and there was a delicious smell of sausages and bacon. They consulted the menu and quickly decided on two eggs, two sausages, chips and beans. They left the drink until later and asked for two glasses of water instead.

The waitress brought the two glasses of water, set them down on the table, and went away. A hum of voices seemed to surround them, with occasional bursts of laughter. They drank some of the water, then they looked at each other and smiled, then they both looked away. They glanced about them with an air of enquiry, as if they really were interested in what other people were doing and saying. Then they looked again at each other and again smiled. They began to talk, then fell silent, then started the talk up again, then again fell silent; looked down at the table, looked into the mirror, across the gangway at the couple opposite, and finally took to studying the menu as if for the first time. They were both wondering what else to talk about when luckily the waitress arrived with their order.

'Sorry it's been such a time. We're very busy.'

They looked down at their plates in surprise. On each plate were three eggs and one sausage instead of the two eggs and two sausages which had been ordered. They thought this mistake a huge joke. The plates were very hot and the contents gave off a faint steam. The plates being on the small size, the chips, beans and sausage were piled up like a mountain, on the top of which the three eggs lay overlapping and precariously balanced, ready at any moment to slither down and onto the glass table top. To prevent this from happening seemed to them a problem created entirely for their amusement and in the process of eating they managed thoroughly to enjoy themselves. Every mouthful tasted deliciously flavoursome. The sausages oozed fat, were round and soft; Jean touched hers with her finger, putting the finger to her mouth and sucking at the grease.

'Oh! It's hot!' she exclaimed, laughing. She had entirely lost her shyness and was full of spontaneous movements.

When they came to order two cups of tea they were filled with hope that two cups of coffee might make their appearance instead. They were disappointed when this did not happen. Every tiny incident that it was in the least possible to find amusing, they found amusing; and they were amused by quite a few that were not funny at all. They both felt warm and full inside with a careless happiness that made them gay, as if nothing serious existed, or could possibly exist anywhere in the world.

On sitting down, Jean had untied her cap, taken it off along with her coat, and given a shake to her head so that her hair had responded with little dancing movements. Now she gave her head another shake and some of the waves fell across her high forehead. Her cheeks had gone rosy and her hazel eyes were shining.

The tea was very hot and they sipped at it slowly. They lingered on between silence and talk. For the first time Stephen was finding himself diffident with a girl. He felt shy – this was a new sensation and he was not able to overcome it. He felt sorry for women because they had not had the luck to be born men and this made him kind to them and at the same time at his ease. Now he was not at his ease; he felt insufficient, although in what way he could not have said.

Jean, who had never felt herself in command of any situation, only felt less so on this occasion. She very much wanted to sit and look at Stephen, taking inward note of his features, his expressions, his build, everything about him, but this was impossible since she could not look at him without also speaking. Evidently Stephen felt the same need for now and then their eyes met unexpectedly and then they both dropped their gaze as if caught out in a secret act.

When Stephen came to pay the bill, Jean handed him her half of the amount.

'You don't need; it's not a lot and I'm not short.'

'I want to,' she replied in a firm voice. He hesitated, but seeing the determined look on her face, he took the money without further protest.

Later, Stephen said, 'I'll see you home.'

'She smiled at him. 'I don't need seeing home.' Adding 'I can take care of myself.' And she gave a little laugh – that little, light laugh which he had come to expect from her, almost to wait for. He was uneasy at her going off alone at night, but there was a decisive note in her voice with which he felt he could not argue. He had found out that she could be stubborn.

Reluctantly, he said, 'Well, I suppose we'd better say good-bye then.' He wanted to kiss her, but did not, partly because he could not find the courage and partly because he could not decide whether it was a fair thing to do. Instead he made an attempt at a joke.

'I can't argue with you,' he said in a light tone. 'It's your determined chin!'

'Have I a determined chin?' she asked laughing. He nodded. It pleased her that he was interested in her character and looks.

They stood on the pavement, still hesitating. Finally, Stephen said, 'I'll see you in the canteen then.' In this not very satisfactory manner, they parted.

After a short walk, Jean reached her home; a terraced house with a well-kept front garden, clean bright blue curtains at the bow window, a whitened doorstep, the door knocker old-fashioned and well polished, but the brickwork of the house was in poor condition and the window ledges showed bare, blistered wood. Jean took out her door key and put it in the lock. She let herself into the unlit hall and stood for a few moments in the dark, listening. No sounds came. Her parents were in bed. She went along the dim passage to the small living room at the far end. She opened the door and switched on the light. The fingers of the clock on the mantlepiece showed shortly before eleven. Her eyes fell on a pair of men's brown shoes leaning against the fender, covered in dry soil, and on the table a dirty cup and plate. Her brother had evidently returned from his weekend camping. Why he should choose to camp at such an inhospitable time of year, she was never able to understand. Now she took up the cup and plate, carried them into the kitchen and washed them. One job less for her mother in the morning.

She unlocked the back door and stepped outside, urged on by a sudden desire to get away from the atmosphere of home. The sky was very distant, clear and starry, the snow on the trees and grass sending out a soft gleam. Everything was still. The garden was the usual size for a terraced house. There was a small lawn, with flower beds; to one side were loganberry and gooseberry bushes, planted years ago by her father, but long since tended only by her mother. An apple tree stood against the far wall; a wall of old bricks richly stained by the weather. The air was crisp. Jean breathed in deeply and felt the air pass into her lungs, cold and clean. Just as in the park, so again now, she felt a need to be active. She bent down, gathering up a handful of snow and sniffing at it. A few flakes flew up into her nostrils, tickling her nose and making her laugh. She wished there was someone with whom she could be merry. She rolled the snow into a hard ball and threw it from her. It vanished into the dark and a second later she heard its soft plop as it landed. She walked up and down the narrow path at the side of the fence adjoining the next-door garden. The sight of her footsteps in the snow amused her. After a few turns she went indoors.

She locked the back door, switched off the light and went very quietly upstairs. She hesitated an instant outside her parents' room. No sound came from within. Opening her own door, she went inside, then listened again for sounds through the wall. Hearing none, she gave a faint sigh of relief.

Without taking off her coat, she opened the window, which looked out on the garden. All she could see was snow and stars and the shadows of trees. She leaned her elbows on the window ledge and closed her eyes. Stephen's face rose vividly before her. She did not know whether she liked him a lot, or not at all, but she did know that he was somebody splendid, unlike any other person whom she had ever known. She felt proud because he had chosen to go out with her. Yet, when she thought about the afternoon, everything that had happened seemed so unlikely that she doubted its reality and his very existence became tentative and unreal to her.

Although she did not know it, at the same moment that she was thinking this, Stephen himself was leaning on the window ledge of his bedroom, doing exactly the same: thinking about her. He had reached his home in the quiet tree-lined street of well-kept, semi-detached houses and gone indoors; into the well-lighted hall and then into the sitting room, with the standard lamp still alight in one corner to welcome him when he came in, and on an occasional table next to an armchair, a tray with a tin of biscuits and a glass of milk which his mother had left out for him. He knew that she and his father would now be in bed and probably asleep. They retired early. He left the tray untouched, turned out all the lights and went quietly upstairs to bed. He sat on the bed, thinking about Jean; thinking about the impression she had made on him as of someone extraordinarily timid and yet at the same time extraordinarily determined, with a kind of vulnerable stubbornness.

He got up and opened the window. He leaned his elbows on the sill and gazed out at the dark garden below and listened to the stillness. He imagined that he could see the creamy white petals and smell the delicate scent of the syringa which always bloomed in the late spring, filling the garden with perfume at evening, which was strange because it was winter and its bare branches were all covered in snow.

CHAPTER TWO

CARRYING her suitcase downstairs, Jean heard her mother call, 'Is that you, Jean? Come and give me a hand.'

She went into the small living room. Her mother was on her knees at the side of an old-fashioned armchair, tugging at the corners of a loose cover which she had washed and was now trying to put back on. She was a short, wiry woman, with dyed reddish-brown hair and a sallow complexion. Her pinched features made her look older than her forty-one years. Tiredness often made her irritable.

'I don't know why you have to keep going out! ' she said sharply, as Jean helped her fit the cover. 'You spend half your time traipsing about.'

'I'm going to see Rita. You remember Rita?'

'Of course I remember her. She used to come here often enough when you were both at school. She ate like a horse – all my cakes!' She went on in an indignant tone, 'We haven't seen a sight of her since she went to the university. Why you want to keep up with her I can't understand.'

Jean knew that her mother resented the fact that Rita never came to visit. She herself thought that her friend ought not to forget the past so easily, but Rita did not live locally now and they were no longer so close; they were held together mainly by childhood memories. The intervals between their meetings had grown longer and longer, Rita now having new friends from the professional classes. Perhaps this latter fact had had an effect on her; Jean did not know, but she thought the neglect due more to thoughtlessness than snobbery. Now all she said was: 'She wrote asking me for the weekend. I don't see why I should break with her.'

'The more fool you! That girl uses people! But then, of course we're not good enough. Although why she thinks so, I'm sure I don't know. Her mother is only a dressmaker – and as for her father, well, nobody knows who he is.'

This was not strictly true. It was well-known in the neighbourhood that Rita's mother had had a romance with a soldier during the war and that Rita was the result. Because of this, Jean's mother took the attitude that her own family was on a higher social and moral plane even though Rita's mother had shown herself capable of weathering the storm, providing a good living for herself and a good education for her daughter out of the proceeds of her dressmaking. She did not marry, although she had more than one opportunity; she liked her independence. She was an ambitious woman and when she discovered that her daughter had academic ability she became enormously proud of her and determined that she should make a showing in life. When her daughter was awarded a scholarship, she let all the neighbours know and boasted about it so often and so much that she made herself unpopular, but this did not trouble her. She had handed on many of her own traits to her daughter with the result that they did not get on all that well.

All the while that they were fitting on the chair cover, Jean's mother went on grumbling about Rita; Rita's mother always had been stuck up. 'Got her head turned altogether when her daughter went to that university.'

The chair cover was finally in place, the creases smoothed out.

'You look tired, Mother,' Jean said. 'Why don't you take a lie down?' Her mother's tiredness was nothing new, but it always saddened Jean to see it.

'If I lay down whenever I was tired,' her mother retorted, 'I'd spend all my life lying down.'

'You're supposed to be convalescing,' Jean demurred. Her mother had only recently come out of hospital after a hysterectomy operation.

'Tell that to your father! He never wanted me to have it done in the first place. He said he'd push it back up for me.'

Jean flushed. 'You shouldn't let Dad speak to you like that,' she said. Her mother's words made her feel sick.

'Don't be so daft! How can I stop him? He does what he wants.' She added, 'You don't know.' But Jean did know. She knew that her father often came in the worse for drink, that he sometimes slapped or hit her mother, that he got abusive if she tried to deny him what he called 'his rights'. She knew this

16

because she could hear him shouting at her mother when they were in bed.

When she was in her early teens, her mother had said to her, not bitterly, but with a quiet resignation, 'Men don't know they're born! Women are ruled by the womb – that's our lot.' It was only when Jean went to the polytechnic that she saw men behaving differently towards women and women appearing to treat men as in no way superior. This made a great impression on her. Besides which, she was an avid reader. She read Olive Schreiner's *The Story of an African Farm* in one long night-sitting, unable to put the book down. She lived the struggles of H.G. Wells' heroine, Ann Veronica. She learned about famous women of the nineteenth century and the suffragettes who followed them. She became utterly absorbed in her new knowledge and tried to interest her mother in all she was finding out about women's lives, so different from what she had been brought up to accept as normal; but her mother took her words in a personal way. She thought her daughter was looking down on the manner in which she lived her life and treating her as ignorant.

'You're still in nappies!' she told her resentfully, adding harshly, 'You want to learn from your brother. He's getting on nicely without all this deep reading.' She was more at her ease with Dick, who had left school at fifteen to take up an electrical apprenticeship. She had always preferred her son to her daughter in spite of the fact that Jean was the one who had tried to intervene on her side when there was a row; Dick had soon given it up and got himself out of the way.

'You silly bitch... You silly cow,' she would hear her father saying and she would want to protest, but when she had protested, the result had been merely a furious rebuke from her mother, 'Don't you interfere, my girl! I can manage my own life.' She had learnt to keep quiet.

Now she said, 'I've got Dick a pair of motorcycle gloves for his birthday, Mum. What have you got?' Dick would be eighteen in three days.

'I'm making him some special cakes, little cream ones – you know what a sweet tooth he is – and I'm paying for him to have a night out with a pal, in London. That will cost me a fine penny!' From the tone of her voice, Jean knew that her mother did not really mind. Although she felt at times a natural resentment at her mother's obvious preference for her brother, she did not hold it against him; she felt for him a genuine, if sometimes exasperated, affection.

Before going out, she wanted to say something kind to her mother, but she could not think what to say. While she stood hesitating, her mother said, in an irritated voice, 'Well! Go on then. Get off! Only don't give *my* love to Rita.' Jean turned and left the room.

Outside the house, she found that nothing could keep her unhappy for long. It was almost a week now since she had been with Stephen in the park. Next week the new term would start and she would see him again. The snow had melted: it was one of those mild January days which often follow on a period of cold; bright and cool, with a pale sky and wintry sun. She did not mind the length of the journey to Ruislip, where Rita now lived.

Rita had written from a new address, 'Richard and I got married some months ago. Like me, he's got a degree and is working with a firm of accountants; we've bought a house here, before mortgages get even more expensive. You'll be wondering about Derek. He wanted to marry me, but I gave him up. He wouldn't be right for the kind of friends I want to make.' She would tell Jean more when they saw each other; if Jean could stay the weekend, she would see Richard for herself. Jean had written back the same day; she could stay, but she wanted to be back on the Monday to greet her brother on his eighteenth birthday. She could not make head or tail of the words, 'He wouldn't be right for the kind of friends I want to make.' Hadn't Rita been in love then, all the years she and Derek had been together?

The two friends had started off living next door to each other. When the girls were in their early teens, Rita's mother had moved some streets away, but by then playing together and going about together had grown into an established habit, which continued into their late teens and beyond. When, at fifteen, Rita started going out with her first firm boyfriend, she had roped Jean in for a cover from the neighbours while her mother was out of the house; she and Derek upstairs, Jean downstairs. Jean had found this arrangement rather boring, but Rita was her best friend and she liked Derek so she did not complain. Derek was twelve years older than Rita, tall, pleasant-looking, and with an affable manner. He worked as a skilled mechanic in a local firm and they had met at a dance hall. But Rita did not seem too young for him; she was very sexually mature for her years.

18

This general maturity put her ahead of Jean. In spite of being one year younger, she had started at university while Jean was still in her final school year. Since then, she had worked as a personnel officer in an engineering firm. Her relationship with Derek had continued and Jean had taken it for spoken that eventually they would marry.

At Ruislip, she went out of the station and looked about her for the green Morris car which Rita had told her she would be driving. After a moment she saw her friend waving to her and ran to the car.

'You look well,' Rita commented, giving her friend one of her quick, shrewd glances before driving off.

'So do you.'

'Oh, me! I'm always well.'

Jean knew the truth of this remark. People who met Rita always remembered her by her energy, which seemed never to tire and by her voice, which had a raspy edge to it.

'Sorry! I can't talk until we're out of this traffic.'

Jean stole a glance at her friend. Rita looked the same as ever in spite of what would have been, for Jean, a traumatic experience. She thought of Rita's affair with Derek as an affair of the heart. Rita was her usual plump self, with plain features and dark hair; very vivacious and sexually attractive, so that her lack of fine points seemed not to matter.

Jean had admired Rita for her energy and quick wit almost from the start of their relationship. (She tended to underestimate her own intelligence.) They passed a line of big, old houses, with large front gardens, then drove through streets lined with modern, semi-detached houses; finally Rita stopped the car outside one such house, newly painted, with white window frames and a pale yellow front door. There was a small, well-planted front garden.

'Our pad!' Rita announced, in a tone of robust satisfaction.

It was a very pleasant road. Rita put the car in the side garage and they went indoors.

'I'll make us coffee,' Rita said. 'Take a look round.' She went off into the kitchen, leaving Jean in the front room.

The front room ran the whole length of the house, with French windows looking out onto the garden. The room was very light, with a plain grey fitted carpet and modern furniture. Jean undid the window latch and stepped out into the garden. There was a shed to one side, a lawn, some evergreen bushes with brightly coloured leaves, and a brick wall at the far end with trees showing on the other side. Jean stepped back into the room and took a look out of the other window at the road. She thought it would be pleasant to live in such a house in such a road. While she was thinking this, Rita called from the kitchen, 'The bicycle shed is coming down. We're going to make a sand pit for the children.' Jean wondered what children. Rita came into the room with a tray and the coffee. As if in answer to Jean's unspoken query, she added, laughingly, 'The children we haven't got!' They sat down.

'I can't remember if you take sugar – help yourself to biscuits.' Rita produced a tin of biscuits from the sideboard. In voice and manner, she was her usual brisk, energetic self. She began to give Jean her news.

She had first met Richard during her final year at university. He was an only child and his parents lived on the south coast. His father owned a small business. They had been ambitious for Richard, but had never put any pressure on him to adopt one way of earning a living rather than another; although, as time went on, they had come to realise that he was unlikely to take over the business, more likely to enter one of the professions. This was a disappointment to his father, but he had accepted his son's preference with a good grace. He was now apprenticed to a firm of accountants in central London. It was not a bad journey; tubes were frequent. Why had they chosen to live at Ruislip? Well, they liked a less built-up place and professional people as neighbours. Also there were good, private nursery schools. Last, but by no means least, there was a new estate, the houses just up for sale, and within their means. Yes, certainly, she was keeping on with her job. She enjoyed it. And Richard would not be earning sufficient for quite a while. There was the mortgage. They both wanted children.

'We think we'll be glad we've got children when we're fifty,' Rita said.

'You do look ahead,' Jean said, faintly protesting at such a large measure of calculation.

'You have to – it's only sensible,' Rita answered. She had no intention of pacing out her mother's destiny.

There was a pause, then Rita said, 'I suppose you're wondering about Derek?' Jean admitted she had been. 'I couldn't understand what you meant by his not being right for your friends,' she said.

'For the kind of friends I want to make,' Rita corrected her.

'Weren't you in love then?'

Rita wished Jean was not quite so old-fashioned. 'Depends what you mean by love,' she answered. 'I was very fond of him. I still am. But I don't want to marry him.'

'Why not?' Jean asked.

'For lots of reasons! To begin with, as I said, he wouldn't feel at home with the kind of friends I hope to make – he's simply not had that standard of education. Then he's twelve years older than myself, which is too much. He'll be fifty when I'm only thirty-eight. Finally, to be brutal – he's got no money! I need money if I'm to pay for a home help; if I'm not to be tied. In our society, women have to buy their way out of domestic slavery – you know what I mean, chores and meals every day, kids all the time. I don't want to finish up that way – without energy for anything else.'

'I can't imagine you without energy,' Jean retorted, smiling.

'I'd end up drained. No! Money is the only escape route.'

'I can see that,' Jean agreed. What she could not see was how it was possible to go with a man for some seven years and then simply say goodbye as if the relationship had meant nothing at all. Hesitantly, she suggested this to Rita.

'Because you enjoy sex with a man doesn't mean that you necessarily want to spend the rest of your life with him,' Rita said. She felt she was talking to someone who could only under-stand if things were put very simply. 'Derek and I were suited sexually. We had a great time together. I shall always be fond of him. He's sorry about it, but he's not broken-hearted. He'll certainly find someone else.' Jean's scarcely concealed dis-approval made her smile inwardly. She found her friend's atti-tude amusingly naive.

'You ought to have a man, Jean. Stop being a virgin!'

'How do you know I haven't?'

'Oh, well!'

This remark annoyed Jean. She was vexed that Rita should take her virginity so for granted. Did it show then to that extent? She was relieved when Rita did not go on asking personal questions; even though she knew her friend was no gossip and could be trusted with a confidence she had a disinclination to mention Stephen.

'I'll show you over the house,' Rita said, gathering up the plates and empty cups, stacking them on the tray, and depositing the lot on the kitchen draining board. As she was leading the way upstairs, she said over her shoulder, 'If you ever want any advice, you know you can come to me. I've had experiences which might be useful.' She did not elaborate. She did not believe in forcing a confidence.

They went over the house. The three bedrooms were light and modern; the third, smaller bedroom was in use as storage for many books stacked up in rows on the floor. Jean expressed her delight at the sight of these.

'Ah, of course! You're a bookworm like Richard,' Rita commented. 'He can sit and read for hours, like you. I need to be more active.' She left Jean to leaf through some of the books while she went downstairs to put out the lunch which was already prepared. In a little while, she called Jean. She had set out a salad lunch on a pull-out kitchen table. She was stirring vigorously at creamed sugar, eggs and flour, in a plastic bowl. 'Richard likes what he calls his "pud" ', she informed Jean. 'When he comes in, he asks, 'What's for pud?' as if that's all he's going to get!' She put the bowl on a side table and sat down with Jean. Jean thought how at ease Rita seemed in the kitchen; as much in her element as when Jean had visited her in her study at the university and found her among her books. While they were eating, Rita gave Jean an outline of her active interests; long walks, photography and musical appreciation classes. She also found time to go on marches for nuclear disarmament, and against apartheid. She could not be blamed for talking about herself most of the time since Jean was more than usually silent. Rita tried more than once to draw her out without success. She stopped herself from making the pointed remark, 'Are you in love?' But she thought it.

At one point Jean did interrupt to say, 'I couldn't diffuse my energies in the way you do! I haven't the temperament. I need to concentrate for a lengthy period on one thing.' That Rita could so successfully do otherwise formed a large part of her admiration for her friend.

Rita gave a laugh. 'In that case,' she said, 'You'd better make very sure you marry a man with a great deal of money!'

After they had stacked away the dirty dishes in the washing-up machine, they went for a walk. The January sun was turning a faint red, the sky hazy. There was a light, cool breeze, making walking pleasurable. They passed a private nursery school, Rita commenting that it had a good reputation. She added that the

22

district was a nice one for children to grow up in – healthy, with a Common close by, and plenty of play spaces.

'It's a lot different from where I grew up,' Rita said, forgetting that Jean still lived there. But she had not meant it in a snobby way, merely as a statement of fact. She never tried to hide her origins.

They got back in time for a leisured cup of tea. The dinner had started to cook itself in the oven. Jean was rather fascinated by the cooker clock; she had never seen that kind of gadget before. But she did not envy Rita. She was living too much in the present for that.

After tea, Rita brought out a book of snapshots. Jean was surprised to come across Rita and Derek holding hands and smiling at each other. They looked very happy. She stared at the snap.

'Do you keep these then?' she asked, surprised. 'Won't Richard come across them?'

'He's seen them.'

'Isn't he jealous?'

'Don't be silly! That's a very old-fashioned attitude.'

Jean was surprised to learn that jealousy was old-fashioned. It was her turn now to be secretly amused.

The dinner in the oven was cooked, the pudding had risen and been transferred to a hot plate; between them, the table in the living room was quickly prepared for the evening meal. Rita put out glasses and a bottle of red wine.

'We don't make a fuss with the wine,' she told Jean. 'We just drink it.'

About six o'clock, Richard came in. Jean heard him go into the kitchen and say, 'Hello, darling.' She thought he was probably kissing her. So they must be fond of each other. Then he came into the room and she got up to take the hand which was extended to her with a cheerful greeting.

'Happy to meet you, Jean! I've heard a lot about you from Rita.' The greeting was just a little condescending. He had long fingers with a firm grasp. She winced.

They sat down and began to chat. To her surprise, Jean quickly felt at ease with him. He was a tall, thin, muscular young man of about twenty-four years of age and had come into the room with a stride rather than a walk. He liked to spend as much of his spare time as possible out of doors so that his complexion wore a healthy tan. Jean guessed that his relationship with his wife was partly a business one, which was not to say it lacked genuine feeling. Jean felt a pang of regret for Derek, but thought that probably Rita and Richard were better suited.

The dinner was mutton with roast potatoes, carrots, and small, round white onions in a creamy sauce which Rita had made at the last moment. There was also cranberry sauce and mint. Richard poured out generous amounts of the red wine. Afterwards came apple pie. When they were relaxing over black coffee, Richard said, 'You remember the chap I mentioned to you yesterday, darling? Well, I'd like to invite him and his wife to dinner. They might come in useful.'

'That's all right,' Rita said, sipping her coffee, 'I'll make something special.'

'Well, try and make the something special taste better than that apple pie,' Richard said, in a businesslike tone and as if he were in the office. 'It wasn't up to your usual.'

'No, it wasn't,' Rita agreed, adding, 'I wondered if you'd comment! Don't worry! I'll be careful.' She said all this in a light-hearted way, not in the least put out by her husband's criticism. Jean had never seen a married couple at home apart from her own parents. Their relationship intrigued her. If she ever got married, was this how she and her husband would act towards each other then – mildly sparring, friendly, yet casual?

The dirty plates were soon disposed of inside the washing-up machine. The rest of the evening was spent chatting, listening to records, and relaxing. Jean found she was liking Richard. If she did not compare him to Stephen, it was because she thought Stephen quite beyond ordinary comparisons.

Sunday was less mild, but still sunny. They ate a cold lunch and then walked to the Common. Most of the time Richard strode on a few paces ahead, rather like a dog on a very long lead, Jean thought. Later they persuaded Jean to stay another night; Rita would see her off the next day. Richard would be away early in the morning, so he said his goodbye last thing at night, inviting Jean to come again; an invitation which she felt was sincere. On Monday, after an early lunch, Rita drove Jean to the tube. Promising to keep in touch, she left Jean to find her own way onto the platform.

Once in the train, Jean found her thoughts returning to her weekend visit in an attempt to sum up her impressions. She liked Richard, but not as much as she had liked Derek; she thought him calculating. Still, she admired him and considered him and Rita well-suited. She did not care for the idea of asking people to dinner because at some future date they might come in useful and she wondered if all professional people were like that. She did not really understand how Rita could abandon Derek with such apparent ease and for reasons which seemed to her inadequate.

She arrived back home about five o'clock and went upstairs to take off her things and deposit her suitcase. Having done this, she tapped on her brother's door. She waited for his usual cheery, 'Come in!' Instead Dick opened the door a little way and looked out with an air of caution, as if on his guard.

'Oh! It's you.' He stepped to one side to let his sister enter, then shut the door quickly behind her.

She had expected to see him getting ready for his evening out, but instead he seemed to be putting vests and trousers into a suitcase, as if he were intending to go on a journey.

'Happy eighteenth birthday!' Jean said warmly, adding, 'And all the best, Dick.'

'Thanks! Oh, and thanks for the gloves! I was really chuffed with them.'

'What time are you going out?' she asked. 'To London, I mean. Mum told me she was treating you.'

'Oh, I'm not,' he answered, putting on a casual tone, 'I don't mean to waste the money that way.'

Jean was a bit nonplussed and looked around the room for a clue as to the meaning of all this activity.

'Does it feel good to be a year older?' she asked, smiling.

He grinned back at her, with a faintly smug air. Then said, 'Now I'm eighteen, I'm off!'

Jean sat down on a chair by the window and looked at him. His fair-complexioned face, with its few permanent freckles wore its usual pleasant expression, his light brown hair and hazel eyes marking him out as her brother. He was wearing an unzipped blue anorak and jeans with brown suede shoes. His hair was combed straight and shone from a recent washing. When he spoke, his voice was mild in tone; there was a slight hesitancy now and then in his speech, just short of a stammer. He looked what he was – a very ordinary, pleasant sort of lad, easy-going and quite devoid of malice.

Seeing his sister sitting gazing at him in silence, Dick was satisfied with the impression he was making. 'I'm going to live in a commune,' he said, in a boastful tone. This announcement did not at all result in the impression which he had confidently anticipated. Instead, to his chagrin, Jean burst out laughing.

'What's so funny?' he asked, piqued. 'Haven't you heard of communes?' He tried to put on a sarcastic tone, but it did not come off.

She went on laughing. 'Of course I have! That's why it's so funny!' She stopped laughing. 'You never even wash up a cup and saucer! How are you going to like looking after yourself and others as well?'

'Home's different,' he retorted loftily. 'You expect to be waited on at home.'

'That's nice for Mum,' Jean answered, a little bitterly. 'What does Mum think, anyway?'

'I haven't told her. I don't mean to. She'll only create and you know how I hate rows. You can tell her after I'm gone.'

Jean was struck dumb by this lack of feeling. Sensing her silent reproach, he had sufficient conscience to blush. In a slightly ashamed voice, he admitted, 'I know I ought to stay and tell her myself, but she'll go on so. I hate Dad for the way he treats Mum, but I can't help despising Mum for the way she submits to him. You can laugh at my choosing to go into a commune if you like, but I've had my whack of the other.' He hesitated a moment, then went on in a more serious tone, 'I know you're the clever one in the family, but I can think too, you know.' There was a long pause, then he continued, 'It may surprise you, but I've been living in a commune at odd week-ends for some months when you all thought I was camping. I like it! It's a much better way to live. Nobody dictates, nobody has power over anyone else.' He repeated with emphasis, 'I like it a lot!' He really meant it.

'About my being clever,' Jean protested, 'It's simply not true! Mum keeps going on about it. I wish you'd both stop. I hate it!'

Not listening, he said, 'I'm going in with a girl. She told me all about communes. She thinks it will give us a much better start.'

Light began to dawn on Jean. She could believe that her brother was sincere in what he had said about power. He had plenty of reasons to be familiar with its drawbacks. But somebody had to introduce him to the idea of a commune. He would never have come to it on his own.

'What's she like?' she asked.

He began to tell her about Betty, where they had met, how long they had known each other, and what their plans were for the future. He could see that at last she was impressed and this pleased him.

'You've really thought it out!'

'Yes.' He seized the opportunity. 'You're always spouting poetry...'

'I'm not!' she interrupted him. He took no notice.

'Well, there's a poem I'm very taken with,' he went on. 'Betty gave it me to read. It's Japanese. I learnt it by heart. Would you like to hear it? It's exactly how I feel.'

If it was how he felt, she did want to hear it. He recited the lines slowly, emphasising each word.

> 'I may be silent, but
> I'm thinking.
> I may not talk, but
> Don't mistake me for a wall.'

He finished, 'The poem's called *Silent, but...*' He was thinking naively, 'That will show her!'

It seemed to Jean that her brother had grown up overnight, as if, now that he was going away, he could afford to reveal something of the more serious side of himself. He turned back to his packing.

'You'll like Betty,' he told Jean. 'She's great! She's very clever, reads all sorts of books and can talk about lots of interesting things. She's taught me a thing or two! She's sporty as well. She has a motorbike and she likes scrambles and football matches. We go all over. She's a great skater as well.' He went on piling up Betty's merits with enthusiasm all the time he was finishing his packing.

When he had shut his case, sat on it and turned the key in the lock, he said, 'I'll get in touch in a few weeks, but at present I want to be left alone. You don't mind?'

Jean shook her head. He zipped up his anorak, pulled on his duffle coat and picked up his suitcase. 'I've had to leave quite a few of my belongings here. There's my camping gear for a start. No one wants the room, I suppose?'

'I suppose not,' Jean agreed.

He stood for a moment looking at her. 'Thanks for standing between me and Dad when I was a kid. You saved me from quite a few hidings. Dad likes you the best, you know. He thinks you're like his mother – clever and bookish, like she was.'

Jean ignored the cleverness bit this time. 'Mum likes you the best,' she replied. She was smiling up at him from where she sat. She was finding parting painful, especially his going away so abruptly and keeping everything to himself until he had to tell her.

'Be seeing you then!' He turned to the door, hesitated, then, half turning back towards her, 'I mean that about power, you know. I don't ever want power over anyone.'

'No.'

Jean continued sitting by the window for quite a while. The room seemed very empty without her brother's presence. When he had been a child, three years younger than herself, she had looked after him, trying to take the place of a father who never seemed to want to play with him or take any real interest. When he grew older, she had stood between the two of them on more than one occasion. Later, when Dick got into his teens, he had drawn away from his sister, adopting a slightly superior attitude towards her and treating his mother with a mild contempt. His good nature prevented anything worse. Now it was as if a guillotine had all of a sudden come down, cutting off that part of their lives and leaving her standing alone. For a while, she felt wretched. 'I wonder what Betty is like,' she thought. She couldn't tell from Dick's exaggerated praise.

She got up. She was going to hate telling her mother. Going down the stairs, she wondered whether Dick had eaten his special birthday cakes before packing. She thought it very likely.

CHAPTER THREE

STEPHEN'S parents had had their first and only child relatively late in life so that his mother was now almost sixty and his father two years older. He had never seen his mother go out to work; his father had always been the sole breadwinner and undisputed head of the family. He had grown up believing this relationship to be the natural one between husband and wife. As he grew older, especially when he went to the polytechnic, he came to realise that there might be other reasons besides the purely financial for married women working outside the home –

28

they might prefer it that way. He found nothing to offend him in this idea. He thought it natural that women should claim a share in decision-making and seek a separate identity. He enjoyed the company of women who spoke their minds and had their own aims.

Still the fact remained that he now found himself more attracted towards a girl whom he had labelled 'old-fashioned' than towards any of the other more assertive young women whom he had previously chosen to take out.

Jean's parents, in contrast, were in their early forties. There had been none of that harmony in Jean's background which Stephen had taken as normal. She had grown up amid openly expressed contempt for her mother. The constantly reiterated word 'stupid' applied to her mother, most often as an adjective standing before 'cow', 'bitch', or 'basket', had seared her feelings over the years. As she grew older she had come to resent her father's use of his physical strength to secure her mother's subservience. It was only when Jean went to work and later to the polytechnic, that she began seriously to question what went on at home. Besides those novels which, early on in her studies, she had read so avidly and which had led her into so much trouble with her mother, Jean studied the more recent laws on property and parental rights as they related to women. She saw that much needed still to be done, but she was extremely glad not to have been born earlier. Then it would have been much more difficult to be emancipated. In spite of her not very helpful early experiences she considered that this was something she had achieved for herself.

However that knowledge did not prevent her from becoming tongue-tied when men were about, nor did it help her to feel free. She mixed with difficulty and suffered from a painful sense of inadequacy which showed itself in an acute shyness, mistaken by many of her fellow students for pride. Because of this, she was not very popular. She noticed men, but they rarely seemed to notice her and after a while she came to think it unlikely that any man would ever take a serious interest in her. In spite of a determination never to marry, this fact caused her some suffering. She was quite unable to go up to a man and start a conversation. Why she should find this difficult, knowing herself an equal, was a problem she never considered.

The winter term started and with it hard work. This did not prevent Jean and Stephen from making time to go about together. They were now friends. Their interests were in some ways dissimilar, but since neither was narrow, they found this fact a stimulus rather than an obstacle and, since each wished to please the other, by the end of the spring term Jean found that the Kensington Science Museum had greatly added to her knowledge of the sciences, whilst Stephen knew more about schools of painting than he would otherwise have been likely to find out. They talked about their family backgrounds. Stephen said his parents had always read a great deal; Jean was ashamed to have to admit that the only books in her home were half a dozen belonging formerly to her paternal grandmother.

'I'm supposed to take after her,' she said. 'At least, according to Dad. She died before I was born.' Then she asked Stephen why he had not gone to a university; she thought him sufficiently clever. He laughed at that.

'Not everyone who is "clever" wants a university,' he said. 'I decided on a polytechnic when I was in the sixth form. I'd led a very sheltered life and I wanted to get a bit closer to new ideas in education.' In his turn, he asked Jean why she had not tried for a university.

'It never entered my mind,' she answered truthfully. It would have riled her mother even more, but she did not tell Stephen that.

One of their favourite haunts was Charing Cross Road with its many bookshops. Stephen soon discovered that once Jean disappeared into any such shop she rarely emerged in under an hour. One Saturday he lost her altogether only to find her again after a search of some minutes – on her knees, down on the floor, her head twisted at an awkward angle attempting to view all the titles on one of the bottom shelves. He felt annoyed that she could so completely forget his presence.

'Do you have to spend the entire afternoon crawling about on the floor, in such an absurd position?' he asked, in a tone more sarcastic than he had intended, bending down and shouting into her ear. She started and jumped up. 'It's a bit stupid, isn't it?' he asked. He saw the pleasure die out of her face at his words, to be replaced by a look of distress. At once he was sorry. He had not meant to sound so scornful.

'Come on! We've got no money,' he said, in an apologetic tone, holding out his hand to help her up. At that moment he felt his power over her, to please or to distress her.

30

His implied rebuke put a damper on her spirits for a short while after they had left the shop. She was silent until they had seated themselves in the pizzeria and placed their order; then she brightened up and became her usual self again.

Her usual self was not what it had been when Stephen had first met her, nor during their early days together. Then she had been very reserved, with a strange kind of hesitation in her responses, a guardedness, as if she were used to concealing her true feelings, only speaking after first being sure that what she said would not give offence and quite often she would turn on him a look as if she were tentatively considering how far she could go with him in openness. It was as though she were subject to sudden frosts when her emotions were covered by a layer of thin ice. Then, after some three months, this reserve had quite suddenly melted away. All her stiff caution went overboard. It was as if she were breathing freely for the first time.

Of course everything was in favour of her feeling and behaving in a light-hearted manner. She was still very young, a student, free from normal adult responsibilities, and her studies were not only progressing well, but giving her a great deal of deep satisfaction. In addition she was experiencing a new dimension to her life; she was no longer going about either on her own or in the company of those who were friends of convenience. She was enjoying life alongside someone who meant a great deal to her. Although living not more than ten miles from the West End, she had seen little of the capital while she was growing up; no one in her family went to London except to shop at sale times. London had remained as strange to her as if she had been brought up in the provinces. Going to the polytechnic was like going abroad for the first time. Even then she had gone about very little; partly because she had not much money, but even more because it made her feel melancholy to wander so much on her own. Her visit to the Royal Festival Hall on that memorable evening had been one of her exceptions.

Stephen, on the other hand, knew the capital well. His parents had not neglected his education in that respect; he was familiar with its theatres, concert halls, museums – and not least, its many and varied walks, for he was a great walker. He had tramped all over the East End, through the Dartford Tunnel, along the river, across to Southwark and Lambeth. He did everything with a guide book, thoroughly. He had a very retentive memory and could recount all he had learned. He had done quite a bit of walking with his parents, later with his father only, and finally on his own. When he got home, he had always been assured of an interested audience. This had added to his pleasure in these solitary outings; he liked informing others and passing on what he knew. He was finding a keen enjoyment in introducing Jean to so much that was new to her. Their weekend outings became a fixed habit.

As time went on, Jean could not fail to realise that her presence gave Stephen pleasure. She began to want to look her best. She changed from wearing pastel shades to warmer colours; rusts and reds, which suited her pale complexion better. She bought herself a dress of a warm corn colour which really set off her brown hair and hazel eyes. She bought and wore for the first time an ornament, a bright red stone hanging from a thin gold chain. She went to a more expensive hairdresser for a better cut. She looked at herself in the mirror and for the first time thought that she looked nice.

One Sunday they walked along the embankment, close to the Strand. They leaned on the embankment wall, gazing down at the fast flowing Thames; gleams of cold, clear light shone on the water. There was a wintry feel, the sky pale and far off. They gazed upstream towards the Houses of Parliament, and downstream to Waterloo Bridge, with the great dome of St. Paul's beyond and the wide curve of the river as it bent towards the sea. As they gazed, the midday chimes rang out.

'When the steamers start,' Stephen said, 'we'll go to Greenwich and take a look at the Cutty Sark.'

'Yes!' Jean answered, feeling as if he had said that they would go to the West Indies.

Another weekend they explored the Inns of Court with their famous lawns and great plane trees. This was a hard afternoon for them both since they could not resist looking up in their guide book every historical and architectural item of interest on their route. In the end they were glad to find a little cafe on the Strand where they could rest and drink lemonade.

'Well, we haven't wasted the afternoon,' Stephen said, in a satisfied tone.

'No,' Jean agreed, adding happily, 'I feel as if I've eaten a good solid meal!'

Yet another time they crossed to Southwark, walking back to Lambeth and passing the Royal Festival Hall on their way. Here they paused.

'That's where we met,' Jean said. It was an unnecessary remark, but she uttered it in a tone which gave it significance.

'Yes,' Stephen answered. He had caught the special tone and it made him feel all at once serious.

Stephen thought that Jean loved him and he did not know as yet whether or not he loved her. He had guessed for some time that her feelings towards him were deeper than the feelings of any of the other young women whom he had previously taken out. As the weeks went by it was impossible for him to miss the effect he was having on her. Seeing him, her face would at once light up, her eyes shine, and she would give him a smile of unconcealed pleasure. He could not help being affected by her delight in his presence; he would have been less than human had this not been so. At the same time her vulnerability touched him and he grew anxious lest he should be tempted to take advantage of her obvious trust.

Whilst they were standing there and he was considering their relationship and puzzling over his feelings, he heard her say, 'I feel free!' And she gave her arms and hands a flap, like a bird soaring.

She did indeed feel free; free and secure. This latter feeling was at the root of her change of behaviour. As soon as she felt safe with him she relaxed. He had slipped up once, at the Charing Cross bookshop, disturbing her sense of acceptance; but, noticing her distress, he had not made the same mistake twice. The memory had faded; she went about with him feeling secure. This new certainty of her own worth created in her a glow of happiness which shone through her. She seemed lit up from within. Of course it was not like this all the time. Sometimes, especially when she had not seen him for a few days, her confidence would falter. She could not really believe that his liking her would last; she did not permit herself to think of it as love. But as the weeks went by these fears diminished. Her apprehensions of disaster became less frequent, especially when she saw a genuine pleasure in his expression on every occasion of their meeting, and when she experienced a kindness and consideration quite foreign to her normal life. Finally, she let go, and felt as she expressed it to him at that moment, gazing towards the Royal Festival Hall, 'Free!' This was one of those moments when she did literally glow with happiness and unconsciously show him most clearly that she loved him. So he was troubled because he had not yet discovered the true nature of his own feelings. Certainly she intrigued him; certainly he enjoyed her company, often a great deal, but did he feel towards her what is commonly meant by being in love? If he did not, he ought to stop seeing her. It was not fair on her. But he knew that he did not want to do that.

Stephen was surprised to discover that Jean could not swim. He at once said that he would teach her in the polytechnic swimming bath. This inability was partly because she had been taken to the sea only on very rare occasions during her childhood, but also because she had somehow acquired a fear of deep water which made her reluctant to make use of swimming baths. However she had no intention of letting Stephen know that she was afraid. She bought herself a swim suit and went down the steps into the water as if she were used to it. When it came to it, she was more afraid of Stephen despising her for a coward than of the water. She learnt quite quickly, trusting Stephen not to let her go under. One day he said to her, 'I think you're ready to swim a length now.' Her body gave a shiver.

'All right,' she said, in a careless tone.

She began to swim, striking out as if she had the Channel to cross and feeling frightened because she could not breathe as she had been taught. She felt that she did not have any directing centre any more; that her arms and legs were detaching themselves from her body and floating away leaving her only a heavy central stump, which would take a plunge to the bottom at any second. She thought she could hear Stephen's voice from somewhere far off.

'I must be over the deep water now,' she thought. Then she heard Stephen's voice, 'Come on! You're almost there. Don't slow up!'

She wanted to cry out that she could not go on, that she was going to sink, but instead she gave a great thrust with her body, with her arms and legs and at once heard the same voice calling out, 'Good! I knew you could make it.' She realised that she had reached the far end and was standing up in the water which was dripping from her arms, face and hair. She received Stephen's congratulations calmly, but inside herself she was conscious of a tremendous sense of triumph. After that she made use of the baths as often as she could until she could swim two or three lengths with ease. It was her first triumph over her own fears.

Sometimes at the weekends they walked through their own local park to bring back the happy memories of their first outing. One day Stephen took a snapshot of Jean while she was sitting on the library bench under the oak tree reading. He positioned himself, waiting with his camera, hoping that she would look up. And she did look up and saw him and smiled her smile of pleasure at the sight of him – that happy, warm smile at recognition of his presence which he had grown to anticipate and be moved by. He was moved by it then and when the snapshot was developed he liked it so much that he had it enlarged to postcard size and framed.

They were becoming used to each other's company as a natural fact of both their lives and when anything of interest happened to either of them, each thought first of the other as the person they most wanted to tell.

They noticed the beauties of nature with sharpened senses. In the winter, in the park, they pointed out to each other the tiny snowdrops with their drooping white heads and bright green petal markings, barely visible among the thick drifts of dead leaves; leaves once dried up and shrivelled, now soggy and wet, drenched with the rain that had followed the snow. In spring, they went to look at the daffodils and narcissi, at the crocuses which had sprung up, overnight as it seemed, on the library green, masses of mauves, yellows and whites, their shiny brilliance set off by light green leaves stripped with tiny white lines; at the hyacinths, turning slowly from dull white to warm pinks and reds and cool blues; and at the tulips, silky to the touch, with bright red lines colouring the ragged edges of the unfolding petals. Pink, almond and white pear blossoms scattered their tiny, soft petals onto gravel paths and grass. On the river bank, close to the golf course, there stood a large willow tree, very tall in spite of its bending branches – whilst other trees were still dark, it showed a pale, clear green, but for its crown which still bore no leaf and on bright days showed bare against a blue sky. It was a moment in the tree's life when the outline of dark branches topping the green presented to the onlooker a double vision of winter and spring in one. All these changing sights, Jean and Stephen noted and enjoyed with keener satisfaction than spring had ever brought to them before. When a warm interlude set in, the couple took their books and studied in the open.

One Saturday they went to an Impressionist exhibition at the Tate Gallery. They stopped in front of a Van Gogh painting of a young girl sitting on a yellow chair against a background of yellow shelves filled with books of the same bright colour. She had dark hair, was dressed in a dark red, satiny blouse and wore a dark green, satiny skirt which reached almost to the ground. She was bent over a book, her eyes cast downwards, an absorbed expression on her face. Against one shelf was propped a yellow ladder and to the far left of the painting was a small square window through which a bright round sun shone into the room. The difference between the girl with her dark hair, dark blouse and skirt, and absorbed expression and the sunlight which glowed all over the painting was very startling. Stephen and Jean stood admiring it for a long time.

'She's just like you!' Stephen commented.

Jean protested, 'She's not a bit like me! My hair isn't black and her features are quite different.'

'True! But she has your absorbed expression when you're reading.' He added, 'I wish I could see the colour of her eyes.' But the eyes were fixed on the open page of the book and he could not see them.

'She won't look up, so there's no point in your waiting,' Jean said, laughing. They moved on.

Spring advanced, bringing with it deep purple clusters of lilac; the creamy flowers with pink spots of the horse chestnuts; white may and golden chain; rhododendrons – huge pale mauve blooms with dark lines edging the petals, blooms of pale pink with bright red dots and blooms of pure white; orange and salmon azaleas. There were avenues of soft, crinkled, fresh green leaves on the tall trees; light green sweet smelling limes, birch trees in a dazzle of sun, twinkling aspens and the soft, warm brown leaves of the copper beeches before the leaves darkened and turned shiny.

At the beginning of the summer term, Jean went down with a slight attack of influenza. Then Stephen felt her loss. She was only away one week, but it was long enough for him to realise how dependent on her presence he had become. This rather annoyed him and he worked more than usually long hours to keep himself occupied.

To celebrate her return to health, they went to an evening of the ballet at Covent Garden. Going to Covent Garden was expensive; it was also something splendid, Jean thought. In the first interval, she went to the front of the amphitheatre and looked down at the stalls and then up at the huge central illumination. It was round, like a globe, and green rays shot out from its centre towards the gold circumference, suffusing the whole with a glistening transparency of green light, like still water hanging magically from the roof of the auditorium.

There were red plush seats and red striped wallpaper and lamps with lampshades of red satin, set in golden candlesticks to light the interior during the intervals. Red plush covered the balustrades. A red and gold velvet carpet concealed the stage. From her vantage point Jean thought the scene magnificent.

'It's very old-fashioned,' Stephen commented, finding none of this to his taste. But Jean liked it. She felt that the whole theatre, with its rather gaudy nineteenth-century atmosphere, was a splendid illusion. In the second interval, they went into the circle bar. There was a strong smell of coffee, people were standing about or sitting, eating sandwiches and thick slices of cream gateau. Drinking her coffee, Jean looked about her, at the smart women, many of them in long dresses with bright shawls and glossy, set hair.

One Saturday, a few weeks later, they decided to go shopping locally and afterwards stroll in the park. It was a mild summer day and it would be very pleasant in the park. They both bought a pair of jeans and Stephen bought a shirt and Jean a blouse. On their journey back through the store they came to a part where there were lots of hats. Jean halted for a moment to gaze at the hats, so Stephen did the same.

'Who buys all these hats?' Jean queried. 'I never see anyone in a hat.'

'My mother wears hats,' Stephen said. 'That hat would suit you,' he went on, pointing to a red velour hat with a large, floppy brim, hung up on a stand.

Amused, Jean said, 'I never wear a hat.' All the same, when she had looked at the red hat she rather liked it.

'Well, you could. I'd like to see you in it.' She looked at the price tag. 'It's six pounds!'

'I'll go halves with you. Why don't you ever let me treat you to anything?' He sounded a bit hurt.

Jean hesitated, then, 'All right! We'll go halves; that's if it suits me. Then it will belong to us both.' The idea pleased her. She put it on with great care and then gazed for a few seconds silently at her reflection in the mirror. She turned and looked at Stephen. Her face, under the shadow of the large red brim was glowing with pleasure, her hazel eyes shining, the upward curve of her parted lips expressive of her happy expectation of his approval.

'Well?' she asked.

And he knew at that moment for certain that he could not let her go out of his life.

They bought the hat and Jean put it on and they finished their shopping and took their parcels with them to the park. They sat on their usual seat under the oak tree on the green and he told her that he loved her and they kissed. He took off the red hat and laid it on the bench beside them so that they forgot it and had to run back in a panic to reclaim it after they had walked away. After that it meant much more to them than just a red hat.

That evening, in his bedroom, Stephen sat and thought a great while about Jean. Now that he had taken the decisive step, he felt much more at ease with himself. He thought about their relationship. He was sure now that he was in love, but a part of his love came from a peculiar sense of having brought her to life; he had found her a shy, withdrawn little thing and had transformed her into a warm, spontaneous, lovable being. Whatever bonds might have been restraining her, and he had no idea what they might have been, he had certainly released her, set her free to give expression to herself. He recalled that afternoon when they had halted their walk to gaze at the Royal Festival Hall and she had suddenly flapped her arms and hands in a funny little gesture, like a bird learning to fly, and had said that she felt free. Another part of his love consisted in his power over her to make her happy or to cause her pain. He did not say to himself that he came first with her, but he assumed it. This almost romantic devotion of hers touched him. He was vaguely aware, which she was not, that she sought a protector, and having been brought up in a home where the woman was 'cared for' this seemed to him natural. He himself was really looking for someone who would understand him and share his hopes and aspirations; someone not too aggressively 'modern', yet intelligent, loyal and able to offer emotional support. When he thought of Jean he thought of her in exactly that way. He knew that she was ambitious to show what she could achieve in life but this did not worry him. He was ambitious himself and could understand.

One afternoon Jean felt a sense of melancholy for the first time since Stephen had told her of his love. Walking back along the embankment and looking at the barges moving up and down on the water, she became aware of a feeling very little removed from fear. It came into her mind to wonder how she could go on living and what she could possibly do to make life bearable if Stephen were to die. Then she told herself that she was simply being silly and that it was natural for people in love to fear being parted by death. It never entered her mind that they could be parted in any other way than by death.

When she got back to the canteen, Stephen was there making notes in an exercise book whilst waiting for her. She stole up behind him and stood tickling the nape of his neck. He turned his head and looked up at her.

'Hello!' he said, smiling. His smile had its usual effect on her. Her fears were banished. She felt happy.

A little while after this they made up their minds to live together and started to look for a bed-sittingroom not too far from the polytechnic and which they could afford. It was not an easy task.

'I think we had better not let my mother know,' Jean said. 'She will not like it; my father neither.'

'We don't need to tell anyone,' Stephen said. 'My parents won't come over unless I invite them. Will yours?' Jean was sure that her mother would not; her father she thought too lazy if they were some distance off. They must look at districts on the other side of London, as far from their homes as possible. They planned to move in for the start of their third and final year at the polytechnic.

On her way home Jean thought how little she would enjoy telling her mother when the time came. She did not want to leave her mother alone with her father. She found herself wondering what her parents had been like years ago, when they were still young and when they had first met before either she or Dick had been thought of. She felt sad because there had never been any real happiness in the home or real affection between her parents since she had known them.

'I wonder if they were once very different?' she thought. Had they cared a lot for each other at the start and, if so, how had they come to their present state of almost total estrangement?

CHAPTER FOUR

ALTHOUGH he left home in such an abrupt manner, Dick had no wish to cause anyone any hurt. He suspected rightly that his mother would not approve of his action. He saw no reason why his sister, who had so often during his childhood stood between his father and himself, should not on this occasion stand between himself and his mother. Jean had the gift of the gab and would know how to handle a difficult situation; education did that for you. He himself had no such gift. It could not be expected of a simple chap.

He saw nothing wrong in accepting his mother's gift of money and eating the little iced cakes which she had lovingly baked for him, without a mention of his impending departure. He certainly had no desire to grieve his mother; on the other hand, he had no desire to give her pleasure if this meant putting himself out. He told himself that his only real demand on life was not to be involved in 'scenes'. He had witnessed enough scenes between his parents. He had an image of himself as a rather nice, easy-going sort of a fellow; which, in fact, he was, especially when he was getting his own way. Could he have known how keenly his mother was to feel this particular action, he would certainly have been surprised and might even have been a little remorseful, but not too much.

Mary did not, as it happens, make a scene. She received the news coldly and said little. She did not wish to confide her hurt to her daughter. Once again, she shut Jean out. Although this was normal, Jean could not help minding.

She minded even more some months later, when she was faced with the need to tell her mother of her own intention to leave home. It was harder for her than when Dick had left, since she felt a responsibility for her own actions which she had not needed to feel for his. She gave her news in a few hesitant words. She wanted to go on to talk to her mother about how she would be placed when left on her own. But her mother would have none of it. If she was going, she was going, she told Jean, adding, 'You must like throwing your money away,' and she gave her little, light sniff of disdain.

'I shall be sharing.'

'I shouldn't be surprised!' her mother answered, in a sarcastic, meaningful tone.

She gave Jean to understand that whether she went or stayed was a matter of indifference to her. This attitude still had power to hurt Jean. She made one further attempt to broach the subject which was causing her concern, but her mother stoutly resisted. In the end she gave it up. There was silence between them until Jean left the house some ten minutes later.

Mary had felt the shock even though she had given no outward sign. She could not accept sympathy from her daughter. It would only have served to add to her already persistent sense of humiliation. Also she had been schooled through many years not to show her feelings; or, if she did, not to expect any sympathy on their account. But so soon after Dick's sudden departure, she was not ready to receive this fresh blow.

Silence had followed Jean's words and her own rebuffs. Now she was sitting alone in the living room and there was silence again. It was as if she had suddenly stopped. She was normally an active woman, both by temperament and necessity, but now she was quite still. She sat in an old-fashioned armchair, facing the half-open kitchen door, her hands folded on her lap, her head erect, her back straight, almost as if she were posing for her photograph. By her appearance she could have been, for she was neatly dressed in a dark blue skirt and red jumper; her hair, dyed a reddish-brown and shining from the hard brushing she gave it every morning, was neatly combed back from off her forehead, the ends lying curled up on the nape of her neck. She had not yet put on her make up and her complexion showed sallow. She looked worn and more than her forty-one years.

She had the strangest feeling of having been all of a sudden cut off, like a plant snipped in half. For years her activities, her thoughts, her anxieties, hopes and fears, had been directed away from herself towards other people. This had seemed natural. Now all at once a door had slammed in her face and she was on her own. She told herself there were other ways of living. Here was her chance. She was not old; in fact, quite young, but she did not feel young – that was the crunch. Years ago she would have welcomed a change in the monotony of her daily life. Now she was aware only of a lack of energy.

Of course she still had Bill. But for years Bill had neglected and ignored her. She kept herself neat and tidy as a matter of personal pride rather than from any hope of pleasing her husband.

There must be a future for her. She tried to glimpse its outline, but she could not visualise a future of which she herself was the centre. When she tried to imagine it, everything went hazy; all she could see was a landscape without contours, a vague, un-inhabited waste. She experienced a sudden panic.

Then she gave herself a shake. This would not do. She had never been one to give in. She got up and with a brisk step went into the kitchen. Once there, she found herself hesitating. It was as if something inside her had come unhinged and was hanging loose. She felt the need of a stiffener. She went back into the living room for a cup and saucer. The familiar sight of the Welsh dresser reassured her. She had loved the Welsh dresser from the moment when she and Bill had bought it second hand when they had set up home together. She loved the hanging cups and plates spread out in double rows, the tea pot, so gay with its painted cottage and bright red poppies.

She made herself a cup of coffee, added two teaspoons of rum and sat down again in the old armchair. She sipped the hot coffee slowly; the rum tasted good. She had a sense of treating herself and this made her feel a bit better. She started to think about her past life.

She and Bill had met at a dance; she had been sixteen, Bill seventeen. He had been very personable then; sturdy, with a broad build, a round, pleasant face, thick dark eyebrows, and a shock of dark hair. At the time they first met, he had just grown a moustache. He was a bit of an exhibitionist. He grew the mous-tache partly to create an effect and partly as a joke. He liked to 'show off' and he liked a jest. He got on well with most people and was liked. He had a good singing voice which put him in demand at parties. He was not one for rows. He enjoyed dancing and liked a drink and what he called 'a tease'. At that period of his life, he never got drunk and he was seldom vulgar. He was shy with girls and it took him time to get started; but once he had got going, he liked to 'cut a figure'. When with a girl, he never swore. He let his mates know all about his 'conquests' and boasted of them, but nobody took him seriously, if only because to boast in this way was the done thing. At that time he was a bricklayer's mate and hoping to become an apprenticed bricklayer.

He had liked Mary because he thought she had 'spunk' and also because, like himself, she was a good dancer. Mary was then in the full bloom of early youth; on the short side, but with a neat, trim figure, very sexy. She had sharp features and a turned up nose, her mouth was full and she smiled often, when her

42

large hazel eyes shone and her face wore a very pleasant look. But she was capable of sharp-tongued retorts and would put on a very haughty air and manner if a partner offended her. Bill found this out to his cost when he said to her, 'You're a sexy bit!', meaning this as a compliment, whereupon she had broken loose and walked away from him in the middle of a dance. After a while, Bill discovered that she was reputed to be 'hard to get', and he found this a challenge. She did, in fact, walk about with a very cocky air and nobody could have guessed from her manner that at home she still went in fear of the strap. Both she and Bill came from homes where there was plenty of loose cash, but much less in the way of affection. When they first met, Mary was serving in a greengrocer's shop.

Mary could still recall everything vividly; all the fun they had shared together for over two years, and during that last pre-war summer of 1939. How gay, good humoured and generous Bill had been and how kind to her. He won her heart. Then she became pregnant and in a panic threatened him. He'd retorted, 'You don't need to threaten me! I mean to marry you.' And he did marry her; partly because he really liked her and partly because of the baby. For he was, in this respect, fundamentally decent. In spite of the wedding being a bit of a splash, neither side approved of the circumstances and afterwards the couple were left to their own devices.

So they became parents at a very early age, both emotionally immature. The start of the war made matters worse. When Jean was born, the evacuation officer wanted mother and child to leave London. 'If our name's on it, we'll go together,' Mary told him. She would keep the family united, come what may. Afterwards, she was proud of this. Bill was not called up at once and within a few months of Jean's birth Mary was pregnant again, but miscarried. Then Bill went into the army, coming home for his leaves and expecting to enjoy himself. A second miscarriage followed. Finally Dick was born. It was not a propitious start to their married life.

Nor did Bill's discharge from the army in 1946 improve matters. In spite of seeing some limited action, he had escaped serious injury and had liked the army life. He couldn't settle to the peace. He got his apprenticeship, but lost it for 'insolent behaviour'. He was lucky, there was plenty of rebuilding work and he got a second chance, but he threw that away too. He put it round that he had been victimised, even though he hadn't joined the Union.

Finally, he was offered a job as a labourer on a building site. He looked upon this as a major humiliation, but he took the job, telling himself it was a purely temporary measure while he looked round. But his references told against him and he never got another apprenticeship offer. He remained an unskilled labourer, going from one building site to another, earning quite good money, but with no prospect of advancement. He felt that life had done the dirty on him. He began to drink more.

Then his sex life took a turn for the worse. He had been used to getting his own way, but with two miscarriages and two young children and a husband to look after, Mary no longer had the energy to enjoy sex; it tired her even more. Matters might have improved had Bill been willing to help in the house or with the kids, but he had never seen his father help his mother and he considered anything of the sort beneath him.

It was then that Mary discovered another side to Bill. She complained that he had started to keep her short of money.

'You keep me short of *my* rations,' he had retorted, 'so I'm doing the same to you.' He liked his sex as he liked his drink, regular.

Thinking back now, Mary said to herself, 'He was always pleasant when he was getting his own way; when he didn't get his own way, that was your lot. And I never saw it! I must have been blind.'

She got up, took her empty cup and saucer into the kitchen, swilled them under the tap and left them on the draining board. Then she brought out the casserole dish and began to prepare the potatoes, carrots and onions; afterwards cutting up the stewing meat and putting it into the dish along with the vegetables and some stock. In the past she had always browned the meat first, but now she cut down on the work. She put the casserole into the oven ready for when it was time to light the gas. She did all this slowly, still thinking about her past. She sliced some apples and began to make a crust. All the while she was doing this, she was thinking, 'Why did I let him get away with it? I could have stopped him at the start. I just let him go on calling me names and of course he got worse and worse. And now its hopeless. I just don't understand why I let it happen.' She hated herself for what she thought of as her weakness more than she hated her husband for his ill-treatment.

She was unjust to herself. She *had* tried to put up a fight, but looking back, it seemed to her that she had not fought at all. Bill had started to use swear words at home chiefly as a means of relieving his sense of humiliation when at work. Mary had objected and he had retorted roughly, 'Don't you tell *me* what to do!' He had enough of being told at work. He had always gone to the pub for a pint; now he stayed longer and drank more. He started to come home a bit tipsy. When tipsy, he would swear at Mary. He had a whole string of words to choose from, all in common use, but he reserved his most contemptuous tone for when he called her simply 'a silly woman', taking care to put an emphasis on the final word. At the start Mary's spirit rose. She wanted to pay him back in kind, word for word. But she discovered that she knew no such words. They were not in the vocabulary. She could call him a bastard and she did, but the word had nothing to do with his sex, it only reflected on him as a person. Whilst all the words he used against her were expressive of contempt for her sex. In the end she had to recognise that she could not compete – the weapon was not there. When she finally acknowledged her defeat, she broke down and cried, with tears of frustrated rage at the thought of his contemptuous language and of her own inability to make reply in kind.

The physical violence came later and was usually the result of some happening at work which had made him want to lash out. At work he had to keep himself under control. He could not afford to lose his job yet again, so he took it out on his wife when he got home. He would find an excuse to give her a push, a shove, or a slap. One evening he came home late and much the worse for drink and beat her up, giving her a swollen face, a black eye and numerous body bruises. Terrified, she ran out of the house and along the street to the police station about three hundred yards away. Two policemen had accompanied her back. By that time Bill had put his head under the tap, had sobered up a bit and was repentant and scared. He had a vague notion that he might be taken off to prison. He quickly discovered that there was no need for alarm. Apart from a rather strong telling-off, nothing happened. Later, among his pals, he found out that his wife must first lodge a complaint against him for assault, and that meanwhile he could continue to live in his own house. Anyway, his pals told him he would most likely only be fined and warned not to repeat the offence. This information greatly relieved his mind. He was confident that Mary would not take him to Court. For one thing, if she did, he would make her sorry. He thought about her situation; she had two young children, no one would take her in with that lot; her parents, he knew, would not want her. Had he seriously thought Mary might leave him, he would have been concerned. He had to have someone to look after him and to bear his bad moods. In the end he decided that he need not worry.

On leaving, one of the policemen had said to him: 'Don't be a naughty boy again, mind!'

This was really the turning point in their relationship. Short of murder, Bill now felt master in his own home. The exercise of power, socially permitted, provided him with an easy way of compensating for his many frustrations so long as he did not go beyond a vague 'too far'. Luckily for Mary, the occasions on which he chose to be violent were not numerous, but since the policemen's visit, there was between them the unspoken knowledge that within the four walls of the home they were on their own.

After that night, for the first time, Mary admitted to herself her total defeat. From then on she turned completely away from her husband to concentrate her interests entirely on the children and the house.

She spoiled Dick without being aware of it. By her lights, she did her best for Jean; although from the start her daughter never meant as much to her as her son.

She kept the house spotlessly clean. She was very fond of bright colours. She collected gold painted vases with high glosses and stuffed peacocks with brilliant tails. The window curtains were a vivid orange, the chair covers a vivid green. Bill was rarely in at nights now, so she did all the redecorating herself. He had turned his back on the home and so, in a way, it now belonged to her. But she never pretended to herself that what had happened was anything other than a defeat. She knew that she could not trust her own body to protect her from assault and that there was no outside agency to which she could turn. She really did have the spunk which Bill had thought he saw in her at that first dance, but she was also clear-eyed. She could not imagine how things could be any different. Now she was considering how she should break to Bill the news of Jean's intended departure. Bill came in at his usual hour, about seven o'clock. She could smell that he had called in at the pub. He was still identifiable as the man she had married years ago, but he

46

had visibly coarsened. Drink had thickened his face. His complexion had become ruddy from constant work outdoors. His dark bushy eyebrows and tufts of dark hair were much the same, with just a touch of grey. He had broadened out and become toughened by all his lifting and shovelling. He was aware of his physique and proud of it.

'That girl is a sharp one!' he said, with approbation, when Mary gave him the news. 'She'll land herself a big fish one of these days, mark my words.' After that he fell silent and got on with his meal.

Mary suffered a pang of jealousy. She knew what Bill was thinking – he expected his daughter to rise in the world. Their own life-style wasn't good enough for her. Ever since Jean had started to bring home 'excellent' on her reports, he had boasted about her cleverness. He thought her 'the cat's whiskers' for getting a degree. He boasted, 'That girl's on *my* side of the family! Takes after my mum she does! A great reader, my mum was.' Mary felt his words as the insult he undoubtedly meant them to be.

After he had eaten, he left the dirty plates on the table and went upstairs to change, a little later coming down in his best suit. Without a word to his wife, he went out. He was going to the pub, where there was a special darts competition; he was a dab hand at the game. He did not think it necessary to say anything of this to Mary. He came and went as he chose. His contempt for his wife had long played a supporting role in his life. He had tied his self-respect to her subjection.

When he had gone, Mary thought to herself, 'I'll look round for a part-time job. Then I won't have to hold out my hand for every penny – just as if I was still a kid!' She had no idea what her husband earned. The thought of some money of her own cheered her up no end. She forgot her recent panicky fears.

She really did have only one alternative: to rely on herself or to go under. Dick visited rarely and when he did he talked little about himself, how he was living or what he was doing. She would have liked to have taken an interest. Bill did not care, she knew; he regarded his son with a mixture of contempt and envy. He would have liked to see him in a job he could have boasted about to his mates, not manual work. But if he was going to be a manual worker then he should have been a labourer like his father, not an electrician. Bill resented his son's apprenticeship. He had done better than his Dad and that wasn't right.

Mary did not mind what sort of a job her son had. It was only a means of earning a living. But she did mind not being a part of his life. Now she was thinking Jean could go if she wanted. Dick had gone and good luck to him! Bill didn't want her – only for meals. Not often even in bed now; he probably had it off on the side. Well, good luck to him as well! She could manage alone. There was a stubbornness in her nature which would not allow any one of them to master her completely.

CHAPTER FIVE

THREE weeks before the start of the college year, Jean and Stephen found a large furnished bed-sitter on the top floor of an old house in East London. The wallpaper and furniture were dingy and old-fashioned, but the room was light with a view of plane trees. They were young and in love so that the atmosphere of general neglect did not affect their mood of happiness.

They had little spare cash, but to brighten up the dingy room, and as a memento of their first walk in the park, they bought a large colour print of an English country lane in summer, full of sunny warmth, trees and grass. They put it up over the mantle-piece facing the double divan, where the light from the window shone on it. They stacked their numerous books up against one wall. Everything they did had meaning. They were to be on their own for the first time. The day they moved in they laid out a little party for two and were very merry.

They were savouring a new and delightful sense of freedom, but the result was not the undiluted joy which each had antici-pated in imagination. They were no longer seeing each other only at college or out of doors with other people close by. They were on their own and this sense of isolation set up an unspoken tension between them so that words and feelings were often at variance. The first night they lay in each other's arms, indulging in kisses and caresses, happily aware that they would not be disturbed. The next night was not a success, with the result that their nerves were affected and in the morning they were aware of fatigue and irritation. Stephen was used to sleeping with girls for whom his feelings were far less strong, with Jean he felt inhibited; Jean herself was apprehensive and clutched at Stephen with sudden nervous movements which did nothing to reassure him.

'Don't tighten up, darling. Relax!' he kept urging, in vain, for the moment his penis touched her she succumbed to unreasoning panic, her whole body becoming tense and penetration unbearably painful. He was gentle and she tried to do as he told her, but his penis was like a sharp instrument jamming against an open wound and she heard herself uttering cries of pain. This so unnerved Stephen that he was unable to go on. He withdrew, rolled over and lay on his back. When she no longer felt the touch of his penis, Jean's panic subsided as suddenly as it had risen. She lay bewildered and exhausted as from a nightmare.

With the daylight, her panic seemed ridiculous. She felt ashamed and apologised. Stephen told her not to worry, many women experienced fear at first. 'Next time you won't be afraid, you'll relax,' he reassured her.

But this did not happen. Always it was the same; while he was merely caressing her, she felt confident, but the instant that his penis touched her flesh panic overwhelmed her resolve. The panic was not connected to any particular feeling or thought. It was fear – a powerful animal without shape or form.

Perhaps she had a dread of the sex act because of the confused sounds, murmurs and distressed cries which she had lain in bed and listened to when she was very young or perhaps it came from when she had come unexpectedly into the living room to find her parents lying on the hearth rug, her father on top of her mother, exclaiming harshly, 'Come on! ... faster... faster... you're not trying, you lazy bitch!' She had turned and fled, not in the least understanding, but with an uncomprehending dread. Nothing had been said to her later although her father had raised his head and seen her. She had carried away with her the image of her mother with her legs spread wide and her arms flailing, her hair lying dishevelled on the rug, rolling her head from side to side and uttering piteous cries of protest, at the same time making pathetic efforts with her tired body to give him pleasure. Or perhaps it was the sex swearwords so liberally used by her father which had linked sex with disgust in her mind.

Whatever the sources of her panic, it was there. If she could have spoken of her childhood experiences, the panic might have ceased, but shame kept her silent. For some months it seemed possible that this obstacle might put an end to their happiness. Finally, it did not. Stephen could understand that a woman might be afraid; he did not take her fear as a personal insult or as a sign that she did not want him. Instead it aroused in him that tender, caring side which was native to him and which had been given a firm foundation in youth. This loving attitude produced in Jean a strong desire to please him. She wanted to overcome her panic not for her own sake only, but above all for his. Finally, together, they succeeded. After this triumph, they could not imagine any problem as beyond their mutual capacity to solve. Their love seemed founded on rock.

The new term commenced with Jean and Stephen well organised. Whoever arrived home first in the evening would start to prepare the meal. They shared the chores on an equal footing; cooking, shopping, cleaning, making out the grocery lists, washing, ironing and so on. They never thought in conventional terms that he should do this and she should do that. 'If things are organised, it's no trouble,' Stephen commented.

At nights, after clearing away and washing up, they would sit down opposite each other at the large round oak table and study. When one or other of the tenants was having a party, the house became very noisy; at other times it was very quiet, with an empty feeling. These were the times they liked the best; they felt they were in the house on their own. Now and then one would look up and become aware of the other seated opposite; Stephen would notice the strands of soft brown hair falling across Jean's forehead as she bent her head over her book and the habit she had when concentrating of raising her eyebrows and sucking at her lower lip; and Jean would notice how Stephen would scratch the back of his head in an irritated manner when he met with a difficulty and give slight sighs when he was tiring. Occasionally they would both look up at the same instant and then their eyes would meet and without the need for words an intimacy would pass between them. A slight smile would come on both their faces.

After some months they arrived at a stage where they were totally at ease with each other – relaxed, happy, and with a warm sense of security. Then everything joined up – the passion, the tenderness, the mental excitement – in one unbroken circle.

They had their first quarrel on a Sunday. It started with an argument over the piles of stacked books.

'I think the best thing would be to leave them on the floor,' Stephen said. 'It's only for one year.'

Jean demurred. They had no real idea how long they would have to stay and shelves were easy to make; a builders' yard would supply the wood. 'I hate to see books on the floor,' she finished.

'Are you afraid mice might eat them while we're asleep?' Stephen asked flippantly. This remark annoyed Jean.

'I don't think that's clever,' she retorted.

'It wasn't meant to be clever,' Stephen answered. He added with a fake seriousness in his tone, 'I suppose you don't fancy the idea of co-habiting with dozens of mice made fat and sleek on a diet of Plato and Aristotle.'

Jean did not answer. Turning away, she sat down at the table, spread out her study material and began to read. Stephen, rather pleased with his quip, followed her example. Silence reigned. By tea time Stephen had forgotten the little tiff, but Jean was unusually quiet and in the end he noticed. They hadn't had a quarrel yet and he felt a quarrel just then would be rather nice. Besides, it was such a silly thing to make a fuss about. He said, in a bantering tone, 'I know! You're still worried about the books. Well, I've got an idea. We'll conduct an experiment; we'll open a school for mice and see if we can teach the brighter ones to read. Then they'll respect the books and not nibble at them.'

She was furious. 'That's just stupid! It's the sort of remark a child would make.'

'I think it's your attitude that's stupid,' he retorted.

'What attitude? I haven't got an attitude.'

'Yes you have!' He was enjoying himself. 'You're sulking.'

'I'm not!'

'You are!' He was delighted to have riled her.

She turned her back on him.

Neither of them said anything further, or took any notice of the other for some time. Then Stephen came up behind Jean while she was standing at the table putting her written work into a folder, and clasped his arms round her waist.

'Come on, darling. Let's make it up. I didn't mean to offend you.'

'Don't do that!' she said, trying to prize his arms loose, but he kept them tightly clasped and put his lips to the nape of her neck.

'Don't!' she repeated, more sharply. 'Let me go!'

'No!' He began to fondle her breast in his cupped hand.

She could not resist him any longer. She weakened and her body softened and leaned against his; then he gently urged her round and kissed her on the lips and they lay down on the divan and made love. In this way their first quarrel ended.

But afterwards Jean was left with a sense of vexation because he had refused to let her go when she had asked. She felt that he had put his arms round her and kissed her and fondled her knowing that she would weaken. And he had been proved right – she had weakened. At this thought, a faint resentment stirred within her.

Towards the end of the term, Jean went down with influenza. It was a morning when Stephen had an early lecture. He was gone while she was still asleep. On waking, her chest felt as if icy water was lying on it. 'Oh dear,' she thought, 'I'm in for a chill.' Then she went off to sleep again. When she awoke a second time, she was hot and sweaty. She sat up in bed with an effort. Immediately the room swam around her. She fell back onto the pillow. As soon as she moved her head even a little the swimming sensation came back. It was some minutes before she became clear in her mind as to where she was. She had imagined that she was back in her old home.

After a while she managed to get out of bed and put on her dressing gown, but she was very unsteady. Her limbs were weak, her head ached and was hot. She would have liked a drink of tea, but any effort seemed too much and so she contented herself with sips of cold milk, but the milk made her feel sick. She sat on the armchair, her head against its back. She closed her eyes.

She was in a very light-headed state. Her mind kept going blank; then she imagined that there were people walking and talking in the room, only they floated instead of walking and never spoke to her. For brief periods she was lucid and during those periods made efforts to get up from the chair, but her limbs would not obey her. From feeling hot, she began to feel very cold. This sense of extreme cold triggered off in her mind a fantasy familiar to her childhood. She imagined that she was falling away from the earth into space. Somebody whispered 'away' and the word terrified her; it seemed to be echoing endlessly in her ears.

When Stephen came back she was still sitting in the chair and still very light-headed. He was at once alarmed, got her back into bed and called in a doctor. She was in bed for some days. During much of that time, she kept up a mutter about falling away. Stephen could make no sense of the words. She seemed so distressed that he took her in his arms in an attempt to soothe her. He thought it helped for she gradually grew less restless and finally, to his relief, she stopped muttering and appeared to drift into a quiet sleep.

When she was strong enough to get out of bed she told Stephen in explanation, 'When I was a girl, I used to be afraid of falling off the earth. I used to think about it walking to and from school. I imagined myself falling outward, almost in a straight line, away; that was what terrified me so much, not the falling off, but the falling away – mile after mile, until no one could see me and I could not see the earth – no people, no shapes, no forms, nothing, and still I went on falling away, more and more distant... It used to scare me a lot; I really believed it could happen.'

She asked, 'Did you put your arms round me when I was rambling on?'

'Yes,' he said. 'You went quiet after that. You went to sleep.' He added teasingly, 'I thought if you were going to fall off the earth, we had better do it together.'

CHAPTER SIX

IT was a Sunday. Stephen was paying his usual monthly visit to his parents. The last few years had brought about so many changes in his life, added so much to his experiences, including falling in love, that walking along he felt his usual sense of surprise at the unaltered appearance of his own road: tree-lined pavements with semi-detached houses, neat front gardens, clean curtains, and doors of pale yellows, mauves and whites. How familiar it all was, and yet he seemed to be looking at it from a great distance.

He was hoping that his mother would not be too upset at the news he was about to break to her. He had not taken her into his confidence and he did not think that she had any suspicion that he might be living with a girl. He and Jean had agreed that he should use the visit to put an end to a secrecy which they disliked. Although he would have liked to be able to give a definite date, their marriage would not be for a while yet.

In other ways he was feeling satisfied. He and Jean had been together now for over a year. They had both obtained good degrees; Stephen had that month started at a Teachers' Training College while Jean was studying for her librarianship examination. They looked on their relationship as permanent.

Stephen's image of his mother was very clear. He saw her as a mild person to whom it would be almost impossible to take a dislike. He was confident that she and Jean would get on. He had never known his mother to fly into a rage, nor even to speak heatedly. He admired that trait in her; he did not like emotional behaviour. He had long realised that as her son and only child he occupied in her life a position of unique importance and he accepted this as in some way his due. He was used to being placed first. When he had come back from an evening out, he had taken for granted that the hall light would be on, and a tray of biscuits and a drink set out on a small table beside an armchair. If he was not going to be very late, he had also accepted that his mother would be up to make him a hot drink. On occasions he had found her fussing irksome, especially during his last year at home when he had considered himself fully grown up, but he had borne with it partly because in some ways it satisfied his ego, but also because his father's own attitude had conditioned him to treat his mother with respect and in the manner considered proper for 'a good son'. As he grew older, she had unwittingly subjected him to various little tests of character from most of which he had emerged with honour; these tests consisting of occasions when desire had conflicted with filial duty – he had quite a strongly developed sense of duty. To his relief his mother had made no objections to his leaving home and setting up for himself.

'Well, dear, you're a man now. You know what you want,' she had answered. When the day came, she had let him go without fuss. Still, he had had some sense of what his departure had meant to her, some sense of her missing him.

His feeling for his father was also one of respect, but the respect was of an entirely different order. He saw his father as essentially a figure of authority and responsibility, without question the head of the family. During all his childhood, he had never once heard his father swear or use a rough tone in his mother's presence. Had anything of that sort occurred, he would

54

certainly have been both shocked and amazed. He had grown up to adopt his father's attitude of formal respect for women. In some subtle way it increased his sense of his own worth.

On leaving home, he had handed in his key. Pressing the door bell and waiting always gave him a slight feeling of strangeness. After a brief interval, his mother opened the door. She had come from the kitchen in her pinafore. She was trim and tidy.

'Hello, dear,' she greeted him. Her voice had a cool note. She was a neat clean-looking woman in her late fifties, with greying hair and an upright, composed manner.

'Hello, Mum,' Stephen responded and gave the smile which she always found so warming.

Closing the front door after him and adding, 'Dad's in the garden,' she went back into the kitchen where she was busy cooking the dinner and making little cakes for tea. Stephen went through to the back garden where his father had been doing some late planting out of wallflowers. He was a broad-shouldered man, very well-built, who on account of his size was not easily missed in a room. He was sixty-three years of age and his dark hair had long since turned an iron grey and receded, leaving bare his high shiny forehead. At work he was a senior maintenance engineer, at home a man of all trades. He did all the decorating, even painting the outside when needed. He looked after the garden as well. His wife restricted her activities to the house; spring cleaning each year with vigour, keeping all the rooms spick and span and cooking excellent meals. When anything in the home needed attention, she would say to Stephen, 'I'll tell your father, he'll see to it.' Now Jim was enjoying himself, perched halfway up a ladder repainting the garden shed a dull green before the wet season set in. He was always cheerful when on a job. He greeted Stephen with enthusiasm.

'I've pruned the currant bushes,' he told him, looking down at his son and pausing in his work. 'Take a look at my wallflowers. I've finished planting them out.'

Stephen looked at the wallflowers, walking slowly along the newly planted rows. Then he went back and stood at the foot of the ladder, chatting to his father. His mother meanwhile was enjoying herself preparing an especially tasty meal. The kitchen was small but had been equipped by Jim in a modern manner so that Mabel could move easily from table to stove to draining board with a sufficiency of shelves at convenient levels. The walls were a light blue, the cupboards a white gloss and a vase of autumn leaves and twigs sat on a small ledge by the window. Her sure movements and clean appearance made Mabel appear almost a part of the decor.

It was clear that when young she must have been handsome. Even now, aided by a discreet application of rouge and lipstick, she made a decided impression. She was of medium height, well-built with a square jaw, lips which tended to purse a little and grey, thinning hair neatly brushed back from off a rather high forehead. Her brown eyes had a reserved look. Under her pinafore she was wearing a classic two piece in fine wool grey material and an artificial pearl necklace. When she spoke she always enunciated her words clearly. Stephen had once said to her, 'You've got a cultured voice, Mum,' which had amused her.

Her house, from top to bottom, was as tidy and well maintained as its mistress.

When young, Mabel had enjoyed sports, especially tennis and swimming; she had loved dancing and been good at it. A remnant of this youthful agility showed still in her upright figure, but now her walk verged on stiffness and her manner had a certain dignified formality which some people found off-putting.

She had married in her late twenties. Stephen had been born when she was thirty-six; she had not become pregnant easily. She had longed for a daughter, but no second child had followed.

A delicious smell was pervading the kitchen. The sirloin was in the oven with roast potatoes and there was a large apple meringue pie for afters. Mabel was slicing the brussel sprouts and wondering why Stephen had never asked her if she would like to see where he was living. Whenever he did anything to puzzle her, she would end up by saying to herself, 'Well, he's a man now.' Somehow that seemed to explain everything.

Now she was thinking, 'Perhaps he's living with a girl'. She glanced into the garden. Jim and Stephen were chatting at the foot of the ladder. They seemed to have plenty to say to each other. Suddenly Mabel felt very left out, excluded from that easy male intimacy. How fast time had gone by! It seemed only yesterday that Stephen had been born. The war flashed into her mind: Jim in a reserved occupation, she and baby Stephen on a Welsh farm, Stephen aged three, Jim wanting her with him in London. Two whole years of her son's childhood lost to her – those precious, irreplaceable early years. If only Jim could have managed without her! For a long minute she contemplated her husband through the kitchen window.

Then, deliberately, she switched her thoughts. Jim did too much for his age, but her words of caution never had any effect. He did not believe in doctors. She had tried saying, 'For *my* sake,' but it had made no difference. He was very stubborn. In her thoughts she always used the word stubborn, never selfish. Now she saw that he had gone up the ladder again; she wished he would not. With a slight resigned sigh, she turned to survey the cakes and biscuits still warm from the oven. What a morning! She opened the window and called into the garden that dinner would be on the table in fifteen minutes. The warning would give Jim time to tidy himself. Both men would be ready to sit down; her cooking enjoyed a certain prestige. At least she knew she could serve up with confidence!

Stephen put his head round the kitchen door. 'Um! Nice smell Mum.' At his words and the sound of his voice, her morning of hard work was rewarded. They sat down to dinner with that sense of easy relaxation which had always characterised their meal times. Mabel had laid the table with care; mats, cutlery, glasses, serviettes, and a centrepiece of flowers. Jean never did anything of the sort. Now that he was again in the old familiar atmosphere, this formality seemed to Stephen perfectly natural and he fell back into it without difficulty. Neither he nor his father started to eat before Mabel had finished serving.

'That was a nice meal, Mum', Stephen said with emphasis after they had all finished.

'I enjoy doing it, dear,' she answered.

After Mabel had washed up with help from Jim, Stephen being left to read the Sunday paper, he ventured on his news. It did not prove as difficult as he had anticipated.

'Well, dear, you're a man now. You know the kind of girl that will suit you,' Mabel added. Jim gave a slight grunt of assent. They neither of them felt the anxiety they would have felt had a daughter been concerned. Stephen was relieved. It seemed that neither of his parents was as removed from the modern world as he had assumed.

Jim was sitting in his armchair near the window. As far back as Stephen could remember, this armchair had been reserved for his father as head of the family. Jim's legs were stretched out. He was comfortably warm and full. His face, round and fleshy, wore a slightly florid look. He often gave the impression that he was by nature indolent, but this was far from the truth. He was both physically and mentally active. And he was used to dominating.

Now, after a pause, he echoed his wife's sentiments. 'You're old enough to know the sort of girl that will suit you,' he said. He never talked down to his son. He treated him as a fully-grown man and his equal. This attitude made for an easy comradeship which mother and son did not have.

A date was agreed for Stephen and Jean to come over. Stephen would have preferred a less formal arrangement, tea instead of dinner, and the actual date left to them. But Mabel would not hear of it.

'I want to know the day you'll be coming,' she told Stephen firmly. When she spoke within her recognised domain it was accepted that she was entitled to lay down the law. After an early tea, which he did not really want, Stephen left. Although he had hoped to spare Jean the ordeal of a formal meal, it was not to be. But anyway, his parents were not people to be feared. She would have to face up to it.

Back in the room after seeing Stephen off, Jim said, 'I don't know why they have to come for a dinner. Why not let them pop in when it was convenient?' He sat down again in his armchair, picked up the Sunday paper and turned over the pages.

Mabel did not answer. It was all right for Jim. He was not responsible for the state of the home. She was and she certainly did not intend her future daughter-in-law to find her in a muddle. By a muddle she meant anything out of its ordered place. She still remembered the occasion when she had taken an unexpected visitor upstairs to admire the new bedspread and they had come across the aluminium pipe from the vacuum cleaner lying on the carpet; she had forgotten it was there. How embarrassed she had been! Anything out of its proper place upset her.

When he had seen Stephen off, Jim had asked, 'All right for money?' 'Yes, thanks Dad,' Stephen had answered firmly. 'You and Mum have done too much for me already. I can stand on my own feet now.' The grant was not large, but with care he could manage. He would not ask for any further financial help. He walked up the road feeling that he had taken a great stride forward. He had a new sense of independence which had been lacking earlier in the day.

Jim had gone back into the sitting room glad that his responsibilities were at an end, but at the same time conscious of having lost something. He was not sure what, if anything, could replace Stephen in their lives.

58

Turning the pages of his paper, he caught a glimpse of Mabel. She was sitting stiffly, a hand to her back, her face showing pain.

Hello,' he said. 'What's up?'

'I've just had such a spasm across my back,' she answered.

'It's Stephen's news,' Jim said. 'Got yourself worked up.' He felt irritated with Mabel. No wonder she suffered spasms. How women fussed! He buried himself behind his newspaper.

Mabel spent a large part of the evening apparently reading, but in reality thinking about her son. She thought about him in a tender way. He had never given her a 'rough ride' like some sons gave their mother. He'd never been lazy or rude; he'd always done any little job she'd asked of him and without grumbling. She started to worry lest this unknown Jean should take advantage of him. To Jim, over supper, she said, 'I hope Jean isn't a career woman,' and added, 'Stephen is used to being looked after.'

Jim made an impatient sound. 'Oh, for goodness sake!' he exclaimed, 'He's been on his own long enough to know how to look after himself. If he doesn't know by now he never will!' He thought his wife stupid. 'He's a man, not a baby,' he told her.

To herself, Mabel said resignedly, 'Jim's right. He's a man now! He does what he wants. You can't tell a man what to do.' Over the years, this was a sentiment she had got into the habit of uttering whenever her husband did anything to which she had expressed opposition or had refused to do something which she had especially wanted done. Now she transferred the saying to Stephen.

Jim said suddenly, 'Women change when they have a child.'

Mabel was startled at this remark, so unexpectedly uttered. She did not answer. She went on feeling uneasy about Jean.

Jim left the table and went back to his newspaper. All Mabel could see of him was the top of his head. She sometimes thought he must be the most knowledgeable person in the country by the amount of reading he did. She would have liked to have talked her silly anxieties out of her. She told herself she knew they were silly, but that did not help. She thought it was unfair that she could not talk about her worries to Jim when in the past Jim had so often poured out his worries to her and always into a sympathetic ear. In the early days of her marriage she had been rather free with her thoughts until she had discovered that Jim took a poor view of the intelligence of most women. Now she preferred to stay silent. She did not care to leave herself open to a sarcastic remark – or worse, a silence. She felt humiliated when she spoke and Jim did not bother to answer. She began to view the coming meeting with a certain dread.

On the agreed Sunday, Stephen and Jean turned up and everything went off smoothly, the only difficulty arising out of the fact that at dinner Jean seemed to be stricken with verbal paralysis. After dinner, she was more at her ease. Jim wanted to know all about her studies and plans for the future.

'Just as if she isn't getting married and probably starting a family,' Mabel was thinking, irritated by all this talk about jobs and openings. She felt a sudden, unexpected bitterness, remembering her own past experience. She heard Jim say, 'You go on with your studies, Jean. Get as far up the ladder as you can.' He added, 'I believe in women being independent.'

Mabel was going to make a remark. She stopped herself just in time. But she thought, 'He's talking to her as if she's the man!' She heard Jean asking him if he supported the emancipation of women. To her annoyance, he replied that he did. She thought, 'He's a nice one to talk!' She recalled his attitude when they had first married. Of course things were different then. Still!

After a while Mabel asked Jean if she would like to see over the house. Jean said she would and followed Mabel out of the room. The two women went up the stairs in silence. Mabel was aware of hostile feelings and so made a special effort to be friendly. As they went into the bedroom, she was telling Jean, 'I was a nurse once; I gave it up when I got married. Women had to then. I didn't want to, I was planning to take exams, qualify to be a Ward Nurse, then a Sister if I could make it.' A note of regret had crept into her voice. 'So I can understand how you feel about your own job,' she finished, trying to sound sympathetic.

They inspected the other two bedrooms. The small one had belonged to Stephen. It held his bed and a table still littered with books. 'I don't touch the books,' Mabel said, with a little amused laugh. 'He used to get quite hot and bothered in the old days if I disturbed anything.' Jean looked and for a moment envied Stephen. Nothing in her home had been sacred.

Mabel began to fidget about the room, showing Jean whatever she could be remotely expected to take an interest in. Bringing out of the wardrobe a much patched and worn pair of dull orange trousers, she said, 'Stephen's old pair of jeans! He wore them when he went fishing with Dad.' She went through the remains of his wardrobe piece by piece. She was finding difficulty in broaching the subject which mainly occupied her mind without seeming to put Jean through an interrogation. At last she forced herself, but it came out brusque, which was just what she had wanted to avoid.

'I suppose you can cook, dear,' she said. She had meant it to be a statement, but it sounded more like a question and Jean took it as such and inwardly resented it.

'Oh, yes,' she replied casually. Then hastily added, 'Not like you!'

Now that she was at last launched, Mabel would not draw back. She went on hurriedly, 'Stephen has been used to being well-looked after. Well, men expect it, don't they? Take my husband now; he can't even boil an egg! When I visit my sister, I have to leave the refrigerator stacked to the roof. It takes me a week of baking! When he runs out, he lives off tins.' As she was speaking, she was aware of a sudden hot current surging through her like a wave. It was her blood pressure. Mabel was frightened. She gave a nervous laugh. Then she steadied herself, finishing rather lamely on the words, 'I can teach you how to make Stephen's favourite dishes, if you'd like.'

But it seemed that Jean did not like, for she did not take up the offer. Mabel felt a keen disappointment. She could not know that Jean was receiving her information with incredulity remembering how Stephen had looked after her when she had been ill; cooking the meals, catering, seeing to everything.

In spite of what Mabel had said about the books, she did turn her attention to them next, making an attempt to sort them out and place them in piles. While she was doing this, she made the remark, 'Stephen has a very good brain, you know.'

'Yes! I know!' Jean said.

'He gets it from his father, of course,' Mabel went on. 'My husband worked himself up from nowhere. Yes. They've both got good brains.'

Jean thought, I wonder if she thinks I'm not intelligent enough for her son? And it was true that Mabel did think that, but she would have thought it of any woman.

Mabel turned back to the wardrobe, taking out the last two garments for inspection, then replacing them and suggesting that they go downstairs for some tea. On the landing, she hesitated, her hand on the stair rail, half turning her head towards Jean, 'You mustn't think I'm criticising Jim, dear,' she said. 'He's a very good husband. I couldn't wish for a better. Only men do expect to be looked after, whatever they *say*.'

They rejoined the two men and conversation of a sort was kept going until the tea was on the table. Mabel insisted on her home-made cakes and biscuits being sampled and was gratified when Jean said she could not do half so well herself. Mabel repeated her offer to teach her and Jean felt that she had inadvertently laid herself open. Soon afterwards they left.

Jean walked up the road alongside Stephen feeling rather depressed. She was not encouraged when Stephen asked, in a slightly irritated voice, 'What was the matter with you? You hardly opened your mouth to Mother.'

She apologised. 'Your mother is a bit overwhelming,' she told him. Stephen was very amused. He saw his mother in quite a different light; a quietly spoken, mild woman of whom nobody could stand in awe. He assured her that once they got to know each other they would get on like a house on fire.

'I'm *sure* we will.' She saw that he very much wanted her to feel that way and so she pretended that she did. But in her own mind she could not imagine getting on easy, still less intimate terms with Mabel, whose priorities were so very different and off-putting. She was haunted for a while by the image of a critical mother-in-law and then consoled herself with the thought that so long as Stephen was not critical of her what did it matter who else was. For the first time she experienced some anxiety as to how he would react to her own home and parents. She had not until that afternoon realised the vast difference in the two backgrounds, but when she thought how Stephen acted in their own home, she admired him the more and was hopeful that all would be well. Still, a part of her was miserable because this was the first time she had found it necessary to lie to him about her feelings.

Meanwhile Mabel was less than satisfied with herself. She knew that she had made a poor start with Jean. At the front door she had gone stiff and her voice had taken on a high, almost unwelcoming note. Just when she had wanted so much to give an impression of warmth. Indoors she had found herself sitting very upright, her hands folded in her lap. She had wanted to be relaxed and friendly, but she had not known how. Then what had possessed her to start talking about Jim's meals? Jean would think she resented having to look after him! How could she have said anything so silly as that he couldn't boil an egg? Of course it was true that he didn't, but that was because she was there to do it for him. He was a good husband. Anyway she ought not to have criticised him in front of Jean. That was disloyalty!

While Jim sat opposite absorbed in a biography, she sat gazing idly down at the open page of her book. She did so hate any deviation from the norm of her feelings. She was unaware that her few words had been sparked off by resentment at what she had overheard her husband saying to Jean. She had thought his remarks hypocritical as if in a mean, sideways manner he had attacked her own way of living all the years they had been together, which, when all was said and done, had added so very much to his comfort and convenience.

She was aware of a confused sense of alarm as if she had stepped outside her own home and unintentionally gone off along an unfamiliar path in the direction of an uncertain future.

Possibly the strength of her alarm, so out of proportion to any of her actual words, was because her son was now lost to her. She knew she was supposed to have gained a daughter, but she did not feel towards Jean in that way; had she allowed herself to be honest, she would have acknowledged that she had taken a dislike to her. But Jean was her son's choice and to criticise her would have been the same as to criticise Stephen for choosing unwisely. This she could not do so she hid her dislike from herself.

Later in the evening she allowed herself the remark that she hoped Jean would be able to combine successfully her role at work and at home. Jim retorted, 'Don't start getting critical now; you women are always having a go at each other!' She shut up quickly.

Besides it was her favourite hour of the whole day and she did not want to spoil it; the hour when Jim finally put away his book and they sat opposite each other with their late night drink, indulging in the easy chit-chat of long acquaintance interspersed with silences that were relaxed and comfortable. She always felt very anchored then.

Jean need not have worried about the visit to her own home. Stephen reacted in the manner usual for a person brought up in a much more favourable environment; his imagination fell short of the reality. He noticed that Jean's parents were less well-off and less well-educated than his own, but he did not consider it their fault and did not consider it important. He thought Jean had not suffered a deprived childhood, by which he meant a lack of the

63

material necessities of life. Another kind of cruelty did not enter his mind. Besides some warmth was shown towards Jean while he was there. He knew that her parents were more conventional than his own parents because Jean had considered it necessary to appear with an engagement ring on her finger; the absence of which had in no way distressed his own mother and father who had turned out so surprisingly liberal.

Both Mary and Bill were determined to make a good impression although from different motives. Mary more from a determination to show Stephen that Jean had had good parents who had known how to bring up children than from any real feeling for Jean. Where her daughter was concerned, she could not overcome her jealousy. Bill was proud of Jean and wanted to boast about her to his future son-in-law who belonged to the 'intellectual' class, the 'brainy ones', and who in this respect was no more than his daughter deserved. So, for both of them, it was an occasion and they dressed up and behaved accordingly.

Jean knew that Stephen had a style quite different from either of her parents, but it was not snobbery that made her fear the meeting, rather a kind of ache, especially for her mother. She wondered how much Stephen guessed of her childhood problems. She had been too loyal to her parents to talk about them.

Mary heard the knock, said, 'They're here!' and went to answer the door. She was curious to see the sort of young fellow Jean had chosen and even more curious to see the sort of young fellow who would choose Jean. Opening the door, she observed that he was good-looking, with style. While waiting, Jean had noticed the scrubbed and whitened front doorstep, the shining brass knocker and the neat edge of the small front lawn. Her hopes rose.

They all sat down in the room next to the kitchen. Mary had wanted to lay out the spread in the front room, which was seldom used, but Bill would not have it. 'We're not going to pretend posh,' he announced. 'If he don't like us, he can lump us.'

But they had both dressed up for the occasion. Bill had shaved, which he did not always bother to do at the weekends, and wore his best brown suit with a striped brown and green tie and a pink flower in his button-hole. His hair, which was still thick, was well brushed, his face tanned by outdoor work and altogether he looked a fine specimen of a man. The only feature which would have given him away to a knowledgeable person was a thickening of the face due to drink.

Mary wore a bright green suit and a white blouse; her hair was still dyed reddish-brown. She greeted Stephen with a warm handshake which concealed the fact that she was feeling a slight awkwardness at first sight of him, but this soon passed. For his part, Stephen was relaxed and at his ease. He thought this was due to his considering everyone as his equal; in actual fact it arose out of an unconscious sense of his own superiority.

When she set herself to the task, Mary was a good cook and everyone could say honestly that they had enjoyed the dinner. Afterwards Bill showed Stephen the garden; the small rose trees near the back door, the flower beds, the allotment with its late cabbages, the loganberry bushes still with some fruit remaining. Stephen admired its well-kept state. 'Weeding is an awful chore,' he said, remembering the times he had helped out his father.

'Yes, it is,' Bill agreed in a hearty tone, pointing out the well-trimmed grass edges. He forgot to mention that it was his wife who did all the work.

Indoors Mary was telling Jean about her new job. 'It's on the Co-op cold meat counter,' she said in a spirited voice. 'I'm kept busy now. I've made a few friends at work, we go to the cinema once a week, and to the pub on a Saturday night. Bill doesn't like me going to a pub, but he has to put up with it. I tell him, it's my own money.'

'You look better, Mum,' Jean said.

'Oh, I am!' Mary told her, with a certain relish in her voice. 'Well, you know your Dad – always at his pub, or with his mates. He made a fuss at first, but much he really cares. It's only his pride that hurts 'cause I've got a bit of independence.' She went on, 'I feel more human now I've got some money of my own. Relying on him for every penny – it was degrading!' She asked Jean about her in-laws.

'Stephen's mother washes up in an old person's home once a week,' Jean told her. 'She has a coffee morning at the church; she arranges flowers.'

'Oh! Does she?' Mary answered, and she gave her disdainful sniff. Jean felt it would have been better if she had not said that. Her mother would think Mabel a prig.

Her mother did not ask Jean about her studies. Jean knew this was a deliberate omission and it hurt her. She did not understand why her mother so much resented her abilities.

Over tea, Bill began boasting about his daughter, much to Jean's embarrassment. 'Our Jean's the bright one of the family,' he said, leaning forward and giving her a pat on the shoulder. '*My* side of the family; takes after my Mum. My Mum was a great reader – she was always at deep books. Just like my Jean.'

'Of course she isn't my daughter as well,' Mary put in, a sarcastic note in her voice. 'She's only *your* daughter, we know!'

'Well, you have to admit, she is my side of the family,' Bill insisted benignly. He repeated, 'Takes after my Mum, she does.'

Turning the conversation onto neutral ground, Jean managed to avert an unpleasant argument. She was relieved when the time came for them to depart without any occasion for further disagreement.

Walking down the street, Stephen commented, 'Your parents are quite a jolly couple.'

' Yes,' Jean said.

Her parents had put on a good face, been polite to their visitor, polite to herself and to each other, told some stories from the old days, even cracked a few jokes and everything had gone on good-humouredly except for the one moment when a quarrel had seemed imminent. She was grateful to them both.

'Yes,' she repeated, 'they used to be very jolly, I believe. When they were young, they went dancing a lot. They were both good dancers, that's how they first met.'

She found herself wondering what they had been like in those now far off days, before either she or Dick had been thought of, when they had both been very young and when they had first met. In spite of photographs, it was difficult to imagine. She thought that the recent afternoon had been in some ways as though one of those old photographs which her mother still kept in a drawer had come temporarily to life, revealing her parents as they had been before they had drawn apart from each other and become enemies.

CHAPTER SEVEN

TWO years passed: Stephen and Jean both completed their training courses. Stephen was to start at a large local comprehensive school in September and Jean at the end of July as an assistant librarian. They decided the time had come to get married; they would take a delayed honeymoon before they became, as Stephen put it, 'wage slaves'.

In early summer they had a quiet wedding at a Registry Office, inviting close relatives and one or two college friends. Dick and Jean had met only very occasionally during the last three years; Jean had not met Betty at all. She was pleased when they both showed up. She noticed a change in her brother. His face, with its freckles, wore its usual pleasant untroubled expression, which with his easy manner still gave him a very youthful look, but he had broadened out and there was something a bit more serious in his gaze when he met Jean's eye, although she did not doubt that he was, in essence, the same easy Dick that she had always known. He introduced Betty as 'my girl friend'.

Stephen had summed Dick up with a look and, apart from politeness, had no further interest in him. However, he gave Betty a few enquiring glances. He thought her a decided personality. She had a shrewd, intelligent face with light grey eyes and straight, almost black hair, worn shoulder length. She was very casually dressed for a formal occasion; bright red slacks, a short sleeved red jersey, white canvas shoes and a shoulder strap bag of a dull blue colour. Her face had no make-up and shone a little. She looked openly at each person in turn as if she was trying to sum them up, but her glances were not unkind. When she met Stephen's eyes she held his gaze until he looked away. After the ceremony, she handed Jean a present from Dick and herself for them both, which turned out to be a couple of very nice book ends. She wished them 'good luck'.

'She's not at all the sort of girl I would have imagined Dick going with,' Jean had commented, 'but they appear to be sticking.'

The marriage had been a disappointing affair for the parents on both sides. For Mary, still resentful over Dick's unceremonious departure and her conviction that he was dispensing with a formal marriage, Jean's affair had been an opportunity to recoup something of what had so far been denied her. She wanted a display much more for her own satisfaction than because she believed it would make any real difference to her daughter's happiness. Now she thought with bitterness how little her feelings counted with either of her children.

In her turn, Mabel would have liked a church wedding; in her view this was right, and a part of her thought the marriage more likely to last if properly solemnized. However she took the disappointment with philosophical calm and did not bear either of the young people a grudge.

Rita also had turned up, her outfit suited to the occasion. Richard was not free, so she had come on her own. Jean thought she looked quite splendid in a dark blue suit with a hat to match, white gloves and white lattice shoes. Stephen put her down as being very conventional, which she was not, and out of their class, which she now was. Rightly he considered her very unlike Jean and wondered at the tenacity of their friendship. Meanwhile the parents exchanged a few words. Mabel thought Bill very agreeable, but Mary rather stand-offish.

When it was all over and they were in the train taking them south, Jean and Stephen looked at each other and began to laugh, then each gave a sigh of relief. It had been an ordeal. After some discussion, they had agreed on a week at the Isle of Wight, followed by a week at Tankerton on the east coast. Jean had long wanted to visit the Island, while Stephen had set his heart on Tankerton solely for the purpose of showing Jean a feature he referred to as 'The Street' and which had taken a grip on his imagination from childhood holidays. It was to be their final splash, they told each other, so they might as well do it properly.

In the early evening, they arrived at Lymington where they were to board the ferry. They had tea and then walked the half mile or so to the jetty with part of their luggage in suitcases and part in rucksacks. Pale greens and yellows were streaking the pearly grey of the sky.

They waited for the ferry to return from Yarmouth. Soon it set out again for the Island, winding its way between the marshes which lay at the mouth of the estuary. The distance was no more than five miles, but to Jean and Stephen leaning over the rail, it seemed to cut them off from England as effectively as if they had been journeying to the far side of the Pacific. It was some little time before they drew away from the mainland and could no longer see the trees close to the shore; dark shapes blending with pale silvery greens. After some twenty minutes they had left the marshes behind and emerged upon open water. The noise made by the paddles was the only sound besides the flapping wings of an occasional seagull as it flew low over the ship, shrieking, or the distant call of a solitary peewee.

Some forty minutes later they were entering Yarmouth harbour, the ferry stopping by a small quay with a grey stone wall.

The sound of paddles suddenly ceased. A strange silence followed, then the hatches were lowered and cars began to make their way onto land. In the evening swell clusters of yachts were dipping gently at anchor, sails furled and laid to rest, tall, upright masts casting long moving shadows on the water which still gave off a pale pink glimmer from the setting sun. The windows of the small, two-storey houses fringing the half-circle of harbour were beginning to light up one by one. It was that short period between the dusk of late afternoon and full evening when objects begin to fade and finally to disappear. As they disembarked, the lighted windows were increasing in number until the whole harbour had become ringed with oblongs and squares of light. By the time they had boarded the bus which was to take them to Totland Bay, dark had come to the Island.

The bus was no more than half full and there was little conversation during the half hour it took to reach their stop. They soon found their hotel, which stood back from the road at the top of a long slope which had been turned into a wooded garden. They picked up their suitcases, pushed open the garden gate and trudged up the steep slope to the house.

'How quiet!' Jean exclaimed, gazing out of their bedroom window at the shadowy hills. Their room was at the back of the house, adequately furnished, but with wallpaper that showed its age and a very ancient gas fire; downstairs there was a dining room with large windows looking out onto the garden and a comfortable lounge. Stephen and Jean were hungry and glad of a meal. Afterwards they made an attempt to explore the garden, but quickly discovered that its many trees made it so dark that they were forced to settle for an early night.

In the morning, after a hearty breakfast, they set out for the day. The walk to the beach was some eight minutes along the village street, then down a road of houses with 'bed and breakfast' notices displayed prominently in many of the windows, reaching finally the tiny pier and the narrow cement walk alongside the sea wall which followed for some miles the sweeping curve of the bay. The sky was now a pale blue, which held a brightness, making it difficult to look upwards for more than a few seconds. White cumulus clouds were motionless on the horizon. The water showed a faint violet tinge which imparted a delicate crystalline gleam to its entire surface. Tiny, white shells lay thickly scattered over the beach giving it a colourless, almost stark look. They took off their clothes, leaving them on the deserted beach and swam naked in the cold, clear water. Then they put on their bathing suits and lay on the hard shells until their bodies had dried. Nothing bothered them, not even the knobbly bits sticking into their backs.

They savoured their youth the whole of that week. One day they chased each other all the way up the steep incline to Tennyson Down, reaching the top breathless and hot and thinking it a great joke. On their right were the chalk cliffs with their sheer drop to the beach; on their left, the downs. They stood looking up at the huge cross placed there to commemorate Tennyson's favourite view; it rose high and bare, outlined against the sky and visible for many miles across the West Wight. They sat at the base of the cross, gazing first inland at the rounded shapes of the downs: brown, green, and bare, receding one behind another into the distance; and then out at the sea where purple fingers ran from the land, betraying in their dark shade the presence of hidden rocks, slimy with seaweed and limpets which with the fall of the tide would emerge to glisten in the sun. Feeling on top of the world, they lay down in the grass and put their arms round each other.

Suddenly Stephen sat up. 'I'm going to run down to the bay,' he said, and sprang to his feet, holding out his hand to Jean. They ran free as the wind, down the long slope to Freshwater Bay.

Their last day on the Island, they swam in the sea, then in the afternoon walked on the downs, ending up in a field. The field was full of rough hummocks. They found a smooth level patch of grass under some sycamore trees and lay down on their backs, close to each other, dozing. They could smell the hot fragrance of cow dung and hear the chirping of birds overhead. A fly crawled across Jean's face. She sat up and looked down at Stephen. He was still lying with his eyes closed. 'He can't be asleep,' she thought, amused, but bending over him she saw that he was. Sleep had smoothed out all the lines of his face; his lips had softened and were slightly open. She could hear his gentle breathing. She lifted the strands of hot, damp hair which lay across his brow and blew them away. She put her little finger under his little finger, raised it and let it go, and it dropped back slack onto his chest. His blue eyes were closed and this struck her as strange. She seemed to know him through the gaze of his bright blue eyes and now that those eyes were no longer visible she thought him oddly removed from her.

She gazed at his still form. Then with the fingers of her left hand an inch or so from his body, she traced his outline on the grass – his feet in their white canvas shoes marked with green smudges, his legs and thighs in their dark green slacks, his chest in its mauve striped t-shirt and unzipped anorak, his right hand lying beside him on the grass, his left hand slack across his body, his face quiet and in repose. She felt that she had marked him out on the earth so that something of him would remain for ever on that spot. The strange idea gave her pleasure. She flicked her little finger mischievously against his cheek. He stirred, opened one eye and asked drowsily, 'What are you doing darling?' 'Nothing,' she answered.

On the way back to the hotel, Jean developed a big blister on her heel. Stephen carried her the last part of the way back to the hotel, tired but glad because he had spared her pain. He was tender and gentle with her as he always was at home when she was out of sorts or tired.

The next morning they left the Island for the east coast. Stephen knew Tankerton well as it had been a favourite holiday spot with his parents during his childhood. It was then that they had introduced him to The Street, the name given by the local inhabitants to an arm of raised sand half way between Tankerton and Whitstable which ran broad and straight for a full mile out to sea. The sand was thickly strewn with shells of all sizes and shapes tossed onto it by the incoming sea and left stranded at its retreat. This phenomenon had been created over a period of time by the meeting of two tides and as a child Stephen had viewed it with awe and delight. Many a happy hour had been spent choosing shells to take home. Growing up, it had remained in his memory. Now he wanted to share this childhood pleasure with Jean.

On their second day, they walked to The Street, about half a mile from where they were staying. The tide was out, a mere faint watery gleam on the horizon; the sand a dull brown desert, but with a soaked look. The Street was visible for the whole of its length, running out to sea as straight as a die, a good foot higher than the rest of the sand and scattered over with pebbles and shells. At first Jean could not understand how such an extra-ordinary phenomenon could have come about.

'You'll see when the two tides come in,' Stephen told her, pleased at her amazement.

They started to walk towards a cluster of black rocks some three-quarters of a mile out. They spent a great deal of time picking up shells, examining them, comparing them, deciding which to throw away and which to take home. At last Jean had collected so many that it entered her head to wonder how she could possibly carry them all home. She decided that she could not and she began to drop the rejected ones back onto the sand. Suddenly she became aware of sounds like tiny splashes; looking down, she saw the shells she had just dropped lying in streams of shallow water. Startled, she turned to the shore. It gave her a shock to see how distant it was. She had not realised how far out they had come. Glancing to each side of her, she saw at once what Stephen had meant by two incoming tides. Looking to her right was like standing on the shore with the sea sounding all along the beach; but instead of the land at her back, on her left there was another sea and other waves coming towards her, sounding along that long second beach. The strength of both tides was evident in their steady flowing towards each other. There was something awesome and magnificent in the thought of their meeting in one great swell of water, running over and submerging The Street until it lay beneath, unseen. Jean glanced down again and saw that the water was deepening, running steadily over the pebbles and the shells. Soon the spot where she stood would be gone. Her imagination conquered her nerve. She turned suddenly, ran and clutched at Stephen's arm where he stood a short distance off, sloshing his feet to and fro in the water. He had taken off his shoes and was holding them in his hand. When Jean came up to him, he had been about to turn back in order to share her delight.

'Isn't it fine!' he exclaimed. But she was in a panic with the sea all about her and her old fear of deep water. He chided her. 'It stays shallow for ages! In any case, you can swim.'

'I don't care,' she retorted. 'I want to go back.'

He was annoyed. 'Don't be silly,' he said.

'I'm not silly!' she said hotly.

'I didn't say you were,' he retorted. 'I said don't *be* silly.'

'It's the same thing!'

'Of course it isn't! If I say, "don't be silly", it means don't act silly. It's not the same thing as saying you *are* silly.'

'It's the same thing,' she repeated, now almost in tears.

'Oh, well! If you insist on being illogical! Anyway, I'm not going to run all the way back – it's too absurd. You can run if you like.' And he threw away the shells in his hand and began to stroll very slowly in the direction of the beach, stopping often and pretending to examine shells as he went. His progress was very slow indeed. He was disappointed with Jean's reaction; he had been so much looking forward to showing her The Street and now she had spoilt his pleasure. The keenness of his disappointment made him harsh and unsympathetic.

Jean left him and walked back to the beach as fast as she could go without actually running, which would have been too humiliating. When she reached the beach she sat down with her back to a rock and waited for Stephen. He rejoined her without a word and together they made their way into the town for something to eat, Stephen making odd remarks and Jean replying as well as her unsettled state would allow. Neither of them referred again to what had taken place.

They bought some sandwiches and orangeade and took them on the beach. Then they decided they had had enough of the beach and would climb up onto the grassy cliffs. They walked along the top for some way, then lay down in a hollow warmed by the sun and out of the wind. Stephen sniffed at the grass; it gave off a warm, scented smell. He wanted to make love, but Jean had been greatly shaken by her experience of the morning and was more resentful than she knew.

'I wish you wouldn't,' she protested, as he fondled her.

'Wouldn't what?' he asked, pretending not to understand.

'You know what... whenever we have an argument.'

'Well, you know it puts you in a good mood again,' he said, as if she were a child who had to be humoured, and she resented this even more.

'I don't want to,' she repeated stubbornly.

But he knew how to make her. It seemed natural to him that he should do this and afterwards they both went to sleep in the warmed hollow. On the way back to the hotel, he put his arm around her waist and it was just as he had said it would be: she smiled at him and was loving. And he thought everything was all right between them.

But two nights later in bed she had a small problem which she could not account for and of which he was unaware. For the first time she was unable to respond to his advances. 'Come on, darling!' he urged, the slightest hint of impatience in his voice. For the first time she did him a favour, and was amazed when he seemed not to know. He was satisfied and rolled over onto his back and almost at once was asleep. She could hear his gentle breathing as he lay beside her. She was thunderstruck. She had thought they were together when they made love. He had not known that she had not had an orgasm, had simply been generous. Was his experience a solitary one then, which only required from her the right physical responses? Was that all the act meant to him? A void between them seemed to open. In the morning, she wanted to speak of her trouble to Stephen, but she found she could not.

On their last morning, Stephen asked in a casual voice, 'Shall we go to The Street and collect a few more shells? You'll probably be used to it a second time.' She knew he wanted to go and she agreed, but her heart had pounded. The tide was in and The Street under water. She experienced a sense of immense relief. They spent the morning swimming and later went to Whitstable and walked along the glistening sand, watching the tide receding. The last night they made love again and everything was all right. Jean began to forget what had happened until finally she seemed to have forgotten it altogether, but it lay at the far back of her mind.

CHAPTER EIGHT

B Y the autumn, both Jean and Stephen were at work and student days seemed far behind. On her free Wednesday afternoons, Jean would take the washing to the launderette, vacuum the flat, and cook their evening meal. Often Stephen would be back first when it fell to him to get the evening meal. While Jean was at the library on Saturdays, he did the weekly shopping and the ironing. Whatever was left over, they disposed of together the next day, but they aimed to keep Sundays free so that they could get out. They had a deep attachment to each other which made being together a pleasure. They thought of themselves as equals.

In November, Jean received a letter from Rita. 'We've got a little daughter, Sarah,' she wrote. 'Come and see her, both of you, then Stephen and Richard can meet.' She added, 'I was pregnant at your wedding!' Jean was not suprised at the news for she knew Rita enjoyed sudden revelations. When Jean told Stephen he made a joke about being beaten a long way from the finishing line. Jean bought a soft teddy bear for Sarah and they both went over the next Sunday.

Rita met them at the station and they sat in the back of the car and listened to her telling the news over her shoulder. Sarah was six weeks' old. Rita looked well and talked away as if she hadn't a care in the world.

They were soon at the house. The two men were introduced and they all sat down in the living room with a sherry. Then Rita went to fetch Sarah and came down with her asleep in her arms. They all admired her and commented on likenesses.

'My mother says she's the image of me at her age,' Rita said, laughing. 'Come on, get in some experience!' handing the sleeping child to Jean. 'She shouldn't wake; she's been fed.' Richard walked Stephen round the garden, then took him to look at their accumulation of books, commenting, 'I don't know where we shall put them when the baby takes over this room. The house is too small for three.' Stephen thought of their single room; if ever they had a child, they would have to find somewhere bigger.

Jean was left alone with the baby. She gazed down at the wrapped bundle on her lap and with her little finger gently touched the soft, warm cheek. The eyes were hidden behind the dark eyelashes, but the tiny face looked out at her as out of a nest. She experienced a new, strong sensation, a melting feeling. She had nursed her brother, but that had been different. She had been very young and not all her feelings had been pleasant ones. She could recall jealousy at all the rapt attention and praise he was receiving from her mother. She had never before held a baby girl in her arms and as she bent over the sleeping child she was aware of a mixture of tenderness and pity. One tiny hand was lying outside the shawl. Gently she lifted the hand and very gently uncurled the fingers. Her heart seemed to melt at the sight of the tiny hand and the tiny exquisite fingers, with faint creased lines visible on the rosy living flesh. The feeling was so strong in her that it was like a pain.

Rita announced that lunch was ready and they all sat down at table and Richard opened a bottle of champagne to celebrate. Afterwards Rita took Jean into the kitchen on the pretext of helping to clear away, but really for the purpose of a chat. As she stacked the dishes in the machine, she told Jean about her plans; she was looking out for a reliable woman with good references and fond of children who would take over the care of Sarah and the house for the greater part of each day so that she could go

75

back to work as soon as Sarah could crawl. 'I couldn't stand being tied to the home! Luckily Richard's parents are very keen on having grandchildren and they can afford to give us quite a lot of help until he gets going.' They planned to have two children spaced out in the recommended manner. 'We don't think one child is fair.'

Starting the machine, she said with a laugh, 'Money may not be a girl's best friend, but it gives a good imitation!' When she had made remarks of a similar nature during Jean's earlier visit, Jean had inwardly reacted in a critical manner, but now she was conscious of stirrings of envy. Then she had had only contempt for her friend's attitude and on the way home in the tube had experienced a sense of moral superiority. She still recognised that Rita's freedom would be based on another woman doing the work, that this was no real solution to the problem, merely a self-centred way out. She knew all this, but she could no longer feel that it was such a reprehensible thing to do.

Rita asked Jean if she wanted a family. When Jean gave an ambivalent reply, she said, 'Well, don't leave it too late. The risks increase with age, and besides, older parents aren't fair on the children. We aim to have our second child in two years time.'

Listening, Jean felt a sense of alarm; she was older than Rita. While she was thinking this, she heard Rita say, in a satisfied voice, 'Now you see how sensible I was not to marry Derek. He's a pauper next to Richard.'

'Do you hear from him then?' Jean asked.

'Very occasionally. He's married.'

'Oh!' Jean said.

'Well, that's life,' Rita answered, with a slight shrug of her shoulders. Her eyes shone a little as she added, 'You don't forget, you know!' and her voice took on a softened note.

When they were getting ready to go, Rita asked, 'Want to have a last look at the baby?' Jean nodded. Upstairs they both leant over the cot with its sleeping child. Jean was pleased when she saw that Rita had put their teddy bear at the foot of the cot. As she gazed at the child, she was conscious of a yearning feeling.

On the way home, Jean asked Stephen what he thought of her friend. Stephen said he thought Rita had a very strong personality, but he had some doubts about the manner in which they both looked at things.

'What things?'

76

'Oh, nothing especially; I think perhaps they're a bit inclined to go after the main chance.' Jean did not think that was a very nice thing to say and they almost had a quarrel.

'Well, they suit each other anyway,' Stephen said, with the intention of pacifying Jean. But she did not like that remark either.

Back home, they only had time for a nightcap before bed. On the Monday there was work and Jean thought she had put the visit out of her mind. Still, she found herself thinking about Sarah. She felt her presence as if she was still holding her in her arms, bending over her, looking down at the tiny person snuggled in her soft warm nest and feeling the touch of the star-like hand. Whenever she felt like this, her heart contracted with longing. Then she would think about what Rita had said about older parents not being fair on children and she would calculate how long it would be before she was thirty and the time seemed alarmingly close.

One evening she asked Stephen, 'Do you think it matters being an older parent – matters for the children, I mean?' Stephen said it depended what was meant by older, but generally speaking he supposed a younger mother was better for producing a healthy baby, and of course younger parents were better for the children. He spoke just like Rita had done.

'But if there are reasons for waiting?' she asked.

'If there are serious reasons,' he said, 'then it doesn't matter all that much. One has to balance advantages against risks.' He went on to analyse the alternatives at some length, talking rather as if addressing a class. While he was talking, she got very tense.

When he had finished, she asked, with a touch of nervousness in her tone, 'But what about us? What do you think about us – you and me?'

He looked at a loss. 'What about us?' he asked. Then when she did not speak, he said, 'I thought we'd discussed it.' It was her turn to be surprised. Had they really discussed it? Perhaps they had; yes, she thought they had mentioned children right at the start. They had agreed that they would not have children until later in their lives; perhaps they would not have children at all. Now she saw that they had simply shelved the question. All they had wanted was to be together.

'I don't think we really did discuss it – not seriously,' she answered hesitantly. 'I think we let it lie.' She waited hopefully for what he might say.

What he said was, 'Well, darling, you know I like children, but you're the one who has to have the child. You must decide.'

He turned his attention back to the book he had been studying before Jean had interrupted his concentration. Now she sat thinking. Was he saying that he would like children, but that he would give them up for her, that her happiness meant more to him even than children, than being a father? And if he did not become a father, would he suffer, would he suffer a lot – or only a little, or perhaps not at all? She looked at him absorbed in his book. She wanted to penetrate his feelings, but she could not. He had spoken in such a quiet, restrained voice and looked at her with such a calm gaze. She did not feel calm at all.

Evidently he had been thinking, for he looked up suddenly.

'Is it Rita's baby that upset you?'

'I'm not upset!' she answered sharply.

'Well, perhaps,' she finally confessed.

For a few moments he was silent, then, 'Think it over!' He spoke in a kind voice. 'After all, we're only twenty-five and your work means a lot to you.' He added, after a pause, 'Think it over carefully. Don't be in too much of a hurry to make up your mind.'

She did not reply and no more was said. He went back once more to his book. Jean pretended to read, but her mind was turning over his words, 'Don't be in too much of a hurry to make up your mind.' *Her* mind, it was her decision then, not their joint decision, but her decision alone? It was the first time since their coming together that he had told her to make up her mind without him. The thought made her feel very alone.

She tried to put the problem out of her head; Stephen had been right to say there was no hurry. The months passed. While she was at work, she was happy and felt fulfilled. It was in the evenings that she sometimes became unsettled and restless.

She was glad when Rita phoned and asked her over. She went on her free afternoon. Sarah was now seven months and sitting up. The play pen had been put in one corner of the large living room and Sarah sat in the middle among her toys, staring up at Jean. She was a happy child and, like her mother before her, advanced for her age. When Jean smiled down at her, she smiled back and gave a chuckle. Jean picked her up, she was quite heavy and plump, and when Jean started to jog her up and down on her knee she gave little excited cries. She slapped Jean's face with her fingers and laughed. At tea, Rita put her into her high chair. All the while Jean was eating, she was noticing Sarah; how she banged her spoon on the sides of the chair, bounced up and down and made repeated, clumsy efforts to feed herself. A little later Rita said it was time for bye-byes and took Sarah up in her arms. 'Want to come and see her in the bath?' she asked.

Rita was very brisk and quick, but she let Sarah splash the water at Jean and Jean splash back before she firmly put an end to their fun. She soon had Sarah dried and in her nightgown. 'She's going to marry a rich man and live a lazy life!' she announced, lifting her daughter up and looking at her proudly before putting her down in her cot.

When Jean was leaving, she went upstairs for a last look at Sarah. She was asleep, the blankets kicked to one side, her little arms and legs stretched out, her face slightly flushed, one small fist clenched in sleep, breathing softly. Jean bent down and stroked the child's forehead and felt herself melt with tenderness.

She got home in the late evening. The house seemed empty with only herself and Stephen in it. She wanted a child. When she was at home she felt this way, but when she was at work she felt fulfilled. Whenever books were returned in a sorry state from rough use, finger-marked, or with dirt or jam smears, she got angry; she felt as if a human being, not merely bound sheets of paper, had been badly treated. When she told Stephen, he said that it was a good sign, it meant that the books were being read and, after all, they were not sacred objects. But Jean felt that they were.

She began to notice babies in prams in a way that she had never done before. She yearned over them and began to want so badly to touch them that she had to restrain herself by an act of will. Then she went into work and felt her normal, fulfilled self again.

She began to suffer nightmares in which she was paralysed.

She tried to reopen the subject with Stephen, but he did not seem able to grasp her problem. 'Well, darling, you'll have to make a choice,' he said in his kind, reasonable tone of voice after he had listened to her patiently.

He told her, 'I can't be the mother,' and explained to her the practicalities of their situation. 'You don't need to become a cabbage,' he reassured her, 'I'd hate that anyway.' He went on to explain to her that once the child had reached school age, she would be free to look out for a job. He suggested, jokingly, that she might consider taking up teaching. Then there was the possibility of a nursery school, which would give her more time to herself while the child was still very young. He went on in this strain for some while, trying his best to be helpful.

It seemed to Jean that he must have taken her hopes, her ambitions, very lightly if he could so easily see her abandon them. She wondered if he himself could so easily abandon his own plans; his interest in educational theories, his hopes of trying out these theories at a later stage in his career, his ambitions for his life's work. She was afraid to put the question to him in case he should again emphasise the difference between them; in case he should say again that he could not be the mother.

After a time she brightened up and told herself that she was being silly. Then she thought how dreadful it would be to give in her notice and not to go to the library any more, to have to put aside her hopes and aspirations which she had thought they shared together. She wanted so badly to talk to Stephen about the confusion in her thoughts and emotions that she made a further attempt, but he began to get impatient and to hint that she was making a fuss about problems which other women found it quite possible to deal with successfully.

When he got impatient, a cold tone came into his voice and his blue eyes took on a cold look, and this frightened her. So she made no further attempts to talk to him about the things that were worrying her, but shut them up in her mind because there they were safe.

On her twenty-sixth birthday, they opened a bottle of wine and Stephen put his arm round Jean's waist and said jokingly, 'We're growing old!' and Jean put her head down on his shoulder and said nothing.

Five weeks later Stephen said to her, 'Did you forget on purpose?' Jean shook her head, which as far as she could tell, was the truth, but she knew Stephen did not believe her. So the problem was finally settled. They added up; it was June, the baby would be born the following March.

Secretly Stephen was glad, for he had always wanted children and it seemed to him natural that a woman should prefer children to a career, however interesting. He had not known that he thought that, he only knew it when the situation arose.

He was very considerate to Jean during the whole of her pregnancy.

'You're spoiling me!' she said when he insisted on taking care of more than his fair share of the chores. 'I'm not ill!' But he only

80

smiled and kissed her on the nape of her neck, which was a favourite kissing spot of his.

When the day came for Jean to give in her notice, she did so with an unreal feeling. In spite of knowing otherwise, she felt that everything would carry on indefinitely in the normal way. When, at seven months, the final Friday arrived, she went to work with a certain dread as to how she would react. The presents and goodbyes upset her a bit, but she walked out still with the feeling that she would be back after the weekend. Her money was paid into her bank account monthly so that she did not handle a wage packet with the knowledge that this was the last of her own money, that after it was spent she would be a dependent, that she and Stephen were no longer on an equal footing. The change was too major for her to grasp at once.

When Monday morning came, Stephen kissed her and left for work, leaving her behind. It gave her an odd, unhappy sensation, but she busied herself and in this way got over it. Besides, it was a relief not to have to carry her burden to work, to be able to rest when she felt fatigued and to attend the ante-natal clinic without an irrational sense of guilt at having time off while others were working. There were occasions when her old uncertainties returned and she was beset by a sudden doubt, almost a panic, as to whether she had done the right thing. She would have liked to talk her doubts out of her, but she knew she could not turn to Stephen because he had already told her that when the baby was born he would help in all ways possible, and she knew that he thought that statement covered everything and that there was nothing left to discuss.

It was a time of expectancy; it felt like a pause in both their lives. Jean lived wholly in the present, for there were a lot of preparations to be got through. She went into town to buy a shawl for the baby. She wanted the shawl to be very special and finally chose one of white merino wool, very soft to the touch. While she was paying for it, she felt the baby move inside her and she took that as a happy augury. She had been in bed when she had first felt the baby and had held her breath and lain very still wondering if she could have been mistaken, so faint had those first movements been. A week later she was quite sure – the baby was alive and kicking. Once when she was at work, it kicked so hard, sticking its little foot against her right side, that it hurt her and she gave the spot a light tap. The kicking instantly ceased; this amused her. When they were both in bed, Stephen would put his hand on her stomach and let it lie there so that he too could feel the movements of their baby.

The nappies and other necessities, Jean bought locally, also the pram. She bought a net to safeguard the baby from cats who might be inclined to lie on its chest, and a canopy to shade its eyes from the glare of the sky. There seemed no end to the unborn child's needs.

'It's our sophisticated society,' Stephen commented. 'Now if we lived in a tribe, you would simply go into the bush and come back with the child wrapped in an old piece of cloth.'

'And it might die,' Jean retorted tartly.

One day he came back from the library with two books: *Baby's First Year* and *Child Psychology*.Later, rummaging among second-hand books during his lunch hour, he came across a paperback: *The Mother's Cookery Book: Suitable Meals for Children up to Five Years*. He read through all these books with keen interest; in the evenings, he read bits out of them to Jean. For some weeks the subject absorbed his spare time. He missed nothing out; he studied how and when to pot a baby, how to sterilize bottles, how to put on nappies, how to avoid rashes, and the best ways of bringing up wind. He familiarized himself with childhood ailments and how to recognise them.

'I had no idea there was so much to it!' he told Jean. Finally everything was in order.

The waters burst at ten o'clock in the morning. Jean was on her own. She phoned Stephen's school and went off in a taxi to the hospital where she had a quick delivery for a first child. Stephen got to the hospital well in time to witness the birth. 'I don't really care either way so long as you are all right,' he had told Jean, but he was secretly disappointed when the baby turned out to be a boy.

After the birth, Jean was very tired and went to sleep. When she awoke, she was on her own. The baby was in a cot at the end of her bed and she could hear it whimpering. She lay for some time listening to his faint calls; then, in spite of weariness, she began to worry lest he should be in any kind of trouble. With an effort, she crawled to the foot of the bed, but she could not tell how the baby was; he was all wrapped up and lying on his side, his face away from her, so that all she could see were a few dark hairs. Then a nurse arrived and shooed her back to bed. 'He's hungry,' the nurse said and she put the baby into Jean's arms and its mouth against her right nipple. At once the baby began to suck.

Five days after the birth, Jean left hospital. Stephen called for her in a taxi. The nurse carried the baby, wrapped in the soft white shawl, and handed the bundle to Jean when she was seated inside the taxi. As Jean took the baby, she was conscious of a sudden qualm, a sudden wish that the nurse was coming with her. The nurse waved a smiling goodbye from the steps of the hospital.

When they got home there were three of them instead of two, and this seemed very strange indeed. Jean sat in the rocking chair which Stephen had bought as a surprise on her return and gave the baby his first feed in his own home. Meanwhile Stephen saw to the dinner; he had gone to special pains. They drank each other's health in white wine and felt happy and relieved that it was all over. Then Stephen washed up and put away, while Jean sat and savoured the pleasure of being again in the old familiar room. Stephen came in with the coffee and sat down opposite and they chatted while they drank, and for a short while it seemed to them both that they were alone; just as before, just the two of them.

Next day they decided to call their son Robbie. At the end of the week, the welfare nurse called to assure herself that all was well. After that, Jean went regularly to the local clinic.

Then the family visits took place; first Mary and Bill, then Mabel and Jim. They gazed at the baby and made the usual comments about familiar chin, eyes, nose, and so on. They left presents and both grandmothers told Jean to let them know if she needed any help. In this way the first few weeks quickly went by and soon mother and child had been home a month. Then Rita and Richard called. Rita said the baby had Stephen's eyes and forehead and Jean's mouth and nose and Richard agreed. Jean said the grandparents had not been able to agree about like-nesses and Rita commented that they never did and they all laughed.

Every afternoon before Stephen came home, Jean gave Robbie a bath. She undressed him, gently lowering him into the warm water, her right hand under his head which looked ab-surdly big for his lanky body and arms and legs. Each time as soon as she started to soap him, he set up a great squeal of rage and clenched his little fists and rolled his eyes in righteous anger so that Jean felt sorry for him, but when she had dried him on her lap, put on his nappy and pyjamas, wrapped him warmly in a small wool blanket and put him up to her right breast, then, as if by magic, the cries and howls of protest ceased and there came the soft sucking sound of his mouth pulling at her nipple and the milk oozing out, spotting her breast and trickling out of the corner of his mouth as he paused for a rest. After some minutes, she would squeeze his nose gently, lifting him off her right nipple and putting him to the other breast, where he would suck again until he was satisfied and his lips became slack. As he lay against her, warm and full, she would smile down at him and he would smile back; sometimes his smile would be a joyous, cheeky smile. Then she felt that she and the baby were one and she was content in a way she had never been content before.

After this last feed and before Stephen came home, she would lay the drowsy child in his cot and then she would stand by the window listening for the sound of his gentle, contented breathing. When it reached her, she would think, 'In the future, when he is grown up, gone away, perhaps very far away, I shall remember these moments.' It was a strong fancy with her, but she kept it to herself lest Stephen should smile at it.

Stephen had other things on his mind. He was in a strange new situation. Only yesterday, he and Jean had shared responsibilities. Now, suddenly, he was on his own, solely responsible for the welfare of two other human beings. He did not say to himself in so many words that he was now the head of the family, but without consciously thinking so he acted and felt as if this was the case. Jean seemed unaware of any problem that did not relate directly to Robbie. Proud as he was of being a father and fond as he was of his son, there were times when he found himself regretting the past. One such time was when he would return home to find Jean seated in the rocking chair, her eyes half closed, gently rocking herself and the baby to and fro. Then he would shut the door quietly and stand for some moments in silence gazing at his wife and son.

He would feel totally excluded. He would feel that he had ceased to count. Suddenly aware of his presence, Jean would rouse herself, put the baby into his cot, and go to prepare the meal. They would sit down at the table facing each other as in the old days, and over the meal she would ask him about his day at school and he would tell her, but he felt that her interest was lukewarm. When he asked her about her day with the baby, she would become suddenly animated and recount every little incident, many of which were boring to him. She seemed to find every tiny detail of Robbie's daily existence engrossing. The truth was that at this stage she was so taken up with the baby as to be quite literally out of herself.

He thought, 'Well, it's only natural,' but a part of him regretted the change in their relationship and was aware of a keen sense of loss.

CHAPTER NINE

T HE baby was named Robert Stephen, but everyone went on calling him Robbie; it seemed friendly.

The birth of their first grandchild was a proud event in the lives of all four grandparents, but their feelings were by no means the same. Secretly Mabel was intensely disappointed that the newcomer was not a girl; how nice it would have been to have had someone of her own sex in the family. Of course there was Jean, but somehow she did not feel towards Jean as she had hoped. It wasn't that she disliked her, more a sense of distrust. She suspected that Jean might have priorities other than Stephen. Then Jean kept her at arm's length – there was no other way of putting it. She resisted confidences between women – and Mabel would so very much have liked that. Mabel was convinced that Jean would turn out to be a careerist so she was genuinely surprised and delighted when told that a baby was on the way. She had misjudged her daughter-in-law: staying at home to rear a family was not after all something Jean considered beneath her.

Mary's feelings were altogether different. She was pleased to be a grandparent. After all, the event so far as the mother was concerned had started with herself and she saw the baby as at least partly her own personal achievement. She was glad it was a boy; she preferred boys to girls and then boys had a much better chance in life.

With Bill, it was simply that he was glad that everything had gone off well for his 'little girl' and he was inordinately proud to have become a grandfather. He boasted about it at work in a rather silly way, causing some smutty jokes, which he did not like, but he consoled himself with the thought that the child was certain to turn out brainy and would not have to mix with 'that low lot', by which he meant his workmates.

Like his wife, Jim too was disappointed that the baby was not a girl. He had fancied a little girl because he could take her about and make a fuss of her, kissing and cuddling her; something which had been impossible with Stephen. With the lad he had boxed and played the sort of rough games where one feigned attacks and defences and, when he was older, he had taken Stephen to football matches where the competitive instinct was given a proper stimulus with badges, rattles and scarves. All that was beyond Jim now. However it would have been quite within his capacity to play ball with a little girl, to float boats on ponds, to engage in some gentle romping and to go walking with a sweet or toy shop in view. Then there was the zoo. Of course he could do some of this with Robbie, but it would not be the same. He would have to feel proud of him in quite a different way.

As always happens in these cases, after a short while both hopes and disappointments were forgotten; the baby took a grip as a real person they could not possibly wish away, or wish different and then, by a kind of unspoken agreement, they left the new parents in peace for a while. Contact was maintained by brief letters and prearranged calls from a telephone box. Mabel wished the couple had not chosen to live so far away, but then she reminded herself that when she had been a young woman she had not wanted to live in her parents' pockets. She accepted it as she had learned to accept most things and, as was usual with her, she looked for the compensations.

When the baby was about two months' old, Dick came to take a look, bringing Betty with him. They came to Sunday dinner. Dick said the baby looked like him; Betty said that was his pride and actually he looked like his mother, which a little annoyed Stephen who thought Robbie had a decided look of his father.

Placed opposite Betty at table, Stephen was able to eye her surreptitiously and make up his mind whether his first brief impression of her at the registry office still stood. She had discarded her rather startling get-up and instead wore orange slacks and an emerald green jersey which admirably suited her black hair and light grey eyes. Her arms, emerging from the short sleeves, were a honey colour. She had an aquiline nose, high cheek bones and an alert look; her mouth was full, but firm. When she spoke, her tone was clear with a decided ring to it and when she looked at Stephen, which she did quite often, she looked at him openly and when she caught his eye she held his gaze so that it became almost a battle of wills as to who would look away the first. Stephen thought her very attractive in a bold way and he wondered what could have drawn the couple together; he had summed Dick up as a very ordinary sort of fellow. His own mind was made up quickly and when he met someone who was slower and less articulate than himself he was apt to write the person off as dull. In spite of considering Betty attractive, he did not think he much liked her and he was quite sure that he would not want to spend a lot of time in her company.

On their way home, Dick commented, 'He's got style. I expect that's why Jean fell for him. We don't have much style in our family.'

'That's not very nice,' Betty objected.

'No, but it's true. And you're all for always speaking the truth.' His voice held a hint of sarcasm.

Thinking of one or two remarks which Betty had made, Stephen said to Jean, 'She's a bit sharp!'

Jean nodded. 'Yes. She's not at all the sort of girl I would have expected Dick to take up with. But then, I never thought he'd go to live in a commune. I expected him to look out for some pretty, domesticated type and settle down with her.' She said this not in a derogatory way, but merely as a statement of how she saw her brother.

Of all the grandparents, Mabel was probably enjoying her new status the most. Having got over her first disappointment, she had already forged an attachment to Robbie which was adding a new interest to her life. She felt strongly that she would like to do something very special to celebrate his arrival. To Jim, she suggested a day out in London, a meal and then a cinema or theatre matinee, but he would not be persuaded.

'I don't like meals out,' he told her.

In the end she went on her own. Sitting in the bus, Mabel found herself wondering how she should order her day. Although she knew from long experience that Jim was very stubborn when it came to anything he did not want to do, she had been hoping that she would be able to persuade him to go with her. Still, he never minded her leaving him at home and going off on her own. He would say, 'You go! I can manage,' but, of course, she always left him a meal to heat up – or, like today, a cold lunch.

The trouble was that she did not particularly enjoy going about on her own and the older she got the more she tended to restrict her outings to nearby shopping centres and local cinemas; occasionally she would venture as far as the nearest suburban theatre. However, on this occasion nothing could hold her back from celebrating, so here she was, sitting in the bus on her way to Manor House tube station, a whole day in front of her to be used in such a way that afterwards she would remember it as very special.

At Manor House, she got off the bus, bought a ticket at the tube station and stepped onto the escalator with a real sense of thrill. She loved the smooth movement carrying her downward. Waiting on the platform for the train gave her another thrill. She had loved the tubes ever since the first time she had been taken underground by her father. She could still recall her amazement at the sight of the moving staircase and her delight at the sights and sounds going on beneath the streets. The noise of the approaching train had alarmed her, making her cling to her father's hand in a minor panic. Her first experience of travelling through the tunnels at what had seemed very high speed and with a continual roar had remained with her to that day. Now she heard the sound of the approaching train in the tunnel with a quickening of her pulse and a little thump of her heart. As she took her seat in the train, she laughed at herself for her childish excitement, but she felt suddenly very free. The train set off into the tunnel and she was away.

But she had a problem – it seemed unnatural, this having no one to consider but herself. She knew that in her past she had experienced that sort of freedom, but it was so far back that she could no longer recall what it had felt like. Even when she went to the library to change her books, she always chose books for Jim first and only afterwards thought about her own choice. Now there was only her own choice to consider and she was finding it difficult coming to a decision. Finally she decided that she would take a walk through one of the large stores as a sort of starter.

The huge department store was very stuffy and she wondered why it was that air conditioning had not been installed; so much more comfortable for customers and staff alike. She started to wander about the ground floor, always her favourite area because it housed what she thought of as the frivolities – and frivolities were what she sought, the sight of them made her feel on holiday. As usual it was packed with people; some buying, others, like herself, just looking. There was a constant hum of voices. The counters, stretching away into far distances, were all piled high with an incredibly varied assortment of goods. There was so much to gaze at, so much bustle, so many sights and sounds, that Mabel felt she had gone inside an Aladdin's cave; only it was too warm for a cave, more like a transformation scene out of one of those old-fashioned pantomimes which she had used to enjoy so much as a child. She lingered at the cosmetics counter, fascinated by the bottles of all sizes, shapes and colours. She had never made up much as a girl; even now she only made up in a way that was termed discreet. She could not understand how so many of the older women could turn themselves into such frights, with bright red lips and bouffant perms; some even went in for pencilled eyebrows and shaded eyelids. It all only accentuated their age. Not that there was any crime in being old, Mabel thought to herself. She lingered quite a while at the cosmetics counter where a young woman was demonstrating the best way to apply make-up. She could not help admiring her efficient manner and the clear tones in which she named each item in turn, applying each to her face as she did so – cleanser, toner, moisturiser, nourishing cream, eye cream, mascara, lipstick, rouge... Mabel lost count. She began to feel quite dirty. The only cleanser she had ever used was cold cream and the only beauty aid Pond's powder. When all the applications had been made, the young woman certainly did look dewy; but then she was very young and would have looked fresh and blooming with the aid only of her own skin. She was decidedly pretty. Mabel thought, 'They know how to choose them!' She moved away and found herself by the handbag counter; a real muddle, people had been rummaging among the many different shapes and sizes – blues, blacks, browns, greens, dark reds, travelling bags, shoulder bags, evening bags. She handled a few for the pleasure. They had looked nice lying on the heap, but really were rather cheap quality, and pricey. At the costume jewellery counter, she lingered; there was a side of her which delighted in childish things. She was especially taken by the poppets hanging in rows from thin metal arms; blues, pinks, ivories, whites. She would have liked to have bought one of the long white poppets; they were so convenient, the way they could be shortened or lengthened at will, she used to wear them a lot. Then she had to give them up, her fingers had stiffened and lost their push power and when she had wanted to shorten or lengthen a necklace the bead had refused to click in, instead it had bent like soft wax. She felt disappointed because there were no necklaces that would go

89

with her rather small wardrobe; the ones she did like were too expensive. Besides, she thought to herself, at her age there was no real point in paying out a lot of money. She had got into the habit of thinking of herself as old.

She moved on to inspect the ranks of umbrellas. What an improvement on the old days when umbrellas were such a dull colour; now they were all colours and even the patterns were varied. One of the compensations of going out in the rain was seeing all the coloured umbrellas, like bright posters or real paintings, but not those awful modern ones with neurotic figures twisting themselves about, or a mumble of flashy lines as understandable as a jig-saw puzzle before the pieces had been joined up. She found herself stopping to watch another demonstrator – a young girl – this time using scarves. What dexterity! The point, it seemed, lay in the clip; if she bought the clip she would be able easily to fix any scarf quite twenty different ways; classic, maxi-bow, half-bow, gipsy bow, neck wrapper, dress tie, flare, great turban... Here Mabel lost count and forgot the names. She stood fascinated while the girl demonstrated each style in turn; draping, whipping off, re-draping for the slow-of-comprehension, tying the scarf with a simple wrist movement into a lovely bow, then one swift pull and the scarf was freed and ready to be redraped. Mabel thought that it would be nice to be able to wear one scarf in so many different ways. The clip was not all that expensive. It seemed less so after the demonstration than it had done before. She bought a multi-clip, as it was called, and, of course, a scarf to go with it; for it appeared that it did require a scarf of a certain shape. She put the purchases into her handbag; they hadn't been expensive, she told herself again, giving the clasp of her bag a decided snap with a sense of having accomplished something.

After the excitement was over, she realised that she must have been standing for over ten minutes and was hot and tired. She went upstairs in the lift to the toilets, then left the store and got on a bus to Oxford Circus. She knew where she wanted to go if the restaurant still existed. She and Jim had eaten there years ago. The fact seemed somehow to make it friendly. She found the place; it had changed to a trattoria and was quite different inside, but she was glad it was still there. It was very crowded, but she was lucky. She found a seat next to the window where she could watch the crowds crossing and recrossing the Circus. She studied the menu. This was a great moment for her. There were some very expensive dishes and she let her eyes flick past these. Finally she settled on what was really her favourite dish: fried fish and chips. As this was a treat day, she decided to order plaice instead of cod, which was cheaper, but not so nice. The waiter came for her order and she gave it with quite a glow of pleasure. It was such a treat to be served – no frying beforehand and no greasy dishes afterwards. All she had to do was to sit and be waited on. It made her think of the time when she had been in hospital for a minor operation; when she was beginning to feel much better and was waiting for the surgeon to come and discharge her later in the week she had lain comfortably in bed wondering what would be for lunch and evening meal. Some of the women had grumbled, but she had agreed with the lady in the next bed that there was no need. Those few days had been lovely. Not knowing what was going to be served up – she had felt like Royalty! When Jim had had to go into hospital, he had taken a very poor view of the food and the cooking. 'I prefer your cooking,' he had told her and she supposed she should have felt complimented. But it was different for him. All he had to do was to sit down and eat! He had never been backward in letting her know his favourite dishes. So, of course, she could understand that eating out was no treat to him; no change, if it came to that. He had been very keen to get home. Of course, in a way, she herself had been keen to get home; in a way, she had. On the evening before her discharge, meaning to be kind, Jim had said to her, 'It's the great day tomorrow!' and she had agreed, but a part of her hadn't wanted to leave the company of the other women. The next morning after her return, when Jim had left the house for the whole day and she was on her own, it had felt very odd. Everything had gone quiet and still. She had felt quite low. And when lunch time had come round, she had missed being given her meal.

The waiter came with the fried plaice and chips and she set to, eating slowly. She wanted to savour her treat to the full. It was still good value, the fish wasn't smothered in batter and the chips were crisp and freshly fried. She was enjoying every mouthful. The room was not all that large, but it had a mirror running the whole length of the end wall which made it appear twice its real size. She thought what a good idea that was, clever. She glanced at her watch; it was getting on for two o'clock, but the trattoria was still almost full and there was a constant hum of voices. Being almost on the Circus, she supposed it must do a day-long trade.

The customers were of all ages and nationalities. She enjoyed looking at them, they were all too engrossed with each other or with their food to take notice of her stares. The waiter did not come with the bill and she felt that no one expected her to gobble down her meal and give way to others. She ordered a cup of tea and when it came drank leisurely. The one amenity the place lacked was a toilet, which she found she was in need of, so having paid her bill and left a good tip for the waiter, she made her way to the public lavatory on the corner of Oxford Circus. It was not something she liked doing; in her past experience, public conveniences were to be avoided if at all possible, but once down the steps, she was taken aback. It certainly was an eye-opener, the place was so clean that she could have eaten off the floor, and really pleasant! The main area contained small, free-standing basins, with warm air machines. The walls, from floor to ceiling, were tiled a glossy, pale blue, a sprig of flowers in the centre of each tile. The whole was spotlessly clean and gleaming. Mabel saw to her hair in one of the many mirrors fixed to the side wall and went back up the stairs feeling that somewhere along the route she must have got left behind. It seemed an odd thing to feel on account of a public lavatory, but she did feel it.

As she hesitated at the top of the steps, she found herself gazing with envy at the many couples. It would have been nice to have had her husband with her. Then she checked herself, 'Jim's a good husband! I've got a lot to be thankful for,' she told herself.

There was still plenty of time left so she decided to take the bus to Marble Arch and have a walk through the park. At Speakers' Corner a few stands were occupied, with a sprinkling of listeners and onlookers. Mabel stood with the rest. One man was talking about Ireland, another about the causes of unemployment, another about racism, and there was a religious speaker. After a few minutes, Mabel walked away, wishing she knew more than she did. She would have liked to be able to stand up to Jim when he made remarks she disagreed with, but it was many years now since she had tried. Somehow he had always managed to silence her. But then, she hadn't a trained mind, he had.

The plane trees were starting to show signs of leafing. It was cool, but she sat down on a bench for a rest. Then she remembered her scarf and took it out of her bag with the multi-clip and the instruction book. Alas! Studying the booklet, it quickly dawned on her that it was less than likely that she would ever succeed in fashioning even a small number of those different styles which had looked so easy when the young woman had been demonstrating them. Mabel sighed a little as she folded her purchase and put it back in her handbag. The clip had not been cheap, although she had pretended to herself at the time that it was. She did not think she would show it to Jim.

But the disappointment could not dim her pleasure for long. It was a still, windless day. She got up and walked some way further along the avenue and then sat down once more. Gazing about her, she thought, 'What a lovely stretch of green and right in the heart of the Capital!' Perhaps she had not missed much by not going abroad. There was a time when she had wanted to travel. She looked at her watch and realised that she was going to be late home unless she rushed; well, she was not going to rush. Anyway, Jim would be reading when she got back. Besides, she would like to buy a toy for Robbie while she was here, perhaps something she could give him when he was a little older. She knew which toy shop she wanted to visit; it had five floors and was famous for the extent of its display.

She found herself drawn first towards the section reserved for girls' toys. This was silly and illogical, but she had to take a look. She found the offerings less exciting then she had anticipated. There were plenty of dolls' houses, nurses' uniforms, washing and sewing machines, ironing boards with their own irons; there were lots of dolls of different shapes and sizes, many with eyes that rolled and some that made mechanical movements; there were cots with quilts and pretty blankets, knitting sets, cosmetic sets, pastry sets, tea sets, sets of playing shop and prams big enough to take a large doll. Mabel didn't think she would have wanted to buy any of these for a grand-daughter. She thought she'd learn all about that side of things soon enough. There were other toys as well; skipping ropes, crayons, slates, paint-boxes, toy telephones, balls, tennis rackets and many different games, but the main emphasis was on the maternal and the domestic. Then she came across some building bricks and farmyard animals, which pleased her more. Still, on the whole, that section was disappointing. She moved on to the boys' shelves which had been her real purpose in coming.

The display on these shelves was much more interesting. There were all manner of mechanical sets replacing the old meccanos which they had bought for Stephen; cars, lorries and vans of all shapes, sizes and purposes, firemen's uniforms with fire fighting equipment, divers' suits, space suits and spacecraft, electrical toys, chemistry sets and tool sets, aeroplanes, guns, and cowboy outfits – a seemingly endless variety. Mabel thought, 'These are the kind of toys to open a child's mind to the world.' But she liked best of all the train sets. They had bought a train set for Stephen, Jim had laid it out in an upstairs room with signals and tunnels, started it up and they had all three gone down on their hands and knees and become absorbed in the game. She had liked best when the train had disappeared into the dark tunnel, coming out at the other end with a rush; she had even enjoyed the collisions. Three trains running at the same time had been best of all. After handling the signals, she had respected the work of signalmen more. As a result of months of working toy trains and a network of railway lines which grew more and more complicated, and took up more and more space, a special relationship had grown up between herself and trains, so that the sight of a real train, or a main line station, still excited her. She had got so much more fun and interest out of Stephen's toys than she had ever got out of her own as a child. She wished now that she had not given away Stephen's collection of dinky toys when he had declared his interest in them at an end. They would have come in handy for Robbie. She had kept a green lorry, had put it on her dressing table concealed by a hand mirror so that it would not be noticed by Jim. Whenever she looked at it, she could see Stephen as a small boy crawling over the carpet and swishing the toy lorries backwards and forwards. She stopped wandering along the shelves, dreaming, and pulled herself back to the present and her purpose. Finally she decided on a small fire engine for when Robbie was a little older and a soft ball for the earlier months. She had made up her mind not to smother the child with toys; she did not believe in it and also she did not want his mother to feel under any sort of obligation.

Her last purchase was a pair of bedroom slippers for Jim. She wanted him to share her happy day. Also she felt a sense of guilt for having left him on his own – which was silly, she told herself, because she knew he wasn't missing her. He would have his head in a book.

About five o'clock she decided to treat herself to a cup of tea. She was not hungry, but she wanted to sit down and savour the pleasure of not having to brew the tea before she could drink it. She looked about her at the other customers and found quite a lot to interest her in the expressions on their faces. She thought that if God existed He must find the human race very amusing. Then she was shocked with herself because she had thought *if* God exists.

On the way home in the bus she was suddenly sad, as if she had lost something. She had had a happy day and it had left her with lots to think about. So much of her life otherwise consisted of doing things requiring little mental effort; washing, ironing, writing out grocery lists, shopping, vacuuming, making beds, preparing meals – keeping others fed and clean. Then she rebuked herself hastily, thinking, 'I've a great deal to be thankful for.' She felt that if she started complaining something dreadful might happen to Jim or to Stephen.

CHAPTER TEN

ONE Saturday afternoon when Robbie was three months old, Jean laid him down in his cot after his feed and drew the curtains across the recess to shade his eyes from the light. Turning round, she saw Stephen seated at the table, pencil in hand, taking notes from an open book. A bright ray from the sun was illuminating his features with their concentrated expression, his dark hair and high forehead, his fingers curled round the edges of the book. For the first time since that evening meal on the day they had brought their baby home, Jean felt his physical presence and saw him as more than merely someone who must be fed and looked after because he was the necessary means of life for herself and Robbie.

She experienced a peculiar sense of his having been away for a long while and having just at that moment come back. This shook her free of her obsession. During those few seconds, she really *saw* him again, but in that odd way, as if he had just returned from a long journey. She was too startled by this idea to do more than cross the room and sit down in the fireside chair which through long usage had become her own. She remained quietly seated. When finally Stephen looked up, making some casual remark, she responded in her normal manner, but she was experiencing guilt, wondering whether he had noticed any change in her and whether perhaps he had been feeling abandoned.

The next morning, when Stephen came in from the garden with the dried nappies and was placing them on the airer, she put her arms round his neck, put her face up to his, kissed him, and said, 'You're very good to us both!'

He was a little surprised that she should think he was acting in any way out of the ordinary. He was quite free from that false pride which makes a man ashamed to be seen pegging out the washing or doing the ironing. So when Jean praised him, he merely answered, 'Well, it's *our* baby,' and kissed her in his turn. And when he said 'our baby', he felt very proud. He was proud and pleased with himself because the only job which he could not do for the child was breast feeding, which, as he said to himself, was not his fault. After the shock of recognising her own absence, Jean was careful to talk more to Stephen, to enquire about his school day, to draw him out so that he discussed his work problems with her and to apply both their minds now and then to what was going on outside the circle of their own two lives, in the way they had done when there had been only the two of them. If her enthusiasm was less, her sense of participation much less, she did her best to hide the fact; if her chief interest and concern remained the baby, she was careful not to make it obvious. And so they came together again in a sense of mutual achievement and caring.

The problem of finding a permanent home exercised their thoughts a great deal. Robbie would soon start to crawl; more space would be needed. Their savings were insufficient for a large deposit, and there was furniture to be bought. After some months, they thought they had found what they were looking for at the other side of their own borough. It was an end of terrace house in a rather run-down state in a quiet road leading off a main shopping centre with the added advantage that the distance from Stephen's school was no further than at present. A fair amount of do-it-yourself work would be required. They decided to take the house if they could get it. After the decision came the nerve-racking waiting period.

It seemed that they were in luck – the house was structurally sound, even the drains were in good order. When, after some further weeks of suspense, the building society's willingness to lend was received in writing, they felt that they had successfully completed an obstacle race. Now they were in a position to decide on a removal date. Since the house was already vacated and they themselves had no property to put on the market, the exchange of contracts was a simple matter.

Once the house was their own, they were drawn back to look over it again; to decide on floor coverings, to measure for curtains, to sum up what furniture was essential. Since they could not leave Robbie behind, they bought a carry cot. Walking down what they now thought of as 'our road', Jean commented on how similar it was to the road in which her parents lived; even the house itself was like her former home. Inside there was the same long, dark passage leading from the front door to a small, square room which led into an even smaller kitchen which looked out on a narrow garden. Behind the front bow window was an elongated room with french windows at the far end, turned into its present shape by the removal of a partition wall so that two small rooms were transformed into one large one, often a way of modernising older types of property. They walked round the downstairs, then they went upstairs and into the two bedrooms, one double and the other single. There was a toilet and bathroom combined, also an outside toilet and a coal shed. The fittings were in good condition even if they were not modern; the sink in the kitchen was an old porcelain one.

'It will keep us busy,' Stephen commented. They did not mind that so long as they were not burdened with debt. They would have to lay out on good floor covering and curtains; they would buy second-hand furniture or plain wood and paint it themselves.

'We'll paint our bedroom furniture white,' Jean said. She tended always towards light and bright colours. They would paint the walls of the front living room off-white to show up their prints. While Stephen set about measuring for floor coverings, Jean brought out her tape and started on the window frames. Finishing first, she left Stephen crawling about the floor of the double bedroom and began to stroll around her new domain.

She had never been in a vacant house before. In the course of their searchings, they had seen over many houses where the owners were still in occupation so that the rooms had all had a lived-in appearance; carpets or linoleum on the floors, furniture, pictures on the walls, often bright wallpapers and old-fashioned mantlepieces. Some rooms had been in a muddle, others neat and tidy, but they had all had an ambience of personality, of life. As Jean moved about the house, she felt its difference: it had a dead feeling. There was no furniture, no personal belongings, no ideas connected with human habitation. Jean walked in and out of the rooms. Standing on the bare floorboards gave her an odd, uncomfortable feeling. She commented on this to Stephen after he had completed his calculations and they were ready to leave.

'It feels as if it's dead,' she said.

'It is,' he agreed, 'but it won't be once *we* get here!'

'After this, I'll look at people's homes quite differently,' she said, as they walked down the road carrying Robbie asleep in the carry cot. 'Until now I've always felt whatever is in a house must always have been there; perhaps because I was born and brought up in the same house and it never seemed to change.'

'So was I,' Stephen said, 'but since I've left home I've got rid of that idea of things going on the same for ever.'

'I'm glad so much needs altering,' she said. She was experiencing a sense of excitement at the thought that it would be herself, Stephen, and of course, Robbie, who would be handing back life to the rooms. She would not have liked to step into a house that was already in a finished state. Now it would belong to them not merely because they had paid money for it, but because their own work would have made it what it finally became. Besides, it would give her jobs to do and things to think about, things to plan.

They decided to take a saunter through their new district. They thought they had done well; besides the nearness of the shopping centre, they were quite close to a doctor's surgery, a primary school, and a park with a lake. They went past the local library, a newish building with a small courtyard in front and seats facing the road. Stephen commented on its nearness to their new home.

'You'll be able to get there without a bus,' he said. His words gave Jean a jolt. She was startled, as if someone had abruptly reminded her of something she ought never to have forgotten.

'What for?' she asked, confused.

'To take out books, of course,' Stephen answered, amused.

'Oh!' she exclaimed.

They went into a Wimpy bar for a snack. They liked doing that because it reminded them of their first outing. While they waited for their order to arrive, their talk came back to the house. Stephen said that when they came to sell, their improvements would up the price very considerably; they intended eventually to make certain alterations which would modernise the property.

'Perhaps we won't want to move,' Jean answered. Stephen saw the district as run-down, but Jean thought it was all right.

'We'll move when I get my Headship,' he said jovially. He was happy that their troubles seemed behind them and they could face the future with confidence. He had no doubts about his own abilities.

But his words annoyed Jean. She said, 'You've got an obsession about that Headship business!'

It was his turn to be annoyed. 'I haven't an obsession,' he retorted.

'Yes, you have! You're always bringing it up.'

'I'm not,' he said, rather hurt at what he considered an uncalled-for reproach. 'You're imagining things.'

She got angry and insisted even more that he was 'always bringing it up'.

He did not want to quarrel. 'All right,' he told her. 'I won't mention it again.' He could not help adding, in a sore tone, 'I can't see what's wrong with mentioning it. A man has to have an ambition.' She did not answer.

On the way to the bus, she began to reproach herself. She did not know why she should have got annoyed. After all, there was no harm in what he had said. She was in the wrong. Up to that point she had been walking alongside him. Now she slipped her arm through his. He understood that it was her way of saying she was sorry. He took her hand and gave it a squeeze.

Without thinking much about it, Stephen had anticipated that Jean would purchase the necessary furniture while he stayed behind with Robbie, but this arrangement was not at all to Jean's liking. She wanted him to go with her. She could not decide on her own, she told him. Couples went about with babies these days.

She was so keen on his going with her and spoke with such earnestness that he had not the heart to deny her, but he silently grudged the time. Jean seemed to think that science teaching did not involve much reading or evening work, but he did not intend to turn into the type of teacher who taught by rote, going on in the same old way all his teaching life. He was anxious to keep abreast of as much of the new scientific knowledge as practicable. Educational ideas and theories were always changing and he did not want to get left behind. He was strongly attracted towards the organisational challenges presented by large institutions; educational, industrial, or otherwise. The truth was he loved a challenge, and his mind was naturally active; if his brain was idle, he quickly became bored. Because of this, he read a lot in the evenings and found that reading relaxed him after the tensions of the school day. He gave in to Jean, but something of his reluctance showed. He trusted her taste, and she knew his, so that traipsing about together seemed rather pointless, but he did not want to appear indifferent. Still, he could not help feeling a certain surprise at the immense seriousness with which Jean went about the business of furnishing their small home with an amount of capital which scarcely allowed them much real choice. He could easily understand that she wanted the rooms comfortable and their home an inviting place for their friends – a place to which they themselves could return with a sense of pleasure – but he was quite unprepared for the degree of intensity with which she pursued her object. They were chasing about from one shop to another, from one district to another, simply in order that her colour schemes were not altered in the slightest degree.

'You've certainly put some thought into all this,' he commented, when, at the fifth attempt, she succeeded in finding a carpet for the living room which was close to the colour and shade she had in mind.

'Of course,' she answered him, rather shortly. He got the idea that his remark, which he had meant to be complimentary, had been taken in a different light. He did not repeat it.

They only just avoided a quarrel over the settee. Jean had decided on a dark blue, which she said would set off the curtains, but the store could only offer brown with no hope of the desired colour becoming available in any foreseeable future. They had been on their feet for some hours and Stephen was beginning to think that enough was enough. He could not resist suggesting that it was not of the first importance whether the settee was of a dark blue or a brown colour since both went with the carpet and curtains.

'What do you mean "not of the first importance"?' Jean asked, in an annoyed tone.

'Well! Not of the first importance,' he repeated, not knowing how to vary his remark. There was a slight pause after he had spoken, then Jean turned to the salesman who was standing patiently by and told him in an abrupt tone that they would take the brown settee. While they were waiting for their cheque to be accepted, Jean turned away from Stephen and began to look at some of the other furniture on view. He could see that she was up-tight, but he did not feel sympathetic. He was fed up and so was Robbie. He had had to take him in his arms to stop his whimpering. He considered his remark perfectly reasonable.

With surprise, he observed that Jean appeared to be placing a primary value on things which, only a short while before, she would certainly have regarded as secondary. He thought it odd and then he thought no more about it.

Robbie was six months old when the removal day arrived; Jean took this as a happy augury. Both she and Stephen were feeling the approaching change. The bed-sitter, humble as it was, had witnessed their first coming together. They must leave behind the table at which they had eaten their first shared meal, the fireside chairs in which they had sat reading opposite each other, the kitchen in which together they had prepared their hasty breakfasts and their evening meals on return from the polytechnic, the bed on which they had first made love. It was the room to which they had brought their first child. These were events and feelings that would never be repeated, a way of life that would never be quite the same again, the expression of a youth that was slowly passing away. They both felt all this without being able to put their feelings into words. It showed in an extra tenderness towards each other that final evening.

But Jean was suffering an added sadness; a sadness which she could not share with Stephen because she could not trace its source. It seemed to rise out of a deep layer of her being and however much she tried to argue it away as no more than a natural nostalgia, it went on persisting with an obstinate strength. A part of her seemed to be clinging to the room, and she felt as if she was having to unclasp herself from it by physical force. This made her tired during most of the last week.

The day was fine and warm with an autumnal glow when they set off in the hired van with the few possessions which did not belong to the landlady. After arranging herself in the front seat, with Robbie in her lap, Jean turned for a last look, but the van was already at the corner and the house along with the road quickly passed out of view. Very soon all the familiar landmarks had been left behind. Then the locality too fell back and they were entering upon new territory.

Twenty minutes later the car was turning into what was now their own road; a road lined on both sides with rows of terraced houses, treeless, but clean and quiet, deserted at that time of day and seeming almost to be sleeping in the warmth of the sun.

The furniture for their new home had been delivered two weeks previously and Stephen had gone over to hang the curtains and arrange things in some sort of order. The laying of the floor

101

coverings had been done earlier by them both. Now Stephen paid off the driver and they went inside, closing their own front door behind them. They were home.

They unpacked only what was essential, then they sat down at the table in the back room leading into the kitchen to enjoy the sandwiches they had brought with them. Stephen set out the plates and made the tea while Jean prepared Robbie's feed. He was now eating baby foods out of small tins, opening his mouth to be fed in a bird-like fashion. He sat in his high chair and gazed around him with a rather surprised, but contented air. The room was a square shape and just big enough to take the high chair, two upright chairs and the table along with a useful second hand, old-fashioned Welsh dresser which reminded Jean of the one in her old home. The kitchen was more up-to-date; they had laid out on a modern gas cooker, a refrigerator and a washing machine. The old porcelain sink faced the window and the long narrow garden.

After their lunch they wandered about the house, Stephen carrying Robbie on one arm and embracing Jean's waist with the other. This was the first time that Jean had seen the house furnished. They had been right – what a difference their furniture and belongings made to the atmosphere! Stephen had put a lot of work and thought into arranging everything as he imagined Jean would like it and he was pleased with her obvious delight. Even the brown settee no longer seemed to cause her concern and he was too tactful to remind her that he had said it would be all right. They went from room to room; the poor decorative state did not worry them. The rooms were no longer dead.

During the succeeding weekends, and in spite of the demands of the new term, they worked together on the rooms, stripping the old wallpapers and preparing the walls for the off-white paint. They tackled the kitchen first; here they painted the walls a light blue and the cupboards a light grey; they had chosen floor covering of grey with bright yellow spots. Jean worked on the sink until all the dirt marks had gone and the surface shone. After that they turned their attention to Robbie's room; soon the walls and ceiling were the same light blue as the kitchen, with grey picture rails and tangerine curtains. A gay striped counterpane covered the bed. The plain wood wardrobe and small chest of drawers were a glossy white and filled with Robbie's clothes, except for the bottom drawer which held his toys. After that everything was white paint, including the narrow, dark passage.

When their bright prints had been put up, the effect was very cheerful; rather like a country cottage. As time went on, snaps of themselves, of Robbie, souvenirs of holidays, including the shells from Tankerton, posters of opera and ballet, began to make their appearance, giving to their home that air of continuous human habitation which, when it had been empty, they had so much missed. They hung the country print over the old-fashioned mantelpiece in the front room. In the mornings, when the sun shone on it, the light seemed part of the picture. They put up bookshelves along the sides of the room so that that part of it looked like a study, although it quickly became Robbie's play space.

After Stephen had left for school in the mornings and especially after the weekends, Jean felt his absence. She seemed to be surrounded by silence and this in spite of Robbie's chatter. He was beginning to talk to himself in his own language; a language which only he could make sense of. He talked away and his talk never broke the silence. It was a peculiar feeling – the talk and the silence existing side by side.

She began to keep a diary of Robbie's development. Buying an exercise book and the feel of the pen gave her pleasure. She experienced a vague sense of satisfied hunger. At that stage every week seemed to bring developments. It had been her own idea to keep the diary, but after a few weeks they had both agreed it was a good idea; they would be able to look back and relive all the interesting phases of their son's early development. Perhaps when Robbie was a father himself he might find it of interest.

Some diary entries – October 8th: On going into R's bedroom, found him *Sitting Up* in his cot! Called Stephen. S. ran upstairs, R. centre of attention; beamed, chortled and waved his arms about with excitement, then quite suddenly fell backwards – *very* deflated! October 20th: *Robbie Talked!* he said da-da – he meant ma-ma, but he got confused in his wording. The diary contained many details concerning weight, height, and what nurse or doctor had said. November 10th: took R. to clinic, sitting up in pram: very windy, cold sun. Passed under trees, bare branches made swaying patterns on R's blanket and across the backs of his hands – very surprised at sight – gazed up fascinated at branches all the time we were passing underneath – very pleased with his new experience. January 20th: *Robbie Crawling* – crawled up the passage – very funny to watch his fat nappy-clad bottom

103

disappearing round the corner into the front room. Getting quite independent! February 28th: *Robbie Walked!* Ran from me to S. in one wild waving-his-arms-about rush, screams of delight and fear, right into his father's arms. Is it a once-off? March 1st: Boy next door, a little older than R., called Nigel came into the house today to play with R. Have left the far side of the front room as a play space. R. has discovered that he can climb out of his play-pen – no peace now! March 5th: The three of us went out together, S. pushing wheel chair. R. very excited and pleased – always like this when we got out together, gets quite red in face with excitement. Walked through park, paused by lake, very cold but dry. S. says his father would have had a fit if seen pushing a pram: S. is proud he has no hang-ups. R. walked a few steps, unsteadily. S. says he is going to be fat and lazy! Said that to tease me. All very hungry on return. R. eating his lunch is a mess! He still can't handle the spoon properly, turns it upside down with the food inside! But he looks lovely – pink satiny cheeks and those clear, bright, shining eyes. P.S. Just come back to reality – he smells awful! Still, can't understand anyone being cruel to children. S. can't either. March 11th: R. showed S. his new shiny red shoes. 'Shoes, daddy!' he said with pride. S. said jokingly, 'Who paid for them, I wonder?' S. very proud of R. March 13th: Took R. over to Mum's, stayed the weekend; then took him to see his other grandparents – very spoilt by both. *Very* sensible not to live in their pockets, they'd ruin him. March 17th: Rita wrote – has had second baby, *a boy* this time, *Richard over the top!!* Dick and Betty called quite unexpectedly last Sunday and stayed for tea. They seem to get on very well together, but are rather mysterious about the way they live. Can't make out if they like it or not, especially Dick. They don't ask us to visit. They seem to live with a lot of other people. Wouldn't suit S. – or me. Our next door neighbours came in yesterday for drink and chat. P.S. This diary is going off the point, it's supposed to be about R. *only*. S. will say I'm not keeping to a method.

Their next door neighbours were a young couple of about their own age; Jack and Daphne, with one child, Nigel, three months older than Robbie. They were friendly from the start. Jack, who was a carpenter, was soon advising Stephen on how to improve the state of the warped window frames and how to rehang a door. This was a stroke of luck.

Jack gazed at the books. 'You haven't read all those books?' he enquired in a tone of some disbelief. He was on the short side, well-built and sturdy, with brown hair, brown eyes and a friendly smile. He introduced them both to his wife, who was also small, with fair hair and grey eyes. Like her husband, she had a friendly smile and manner. Jack's help proved a real boon to Stephen, enabling him to get through the essential repairs much sooner than he would otherwise have done. When Stephen discovered that Jack's chief hobby was fishing, he gave him a fishing rod, which, although Jack said it was not necessary, pleased him.

Unequal in education, they found that they had quite a few interests in common. They talked about gardening, the local football club of which Jack was an ardent supporter, carpentry, income tax, strikes, and what was going on generally. Jean was surprised to discover that Stephen could find so much common ground with Jack. Daphne was not interested in football, or in any sport except swimming; she made regular use of the local baths.

'I get bored with football,' she confided to Jean. 'Jack makes such a fuss over who's winning and who's losing. Like a baby! I can't have anything on for myself if it interferes with his precious game.'

'It worries me when they talk about nuclear war,' she told Jean, 'but I can't do anything about it, so I try to put it out of my mind.' Her chief interests were her children, her home, dress-making and cookery. She went to cookery classes and enjoyed trying out new dishes. 'I don't think Jack notices,' she confided to Jean, with a laugh, 'he's set in his ways.' She was glad to have a young woman to chat to; the woman on her other side was elderly. In those first weeks, she chatted a lot to Jean about Nigel, Jack, food, clothes, men, and make-up, in that order. 'I make all Nigel's clothes and my own dresses,' she informed Jean proudly.

Daphne invited Jean to watch her favourite television programmes as they had not yet a set of their own, but Jean found that the series Daphne liked best held little interest for herself; one episode was very much like another. She enjoyed the gardening programmes the most and made up her mind to give the garden serious attention when the weather improved. In fact, she was always thinking up something to do, even when it did not need doing.

In this manner they went on until they had been a week short of six months in their new home and Robbie's first birthday was almost upon them. During this period, they had applied themselves to the house so consistently that none of the urgent work remained to be done. The rest could be taken at their leisure. They found themselves one evening discussing this with some self-congratulation.

'The labours of Hercules are at an end,' Stephen said, with a laugh as they sat down to their evening meal. He had chosen his remark with care. He was secretly glad. He was still at that stage in his school work when he needed all his energies for his job. Besides the house came very secondary with him; its appeal was mainly functional. But he did not enlarge upon the reasons for his satisfaction. He had learned from experience that Jean could flare up at remarks which to him were entirely innocuous. He could find no logical reason for this but it had taught him to be cautious. After the meal was finished and cleared away, they retreated to the front living room, which they always frequented in the evenings. They sat opposite to each other as they had done in the bedsitter. They were both reading, as they had done then. After a while, Jean gave an unconscious sigh. When she had sighed more than once, Stephen looked up.

'Tired?' he asked.

'No,' she answered, looking across at him surprised.

'You were sighing.'

'Was I?'

'Yes.'

'I didn't know.' She added, 'I'm studying this book on gardening. I got it out of the library.'

Stephen reminded her that he and Jack would have to dig over the garden before any planting could be done. The soil was either trodden down or full of weeds.

'It will need trenching,' he said.

'I can trench,' she retorted. 'I'm not a cripple!'

He retreated into silence.

Robbie's first birthday arrived. When Stephen came back in the late afternoon they held a special birthday tea. Jean had made a sponge cake, decorated it with pink and white icing, and in the middle placed a single candle in a little silver container. She stood it on a cake stand, a present from her mother, after having first spread a lace cloth on the table, a gift from her mother-in-law. To one side, she placed a vase of daffodils. The effect was pleasing. Jean was proud of her effort. She did not often bake cakes. Near Robbie's high chair she put a large plate of pink and white iced biscuits which she had cut into various animal shapes. 'You're getting very clever,' Stephen commented, admiring the result. He never would have thought that Jean would turn out to be so practical.

Robbie used to be a fat baby, but since he had learnt to crawl and stand with the occasional totter, he had become much leaner, with sturdy knees and signs of an impatient temperament. He liked throwing his toys about so that expensive ones, such as his fire engine, got broken and Jean found she needed to curb this particular hobby by not replacing whatever had been broken. This annoyed Robbie, but in the end the method worked. Now he was seated in his high chair, in a bright blue woollen jersey and trousers, a shade darker than his own eyes. He had thick black hair, which was standing up on his head and his cheeks were round and pink with that satiny glow which showed both his age and his health. He was busily engaged in trying to get rid of the strap which prevented him from standing up. He was talking incessantly to himself. Neither parent could make out what he was saying as the words were all joined together, if indeed they were words at all and not just Robbie enjoying the sound of his own voice. When Jean lit the one candle, he stopped talking to himself and fixed his eyes on the flame in wide-open wonderment. He strained forward in his chair and tried to seize hold of the flame with the fingers of his right hand and when he could not reach he made impatient noises. Then he got angry and gave a yell. But when he was given a piece of the iced cake and some pretty biscuits, he stopped minding and concentrated his attention on eating. After a while he began to yawn and finally fell asleep, his head on his chest, whereupon Jean took him off to bed.

Later in the evening, Jack and Daphne came in. They had been invited for a drink to celebrate the occasion. Daphne handed Jean a small red bus for Robbie. She brought Nigel asleep in her arms and he was laid on an upstairs bed. Then the four parents sat in the living room, finishing off the cake, drinking and talking. The couple stayed until almost midnight.

In the bedroom Jean commented, 'It's difficult buying for so young a child,' thinking of the two brown teddy bears which had arrived from the grandparents and which they had that morning named Nod and Nick, because one wore a dreamy expression and the other looked rather sharp.

Looking round the pleasant bedroom with its white walls and

furniture, Stephen said in a satisfied tone, 'A bit different from when we first arrived. What a dilapidated state!'

'Yes,' Jean agreed, sorry that it was all finished.

In bed, in the dark, Jean heard Stephen's voice saying, 'Robbie will soon be a little person in his own right!' He repeated, 'a little person,' and his voice had a proud note.

Jean went to sleep and had an unpleasant dream. She was running up and down a narrow, dark corridor on each side of which were a great number of closed doors. As she came level with each door she stopped, turned the handle, pushed open the door, which seemed to yield grudgingly, and glanced inside. Each room she looked into was empty; there was nobody inside, no furniture, no pictures on the walls and the floor was bare floorboards. The light was very poor and she could not see the window. She kept opening door after door and the interior of each room was the same. She seemed all the while to be running and in a great hurry... When she woke it was morning. She lay for a while trying to shake off the unpleasant sensation. She interpreted the dream as an image of their house as it was when they had first walked round it. Still, she was glad to get out of bed and start the day's activities.

CHAPTER ELEVEN

ROBBIE celebrated the start of his second year with daily sniffles and snuffles; then, more alarmingly, measles. By the time he was quite well again he had got used to being the one who mattered. A series of tests of will began between himself and his mother. He was like his father in that he never relinquished easily a goal on which he had set his heart. This time it was the contents of a bag of sweets.

'No more!' Jean told him firmly. She put the bag into a tin and the tin on the top book shelf and left him to his angry mutterings. Coming back a few minutes later, she found him clinging with his left hand and both legs to the shelf, his bottom bulging outwards in a ludicrous manner, his right hand stretched up feeling for the tin. She seized hold of him, pulling him free by force, for he clung on with all his might.

'Lemme go!' he yelled indignantly. With much difficulty and struggle, he had dragged an upright chair across the floor, pushed it up against the bottom shelf, climbed onto it, and from that platform had made his way, puffing, upwards. Ignoring his yells, Jean deposited him on the floor, returning the chair to its original position and went back into the kitchen to finish preparing the casserole. Returning, she found the child again half-way up the bookshelf. Again she pulled him away and again put the chair back where it belonged, whereupon Robbie trotted across the room and deliberately pushed the chair over, sending it to the floor with a bang. Then he stood, legs apart, looking up at his mother with defiant face.

'Pick it up!' Jean told him, pointing to the chair.

'Won't!'

When Stephen came home, she told him.

'Good!' he said. 'He's going to have a will of his own.' He was pleased that his son knew what he wanted and was determined to get it.

'I gave him a good smack,' she said. 'Then he sulked and wouldn't eat his dinner.'

'Did Mummy smack you then?' Stephen said and gave the child a kiss.

'If you had him all day, you wouldn't be so soft with him,' Jean objected. 'He knows you're admiring him.' But Stephen only laughed.

'What's for eats?' he asked. 'The school meal wasn't worth having – I'm starving.'

This was a question he would have known the answer to in the old days when they had shared equally all domestic tasks, including the catering. Now, unrecognised by either, both their attitudes were changing in response to the changed circumstances. Moving out of the bedsitter and into a house had made a great difference. It was not that before their move Jean had been free. She had been tied to Robbie since his birth and for the first few months had been totally absorbed in him. It was rather that the atmosphere of the single room was lacking. There all the old memories had been vividly present; books had lain about everywhere and the smallness of the space had brought all their interests within constant view. In spite of Robbie, the former life had continued to live on in their feelings.

In their own house, this ambience was lacking. There were too many rooms, too much space. The house, although not large,

109

made daily demands. Inevitably it was Jean who met these demands. She scarcely noticed her books. There was a great deal more essential housework. She knew now what was meant when mothers talked about the incessant demands of child-care, she seemed always to be moving about, while taking Robbie out was an important part of each day. So gradually it was the old life which took on an aspect of strangeness and the new life which came to seem natural.

Still, there were times when there came back on Jean the sadness which she had felt on leaving their one room – that intense sadness which had seemed to rise out of a deep layer of her being and which, however much she had tried to argue it away as only a natural nostalgia, had gone on persisting with an obstinate strength, until a part of her had seemed to be clinging to the room, so that she had felt she was having to unclasp herself from it by physical force. Every now and then the sadness came back, but she fought it off.

And Stephen too began to feel differently. This alteration in both their feelings was the outcome of their activities gradually falling into the conventional pattern. Stephen was now the breadwinner, the person upon whom Jean and Robbie depended. This gave him an added prestige in Jean's eyes; a prestige which he acquired without her consciously thinking about it or even being aware of the change. She simply felt that the responsibility lay with her to make sure that her husband had everything he needed to keep in good physical and mental condition. She was careful to time her activities so that when Stephen came home Robbie would not be in a demanding state and the house would be quiet for him to relax after a tiring day; she began to see the house as a kind of cave with windows into which her husband retreated each evening to recuperate himself for the next sortie into the world. Stephen himself saw his home in a very similar way.

In both their eyes, it became a retreat, which Jean kept in the necessary good order. Except to a very minor degree, the chores were no longer shared. Jean cooked for Stephen, washed and ironed his clothes, saw that he had the quiet he needed and was always ready to listen when he spoke about his worries. She took quite a grave view of this responsibility, whereas, formerly, when they had both worked and each given the other moral support, she had done her part lightheartedly. But she no longer remembered how she had felt in those days;

110

although they were scarcely more than twelve months away, they seemed very far off.

Stephen did not remember those days either, partly because he had little time to spare for looking back, and partly for other reasons. Among the latter, by far the most influential was his childhood. During those impressionable years he had been used to seeing his mother at home, looking after his father and himself, while his father held the status and responsibilities of the breadwinner. He had known even as a child the importance of that duty, just as he seemed always to have known that his mother too had recognised that importance and had treated his father accordingly. When he grew older and went to the polytechnic, this set-up had taken on an old-fashioned aspect; he assimilated the new ideas regarding the equality of the sexes and thought them sensible. He was perhaps unusual in that he did not like the idea of being in any way privileged.

But he had not considered the question of children. This was strange for a mind as analytical as his. Immediately on Robbie's birth, in that one day, so it had seemed to him, he had taken on sole responsibility for the welfare of two other human beings. He had become at once the real head of the family. So long as the baby was not there, he was able vaguely to feel that Jean would somehow soon be returning to work, just as Jean herself had felt this way. It had come as a shock to him that he was now on his own, but he had soon adapted to it. It was only later that he began to question how his previously held convictions fitted into this new reality and he quickly perceived that they did not fit in at all. Formerly he had thought his parents' conception of family relationships very old-fashioned. Now he saw that the concept was rooted in necessity. A lot of the ideas that he had listened to at the polytechnic and had thought adapted to modern life, had been no more than student talk. Real life was different. It was not, as he had previously thought, his parents who had been out of touch, but himself.

He felt grown up and he felt proud of his new status. He felt proud of his wife and his son in a way that he had not felt proud previously of anything in his life. It was a possessive feeling. He recalled how well his father had done the job of provider and he made up his mind to do the same job no less well. He did not mention any of his new thoughts and feelings to Jean. He kept them to himself. He treasured them. After all, he said to himself, wasn't it only fair that he should rate himself highly? If he were to

111

fall ill, be unable to continue at work, where would they all be? The entire burden of ensuring the family's security now fell on his shoulders alone. He took out an insurance policy.

The added attention he was receiving seemed no more than his due. He looked after Jean. She looked after him. It was a fair exchange. However, along with his satisfaction there went a vague but quite powerful sense of having lost something. When he was busy with school work in the evenings he was not aware of this sense of loss, but when he did not bring home work to correct, or only a small amount, he became aware of it. Suddenly there seemed little that he and Jean had to talk about and he missed the former spontaneous exchange of ideas and information concerning the day's activities. Of course there was Robbie, but he did not want to talk all evening about Robbie, fond as he was of him. He talked about his job, but somehow it was not the same. When Robbie had been only a baby, Jean had lost her interest and he had felt left out. Now that he was older, her former interest had come back, but her lightheartedness had gone. Jean listened to him with an intensity that made him feel less rather than more relaxed. He asked her about her own day, but it did not hold his interest. He knew it all before she spoke. Then he felt guilty and did his best to make conversation around all the little items which made up her day. Nevertheless he missed the liveliness and happy glow which she had formerly given off. She had always been to a certain extent serious, but this element had never been the only one in her personality. Mixed with it had been a lightheartedness and sense of fun. She had always known how to get rid of the seriousness, to use it up. Now she gave him the impression that it was there all the time and had become more intense, as if locked up inside her, stagnant. He could not make out what produced this impression on him and he did not know how to question her. As always happened with a problem he could not solve, he became irritated with himself. In the end he found the solution in her new maternal responsibilities, a temporary effect which would wear off as Robbie got older.

One evening, when they were seated as usual in the front room, he said to her, 'You don't do much reading these days.'

'Yes, I do,' she retorted quickly, looking up from her book and across at him where he sat on the opposite side of the hearth.

'Only do-it-yourself books,' he commented. He knew she was reading a gardening book.

With a note of resentment in her voice, she returned, 'I'm concentrating on the garden. I like to concentrate on one thing at a time. You know that.'

'You certainly are doing that,' he replied, amused. 'That's the fifth garden book you've read.'

She was surprised that he noticed what she read.

'Of course I notice,' he said, annoyed that she should think him indifferent.

There was a silence. Then she said, 'Someone has to see to the garden. There's a lot to learn. I want to do it properly.' The soil had been dug over, the weather was now mild, and she was spending most of her spare time planting out.

He thought she looked tired. 'Give it a rest,' he said. 'I'll help you at the weekends. There's no need to keep at it every day. You look tired.'

He spoke with concern. She did not answer. She turned again to the book. She had wanted to make a sharp retort, but had checked herself. She did not want a dispute, including a possible reproach that she was not being reasonable. She knew from past experience that she would not be able to stand up to his logical arguments. He would tell her exactly what she must do in order to make her life run on sensible, satisfactory lines. He would do it with the best of intentions, which would make it so much worse.

There were times when she wanted strongly to quarrel. This desire came out of a sense of resentment which she could not attach to any particular cause. If she could have pinned it down and said, 'It's this,' or 'It's that,' she would have felt less angry, but she could not. It was a diffused resentment which refused to attach itself to any one object.

It was not only the relationship between Jean and Stephen that was altering. The relationship between Jean and her son was also in a state of flux. During the first year Robbie had been everything to her; for the first few months Stephen had seemed almost not to exist. Then there had been the start of the second year and for a while Robbie's development had gone on at a pace sufficient to keep Jean's daily interest. She had enjoyed writing up the diary. He was a very intelligent child, people had commented on how advanced he was for his age. This had pleased Stephen, but by fourteen months the phase of rapid development was over and Robbie was acquiring facility through daily repetitions. Watching him was no longer all absorbing. About this time Jean ceased to keep her diary each day. Instead she entered items weekly, then every other week, then only when it entered her mind. Finally the entries ceased altogether and she put the diary into a drawer and left it there.

Robbie no longer spent most of his time with his mother, although he continued to demand that she be on call. His first thought on waking appeared to be how soon he could get together with Nigel. The two lads now spent the greater part of each day either in Jean's garden or in her house. Nigel had acquired a second home.

Jean had more leisure, but somehow the leisure got swallowed up. She could not have said how. It was because of this that she started to answer Stephen vaguely when he enquired about her day. She could not have told him what she had done. She did not know. Stephen found this new reticence a relief. Gradually, from an earlier sense of loss, he progressed to the stage where he started to forget that there had once been a time when he and Jean had found no difficulty interesting each other of an evening and instead he settled down to a quiet time with a sense of relief after the hubbub of the school.

When he came home tired, which he often did, Jean would feel guilty at seeing him washing up after their dinner, while at the weekends she felt he needed a good rest. So gradually the chores became more and more her total responsibility, whilst, of necessity, his paid employment became his top priority and their relationship altered to fit in with the new reality.

'I'll lend you some of my magazines,' Daphne told Jean one morning when the two children were playing in her kitchen and she had asked Jean in for coffee. 'I keep a pile,' she added. 'I look through them when I need advice.' Daphne read every bit of print in the two women's magazines she bought each week; not only the serials and short stories, but the articles on child care, clothes, cosmetics, cookery, keep fit, holidays, medical care, letters in the agony column, even the advertisements – this was her sole reading matter. She made use of some of the recipes and knitting patterns and kept notes of useful household hints. She thought the stories good and recommended them to Jean. Jean thanked Daphne and took the large pile she was lent.

When Robbie was upstairs for his reluctant afternoon rest, Jean leafed through some of the pages. She tried a story, but soon gave it up. Unexpectedly she found herself drawn towards the cookery recipes and to the pages which showed seasonal

114

fruits and vegetables in brilliant colours. It was the colours and shapes that fascinated her. The firm round ripeness of the tomatoes, oranges and apples could be felt almost as if handled, their red, orange and green glossiness shone on the page. Nectarines and peaches showed smooth and silky, with a reddish glow and dull purple sheen, delicious fruity smells seeming to rise to her nostrils and make her mouth water – a treat for the senses. Other pages showed risen, pale golden souffles, jam puddings with bright red jam oozing from the sliced portion, crusty apple pies with shiny surfaces and baked apples topped with runny syrup, so that she could almost smell the warm, cooked flavours. Then there were jars of home-made jams and preserved fruits in neat, labelled rows; fish dishes with rice and prawns, olives, cucumbers, parsley and red peppers; mutton and beef joints in oblong dishes, surrounded by crisp roast potatoes, parsnips, and small, round, browned onions, glistening with heat. There were amber-coloured steamed puddings in little dishes and savoury omelettes, pale golden; and newly baked crusty breads; and pineapples, strawberries, gooseberries, red and black currants – according to the season and festive occasion. Jean kept on leafing through the pile of magazines, feeling herself drawn towards this world of brilliant colours, shapes and smells; a world which promised creative possibilities.

She began to cut out and send for cookery book offers, posting the coupons with a sense of satisfaction. In a short time, she had collected quite an assortment. She had already cooked successfully for some years without any of this fuss and she was aware of the absurdity of collecting so many recipe books especially as, when it came to it, she felt no real desire to try out any of the suggestions, but she continued to send the coupons and to anticipate with some eagerness the arrival of the latest book or leaflet. When she went out and passed a book shop, she would go inside and look at the cookery books. Turning over the pages and fondling the covers gave her a feeling of satisfaction.

One morning she bought a book called *Appetising and Nutritious Meals with Liver, Kidney, Heart and other Offal*. She also bought an exercise book and began to write out recipes she had tested and might want to use again. The writing out and the sight and smell of the exercise book gave her a sense of pleasure; she enjoyed the feel of the pen between her fingers.

She persuaded herself that it was her duty to provide Stephen with a more varied diet. She began to try out more of the recipes.

She kept her collection on a shelf in Robbie's playroom. Although she went to the shelf quite often to take out or to put back a cookery book or leaflet, she never once glanced at any of her other books, although these were books which in the recent past she had highly valued.

She began to ply Stephen with fresh dishes, one or two each week. After he had eaten, she would ask eagerly, 'Well, how does it taste? Do you like it?' He was able to say with truth that he did like it, for through sheer perseverance she had made herself into a good cook, but he did not much care what he ate and he thought that Jean was wasting her time with all this labour in the kitchen. He was aware of disappointment because she had shown herself to be so easily satisfied.

He had expected that now Robbie was not at her heels all day she would make use of her greater freedom to do some serious studying. He did not ask himself what the purpose of such study should be. He could not help noticing that she was starting to read Daphne's magazines, although she had told him she took them only so as not to offend by a refusal. She seemed to be reading them more and more often. He did not mind that, but he could not understand how she could restrict her reading in this manner and it annoyed him. He checked himself lest he should provoke resentment. He knew by now that she reacted strongly to any remark which she considered to be critical. Besides, he felt that it would show disloyalty.

One evening, when she had prepared a very special dish Stephen did not come back at his usual hour but sent a message by a colleague who was passing the door to let her know he would be late and not to wait for him. He would eat out. Her disappointment was intense, almost bitter, and out of all proportion to the offence. She did not eat any of the dish herself, but let it go cold on top of the stove. It was quite spoiled. When Stephen came in about nine o'clock, she could not contain her sense of outrage.

'All right!' he said. 'I'm sorry! I forgot to tell you. It slipped my memory. But do you need to make such a fuss? It's only food.'

'I made a special dish,' she said.

'Well, you didn't need to,' he retorted. He was tired and had no patience. 'Food is something I eat to keep myself going. We were quite healthy with simple meals in the bedsit.'

The mention of the bedsit caused her a sudden, sharp pang. She turned away so that he should not see the tears in her eyes.

116

But he knew that she was upset and he put an arm round her waist and gave her a squeeze.

'Don't be silly, darling,' he said gently.

'Let me go, please.'

'I will when you stop being silly. I had to go to a school meeting. I couldn't say I wouldn't go because I'd forgotten to tell my wife!' He kissed the nape of her neck and fondled her. And she wished she had the strength of a man to turn round and hit him hard so that he would have to let her go.

After that she did not cook any more special dishes but reverted to the recipes they had used in the bedsitter, which were all based on spending as little time in the kitchen as possible.

'Why don't you learn to knit?' Daphne asked her one morning. 'I know how frustrating it is if the man in your life doesn't notice when you cook something very special. I don't mind because I enjoy cooking and if Jack doesn't want it, if he prefers his old sausages and mash, then there's more for me! But if it's a chore, you might as well keep it simple.'

So Jean let Daphne teach her how to knit and she made Robbie a little scarf of blue and orange. Robbie liked it and exhibited it proudly to his father.

'Mummy made this!' he announced, holding it out to his dad with pride.

'Well, we have got a clever Mummy!' Stephen said.

'Yes! We have,' Robbie agreed, in a tone of great admiration.

Later on, Daphne taught her how to cut out viyella material to make blouses for Robbie. She managed this too, although when it came to the trousers they looked rather odd because she had not put the pieces together correctly; still, they would do for indoors and the garden. After a while she abandoned her attempt to conquer this particular skill. The effort made her tense and gave her a headache. She liked knitting, it soothed her nerves, but when it came to a jersey she had to give up the attempt because her tension was not even – her stitches were either big and loose or much too tight. When she wanted to soothe her nerves, she would take to knitting yet another scarf as it did not matter so much what it came out like.

Robbie was very pleased with his first blouse. He had taken a keen interest in its making. When his father came in, he ran to him, 'Look Daddy,' he shouted, 'Mummy's made me this.' And he threw his arms wide so that his father could take a good look.

117

'Well, we have got a clever Mummy, haven't we!' Stephen said. And Robbie nodded his head vigorously in agreement.

To Jean, he said, 'You're very clever with your hands these days, Jean.' When he congratulated her, she wanted to scream. She was not clever with her hands and the effort to be so wearied her.

She relaxed when she was working in the garden. She had laid down a perennial border, marked out an allotment area and manured and seeded the soil, planted half a dozen raspberry bushes and put in a few standard roses. She was hoping later to have a greenhouse at the top end. She watered the growing vegetables and plants with great care and looked every evening to see what progress they were making. She experienced an impatient feeling when no progress was noticeable.

Every day there was a special time to which she looked forward; it was when she had put Robbie to bed and was reading his bedtime story. This was something she loved doing, so that when he plagued her for another and yet another story, she readily acceded to his pleas. She read aloud the adventure and fairy stories suited to his age as well as some poetry. Sometimes what she read was too old for him, which at least had the advantage of sending him to sleep. Often she did not realise that he had gone to sleep, but went on reading aloud for her own pleasure and because handling a book gave her a very special kind of satisfaction. When he pleaded for just one more story, she always humoured him, so that she was often spending a full hour upstairs.

One evening, when she came downstairs, Stephen asked, 'What on earth do you do up there? You've been over an hour.' He spoke irritably.

'I was reading to Robbie.'

'You spoil that child,' he replied testily.

'Nonsense! He's still only a baby.' She did not want to say that she looked forward to the hour upstairs reading to Robbie as the one hour in the day that gave her real pleasure.

'He'll remain a baby if you have your way,' Stephen retorted. 'He's a boy. He needs to grow up to be independent. You smother him. Look at the way you carried on last weekend.'

She knew he was referring to her having stopped Robbie from climbing up a ladder placed against the outside wall of the house. 'He might have fallen on to the concrete,' she argued. As she was speaking, she was resenting his remark about independence.

'You're not a careful person yourself,' she told him. 'You don't go to the doctor when you ought.'

'I don't see the need to go off to the doctor every time I have a cough.'

'Oh!' she said, with malice. 'You're jealous!'

'Don't be silly,' he answered. But she knew he was.

'You are getting into a fussing habit,' he accused her, and returned to the book he had been reading. He had spoken in an abrupt tone. She was developing an irritating tendency to mother him. He did not want that. He wanted his meals on time and his clean clothes when he needed them, but he also wanted to feel that he retained his independence. He tried to suppress his irritation and reply kindly when she kept on about what he should wear in the cold weather and what he should eat for lunch and the need for him to gargle and to go to bed before midnight, but he had discovered that when he spoke abruptly it always put a stop to her fussing, so that he was more and more tempted to take this easy way out.

Another wearying habit she had developed was that of plying him with questions when he came home after school. She pressed him for every little detail. In one week they would go through a catechism of questions and answers; what had been discussed at the staff meeting, how had the children behaved in class, which children were difficult and in what way, what did they talk about during staff breaks, how much did the teachers know of the children's backgrounds, what did they have for lunch and did he eat it, when was it his turn to supervise, was the Head in a good or a bad mood, how did members of the staff get on, any cliques, was he especially friendly with any of the teachers – and many other, trivial, questions. She would have questioned him about his class work if she could have understood his subject.

His working hours were a struggle. He did not want to have to live them over again in his own home. Also, as he became more and more a part of the school, so he found that only someone familiar with teaching and the problems it brings could appreciate what these problems were and what his working life was like. He felt that Jean could not enter in, and that what he said to her lacked the essence of his situation. Talking about his work came to seem simply a waste of time and an unnecessary weariness just at that period, towards the end of the day, when he was most tired and needed most to relax. So, gradually, he began to come back at her, asking, at first simply as a way of passing the necessity of a reply over to her, 'And what did *you* do today?' After a while, he noticed that this query acted as a stop to further questions. She would fall silent and not give him an answer so he began to make use of this observation to prevent her from continuing with her questioning. The tactic proved successful. Finally she stopped asking him about his day at school.

He did not understand that she was attempting to feed herself off his life. What he had done in silencing her did not seem to him unreasonable. He was conscious of doing his duty as a husband and a father – perhaps a little too self-righteously so. He thought many men demanded much more of their wives than he did. He made a point of not placing any unnecessary burdens on Jean. He did not ask for or desire a variety of cooked dishes – he ate only to keep alive. He did not in the least care whether or not the furniture was polished. He did not like dust or dirt because it was unhygienic. He only wanted the house kept reasonably clean. He wanted his home to be a place where he could rest, relax and be at his ease. That was not an awful lot to ask.

Weeks passed – Jean was beginning to develop a fear of time. When she had been at work she had not given time a thought except insofar as there never seemed enough of it. She had known exactly how it would behave – she could rely on it to make her hurry. She was used to time racing – getting up in the mornings, getting to work, at work, getting home, meal-times, and at nights. The weekends were a little more leisurely, but not much. What she was not used to was time dragging, still less to time seeming to stand still. It unnerved her.

This sense of being unnerved by time was really the result of boredom. Jean had never experienced boredom before, it was something new in her life. It was an affliction. It made her tense and unhappy. She did not know how to cope with it.

It made her afraid. For alongside her natural feeling for her husband and son there ran, keeping pace, another feeling – a feeling that even when she was at her busiest, nothing at all was happening. She was moving about in a kind of unaltering eternity. The two feelings ran steadily side by side. She was fearful of what might result if the feeling for her husband and son should weaken and leave her alone with that other feeling of unchangingness.

She really was beginning to suffer. She was like a person thrust into a small space where it was impossible to stand or sit and who after some hours begins to experience cramp together with a longing to stretch to full height. Only in her case the longing was to stretch mentally and the suffering was of a mental nature.

However she was the sort of person who was not easily beaten; in this she was like her mother. She searched for an escape hatch and thought she had found it. She told herself that she had been foolish to make such efforts at cooking, knitting and dress-making; Stephen did not expect it of her. He knew she was unsuited. She made up her mind to give up what she now saw as an absurd attempt to remould her nature. Instead she decided to reserve a portion of each day for herself. She would make a space – a space that would belong to her and to no one else.

Looking again at her books gave her an odd sensation as if a part of her mind had been anaesthetized and was waking up and she began to feel pain as from an amputated limb. Since the room had become Robbie's play area, she had been close to the books on many occasions, but she had never once paid them any attention. She had not even glanced at them. Now she felt the cleavage their absence had made in her life. She knew too that her ig-noring of them had not been accidental, but the result of an unconscious guarding. She had wanted them so much that she had had to pretend they were not there. Now she took down her favourites and stood leafing through the pages, then sitting on the floor and piling them up on each side of her like old friends who had come to renew their friendship, long ached for, and joyfully received back. In one of the books she came on notes tucked inside the flap; they were notes on the history of England in the fifteenth century, a period which had interested her so much that she had thought seriously of doing a thesis once she had got herself settled in the kind of library she had in mind. She paged through them and then she wept.

Afterwards she began to read. She sat on the floor, her back against the bookshelf. She read and read, forgetful of where she was, unmindful of the time, totally absorbed until Robbie came running in from next door for his dinner. Then she sprang up in a state of confusion. She had forgotten all about Robbie and his dinner. For a brief moment, seeing his flushed face, eager eyes and look of expectancy, she wondered who he was and what he could want with her. Then reality returned, and with it a sense of guilt.

It was then that she made her discovery about time. The long hours had been largely an illusion. While she had been cooking, dressmaking, knitting, the time had been long because she was bored. As soon as she settled down to something which held her interest, time ceased to be a wide plain extending into an indefinite distance, and instead contracted, breaking up into small, separate plots of earth. She was made aware that her day was hopelessly fragmented so that the sight she had seemed to glimpse of a satisfying space for herself was only a mirage. Tasks presented themselves one after the other for her attention, as if on a conveyor belt. Each on its own was trivial and yet without their totality the domestic routine could not successfully continue. This conjunction of the trivial and the essential was inescapable and at the same time agonising.

She did not mind the actual doing of the tasks so much as their constant pressure on her thoughts. She felt that her mind had been taken over so that no part of it was left belonging to herself to give expression to her own will. Even while she was reading, with the hope that perhaps she might be able to venture on some worthwhile project, even this short time was invaded and colonised by the before and the after. She struggled to free her thoughts, to concentrate, but her thoughts insisted on returning either to what she had just done or to what she had still to do. The meals harassed her mind, the need for them to be ready at the right time. The right time crept into her thoughts, displacing them as effectively as cancerous cells. She was made to realise that her escape hatch had never been workable. All she possessed of her own time was small remnants left over from other people's needs.

She began to experience strong feelings of resentment. These feelings frightened and alarmed her so that she made tremendous efforts to suppress them, but whenever her real interests had to give way, which was often, they came back. After a month, she gave up the struggle. She returned the books she had been attempting to study to the shelves. She stopped taking them out. She stopped looking at them. She wiped the books and their contents from her mind. She put out of her life everything that stirred old desires, everything that set up a painful longing. By this means her life became again governable.

But the problem of time remained with her. For that same time that had contracted from a wide plain into small plots of earth, sometimes mere stepping stones when she had sought to make use of it for her own needs, now that she had abandoned the attempt once again extended itself into the distance – a distance without end or horizon. Minutes disappeared, reappearing as hours; the clock on the mantelpiece began to play tricks with her. When she had been trying to study it had raced ahead, bringing her to an abrupt, painful halt. Now it ticked away, more and more slowly, like a heart nearing death. On some especially bad days, it seemed to stop altogether.

Waking in the mornings, she got up, aware of a lack of interest and a sense of absence of aim, which, on the face of it, was absurd, since her daily activities were anything but without useful purpose. She started to reproach herself for her stupidity and to feel guilty towards Robbie and Stephen because a part of her wished they did not so consistently need things doing for them. When this happened, she became frightened and hastily suppressed the wish lest it should bring calamity.

During the summer months she spent a great deal of each day in the garden, weeding and playing with Robbie. She took him to the park where the local council put on shows for the children. Sometimes she took Nigel as well, but when the colder, late autumn weather set in, she was forced back on the house.

And the house provided her with a purpose. She became aware that it needed attention; there was dust on top of the wardrobes, mixed with fluff underneath the beds, behind the settee in the living room. Dust lay on the window panes, showing up whenever the sun shone, even the framed snaps and wall prints needed dusting. The net curtains had a grey look, the table top was dull and much of the furniture smeared with Robbie's finger marks. Loose change, keys, odds and ends, lay scattered about the sideboard and on the mantelpieces. There was no actual dirt, but evidence of neglect was everywhere. Jean felt ashamed.

She now had an aim; to get everything in the house into a well-kept state and then to keep it that way. Having an aim again provided her with a measure of satisfaction. She set about fulfilling her new task with enthusiasm. It was not in her nature to do anything by halves. She undertook an old-fashioned spring cleaning. No corner was left undisturbed. This assault lasted for a full three weeks. All that then remained was to organise so that the house kept its cared-for image, but this turned out not to be the simple feat which she had imagined. It appeared that everything had an inbuilt tendency to degenerate. In the end Jean found herself working twice as hard as before. She vacuumed every day instead of once a week so that the crumbs were not trodden into the pile, she dusted throughout the house every morning. Once a week she polished the furniture, giving special attention to the table top and the arms of the chairs, wiping off greasy finger marks. When she polished she did not use the modern sprays, which left only a dull shine, but the older wax polishes which had to be spread on and then well rubbed. She kept an eye on the net curtains, taking them down and washing them whenever they lost their white look; she no longer hung them without first ironing. Leaving the creases to come out of themselves now seemed to her slovenly. When she cleaned the windows, she added vinegar to the water, while formerly she had not bothered. She could not bear to do a poor job.

The beds were made each morning with care, instead of the blankets being thrown back on until they began to touch the floor.

The bath and toilet were kept spotless. Every few days she threw buckets of disinfectant down the drains. As soon as the cushion covers or cotton headrests showed signs of wear, she changed them. The outsides of refrigerator, washing machine and gas stove were weekly washed down. She paid especial attention to the sink. As she went about her tasks, she found she was all the time adding new items. During this period, she made a literal truth of the word 'housewife'. She was married to the house.

She decided that they had been living in dirt. She took to cleaning the carpets and mats. She wiped down the doors. She began to wash the paint on the walls. She told herself the walls must be dirty even if the dirt did not yet show. When Daphne commented, 'You make me feel ashamed of my place!' she was gratified.

She had achieved her aim, but somehow the result depressed her. It was so entirely negative. Robbie took no interest in her polished furniture, he got annoyed when she told him not to smear it with his jammy fingers. True, at first Stephen did comment that the house looked better, but after that he took the new look for granted. It seemed to Jean that her labours only became noticeable when she ceased to perform them – Stephen did not like dust or dirt. She began to feel that her husband did not appreciate the immense amount of care and energy she had to expend in order to keep the home ticking over. She suspected that when Stephen came home in the late afternoon, he wondered what she had been doing with herself all day – that is, if he thought about it at all. Yet she was glad when he did not ask because she knew she would not be able to explain.

'I'm doing the same things over and over,' she told Daphne in one of her rare complaining moments.

'That's right!' Daphne agreed cheerfully.

It occurred to Jean that her life consisted of constant repetition. She made out grocery lists – they had to be made out again. She filled the refrigerator – it needed refilling. She prepared and cooked meals – they were eaten and had to be prepared and cooked again. She washed and ironed clothes – they needed washing and ironing again. She changed sheets and pillowcases, curtains, cushion covers, head rests – they needed changing again. She cleaned and dusted – she cleaned and dusted again. Her list of tasks was always the same – repeat, repeat, repeat.

She decided that for the first time she understood what was meant by the labours of Sisyphus and yet she needed her ceaseless physical activity as people without hope need opium.

Her mental faculties became affected by the monotony. When at nights Stephen put on records, or the radio, her mind would not concentrate. She found it difficult to follow an argument or listen to serious music. When Stephen remarked, 'I like that music,' she would answer, 'Yes! So do I,' but she had no idea. When he commented on a radio discussion, she made an effort to respond with her own comment, but her mind shrank from applying itself to meaningful talk, or to any of her old interests. She made an exception of reading to Robbie. This was permissible reading.

She found herself waiting for something to happen in the evenings after Stephen had come home; something towards which the whole day had been leading. She felt it must. It did not – but she went on anticipating. She lived in a state of unfulfilled, illogical expectations.

One Sunday, after dinner, Stephen said irritably, 'This house is getting to be like a museum. I'm afraid to put anything down in case it makes a mark.'

'That's nonsense,' Jean retorted, annoyed.

'No, it isn't! You just snatched up my cup because it might make a mark on the table.' He added, 'You're always on the watch.'

'You'd soon remark if I didn't keep things in order,' she told him. 'You'd say I didn't know how to organise.' She remembered the one occasion on which she had let him run out of clean shirts and he had had to go to work with his collar showing a mark.

'I have to stand in front of a class,' he had told her. 'I have to look neat.' Which remark she had thought ridiculous going by the way his pupils looked on the rare occasions when she had seen any of them. She had thought them a rather scruffy lot. She had discovered that Stephen was quite finicky about the way he dressed. She came to the conclusion that his mother had spoilt him, he expected everything just how and when he wanted it. Yet he had had quite a different attitude when she had been working as well, before Robbie was born. He had not minded even ironing. Then she told herself that it was only natural that he should expect more of her in the way of attention to his needs when she was at home all day. And she ended her interior monologue in the usual way, feeling guilty.

She did not realise that Stephen thought she liked all this domestic work. He was disappointed; he had expected something different from her. He thought that she had become a less interesting, less vital person. Her intellectual and artistic interests seemed to have been shoved to one side and she had lost most of her former sense of fun. He could not think how she spent her day if she had to take up knitting and sewing blouses for Robbie in the evenings, and when she was not doing this, she was apparently absorbed in women's magazines or do-it-yourself books. It had seemed a little while back that she was getting over that phase. She had started reading serious books again. She had gone back to her own subject. Then suddenly she had stopped doing that and taken up again with her new ways. He thought her a decidedly duller person than when he had first met her and when they had been living on their own.

Then he told himself he was being unfair. After all, wasn't this what women were like? Their maternal instinct, their instinct for home-making, overrode all else when it came to the point; intellectual interests were more superficial, filling in the time until marriage and children. He thought to himself that a woman's sense of identity must be much weaker than that of a man – didn't women surrender easily their own surnames on marriage, something no man would be willing to do, and didn't they easily give up their jobs, settling for part-time work, and this even after years of training and study? The husband and children always came first with women. He had known quite a few intelligent, educated women who had gone this way. Jean was no exception.

126

He decided that those women could only have appeared to be absorbed in their work, that their work could not have meant anything serious in their lives, could not have been a basic part of their personalities. No man could so easily give up work which interested him and after years of study. Intellectual effort was a kind of froth on a woman's being which disappeared as soon as the substance was reached.

All the ideas about women which he had formerly put away from him as old-fashioned began to re-assert themselves. He remembered that his mother had been satisfied to devote her life to his father and himself. The ideas about women which he had absorbed emotionally during the years of his growing up claimed again their old influence over his feelings, whilst the new ideas weakened because they had never been more than an intellectual part of him.

He had come to think women illogical. He did not consider he himself was being illogical in expecting Jean to see to all his needs and at the same time remain a lively, interesting person.

Then he felt guilty and tried to make amends. 'You've got a fine collection of cookery books,' he commented one evening, running his fingers across their bindings. 'Why don't you try out a few new recipes again?'

'You said you weren't interested,' she reminded him.

'I didn't want you tied to the kitchen,' he answered. 'But if you enjoy cooking, I shall enjoy the results.' He added, 'You're a very good cook.'

He had made a sincere effort, but she knew him too well to be deceived. She knew that he was trying to say the right thing and she felt that he was patronising her. She did make a few new dishes, but her old enthusiasm did not return. She spent hours on their preparation and they were eaten up in a few minutes. She grudged the time without any clear idea of what she would otherwise have been doing. When Stephen praised her efforts, she felt gratified and resentful at the same time.

Things might have changed either for the better, or towards an open crisis, if she could have spoken out honestly, but she could not. The strongest can be overcome when they struggle inside a net. She was caught in a net of guilt.

She made an effort. It came about this way. She was beginning to neglect her personal appearance. Stephen did not like this. He cared about appearances and she had always showed a sense of what suited her. Now she wore the same trouser suit day after day. She no longer changed at weekends into something different. Her vitality seemed drained away. She always looked tired. And yet, now that Robbie was a little older and spent a large part of the day with Nigel, she had more time to herself. Many women did part-time work. He did not want her to go out and leave Robbie in the care of another woman, but he could not see that she had so much to do that it showed. He felt that in some way she was being unreasonable.

'You need to get away from all this housework,' he told her over their late night drink. 'You need mental stimuli.' He made the suggestion that she went to an exhibition or a matinee now and then. 'Daphne won't mind,' he said. 'You can do the same for her.'

'Daphne wouldn't thank you for a day in London,' Jean said. 'She hates going about on her own.'

She could see that he was about to produce sensible suggestions as to how she could improve matters for herself if only she would take the trouble. He was going to apply his cool, calm, logical intellect to the solution of whatever might turn out to be her problem and this frightened her. She was afraid that he would start to judge her. She would not be able to stand that. She waited for Stephen to mention organisation.

'You need to organise your day better,' he told her. 'You could manage a time to yourself each day.'

She wanted to reply that time to herself was just what she was seeking to avoid; that she had tried it and that it did not work. She did not know how to concentrate in a leap-frog manner, jumping from the job she had just finished to the next job needing to be done, concentrating for the brief moment she was in mid-air. She wanted to tell him that she could not bend her mind to a serious purpose in a living space no larger than a series of small puddles; and the puddles themselves colonised by the before and the after. But she was afraid to say that, for it would be equivalent in his eyes to her saying that she did not want to look after himself and Robbie, and to him that would be the same as saying that she did not care for them any longer. She did not know how she knew this, but she did know it. She loved them both, but she did not want to spend her day looking after them. He would think this illogical. He thought it logical that only the mother should be responsible for the daily care of *their* child.

Even then, in her distressed state, she saw the problem clearly – he had not the life experience necessary for understanding. What ages it seemed since they had shared their lives. But she

128

made the effort. 'I have to have a period of time in which to concentrate,' she said. 'My mind was trained that way. I can't! There's always something that has to be done or I'm thinking about it.' She hesitated. 'It upsets me, you know, to keep starting and stopping. I'd rather leave off altogether. I can manage that way.'

It was the nearest she got to telling him that mental stimulus was the one thing she dreaded; that it aroused desires in her that she could not satisfy.

He was silent. He seemed to be pondering over what she had said. Her hopes rose a little. Then he said, 'You must have known all about this when you chose to have a baby.'

'I didn't choose,' she said. 'And you can't know.' But he thought that an excuse.

After another pause, he said, 'Well, you only have to ask if you want help. I'll always help.' He went back to his reading.

He did not understand the difference between helping and being responsible; the latter sucked in. She wanted to tell him this. But she, who was so emancipated, could not bring herself to say it.

Her anxieties began to affect her sex life. She did Stephen a favour more and more often. When he did not seem to notice, she was upset and relieved at the same time. She remembered her experience during their honeymoon after the episode on The Street, when she had feigned orgasm and he had not known and how unhappy it had made her.

Stirred by his reproaches, she made another effort to read, but left off because it caused her too much pain. She went back to the magazines.

She suffered a nightmare in which she was reading a book; the book started slowly to alter shape, leaves sprouted out from around the edges. The leaves were thin, elongated, sharp pointed, and a vivid green. The vivid green scared her. She dropped the book. It fell to the floor with a heavy thud. Gazing down, she saw that it was altering its shape, turning into a huge cauliflower, with a dead white centre, and bulging, so that she thought it must be pregnant. She woke up with the feeling that comes with nightmare.

She began to have trouble remembering the order in which things had to be done. She told herself that she would see more people in prison during a day than she did at home.

She looked forward to Stephen coming home, but he gave her

no items of interest which could sustain her. If she had been suffering physical starvation he would have rushed to her aid, but she was suffering from mental starvation and mothers did not suffer in that particular way. It was not allowed.

She would have felt more normal if she could have identified an enemy. But she had no enemy and no ally.

When she did attempt to read, she found that spaces were appearing between the letters. She went to an oculist, but he told her there was nothing wrong with her eyes.

Meanwhile Stephen could not help being irritated with her. He experienced her unhappiness as a personal insult. She had no right to be unhappy. His sense of disappointment sharpened and this time he made no effort to conceal it from himself. She was less lively, less interesting than he had a right to expect. He was working hard to look after her. 'What about a cup of coffee?' he would say, after his dinner. He said this not because he wanted the coffee, but because he was annoyed with her for not living up to his expectations. When she got up and made the coffee, handing him the cup without speaking, he was even more annoyed. He did not think of the fact that he himself was often silent for long periods with a book.

Because of his disappointment, when he saw her reading a women's magazine, he would make deprecating remarks about the contents. 'When are we going to see some results from those wonderful concoctions you're studying?' he would ask. He made his remarks in a sarcastic voice. She began to think of him as her judge.

Then another year had passed. It was late March and Robbie's birthday. There were two candles, instead of one, on the birthday cake. Again Daphne and Jack came in for the celebration. Later the same evening, Stephen said, 'It's only a short while to the spring holiday. You need a change. We'll get one of the Mums to look after Robbie and we'll go away for a long weekend.'

When he was being kind, he had a special gentleness. Now he spoke gently, put his arms round her and kissed her and she turned and clung to him as if she were about to lose him.

CHAPTER TWELVE

So during the summer holidays, Jean and Stephen went for a long weekend to the Broads, leaving Robbie in the charge of a delighted Mabel – Mary was now at work all day. They hired a boat, took stores on board, and after a minimum of instruction left the quayside at Wroxham for four days afloat.

It was like stepping into another dimension of life, satisfying and relaxing. The water flowing each side of the boat acted as an insulator so that the land, although no further off than a few feet, seemed part of a different existence. On board, troubles no longer had meaning. To the accompaniment of much hooting from crafts of various sizes and shapes, their boat passed under Wroxham Bridge. All the world seemed on the water – and yet the world was oddly absent. It was strange that with so much human activity, there was yet no aggravation, no jostling in a crowd; on the contrary there was a sense of effortless, forward movement.

They both took turns to steer. They had neither of them been to the Broads before and the new experience delighted them. 'Mum was right when she suggested the Broads,' Stephen said, steering with cautious ease. 'She and Dad went quite often when they were young. She said it was a world on its own.'

'She was right,' Jean agreed, with enthusiasm. She was already feeling better, more relaxed, less tired.

They made a leisurely way upstream towards Horning. A slight drizzle was setting in, but nothing could dampen their spirits. On all sides, there was something of interest – two large, white swans with six grey, fluffy cygnets nesting on a low bank, a tiny moorhen with a bright beak, peeping out from under reeds at the river's edge, a scatter of water lilies in a quiet corner, and clustered at the edges of the bank, early, vivid blue gentians. There were willows everywhere, most of them pollarded.

'I don't care for pollarded trees,' Jean commented, 'they look odd.'

'They look odder still in the winter. Little, bare arms sticking up.'

'How do you know?'

'I've seen them in Epping Forest. Dad and I used to walk there.' Jean always experienced a queer feeling of disbelief when Stephen talked about his parents in that easy manner.

They found a corner where they could anchor the boat. They sat on deck, eating sandwiches and drinking cider, watching the other boats pass up and down. On each side of the pale, rippling water lay a flat, open landscape of misty, green, low-lying fields stretching away into far distances, with overhead a pale, luminous arc of sky; the spreading view was broken only by square church towers and an occasional windmill, long silent. They did not go far that afternoon, but lazed. After an hour, the drizzle had ceased. As dusk fell, they tied their boat to a bollard, went ashore, strolled along the one street of the little riverside village, drank at the pub, listened to the chatter of the locals and holidaymakers, returned to the boat, took one final gaze around at the dark river, the misty banks, the starless sky, and went below to sleep until late morning. The rays of the sun through the cabin window finally woke them. They made breakfast and went on deck again.

On their first full day the weather was fine, if with a damp feel. They came to detached houses set well back from the river bank, with gardens running down to the water's edge and often a pool to one side where a boat lay at anchor. There was a slight mist and, as they went by, each house and garden emerged as if out of a dream. They chugged past riverside villages with houses of pale greens and browns, unspoilt by change. They kept passing sights which told them that they were in a different world from the one with which they were familiar – a heron with a long, extended beak, rising with sudden rush into the air, the blue flash of a kingfisher, banks thick with reeds, early spring flowers, pale yellows and bright blues shining out of the shadows cast by reeds and rushes. They passed a second heron, silently stalking its prey, swooping on it without warning from above. They leant over the side of the anchored boat and watched the ripples of water as fish moved and darted just below the surface, and they ate their lunch in a marvellous silent backwater, out of reach of the mainstream of boats.

Once they passed two fishermen seated silently on a bank at a quiet spot, waiting patiently for a bite, with a wary eye to the approaching vessel, so that they slackened speed as they went by. When dusk fell, they tied up at another unspoilt village and again went ashore, ate supper at an inn, drank cider and listened to the talk. They told each other that the cider tasted better than it had tasted anywhere else.

The third day they ventured on to one of the broad stretches of

132

water which gave the area its name. It was like venturing on an inland sea. Towards early evening a wherry with a huge, black elongated sail went by, signalling its passage with only the faintest rippling sounds. They stood on deck admiring a sight now seldom seen.

On the last day of their stay they drew the boat up close to the bank under some willow trees in a quiet spot and lazed on deck. The sun had come out after hours of greyness and was making the water sparkle and ripple shiningly past them in the light breeze. Stephen began to talk seriously about their return home. He argued with a cool reasonableness against the manner in which she was coping with her situation.

'You don't have enough mental stimulus; that's why you're always tired,' he told her. 'You should get out more. Daphne would look after Robbie while you went to an art gallery, or a matinee; then you could do the same for her.'

'Daphne wouldn't thank you for a visit to an art gallery,' Jean responded, with a laugh at the thought.

'It doesn't have to be an art gallery,' he replied, with just a hint of impatience in his voice.

'You could learn to play the piano,' he suggested. 'You like music. We could afford a second-hand one.'

She hesitated, as if about to say something, then changed her mind.

'Yes. I could,' she said, aware of his impatient tone.

'We could try and find a nursery school where Robbie could go for an hour or so,' he said.

'Yes, we could,' she said.

'You ought to take advantage of your free time,' he said. She had an opportunity to increase her knowledge and skills which would not present itself to him until he retired. He did not say this, but she guessed he was thinking it.

He told her, 'Mother used to go to the Townswomen's Guild. She said she learnt a lot from the talks and discussions.'

'I expect she did,' Jean said.

She knew she was not responding in the manner he asked of her. And she knew he knew it. She made an effort.

'I'll try,' she said. 'I'll get out more. I'll go to some classes.'

He was pleased at her promise.

At that moment it did not seem an impossible promise, stimulated as she was by change of scene and interest. She told herself that she had been making a mountain out of a molehill, but she

133

was relieved when he did not pursue the matter any further. That night, in the little cabin, they made love – and their love seemed as strong as at the start.

When they went to pick up Robbie, he was pleased to see them, but by no means rapturous. He had been very spoilt by both his grandparents and for a week after he returned home he was difficult to discipline.

Stephen went back to grapple with the summer term and exams and Jean set herself the task of carrying out her promise.

On Tuesday afternoons she went to a Townswomen's Guild, while Daphne kept a willing eye on Robbie and Nigel. There she listened to a variety of speakers on a variety of subjects from holidays in the United States and Iceland to problems of bureaucracy in local government. Each talk was of interest on its own, but the subject snapped shut once the couple of hours had come to an end. She was not used to such abrupt dismissals. She joined a sociology group, taking part in a project about everyday life in Guatemala. Later she gave a talk on Latin America as her contribution to the group. One evening she attended a class on the history of painting in the Netherlands, then signed up for twelve lectures at the local school. She brought home books from the book box supplied by London University and took to reading them in place of women's magazines. She wrote an essay on the relationship of the Netherlands to Spain which the lecturer marked 'Excellent!' Now and then she went to exhibitions at the Tate and Hayward galleries. She went to an occasional matinée. About this time, she finally managed to get Robbie into a play-group where he went from ten o'clock to twelve, twice a week.

But instead of all this mental activity reducing her tired feeling, her fatigue increased. She began to feel more and more weary. She got up tired in the mornings; even when she went to bed early she woke up tired. She suffered a chronic tiredness – as if she was old instead of being only twenty-nine. She tried resting in the afternoons while Robbie took his nap, but she got up from her rest more tense than relaxed.

She persevered with the Guild, but she missed depth of study and an aim. It all seemed merely a means of filling in time. She went with the Guild on an outing to Eastbourne and enjoyed the sight and sound of the sea, but the chatter of the women got on her nerves and she blamed herself.

When the History of Netherlands Painting finished she went

134

instead to a series of lectures on the Nineteenth Century. She took a book out of the book box, brought it home, and turned to it during free moments. She had read half way through the book when she began to sob and put the book down. She gave it back the next time she went to the class and she did not go to the class any more. She went out of the house as usual and spent the two hours wandering the streets, sitting in a night café, pretending to Stephen that she was still attending the course.

For she dared not say to him that the lectures and the reading aroused in her desires which she could not satisfy alongside the carrying out of her duties as a wife and mother, nor that these desires were so painful that they were wearing her down, wearing her out, bearing on her nervous system so that it could hardly sustain the strain, because then he would think that she did not any more want to look after Robbie and himself. And this would be the same to him as her leaving off loving them – for food and clean clothes, and attending to all their needs, equalled love in his eyes.

And she thought, 'Perhaps it would help if I went to religious classes.' She longed for her mental needs to wither then she would not have to live any longer a life sliced in two – one half living, one half struggling to stay alive.

She tried brushing up on her French, but the thought of France made her aware of movement, of purpose, of people, of the flow of life. When she took up the grammar book, she discovered that everything she had learned the previous day was wiped away. Her mind was a blank. This kept happening until at last she abandoned the effort to learn.

Her mental fatigue went on growing and growing. The more mentally active she became, the more her fatigue grew on her. Her mind seemed to be whirling round aimlessly, like a piece of machinery disengaged from its source of power; the free wheeling seemed like a physical hurt.

She became easily irritated. She started to speak to Robbie in a rough tone and to smack him for trivial offences. Once she hit him on the top of his head with a spoon, a real hard smack because he was making a fuss eating his dinner, and when he yelled and screamed, she felt she could kill him. She calmed him down, then anxiously examined his head for a bump and was thankful when none showed for she had no idea how hard she had hit. She waited for him to say something to Stephen, but by the evening he had forgotten his tantrum and its result.

But she could not stop irritation with Robbie welling up in her.

'You shouldn't shove Robbie away from you,' Stephen said one evening angrily, when she was preparing Robbie for bed. 'You're always pushing him away.'

'If you had him all day,' she retorted, 'you'd be less lofty.'

'You're always talking to him in an irritated tone,' Stephen objected, adding, 'You shouldn't have had a child if you didn't want to look after him.'

He turned to Robbie, 'Mummy doesn't want to bath you,' he said. 'Daddy will bath you instead.' He lifted the child and carried him off to the bathroom; a little later Jean heard Robbie's delighted shrieks and Stephen's laughter. The sounds made her feel left out and guilty.

Soon after that incident, Stephen started to develop a tendency to concentrate on Robbie at the weekends, he played with him in the garden and took him off to the park with a bat and ball. 'I'll take him off your hands,' he said to Jean, 'and you can get on with something of your own.' But he did not say it in a nice tone of voice. She felt she was being punished.

That night she lay in bed thinking about the past and listening to Stephen's soft breathing beside her in the dark. How strongly she had wanted a child! She recalled the moment when she had first unwrapped the small bundle and gazed in awe at his tiny star-like fingers which had closed so tightly around her own little finger and the bliss she had felt when she had held the baby close to her breast and he had sucked her milk, and his birthday with the single candle shining, and all the joy of the first year. All that – and none of it was worth what came after, and went on and on and on....

She wanted to talk about her feelings to Stephen, but she dared not for she feared that he would take it as proof of a lack of love. She knew then the special quality of a loneliness that comes in the presence of a loved one with whom it is no longer possible to communicate.

About this time they had the phone installed. The first person to contact her after the relatives was Rita. Notoriously bad at writing, Rita liked a chat over the phone. It was a Sunday afternoon and Stephen was out with Robbie, playing in the park. Rita was full of news. Her crisp, decided tones came clearly over the wires.

'I'm teaching part-time at the local polytechnic now,' she told

136

Jean. She had been very lucky. She had found a widow woman with two grown-up children, a responsible woman, who could give her five hours a day.

'When I get back, she has the lunch ready. Then I take over the house and she fetches Ian from nursery and Sarah from the play centre.'

'We passed the nursery,' Rita went on. 'Do you remember?'

'Yes. I remember,' Jean said. How long ago it seemed since she had sat in that train. Another time – another life.

'Do you like your job?' Jean asked.

Rita said 'Yes,' it was interesting – not what she would have chosen, but it got her out of the house and away from the children – and she met all kinds, from all over the world.

'And what about you?' Jean hesitated. Then she launched into details of her various activities.

'My goodness! You do manage to fit in a lot. All that talk about not having any energy!' Quickly Rita added, 'I must be going now. I'm frightfully busy. I never have any leisure at the weekends. But it's a great life – if you don't weaken!'

'Yes,' Jean said.

'But you're not doing badly. Remember me to Stephen. Both of you come over some time. Just give us a ring.' She was gone without waiting for an answer. Jean put down the phone with the odd sense of having talked to a stranger. She told Stephen about Rita's call and he made the remark that they were a couple who would get on.

'I don't see the need for being nasty,' Jean said. 'What's wrong with "getting on"?'

'I didn't say there was anything wrong with it,' Stephen retorted. His tone had held a reproach, and Jean recalled the time when she herself had felt that way about Rita and Richard. Now she thought they had a realistic attitude to life. She also thought that Rita was rather wasting her abilities. Rita had insisted that a woman had to buy her way out, but Jean was not sure that Rita had succeeded.

Twice a week, Jean took Robbie to the playcentre: one day she left him to go shopping, the other day she stayed with the mothers, had a cup of tea, listened to their talk about children and their ailments, about what food was available in the shops and at what prices, about husbands and their failings and virtues, about problems with older children, and she tried to join in.

When she was with other women, listening to their chatter, she

137

longed for solitude; when she was alone, she longed for company. She dreamed of an interesting conversation as the starving dream of food. She thought that if she was covered in irritating spots, she would be pitied, but as it was she could expect no sympathy – her kind of misery was not real misery. Then she pulled herself up. She was becoming self-pitying and she did not want that.

She began to develop a sense of resentment towards Stephen, especially when he turned his attention more and more to Robbie, leaving her out. Inevitably her sex life was affected. She began to hold back, to make excuses. When he talked about the time when she would be able to take a morning job, which he did with the intention of cheering her up, her resentment increased, because he saw her future in terms of subordination to himself and his son. The more she reproached herself, crushed her resentment and tried to respond to his advances, the less she was able to do so. Her tiredness was always with her.

'You make me feel as if I'm raping you,' he reproached her bitterly, after one especially unsuccessful attempt.

On another occasion, he said out of the darkness, 'You make me feel less than a man!' He thought it a slur on his manhood that he could not make her want him. He felt sexually rebuffed, his pride was hurt and this made him hard.

Because he was disappointed in her, he became even more critical and looked for opportunities to disparage her. 'It's time you paid more attention to your appearance,' he told her. 'Your hair looks as if it's a pantomime wig – all over your face.'

And on another occasion, 'Your blouse is hanging out – why don't you tuck it in and try to look neat for once in a while.' She did not answer him, but his words made her feel inadequate in body as well as in mind.

She was starting to forget things; she forgot that they had run out of salt, even though she had it on her list. As it was a Sunday, she had to borrow from Daphne. She felt humiliated. 'You should take a few hints from Daphne,' Stephen said, when she returned with the salt. 'Daphne knows how to organise a household.' She felt inadequate.

A few days later, he came home with a memo board which he put up in the kitchen. 'There you are,' he told her. 'That's all there is to it!'

She could no longer pretend to want him. 'Give yourself to me, darling,' he would urge her. She would lie without movement,

138

thinking, 'I've nothing to give!' and feeling empty. Then she would suffer a sense of guilt and apologise, 'I'm sorry! I don't know what's the matter with me.'

And he'd answer, 'You're cold!' and turn away. She would weep silently while he slept. The time when they had been happy in bed and loved each other seemed aeons in the past.

Stephen thought to himself resentfully, 'Women are illogical; give them what they want and they want something else.' Jean had wanted a child and now she had a child she wanted the kind of life only single women, or childless women, could have. There was no arguing with women. He thought with envy of his father's contented home, with a satisfied wife and mother who had never bothered about exams and all that sort of thing. He thought, 'Well, if she doesn't want to act sensibly, if she wants to make a martyr of herself, she'd better get on with it.'

His pride was offended. He felt affronted. Her responsibilities were very small next to his. She ought to have his problems to face each day. Did she have the least idea of how stretched he often was? He asked her this. All he got in reply was, 'You're lucky!'

'You're lucky with me,' he retorted resentfully. 'The things I do for you, most men wouldn't do. Most men think it's the woman's place to look after the home and the children and their place to earn the money to keep them.'

She did not answer him.

He went on turning over his grudge in his mind. His mother had not gone to a polytechnic, or got a degree. She had left school at fifteen and gone into nursing. When she had married, she had been happy. And he compared the happiness and serenity of his parents' marriage to his own. He came to the conclusion that a specialised education for women was a mistake, it only made them unhappy. It made them ambitious and unrealistic. What was needed was an education that would help them to be flexible. After all, men couldn't bear children.

One evening, he said to her sarcastically, 'When you had your ambition, you wanted a baby. When you had a baby, you wanted your ambition. Whichever you had, you'd want the other!'

'That's right!' she answered him.

She could not choose between two equally powerful needs – any more than if she had been the mother of two children she could have chosen which child should live, which child must die. She was thinking this while there was a silence between them.

Then he said, again sarcastically, 'Perhaps you'd like me to stay at home and mind Robbie while you go out to work?' He thought of her as belonging to another species and that what applied to him did not apply to her.

They spoke only a few words to each other for the remainder of the evening and when they went to bed they lay side by side like strangers forced to share a bed.

Her increasing forgetfulness irritated him. She used his memo board and still she forgot. She forgot the bread, she forgot the potatoes; she forgot to iron his shirts so that he ran out; she forgot to defrost the fridge so that, when she did, the water ran over the floor; she forgot to change the sheets when they needed changing; she let the curtains, the cushion covers, the head rests get grey and soiled so that when he invited a friend home from work, he was ashamed at the look of the place. Yet when the home had been tidy, clean and bright, he had thought much of her work unnecessary. She did not forget or overlook everything all the time, but there was always something which she had neglected. And, he thought, he wouldn't keep his job for long if he forgot to prepare his lessons, mark the children's homework, return it to them on time, give out the next lot of exercises and be on hand when it was his turn on the dinner rota. He had a hundred and one daily responsibilities.

When he came home after a hard day's work, he had to wait for his meal because she had forgotten to put on the potatoes at the right time or she had let the pan boil dry and the vegetables tasted half burnt. This did not happen all the time either, but he thought it should never happen and he showed his displeasure when it did.

He thought she had turned into a dull, uninteresting person, grumpy, often a nagger, the kind of woman men made jokes about and got away from into pubs and clubs. He did not think to ask himself whether it was reasonable to expect so much from her – interesting companionship as well as all the normal duties of a wife and mother.

The thought that he watched her, noted her failings and weighed her in a balance, made Jean nervous. She lost the remainder of her spontaneity, all her former gaiety, her sense of fun, her outward warmth. She shrank from him as from a judge. And she could not cure either her forgetfulness or her tiredness so that she could not avoid irritating him. Because of their mutual disappointment, they no longer cared if they wounded

140

each other. When they were in bed and he turned to her, she told him that she could not, she was menstruating. He answered, 'Well, it hardly makes any difference now, does it? Except that it puts you in a bad temper.'

'It does not,' she answered.

'It does,' he insisted. 'I can always tell.' He meant to hurt her. After that, she kept a tight control over herself during those times when he could put her nerves down to a period. She shrank from seeing the superior smile on his face. And as she menstruated every few weeks, she was rarely free from a guardedness in his presence. His words gave her a sense of bodily inferiority. She began to lose confidence in her body. Without confidence in her body, there was no possibility of confidence in herself.

She began to think of the penis as an instrument upon which she was impaled, so that when he tried to approach her, to soften her, to urge her to give herself to him, she lay rigid. 'I won't! I won't! I won't!' she repeated silently to herself. Frigidity replaced her former generous giving; remembrance of his superior smiles froze her responses. She saw her body as an object to be taken and he as the subject who took.

Being dependent upon him became for her a degradation. She avoided asking for money unless it was absolutely unavoidable. She bought herself as few clothes as possible. When she picked up the bank notes which he had left on the sideboard, she felt humiliated.

'You either neglect the house, or else you spend much too much time on it,' he complained. 'I could keep the house clean in half the time you take.'

She asked coldly, 'And what would you do with the rest of the time?'

'I should have thought, with your education, that would be no problem,' he answered.

On her birthday, he got her some hand cream. 'I didn't know what to get you,' he said. 'You don't read now – you don't do much of anything.' It was true that she had gradually given up her outside activities. She no longer went to the guild, or to classes. She thanked him, but she was outraged.

One morning, when Stephen was at work and Robbie at the play centre, she stood in the middle of the front room and screamed and screamed and screamed. Daphne came rushing in, 'What's the matter?' she called out as she came into the room. Jean had forgotten all about Daphne.

'Oh! It's a huge spider, a monster!' Jean answered. She had fallen on her knees and was pretending to be looking for something under the settee. When they could not find the spider, Daphne insisted on Jean going over to her place for coffee. 'I'll put some brandy in it,' she said. 'It's nice and will do you good.' She looked at Jean with a worried expression. She thought Jean looked odd.

After that, whenever she screamed, Jean buried her face in a pillow. She would put on the radio, then she would turn it off. She thought to herself that if she had committed some great crime, she would not have been sentenced to solitary confinement; not in England, anyway.

Once, when she was shouting at Robbie, a habit she had developed, Stephen said, 'Why did you have a child, if you didn't want to look after him? Why did you marry in the first place? Women who love their family don't mind putting them first.'

'I wish I hadn't married,' she retorted, adding, 'I wish I'd never met you.'

'If you don't care about me any more, at least care about Robbie,' he told her. 'Look after him properly.'

'I wish I had never had him,' she answered and turned away from his indignant gaze. Without realizing that she was acting in this manner, she stopped looking at him when he was in the room. She looked at him only when it was unavoidable.

She began to pity herself, a fault to which she had never before been addicted. One day, as she was standing at the sink after breakfast and Stephen was putting on his coat to go out, she suddenly said, 'I wish I could go into hospital and have my brains taken out.'

He was shocked. 'You shouldn't say that!' he told her. After he had gone, she wept into the washing-up water. When she went to put the peelings into the dustbin, she wished she could have wrapped her brains in the same piece of paper and left them inside the bin.

After his failure on that occasion, when she had made an indirect appeal for his help, she became vindictive. She started to imagine in what ways she could hurt him, take revenge. When he asked for a cup of coffee, while she was getting it she was thinking, 'I could put poison in it.' She imagined him taking the cup from her, unsuspecting, confident in his ability to control every situation. Beyond that point her imagination did not go. She simply wanted to feel that it was within her power to destroy him.

'Can't you get your own coffee?' she asked, on one occasion.

'That's what you're here for,' he answered, without looking up from his reading. It was on occasions such as this, that she indulged her fantasy.

About once a fortnight, Mabel would phone. The conversation always took the same course.

'How are you, dear?'

'Oh, I'm all right.'

'And Stephen?'

'He's all right.'

And then it was all about Robbie. How was he? Was his latest cold better? Did he still like his playgroup? Did Jean think she would like a knitted jersey for Robbie next winter? What colour would she like? What about two, one got dirty so quickly, especially with a boy? She knew this because of Stephen. Sometimes there followed reminiscences about Stephen's childhood. Then, what about herself? Had she done anything exciting recently? She did still go to the Guild, didn't she? And so on and so on...

'What about you and Dad?' Jean would ask, to check the flow. 'What have you two been up to?'

'Oh, not much at our age, dear!' Mabel always spoke as if she and Jim were eighty.

When she put down the phone, Jean thought, 'I can't stand that woman! Always rooting! Still, she did look after Robbie when we were on holiday; and it's not her fault that the truth isn't what she imagines.' But she could not overcome a shrinking feeling when she heard Mabel's voice. She wondered what Stephen talked about when he went to visit his parents once every few months. She often found an excuse for staying away and left Stephen to take Robbie on his own. When she did go, she talked very little. Her mother-in-law's confident tones made her ill at ease.

With her own mother, she was much more relaxed. Mary did not fuss over the phone. She simply asked if they were all well and was satisfied with a bare 'Yes' for an answer. She had never pretended that her daughter was a favourite with her. 'Don't think I don't know why you've gone the other side of London,' she had said to Jean when they had first moved. And Jean had not tried to deny the implied accusation. To that extent, her relationship with her mother was an honest one, but Mary was genuinely fond of her grandchild; she had always preferred male

143

children. In spite of the treatment she had received from her husband and Dick's neglect of her, she still looked up to men as the superior sex.

So the months passed – again it was Robbie's birthday, and there were three candles on the birthday cake.

CHAPTER THIRTEEN

JEAN woke one morning in a panic. She said to Daphne, 'I felt bad! I felt as if the house was on fire and I couldn't get out.'

She sometimes talked to Daphne. Daphne never told her she was silly, nor did she give advice. 'I take people as they are,' she had once told Jean. But the acceptance had its drawbacks. Daphne did not enter in. She listened sympathetically, but after a little while she turned the talk into other channels. In the end Jean gave up the attempt to communicate. Her friend was satisfied with the way she lived. She could not understand why Jean was not the same. To Jean it was as if there was nobody anywhere who felt as she did. This sense of being in some way odd was the hardest of all to bear.

Shortly after Robbie's third birthday, she began to suffer bad insomnia. She had to go to her doctor. He gave her pills. Then she began to develop phobias. Like in most houses, but especially those of an older type, mice and spiders made an appearance from time to time. Jean had never much liked either. But she had tolerated both. Now her tolerance threshold suffered a sharp fall. One morning, as Stephen was getting ready to leave for work, her eyes fell on a large, black spider rapidly crossing the living room floor. Immediately she gave a loud scream and implored Stephen to find the spider and destroy it. He did his best; he searched all round the floor, moving the table and chairs and peering into the dark corners, but all to no avail. The spider had disappeared as suddenly as it had appeared.

'If you paid some attention to the dust, you might not get so many spiders,' Stephen told her, irritably. 'Anyway, it's gone now.'

'No, it hasn't gone!' Jean insisted. 'It must be under the sink. I saw something go into the kitchen.' She had not seen anything, only a flash across her eyes, which was probably nerves, but the brushes and buckets had to be taken out and examined one by one in case the spider was sitting on one of the brushes or had got inside the bucket.

Finally Stephen said, 'This is ridiculous! It won't bite.'

'I know it won't bite,' she shouted back at him. 'I just can't stand the sight of it.'

'Well, I can't waste any more time,' he retorted, exasperated. 'I'm late already.' He got up from the floor, brushing the dust off his trouser legs.

'What am I going to do if I see it?' she asked, almost weeping.

'Tread on it!' he answered, as a way of finally disposing of the problem.

'I can't stay in the same room.'

'Nonsense!' he retorted, adding, as he got to the door, 'see you tonight.'

She hated him then.

When she saw a spider in the bath, she shrank from the sight of it and wanted to call Stephen to dispose of it for her, but she feared he would make a joke about her phobia, so she forced herself to try and wash it down the plughole. But if it started to run about the bath, she was forced to call Stephen and then she felt humiliated.

She tolerated mice a little more, but she dreaded the sight of one. When she thought she heard a scuffling in the kitchen cupboard, she was convinced she would see a mouse if she opened the doors and she could not bring herself to do this, which involved her in all manner of difficulties.

Her phobias gradually became more severe. From a violent reaction to the presence, or suspected presence in a room of either spider or mouse, she reached a stage when she became convinced that she was being victimised, that they were engaging in a vendetta against which she was powerless. She developed a sense of paralysis in relation to this threat; a numbness, an inability to take any sort of counteraction. Her suffering was very real, but to Stephen it seemed a sheer nonsense; a hysteria which she could control if she had a mind to. The fact that he did not intend to be cruel made his impatience none the less hard to bear. It imparted itself to Jean as yet another example of his scorn for her general inadequacy.

Slowly the sense of persecution became transformed into a generalised sense of fear. This was even harder to bear. At least, before, her fears had been attached firmly to two familiar creations of the natural world which commonly aroused revulsion. Now fear floated in the air, unattached to any specific object. She was afraid without knowing why. Fear was everywhere.

Her feelings towards Robbie began to oscillate violently. One moment she was screaming at him, the next moment she was filled with remorse and was flinging her arms around him and smothering him in kisses. He hated the embraces more than the shouts.

'Lemme go! Lemme go!' he would yell, and breaking free, his face all red and angry, he would run off and hide or, if it was fine, into the garden. He started to throw tantrums and to jump up and down in paroxysms of rage, just as he had done when he was growing out of babyhood. When his father came in from work, he would run to him, pointing a finger at Jean, announcing accusingly, 'She's nasty! She's nasty!' Then, later in the evening, when Jean was putting him to bed, he would cling to her and start sobbing. All this upset Stephen and their relationship became even more strained.

There were times when Jean was certain that she loved them both; other times when she wished she had never set eyes on her husband or borne her son. When she felt the latter, she also felt very wicked.

About now, she had a bad nightmare. In her nightmare, there were two men with sharp, short, broad-bladed swords, fighting each other and one of the men sliced the other man's throat with his sword right down the middle and the blood poured out in a dark red stream and the wounded man, whose face could not be seen, only his neck and the stream of blood, made horrible, gurgling sounds. The dream was very vivid and when Jean woke up her heart was pounding and she felt very sick. She said nothing to Stephen about her dream.

To make up to Robbie for his mother's behaviour, instead of trying to find the reason for it, Stephen tried to take Jean's place. He spent an increasing amount of his free time playing with his son. More and more often he put him to bed. Then he would sit and read to him, cutting Jean out. At the weekends, he would take Robbie to London, to a children's theatre or a children's part of a museum, but he never asked Jean if she would like to go with them and she felt that she had been cut out of their lives.

Once she said to him, 'You never ask me if I'd like to come with you.'

146

'I'm giving you the opportunity to do what you want,' he answered, adding, 'without Robbie getting in the way.' And she knew it was a rebuke. His rational approach to everything drove her to despair.

Once, when she was having a bath, he came into the bathroon for his dressing gown, which he had left hanging on a hook, and she was filled with an unreasoning panic lest he should see her naked body. She tried to immerse herself in the water so that nothing of her body was visible, but he did not glance in her direction. Instead he went out, closing the door quietly, as if she had not been there at all. In the old days, he would have come over to her. She felt that he had cut himself off completely from her and she was relieved because she could no longer bear him to touch her. Yet, at the same time, she felt grief.

She began to dream more often or else she remembered her dreams more. Sometimes they were very pleasant and when she woke up she was sad. One dream especially kept on recurring – she was standing on a spit of land, gazing out over the sea, which was very calm and extraordinarily lovely, pale green, clear and still, like a lake. Looking at it, she was aware of a sense of complete peace, untouched by remorse or sorrow.

Then she had a different kind of dream; in the dream there was a huge plaice and someone was tearing the plaice into pieces and stuffing the pieces down another person's throat until the throat was choked with fish right up to the cavity of the mouth, and the throat was transparent so that she could see clearly the pieces of fish and they were glistening like phosphorescence. Then she dreamed again the sea dream and when she woke up she felt sad.

Her tiredness grew so that when she was on her own she would totter to a chair, fall into it, and lie there, lifeless.

She developed an illogical fear that something dreadful would happen to Stephen or to Robbie and that it would be her fault; this fear was interspersed with vivid feelings of vindictiveness. Then she would fall again into a chair and lie there, too ex-hausted to worry about anything.

In early June, when the weather was warmer and more settled, she took Robbie every day to the park and sat on a bench while he played on the swings and roundabouts. He would shout across to her and she would come and push him on the swing, high into the air. She took lunch and they picnicked and she tried to make up to Robbie by doing everything that he asked of her. They played ball; she put up stumps and they played cricket. He ran and she chased him round the trees. He joined with other children and she sat for long periods while the children ran about, jumping, running and shouting. They walked to the paddling pool, where Jean sat again while Robbie splashed and screamed and all the other children splashed and screamed. They went to the lake and Robbie fed the ducks and drakes. Then Jean took Robbie to the open-air cafe, where he ate ice cream and licked a lollie and she ate an ice cream too. They went home in time for Robbie's tea and to prepare Stephen's meal. As long as the weather remained fine, they went to the park every day.

As the summer wore on, Jean sat in the park day after day. She became familiar with other mothers, especially at the paddling pool. They greeted her and chatted to her to while away the time as their children larked in the water and chased each other round the edge of the pool.

Jean felt that they were human only in shape, that in reality they were living on a sub-human, biological plane. She thought of the park as a kind of zoo where a special female species took their young, whilst the human species was elsewhere.

In late June, Mabel asked if she might have Robbie to stay for a week. She would take him about while the weather was fine and before the summer vacation came and Stephen would want him. It was agreed and Robbie went to his grandparents. He was glad to go because he knew he would get his own way.

Now, when Stephen left the house in the mornings, Jean was on her own. For the first couple of days Robbie's absence was a relief. The routine, except for Stephen's evening meal, was gone. She got up late. She excused herself to Daphne. She ate a sandwich for lunch. Then she lay down on her bed with a sense of relief. She lay on the bed for longer and longer periods. She thought she was taking a kind of holiday and that she would be less tired afterwards. For she was always tired. She had grown accustomed to being tired.

After some days, Mabel phoned to ask if Robbie might stay a little longer than the week. She had promised to take him to the Tower of London and Battersea Park.

'Yes. Of course,' Jean said. She forgot to ask if he was enjoying himself.

'Would you like to speak to him?' Mabel asked. Before Jean could answer, she heard Mabel calling, 'Robbie! Mummy wants to speak to you.' There was a pause, then Mabel's voice spoke again. 'He's run into the garden, the naughty boy. Shall I go and get him?'

'No. Leave him,' Jean answered. She put down the phone with a sense of relief. For a little longer she would not have to pretend cheerfulness.

One morning, she woke up very late. Stephen had left the house. Everything was very still. She could not think why she had to get up, or what day of the week it was. It could not be the weekend, otherwise Stephen would still be in the house.

Another morning, on her way home, she turned aside into a small graveyard which she passed on her way to and from the shops. She had never been inside the gates before. There was a bench and she rested her shopping. The graveyard was tidily kept with small shrubs between the graves and the grass edges neatly trimmed. It was very quiet – no one was about. Leaving her shopping, she wandered among the graves. Some of the stones bore interesting inscriptions. Other stones were covered with moss and the words quite obliterated. She liked the look of the green, moss-covered stones. After a little she went back to the bench and sat down.

She felt very at peace. There was nobody to tell her what she ought to think, how she ought to behave, how she ought to feel. The dead accepted her as she was. She took to going there every afternoon, instead of lying down, and it seemed to do her good. She felt less tired.

Then one morning, when Robbie had been away a full week, she got up and could not think who she was or what she was doing in that house. Then she remembered, but she was very frightened. She made herself some strong tea with whisky and sat at the kitchen table. Slowly, with an effort, she ticked off on her fingers everything she knew about herself: her name, her address, her age, her actual birth date, the date of her marriage, the school she had attended, the polytechnic, her parents and where they lived. She knew who was her husband and who were her in-laws. She knew she had a son, his name and where he was now. But when she turned her attention to herself, she felt as if she had reached the edge of a cliff. A step further – and there was nothing.

'I don't know who I am,' she said aloud, frightened again.

And she asked herself. 'Who am I?' And she could not answer the question.

And she said out loud, 'I feel as if I don't exist.'

Then she took a knife and made a small cut across the palm of her left hand and when she saw the blood she knew that she existed.

Robbie came home two days later and she ran to him, covering him in kisses and smothering him in embraces, which made him grimace, for he did not like her all over him. She was relieved and happy and grateful to him for restoring meaning to her life.

She became quite gay and Stephen thought that she was being realistic at last. She herself thought that Robbie's absence had done her good. It had taught her who and what really mattered in life, but every now and then she went through periods when she seemed not to be there. She began to dread these times, but she managed to behave normally and no one suspected that anything might be amiss.

The summer vacation came and Stephen took Robbie out and about; sometimes Jean went with them, but mostly she did not. Sometimes she was asked, often she was not. She remained behind on her own. When the two came back, Stephen never asked her what she had been doing while they were away. They went for a week to the sea and played with Robbie on the sands, but their relationship had become too strained to make it a pleasure.

One afternoon, when father and son had gone to one of the science museums, and the day was warm with a blue sky, summer in full bloom, Jean suddenly made up her mind to go to a local flower show. She loved flowers and it would get her out of the house. When she got to the park, she found a large tent pegged down on the grass – inside, the stalls were loaded with flowers, the air filled with their scent. There were masses of fragrant roses of deep orange, peach, bright lemon, coral red and light gold, with fresh green leaves and beautifully shaped petals. All the roses were grouped together at one end of the large tent. On the long, middle benches were miniature gladioli with delicate red and white markings, morning glory, a deep, vivid blue, with slender, pointed leaves, groups of sweet-smelling white flowers with serrated edges, Tibetan poppies with a blue shimmer, and dahlias with enormous, shaggy, scarlet blooms. At the opposite end to the roses, there was a bench devoted to the Japanese way with trees – minute specimens of oak, lime and beech, perfectly formed and shaped.

Jean walked round the sides of the tent and along the centre benches, so that she would miss nothing of what was on display.

150

There were tickets attached to those of the exhibits which had won prizes. She halted at each such exhibit to take a closer look. Then she went outside and gazed up at the scented lime trees fringing the side walks. She walked slowly along, gazing at the tall, pale pink grasses in a neglected area of the park and at the fountains playing their sprays of sunlit water near the beds of red scabious close to the old-fashioned band stand. There was a bed of pale mauve phlox with white centres to one side of the open air cafe, and near the pond, with its flashing goldfish, bushes of yellow Roses of Sharon.

She felt nothing – it was just as if none of all this existed. She sat on a bench in the half sun, half shade. About her was the warmth and glow and colour and scent of summer, and there were people seated near her, lots of people, children with balls, babies in prams, young couples hand in hand, fathers and mothers, grandmothers and grandfathers, with their families, for it was a Sunday.

It was just as if nothing of all this was real. It was as if the threads of her nervous system had been drawn out, one nerve thread after another, until there was no single nerve left anywhere in her entire body with which she could feel.

She could feel nothing at all. Her nervous system had simply packed up on her, like a battery that had finally run down.

It was an inner deadness.

She got up from the bench, went home and behaved normally.

At first the lack of any sensation was a relief, a boon, but after a while, she began to wish that she could experience some feeling, even if painful, even the feel of a sharp saw or a knife. But she felt nothing at all.

'I don't exist,' she told herself. 'I'm not real!'

All this time she behaved in a rational manner, automatically carrying on with her usual duties – feeding Robbie, feeding Stephen, making out grocery lists, shopping, washing, ironing, answering her child when he spoke to her, playing with him, reading to him, kissing him good night, tossing him the ball whenever he demanded, listening to Stephen when he spoke to her, answering him, speaking herself. Her former forgetfulness had left her. It seemed to Stephen that she was behaving much more sensibly. The truth was that she knew what was expected of her so thoroughly that she was able to act it out with an automatic precision, without the need of any spontaneity.

And all the time she knew she was not real. She lived a strange existence. Nothing aroused in her the least stir or ripple of emotion. The sense of a hollow within her was the nearest she came to a feeling.

The weeks passed and the leaves of the trees were tinted with autumn colours; a mild sun shone from a pale blue sky. The weather held a late summer warmth. Jean and Robbie still went to the park. In order to be seen to be engaged in something and to avoid being drawn into one or other of the groups of women seated by the paddling pool, Jean would sit on a bench a little way off with a book laid open on her lap. She would drift off into a vague emptiness, just aware of what Robbie was doing. She picked a book at random and afterwards returned it to the shelf without knowing which book it was.

Until one mild, late September afternoon, she did idly glance down at the book open on her lap and did idly flip over the pages. By mere chance she had picked up a book on Twentieth Century paintings. There were many bright prints. She was dimly aware that a few of the prints were familiar to her. For the first time for many months a lukewarm interest was aroused in her. Without reading the text, she fixed her eyes on the print. After a while, she turned over a page and found another print. In this way, casually, and without any special effort on her part, she began to pay some real attention to what she was gazing at. The brightness of the prints, their vitality, their designs, their colours, had an effect on her. She started slowly to read. She read on and on and on, unaware of anything that might be happening around her, of where she was, utterly absorbed.

A part of her that had been held down, had suddenly prised itself free.

After what seemed a short while, Jean looked up from the page. As she did so, she became aware of a change in herself. Her fatigue was gone. Her brain was fresh as if spring had come to it. She felt as though her mind had been recharged – all its mental tiredness was swept away as if by a strong wind from off the Downs. It was an exhilarating sensation. For so long now, she had felt only half alive – worn out, old and tired. Now suddenly she was young again – young and full of life.

'I'm alive!' she thought, with a rush of joy. 'I'm alive!' All her feelings had come back in a rush.

And then, 'I'm young! I'm young!'

She experienced an intense desire to put right what was wrong between herself and Stephen – to retrieve the days when they had understood and loved each other, the days when she had loved Robbie without regrets. It must be possible, she thought. It must be possible to make all that love and tenderness and trust live again.

At the thought of Robbie, she gazed round for him. She could not see him. The park was strangely silent, the rays of the sun very long and low, the luminous sky fading slowly into a pearly grey, scent from the flowers rising, a bed of phlox showing pale yellows and mauves.

Alarmed, she looked at her watch. It could not be right. The mothers and children were gone, she had been sitting on the bench for almost two hours. She let the book lie on the grass where it had fallen when she had sprung to her feet in a fright. She ran all over the park, she ran calling Robbie's name, 'Robbie! Robbie! Where are you? Robbie!' She got out of breath, but she went on running. She got into a state where her energy began to give out. She ran a few yards, then halted, then ran again for a few yards, then halted, and so, running and halting and calling she went wildly round the park, searching for her child – until a keeper caught hold of her and made her stop.

After that, she remembered very little until the moment when a policewoman, accompanied by the same keeper, took her hand and she pulled her hand away.

'I can't go in! I can't look!' she said.

'It may not be your child, dear,' the policewoman said gently. 'It may not be your child.'

But it was. Robbie had fallen into the lake and drowned.

'Are you telling me that you sat reading for two hours without once looking up to see what Robbie was doing?' Stephen asked.

He was pacing up and down the living room, too agitated to sit down or stand still for an instant. He had loved his son dearly. He could not and would not believe that he was dead, even though he had seen his body.

After a long pause, Jean answered him. 'Yes,' she said. 'I forgot.'

'Forgot?'

'Yes,' she repeated. 'I forgot. I forgot Robbie.' She made this statement in a calm voice.

He was in a state of shock at Robbie's death, but he was stunned by her cool tone and manner. He began to pace the room

153

again. 'She's mad!' he said, as if to himself. 'There's no other explanation for it. She's mad.'

'Yes,' she said calmly. 'I am mad. Didn't you know?'

'No!' he said. 'You're not mad, Jean. There's only one thing the matter with you. You're not a normal woman. A normal woman wouldn't sit reading while her child drowned. You were always unfit to be a mother.'

She got up from where she was sitting, she went up close to him and looked him in the eyes.

'I hate you!' she said.

CHAPTER FOURTEEN

'SEE she takes the tranquillisers and don't leave the bottle in the room,' the doctor said. 'Try not to worry, it always takes time to recover from shock – she's had a great shock. But she's young.' At the door, he added in an encouraging voice, 'And she's got you.' He left promising to make another call in a few days.

Stephen closed the door and went back into the living room. He sat down in the chair where he spent much of his time. The doctor had dismissed the idea of his presence worsening her condition, but he knew better. 'It's a nervous reaction,' the doctor said. 'She's suffering from feelings of guilt; mothers always do when anything happens to their children, even a minor illness.'

Continuing his rounds, the doctor was thinking to himself that a sense of guilt was understandable, if almost certainly exaggerated. There did seem an element of neglect in the case. He made no effort to understand the full circumstances, these tragedies happened every day, in one way or another, and people always said, 'If only I'd done this instead of that, if only I'd foreseen,' but it wasn't so easy to foresee; one only thought afterwards it was. With words which sought to make the tragedy appear an everyday occurrence, he had done his best to reassure the husband. But Stephen knew better than to believe that a nervous reaction explained his wife's shrinking from sight or touch of him. The doctor had not seen the hate in her eyes as he

154

had seen it – he had not heard the hate in her voice as he had heard it. She had not come up close to the doctor and looked and spoken as she had come up close to *him* and looked and spoken. It had added up to one strong impression – an impression of pure hate.

He had done nothing to deserve the hate. Indeed, the opposite was true. He could be excused if he felt hatred towards her. It was she who was at fault – a mother who had allowed her child to die as a result of sheer negligence. Because she had been reading! Books were more important to her than her own flesh and blood, her own son. While he was alive, she had pushed the child away from her, had been rough with him, upset him, shouted at him. Yet she need not have borne him in the first place – he had not forced the child on her. He could have understood her resentment if he had done that. He had left her absolutely free to choose and she had chosen to have a child. He recalled the early days, the first year, when she had been all over the child, putting himself well second, when he had seemed scarcely to exist for her – and her books nowhere at all. Then suddenly, or so it seemed to him looking back, it had all changed. It was as if she had only wanted a plaything, a large doll. Then she had tired of the doll. She had tired of himself too. In the end she had resented everything she did for either of them. She hadn't even looked at him, she had walked about the room as if he were not there.

The symbols of happier days lay all about him, but he tried not to look at them. He averted his gaze from the mementoes of outings, the snapshots, the books, the rocking chair. But he could not help recalling the time when, returning from work in the evenings, he had opened the door to see her seated in the rocking chair, half asleep, with the baby nestled in her arms.

A short time before it had happened, she had said, 'I wish I had never met you.' And he had answered, 'If you don't care about me any more, at least care about Robbie. Look after him properly.' But she had not looked after him properly, she had not looked after him at all. If she had done, he would not now be dead. She had said, 'I wish I had never had Robbie.'

He wanted to ignore the snapshots, but they drew his eyes towards them – one snapshot especially, which he had had enlarged and framed, showing Jean seated on a bench on the library green, reading a book and waiting for him. He had stood with his camera poised, hoping she would look up, and she had looked up and seen him and smiled and he had caught the smile and the look – a look of love. He had no idea, not the glimmer of an idea, as to how and why that love had changed into hate.

All he knew was that now she did not want to look at him – it caused her distress to meet his gaze – she shrank away if he tried to touch her by so much as his little finger.

She had said, 'I wish I had never met you.'

He could have understood if he had gone with another woman, but he had never so much as looked at another woman. He had absolutely no clue.

He got up and went into the bedroom, but he came back quite quickly. It was a bitter truth that his presence there made her worse. He had taken the red hat from its hook on the door and wept over it. She had seen him doing it – when he turned, he had caught her eyes gazing at him and at once she had closed her eyes and turned her face to the wall. He did not know whether he still loved her or whether he hated her, as she hated him.

The days passed, Jean got up and sat in the living room by the window. She said nothing. If he spoke to her, she ignored his words, but she ate the food he prepared for her. He phoned the relatives, 'Please don't come over,' he told them. 'The doctor wants Jean kept very quiet for a time.'

When he thought she could be trusted not to do anything silly, he went back to his job. In the evenings, he did the cooking; at the weekends, he shopped and cleaned the house. He knew how to manage everything efficiently.

After a while, he found his dinner cooked and ready for him when he came back in the evenings. Gradually Jean took over her old duties, but she spoke to him as little as was possible. When he tried to bring up the past, she did not answer.

In the end he could not bear it any longer. It was more than he could take – the silent evenings, her avoidance of his gaze, her shrinking from him. One evening, he said, 'I think we'd better part, Jean.' It was five months since the tragedy. 'We can't go on like this – I can't anyway. Once you feel strong enough to be on your own, I think we should go our separate ways.'

She spoke at once, just as if they had been speaking normally during those five months during which she had scarcely opened her mouth, or so much as glanced in his direction. 'Oh, I'm quite able to look after myself now,' she said in an almost cheerful voice. There was no mistaking the tone of relief. It was as if she had been waiting for him to utter those words. And, indeed, she did experience the most immense relief. It was coming to an end – it would be over at last.

He gave her up then – in his thoughts, he gave her up for good. Her immense relief was too awful. He saw to everything: selling the house, paying off the mortgage, finding separate accommodation for himself and Jean, the financial arrangements, for she would have to be supported until she was well enough to work again, dividing up the furniture, and all the seemingly endless details involved in a separation.

At last everything had been attended to in a satisfactory manner. In the middle of March, two weeks before what would have been Robbie's fourth birthday, Stephen took Jean to see her new living quarters, a small first floor flat not very far away. When they got there, he made her some tea, while she sat down. He poured out a cup and handed it to her. He thought, with a sense of disbelief, that this was the last service he would do her. The same thought entered her mind, but it was a deadened pang. Then he pulled on his coat and stood hesitating.

'Is there anything else?' he asked. Turning at the door, he said, 'You'll be able to go back to your library work as soon as you're well again. Perhaps they'll take you back at your old library – it's not so far from here.'

She did not answer.

He added bitterly, 'Well, you've got what you wanted now.' They were cruel words.

He went out of the room, closing the door quietly behind him. She heard his steps down the stairs. She sat quite still, her eyes closed. She had not flinched at his words. Everything inside her was dead. She heard the front door shut.

He was gone. Their life together was at an end.

CHAPTER FIFTEEN

WHEN, at his wedding, Stephen had looked at Betty in her red suit and white canvas shoes with red laces, noticing, with appreciation, her honey-toned skin and light, grey eyes with their steady gaze, and listened to the clear, bell-like sound of her voice, he had felt for her an admiration tinged with a slight

157

disapproval. He had thought her rather bold. He decided that in spite of her attractiveness, she had an unsympathetic personality. This was an impression she often made on those who did not know her well, due to an upbringing which had left her with a strong distaste for any outward display of emotion. She did, on occasions, even to those who knew her intimately, appear unkind, abrupt, even tart.

Her parents, temperamentally unsuited, had married only because a baby was on the way. In bringing up their child they had acted on the belief that they could conceal from her their mutual incompatibility – the result had been to envelop her in an ambience of false emotions. Left to his own common sense, her father might not have taken this course, preferring instead a franker path, but in this one all-important instance, as in no other, he had accepted and acted on his wife's prompting, mainly on account of his sense of guilt.

At the time of her pregnancy, Margery had been twenty-two years of age, still living at home and working at a local drapery store as an alterations hand. An only child, she had been brought up to think it a sin to swear, drink, or go to a cinema or dance hall. As she got older, she began to take such teachings less seriously, but she could not escape a sense of guilt whenever she was enjoying herself or cease to feel that whatever she did ought to be done for a good purpose. Then, according to her lights, she really did sin and in the worst possible way, since the result could not be hidden. She was in her twenty-first year when she first met Fred, who was two years older. She had been walking up and down outside a cinema with a work mate, waiting to be 'picked up'. She was so innocent that she had no idea what her companion was about and although she thought it a little odd when they were accompanied into the cinema by two young men whom they had not before set eyes on, she was satisfied to be guided by her friend who told her it was 'the usual thing'. After the show they all four went to a coffee bar, then Margery ran all the way home. She was as scared as if she was still a little girl. Before she was allowed to go to bed, she had to listen to a long sermon on the sinful nature of cinemas and coffee bars. Although she had been too naive to lie, she possessed a sufficient sense of self-preservation to leave the two young men out of her account.

Margery had a doll-like appearance, a petite, well-proportioned figure, with small firm breasts, and the look of a 'boy' so attractive to some men. Her hair was almost flaxen and her eyes a pale grey with large light irises. Fred on the other hand was of broad build with a well-tanned out-of-doors look, thick dark hair and eyebrows, and a pleasant voice and smile. He had an easy-going, relaxed manner and he made an immediate appeal to Margery. He was the exact opposite to her own parents with their strict, unsmiling ways and stern judgements. There developed a strong mutual sexual attraction and it was not long before Margery discovered in herself a quite unsuspected capacity for deceit; at first shocked at this self-revelation, she quickly adjusted to it. Difficult though it was, she worked out secret meetings and became adept at clever little lies to cover up her traces. For the first time in her life she learnt the meaning of sensual pleasure. Until then all her sensuality had been diverted into religious paths. She had gained her greatest satisfaction from singing hymns of a pathetic kind; pictures of Jesus in various attitudes, including a large print of the crucifixion, had adorned her bedroom wall since early childhood. Now she had found another and more powerful outlet for her sexual energies. She behaved as any animal would behave whose instincts had been kept behind bars. With Fred naturally careless of the morrow and Margery totally ignorant, the outcome could be safely predicted. She was terrified and began to threaten him.

'You needn't threaten me,' he answered her resentfully. 'I mean to marry you.'

She was not the first girl he had had and he was already beginning to send glances elsewhere, but he would have considered abandoning her an act of dishonour. Besides, he had his small scrap-merchant business to think of, he could not easily go elsewhere and he knew sufficient of her parental background to be fully aware of the likely uncomfortable consequences to himself of any attempt on his part to evade his 'duty'.

A fearful row followed Margery's announcement of her intention soon to marry. Her parents suspected the reason, but the fact was never stated. The couple went to live in a small house in Haringay which belonged to Fred and was attached to his business premises; the scrap yard was next door. Betty was born seven months later, a 'premature' baby. After that Margery saw little of her family – they more or less discarded her. They considered the scrap yard business the final degradation.

Apart from sexual attraction, there was nothing to draw them together and this single genuine bond weakened with time. They continued a mild enjoyment in bed, but during the day the dissimilarity showed. They might have become more compatible had Margery been able to throw off at least a part of her early conditioning, but her defiance seemed to act on her more as a deterrent than an encouragement. She carried about with her a sense of shame which was a part of all she did and said. It stood between herself and her husband's good nature.

The thought that Betty might one day discover the truth terrified Margery. She took it for granted that her daughter would despise her and since she believed that love had to be earned, this was a fearful thought. Always easily frightened, she became jealous of her sister-in-law who lived close by, visited often, and was, like her brother, uncensorious and warm hearted.

Betty had learnt that every good girl loves her mother – if she did not love her mother a lot, she was not a good girl. At what age and by what means this important piece of information had been conveyed to her, she could never recall exactly, but looking back in later years, she thought it came from about the age of six – from the day when she had flung her arms round her aunt in the hall, hugging her and receiving a very warm hug in return. After Auntie Clare had gone, her mother had called her into the living room and, sitting down beside her on the sofa, had asked, in a solemn tone, 'Who do you love best, me or Auntie Clare?' Knowing in an intuitive flash what was expected of her, Betty had looked up into her mother's eyes and answered in a firm, slightly surprised voice, 'Why you, *of course*, Mummy.'

'I hope you do!' had come the reply, uttered in a reproachful tone, a tone which left no doubt in Betty's mind as to where the moral obligation of loving lay. This first early lesson in the necessity of emotional deceit had remained vividly with her throughout her childhood and growing up, guiding her behaviour and responses into safe paths. It was not until she had left home for some years that she decided to stop this once and for all by adhering in future to a strict policy of honest responses. Life not being that simple, it was perhaps not surprising if, on occasions, this deep-rooted desire for emotional sincerity caused Betty to overreach herself, giving the impression of a personality lacking in sympathy.

When Auntie Clare married and went away to Australia with her husband, Betty wept bitterly. 'I wonder if you'd cry like that if I went away?' her mother asked her.

Once the constant irritant of Auntie Clare had gone, mother and daughter got on much better outwardly. Betty was about

160

eight years of age then. For quite a while she missed her aunt a great deal, but, like any child, she had to find ways of living with her situation. Life settled down into a calm broken by regular squalls between the parents, but not directly involving Betty.

'At least our daughter is enjoying a happy childhood,' Margery would console herself whenever her irritation with her husband threatened to exceed tolerable limits and she made great efforts, when the three of them were together, to act out a happy family lifestyle. She believed that she had been successful. They often rowed at nights, but only after Betty had gone to bed.

'Keep your voice down! Betty will hear,' Margery would remonstrate and Fred would lower his voice. They did not think that the low, if often fierce tones in which they indulged their mutual frustrations with each other could reach to Betty's bedroom on the first floor of their old-fashioned house. Yet Betty's quick, inquisitive mind and lively imagination could not fail to sense an unuttered something in this atmosphere. It produced in her a sort of fog of apprehension through which objects and events loomed menacingly, devoid of firm structure. She felt herself groping, uncertain of what she might find, but one truth she early discovered – her parents did not love each other. They acted out their parts while she was present, rowed at nights in her absence. Unsuspected by her mother, it had become a habit with her since she was about eight years old to crouch half-way down the stairs in the dark, her hands hugging her knees, her head bent forward, listening intently to what was going on below. Her hearing was sharp and her movements, like those of a scared animal, so quick in response to any warning sign from below that she was well back out of sight before anyone emerged from the downstairs room. She was never discovered and continued the practice right up until her middle teens, when she gradually abandoned it as being beneath her dignity.

This childhood espionage arose out of an intense need to discover the reasons for her parents' quarrels. Early on, the child gathered that her father was vulgar. 'You're so vulgar! I hate going out with you,' her mother would say. 'What is vulgar?' she wondered. She thought it must be something nice if it was connected with her father. Time and time again, the word surfaced.

'You talk in such a vulgar way; swearing and making vulgar jokes.'

'They aren't vulgar jokes,' she would hear her father retort. 'It's you! You've got a dirty mind.'

161

'How dare you!' her mother would explode, her voice enraged.

'Well, it's true! Sex is healthy. You make it seem dirty.'

'What's a dirty mind?' Betty wondered. For a long while after she had crept back to bed, she kept turning the phrase over and over in her thoughts. She could make no sense of it.

Another time, she heard her father say, 'Well, what does it matter if I have a bit on the side? You can do the same if you want.'

She was nearly caught on that occasion, her mother storming out of the room and slamming the door behind her, caution forgotten in her rage. Lying back on her pillow in the dark, Betty wondered what a bit on the side could possibly mean.

But already she had become cautious, she knew better than to ask awkward questions. She did not know why they were awkward, but she did know that they would fall under that heading. She had once asked her Auntie Clare what 'vulgar' meant, and Auntie Clare had pursed her lips, hesitated, then said, 'Well, that's an awkward question,' and gone on quickly to talk of something else.

Some years later, she learnt what vulgar meant. A circus came to their district. In spite of Margery's objections and to Betty's intense joy, Fred insisted on taking his daughter. A big tent was pegged down in the middle of a field of very rough grass. Inside were rows and rows of plain wooden benches, backless, rising high up, almost, so it seemed, to the very roof. In the centre a large sward of grass was sealed off from the audience by a narrow, round metal ring. They climbed up wooden, rickety steps and sat down about half-way back, but still much closer to the ring than in an ordinary indoor circus, except in the very best seats. The tent was soon crammed with children, some with a parent, and it got hot, stuffy, full of the sound of voices and the laughter of the very young and smelt of sawdust and sweat. When the horses came on, prancing round the grassy ring, Betty felt that she could almost touch their thick, black manes. She had been to a circus before, in London, in a huge arena, but this was quite different – much more immediate and exciting.

She recounted it all to her mother over tea. 'It was lovely, Mummy!' she told her. 'You were silly not to come.' She added, 'I was sweating, it was so hot.'

'Perspiring, dear,' her mother corrected her, smiling that peculiar, sweet smile which Betty had begun to distrust.

162

That evening, eavesdropping, she heard her mother say, 'You shouldn't take her among such vulgar people.'

Now she knew what vulgar meant. It meant the kind of person who was comfortable – by comfortable, she understood relaxed, like a soldier standing at ease. At ease was what she so often did not feel when she was with her mother. Sometimes she felt as if she was about to get the cramp. This feeling would come on especially when they went out together for a walk, when suddenly, with a wild whoop of delight in her power of quick movement, she would leap ahead and along the path, only to be recalled at once by her mother, with the reproof, 'Don't run ahead shouting; you're not a savage on the warpath!' She got an awful feeling of cramp in her mind then.

In later years, looking back at her childhood, all her memories of happy times were linked to her father. They were all small occasions, but none the less happy for that – in fact, their everyday smallness really made for the happiness. When out with her mother, she always had to eat slowly else she would be told, 'Don't gobble! You eat as if we starve you!' She knew she must not take a second cake without first asking. Sometimes, after she had asked, her mother would answer, 'That's being greedy!' and refuse her so finally she stopped asking and took only what was offered her. But when she was out with her father, it was quite different. She could eat as many cakes as she liked. She had a passion for vanilla slices. Her father would take her into a tea shop and queue up while she sat down guarding two seats; when she saw him coming from the self-service counter with the laden tray, she would call out, 'Any slices, Dad?' and he would nod and grin. He never told her not to shout. She would clap her hands with glee. She was about nine years' old then. He would set the tray down and hand out the cakes and cups of tea, enjoying the pleasure on his daughter's face as much as she was enjoying the cake which she had snatched. She would gobble one slice thick with oozing cream and jam, leaving smears all round her mouth, something never encouraged by her mother, who would say, if she was present, 'Wipe your mouth, Betty! There's jam round it.' When alone with her father, she would take a second slice without first asking. Once her father said, pointing to the remaining slice, 'Go on girl! That's for you. Eat up!' She had hesitated, asking, 'Isn't it greedy, Dad?' He had laughed. 'Greedy? So what? Be greedy! It's nice, isn't it?' Yes, she thought, being greedy was nice, all right! But when she got

163

home, she didn't tell her mother that she had found out it was nice being greedy.

Now and then they went to a fair ground, which Betty especially enjoyed. She loved wandering about in a dark lit only by hundreds of brightly coloured lights; she loved the moving crowds, the fun fair, the side shows, the fortune teller who told her she would marry a tall, dark man and get appendicitis, the jugglers, the roundabouts, the air balloon which frightened her because it had a flame underneath. Fred had a simple side to his nature and enjoyed the fair as much as his daughter. They were more like two children wandering around than an adult and a child.

'Would you like some floss?' her father asked, as they came up to a stall with the stuff on display. He was always generous. 'They spit into it to make it stick together,' he added in a serious voice.

Betty's eyes opened wide. 'Do they?' she asked innocently.

'Rather!' her father answered solemnly. 'It's good for you,' he added. He bought Betty a great piece of floss on the end of a stick. 'Go on!' he urged jovially, watching her eating the soft, woolly stuff, 'Spit into it!' So Betty spat into it with immense joy.

When they got home, she said to her mother, 'I ate floss, Mummy. It's lovely! You spit into it to make it stick together.' 'Oh, what fun!' her mother answered, giving the sweet smile which the child had come to think of as somehow strange and odd, and to dislike. Later, when she was older, the dislike turned into distrust. For in spite of her father's efforts, she was not a happy child. She knew that all was not well, but she did not know why.

Fred went on taking his daughter to places of which his wife did not approve. One evening, when she was eavesdropping, they had a real row. 'You teach her dirty habits,' her mother was saying, referring to the floss. 'And you take her into unhealthy places. You've no sense of hygiene!' Within the next few minutes, Betty learned that it was unhealthy to buy chips, sprinkle them with vinegar and salt from the counter, take them, wrapped up in paper, into the street and eat them together with a large white pickled onion, while walking along. The onion, it seemed, was particularly undesirable for a reason Betty could not grasp. To act in this manner was certainly vulgar, but it was also unhealthy. It was unhealthy to go into one of those many side-street cafes and drink tea out of cups which were not properly washed and eat sandwiches which the man behind the

164

bar extracted from inside a glass case with hands which almost certainly were not properly clean.

'Nonsense!' her father retorted, in a scornful voice.

But when, the next time they went out together, her mother made an objection, he did not repeat his scorn. He never criticised his wife in front of his daughter. 'She's right, really, you know, your Mum,' he said to Betty in an apologetic voice as they were walking down the street. 'You don't want to go and get a disease.' Betty thought to herself that they had not got a disease yet. She loved the off-beat walks they took together down by the docks, the odd, little cafes, the fish and chip shops, the riverside districts; she dragged her compliant father down every side street which took her fancy. In this sauntering manner, they discovered many an unpublicised, half hidden nook and corner of the great metropolis. It was all very exciting to a young child.

'I think you'd have done well as a docker, Dad.' she said once.

Her father nodded. 'I think I would,' he said seriously. Any outdoor work appealed to him.

'Or a sailor?' Betty suggested further.

'A sailor would do,' he agreed, with a nod of the head. Before the afternoon was out, they had fitted him up with quite a number of suitable jobs. 'But I'm a scrap merchant,' he said finally and he gave her hand a little squeeze as if to say that he might have done worse.

'That's a lovely job!' Betty responded with enthusiasm. She liked the scrap yard, full of all manner of odd bits and pieces. She knew her mother hated her going there, but she went there all the same and rummaged without hindrance.

Fred could be very stubborn; a trait which, without his daughter at that stage in her life being aware of it, he had transmitted to her. But for the one exception, he behaved as he chose, ignoring his wife's complaints. She bitterly opposed his taking Betty to the races, she considered betting to be a vice, but he took her nevertheless and she loved it. She loved the speed, the riders bent low, wielding their sticks, the thick, firm green turf, the sweating horses at the finish, the excitement as to who was going to win. Most of all, she loved the thundering hoofs. When her father won, he always gave a part of his winnings to his daughter. He only put a small amount on a horse, so Betty's winnings were never large. All the same, he said to her, 'I don't think I'd tell your mother. You know she fusses.' That was the nearest he ever came to openly criticising his wife. Even then his tone was apologetic.

In her early teens her father started to take her to the cinema. They went every Tuesday. Betty looked forward to the weekly outing and mourned if anything happened to prevent them from going. 'You shouldn't take her to those dirty sex films,' she heard her mother saying reproachfully as she was coming into the room, ready for their Tuesday evening out.

'Why not?' he retorted. 'You listen to *Carmen*. That's about sex.'

'That's different,' she answered angrily. 'It's great music!' She added, not noticing Betty, 'You've got low tastes.'

Without answering, her father went upstairs to get his coat. Turning on her mother, Betty asked, 'Why are you always so hateful to Dad?' and burst into tears. Margery was stunned.

'What do you mean, child?' she said. 'I'm not nasty to your father.' She did not think she was. She thought it was the other way round.

But Betty could not contain herself now. 'He hasn't got low tastes,' she screamed across at her mother. 'He hasn't! He hasn't! He hasn't!' And you *do* treat him hatefully.' This incident signalled the start of the stormy years.

At that period of her life, when she was only thirteen, she was much more often confused than clear in her feelings, but there was one part of her daily experience about which she had no doubts – a side she especially disliked. It was the kissing ritual which took place between her parents each morning when her father left for work and was repeated each evening on his return. Then there was her own bedtime, she had to kiss her parents before going upstairs. She did not mind kissing her father, but she hated kissing her mother. There was growing up in her sensibilities a distinct impression of her mother being in some peculiar way different from the image which she was at pains to project. This did nothing to give her a sense of security.

Then the occasions on which she went out with her parents were not always happy. Fred often embarrassed his wife, especially in a cafe. She thought his table manners verged on the uncouth. He had a gusty laugh, very loud, which sometimes caused people to glance in his direction. Then Margery would whisper in angry embarrassment, 'Don't laugh so loud! People are looking at you.'

166

'Nonsense!' he would retort, in a voice as loud as his laugh, so that everyone heard.

His chatty ways with women and young girls, whilst making her uneasy, also reminded her of her own lapse, so that she was doubly ashamed when they were together, both because of his lack of fine manners, as she defined them, and his easy approach to other women. Once, when Betty was still only nine years old and all three were eating out, two teenage girls with their parents seated themselves at the next table and he bought two small bars of chocolate and gave a bar to each of the girls. Margery was covered with confusion. 'What a fool he's making of himself,' she thought angrily. 'Can't keep his hands off the young girls! What must the parents think?'

That night they had a row of which Betty, on the stairs, could make nothing. 'Looking at young girls like that!' her mother was shouting in a kind of low, suppressed fury. A rumbling argument went on for a long while after that; a kind of drawn-out, distant thunderstorm – no loud, overhead crashes which would leave the air fresh. The next morning at breakfast Betty looked for signs of the last night's disagreement, but her parents were all outward cordiality and bonhommie. This made her feel worried without knowing where to pin the worry.

However, in spite of often not feeling comfortable in her mother's presence, Betty did have a great admiration for her. She thought her mother very clever. Especially she admired the dexterity and artistic taste she showed in stuffing and dressing dolls for charity and church bazaars. 'You *are* clever, Mummy,' she would say, sitting down on a chair and staring entranced at an array of dolls of all sizes and in all manner of costumes, national and fancy free, which stood in rows on a side table ready to be put into a large cardboard box and taken to a local bazaar.

'I'll take you to a costume museum one day,' her mother promised, not displeased with her daughter's admiration. 'I get ideas from magazines and displays in shops, sometimes exhibitions.' She would fondle the dolls, stroking their fine, silky hair and the sheen and softness of their bright dresses. All this handling gratified the sensual side of her nature whilst avoiding reproach as it was all in a good cause. She would go up to Oxford Street, ostensibly to 'get ideas' from the items on display in the big stores and to buy remnants, but really to wander round the dress and haberdashery departments, fingering scarves and gazing at evening gowns. Sometimes she took Betty with her.

Betty liked to remember that she had shared this particular slice of her mother's life. After one such outing, she asked, 'Mummy, why don't you go to the theatre? There isn't all that difference, is there?'

'There is,' her mother replied without hesitation. 'I make these dolls for charity. You don't go to the theatre for charity, only to enjoy yourself.'

'But you enjoy making the dolls,' Betty persisted.

'Yes, but it's for a good purpose,' her mother replied.

Betty wondered why her mother always had to have a good purpose for doing anything that gave her pleasure, but she did not know how to phrase the question.

There was another fact about her mother which puzzled and sometimes distressed Betty – she was not allowed to buy her presents. When she was eleven, her mother showed her a very pretty china plate with birds and flowers round the edges, which she had bought to give to a friend. There had been two identical plates in the shop in the local high street. Margery was full of admiration for the plate, turning it round and round in her hands.

'Do you like it a lot, Mummy?' Betty asked.

'Oh, yes!' her mother answered, holding it admiringly. So Betty emptied the contents of her money box and bought her mother the twin, still in the shop window. She wrapped it in coloured paper and handed it to her mother, then stood by with a joyous impatience while the gift was unwrapped, anticipating an outburst of delight and thanks. Instead, her mother spoke angrily.

'You shouldn't have bought this for me,' she said. 'You ought not to have spent all this money on me.'

'Why not on *you*, Mummy?' Betty burst out. She ran out of the room and up the stairs, her face wet with tears of rejection and incomprehension.

It was easy to give a present to her father; he gave and accepted gifts with ease. She had never seen her parents exchange presents. It happened at Christmas, but then the presents turned out to be of a useful nature, which made them non-presents in Betty's eyes.

Her adolescence was not easy. After the outburst when, without in the least intending it beforehand, she had told her

168

mother that she treated her father in a hateful manner, Betty had never again let herself go. The result had proved too highly emotional for her taste. Instead she suffered a kind of dark shadow which settled down a little distance above her head once the evening set in, causing her silent distress. This went on for some years, only clearing up finally when she left home.

She went through a hyper-sensitive stage during which she became acutely aware that in response to her coming into a room, her parents at once altered the tones in which they had been speaking – the pitch of their voices, their conversation, even the way in which they were standing, sitting or looking at each other. This sensation was very frightening. Finally she came to feel that they were all three acting parts in a play. This made her wretchedly uncertain and insecure, as if nobody could be trusted, least of all adults.

It was from these childhood experiences that her passion for emotional honesty, almost her obsession with it, took its roots. They were to be deep, permanent roots in her life to which she was to remain faithful even when, later, this loyalty was to cost her a painful sacrifice.

When Betty was fifteen she left school and went to a training college. Her first job was in a local office as secretary. She continued to live at home for the next two years. Then, when she was eighteen, she found the courage to face up to her mother. She knew she would meet with determined resistance in her resolve to leave home, but as she had learned determination herself, the battle finally ended in a compromise. Margery agreed to Betty having her own bed-sit provided it was near home and she herself had first vetted it as respectable. She also insisted that her daughter come home each weekend. In this way she hoped to keep an eye on her. The arrangement meant a great restriction on Betty's freedom, but further contest only resulted in tears and recriminations so she thought it wise to give way, especially as her father did not support her. She felt his silence as a betrayal and it was some years before she fully forgave him.

Surprisingly, Betty found that instead of being chafed by the arrangement, she was relying on it for support. She could not understand this sudden change in her feelings and reproached herself for weakness, but it was very natural, taking into account her upbringing and youth. She had for so long resisted her mother's emotional sway that, in a very real sense, she had

169

become dependent on it; once on her own, she felt the lack of an emotional thrust in her life, even if one of opposition. It was strange to come back from a busy office, where the noise of typewriters and sound of voices was constant, to a silent room. After a few months, she found she was tending to talk aloud while preparing her evening meal or taking her bath. She was struggling to adjust to a life without either constant support or constant irritant. She had anticipated this being easy – it was not. Instead she was looking forward to going home at weekends. On finding herself sincerely missed, she also found herself recognising for the first time since her early adolescence that there might be a genuine side to her mother which she had overlooked.

The atmosphere of a professional office did not aid her in what was, in essence, a maturing process. She became aware of the same insincerities as at home. Moreover, a lower middle class snobbery prevailed with a sense of superiority over those who worked in a factory, or even a factory office. After a while, Betty could not tolerate the atmosphere any longer and found herself a job as secretary to a shop-floor manager in a local engineering firm.

She found this job more meaningful. She liked to think that she was aiding in the production of articles necessary for living. For the first time the words shop-steward and shop-floor acquired significance. She thought the office workers were less of a race apart, less inclined to look down on manual work. She began to make a few friends. By her twentieth birthday, she found herself less reliant on her home for support in her spare time. Margery complained that she could not understand her daughter any more. Why did she need to leave a professional office with a good class of person to work among people with whom surely she could have little in common? When Betty ceased to come home every weekend, she felt aggrieved. Without actually putting the idea into words, she thought that her daughter had an obligation to love and cherish her, a kind of unsigned but binding contract entered into at her birth.

Over months, Margery became resigned to a visit from her daughter every other Sunday. This new arrangement afforded Betty much more free time. She started to go to evening classes. At school, she had taken little interest in her lessons, now she discovered that she liked reading. But her main pleasure was in using her hands. She went to pottery classes and basketry. She took home to her mother objects which she had made and Margery at last began to feel pride in her daughter's talents.

'She takes after me! She's clever with her hands,' she told her neighbours and friends. It afforded Betty quite a deep pleasure to know that her mother was at last finding something in her to praise. This aided her growing up. She gradually came to assume in the family the status of an adult, instead of a difficult child.

Dick first noticed her as an animated, high-spirited girl, skating rapidly round an ice rink. Just as his father had been attracted to his mother by similar qualities, so he was attracted to Betty. By then she had left her flat in Harringay and gone to live in a shared house in Camden Town occupied by a loose-knit community. The large, formerly empty house, was owned by the local council who had rather reluctantly rented it out for an indefinite period. There were four couples, two with children, besides Betty and her room-mate, a single girl of similar age, who was also working in a factory office and had introduced her to the idea. There was an agreed list as to who was to do which chores, including shopping, a weekly get-together, a genuine interest in each other's lives, and a willingness to help each other out in difficulties. It gave Betty what she wanted – a sharing which made her part of a larger whole and yet not so intimately connected as to be emotionally oppressive.

At this stage, Betty was in her early twenties, her lively mind eager to sample anything new which life might put in her path. She began to blossom out, to use make up and eye shadow, to dress in vivid colours, to have her hair set in the latest styles. It was a phase she was going through later than normal. Her mother protested in vain. She was feeling free for the first time in her life.

'I wish mother was less anxious,' she found herself thinking one evening in her room after a visit home. 'Perhaps one day I'll be able to help her.' The self-confidence of the thought marked out how far she had travelled from that point where life had seemed to offer only two alternatives – a lonely existence in a bed-sit or a home so clingingly stuffy that she could not breathe freely.

She had normal instincts and felt the need of sexual experience, possibly a mate, even if a temporary one. She liked Dick. She knew that his mind was not as lively as hers, but she quickly discovered that he was by no means slow or silly. She

171

liked his lack of tenseness, his ability to enjoy the moment without the need to hug it to him. When Betty told him that she lived in a shared house, he did not know what to make of it. He started to visit her.

'Is this what is called a commune?' he asked, with a vague idea that he had heard the term before and that it might apply here.

'Well, sort of...' Betty said hesitantly, 'but a lot less close.'

One evening she told him, 'There's a small, empty room at the top, under the roof. You could have it.' She added frankly, 'Or you could come in with me – my original sharing mate has gone. We like each other. Why not? It doesn't have to be for life.'

He considered the offer for some weeks, then said he thought they could make a go of it; at least for a while. Betty rejoiced at his tone. He would not be a limpet.

'Of course you'll have to do your fair share of the common tasks,' she told him firmly. 'We take turns to go to a wholesale market and buy for all of us; we've got a van. Then we take turns to look after the kids while the parents go out and they do some of our jobs about the house in return. We've got everything worked out – we all share in the cooking, cleaning, washing, and so on. The men as well.'

This did not appeal much to Dick, especially the 'men as well' part. he took some further weeks to consider the question. He remembered that Betty had said it need not be permanent. He liked her. He wanted to get away from home and he was much tickled by the thought of how Jean would react when he told her he was going to live in a commune – to look on the set-up as a commune fed his vanity.

'I'll give it a try,' he told Betty.

'OK' she replied, off-handedly, but she was delighted. His sense of fun, his kindness, his generosity, his relaxed ways reminded her of her father. Their stay was to last almost eight years, an outcome anticipated by neither at the start. For the first three and a half years, the couple were childless, then Tina arrived. Very shortly after that event, Dick's long-smouldering dissatisfaction with their style of life came to a head in open rebellion. He wanted them to get married, he wanted them to have a home of their own.

'It's a more natural way to live,' he told Betty, forgetting his previous opinions. 'Almost everybody lives in their own house.'

172

'There's nothing natural about it,' she retorted. 'You mean you're tired of the common work load! Well, you've never been exactly an outstanding volunteer.'

He answered her defiantly, 'It's no fun looking after other people's kids. We've got one of our own now.' He was a fond father.

'That ought to make us more interested in all children,' Betty argued stoutly, but he would not give way.

For a considerable time Betty resisted his attempts to pressurize her. The style of life exactly suited her temperament and general attitudes. Dick had never been a very satisfactory member, he had been tolerated for her sake. In the end, Dick won. His strength lay in the fact that when it came to the point, although he liked Betty quite a lot, his early total enthusiasm had worn down. There were times when he found her, as he put it to himself, 'a bit much'. While Betty, to her own surprise, when it came to the same point, discovered that she felt quite a deep attachment to Dick. She was at ease with him. This was very important to her. She could overlook other defects. She did not see herself doing any better – but she would not consent to marry him.

'We'll see how things go on in our own place,' she said cautiously. She was just as firm on that point as he was on leaving the house. In the end each gave way to the other. But agreement was only the start. It took them a little short of four years to save up sufficient to put down the deposit for a reasonable mortgage. They moved just in time to avoid Tina having to change schools.

'We can get a run-down place and do it up ourselves,' Dick had said cheerfully.

Betty had at once objected, 'Not too run down!' She knew Dick did not like putting himself out and she was determined to avoid being the do-it-yourself Chief. At last everything was settled and they were able to move into a small, upstairs maisonette in the same borough.

All these years Dick had kept in touch with his parents and sister in a very off-hand, casual manner, sending birthday and Christmas cards when he remembered, which was by no means always, visiting his parents about once a year. He never forgot Robbie's birthday and was always generous with his presents, but he did not put himself out to see much of his nephew. He had not seen Jean or Stephen for more than two years and then had only popped in one evening with Tina for a couple of hours, spending most of the time playing with Robbie, while Jean and Stephen made friends with his daughter. He had sent the usual change of address card, but had given no reason for the move.

It was a Saturday morning. They were sitting over a late breakfast, Tina playing with her toys on the floor, when Dick slit open the envelope with his mother's handwriting. His nature did not predispose him to expect bad news. He was silent for some moments, reading the few lines written on the one sheet of paper.

Then, 'Good God!' he exclaimed, in a shocked voice, looking shaken. 'Robbie's dead – drowned!'

CHAPTER SIXTEEN

'ROBBIE dead?' Mabel repeated the words in a stunned, incredulous voice. They were at breakfast and Jim had read aloud Stephen's brief letter. There was a silence. Then she said, in a voice of vigorous denial, 'Robbie drowned? Oh, no! It can't be true! How could it?'

Everything that happened after that first shock seemed to Mabel to lack sense and she found herself thinking that the tragic event must have driven both her men out of their minds. This sense of absurdity began with Stephen. His few lines had told them only of Robbie's death, not how it happened. She phoned him, of course, what mother wouldn't? Her own son! And what had happened? He had spoken to her as if she were an inquisitive stranger who had to be kept at bay and got rid of as quickly as possible.

'Jean didn't notice,' he told her. 'Robbie ran off. That's all. There's no mystery about it, Mother. These things happen every day.' He had put the phone down on her. She was stunned. She could not believe that he had gone. And his tone – so aloof, so cold. She could sense him almost physically thrusting her away.

After some days, when she had managed to collect herself a little, she went to see Jean. And what happened? She was met at the door by Stephen who would not let her put a foot inside the house. Jean was suffering from a nervous breakdown, he told her; the doctor had forbidden visitors, even from the family.

'But I wouldn't stay more than a few minutes, dear,' she said, tears coming into her eyes at his tone and look. He shook his head.

'Poor girl! She must be in an awful state. She must need support, she'll think I don't care about her.'

'She won't think about you at all, Mother,' he answered callously. 'And she's not in need of consolation.' He added, in a cold voice, 'Far from it!'

She thought she could not have heard him correctly, but his look and the tone of his voice told her that she had. She was dumbfounded. He met her amazed, incredulous gaze with an utterly off-putting look.

All the way home, she kept repeating to herself the words, 'She's not in need of consolation. Far from it!' What could he have meant? A mother who had lost her only child and in such sudden, tragic circumstances, not in need of consoling? Far from it? Those three words seemed as if stamped on her mind. She could not stop repeating them over and over, recalling the cold, hostile look with which Stephen had uttered them.

She told herself, '*He's* in a state of shock!' Shock made people act in a very odd manner. Yes, of course, that was it. Yet she remained uneasy. Something was not as it should be. Perhaps Jean would let her call later on, when she was feeling less distraught, might even then welcome her sympathy. She did so ache for Robbie and ache for Jean. She sat down and wrote a few brief lines to her daughter-in-law. 'I *am* the child's grandmother,' she told herself. When no answer came, she thought it only natural. It did not worry her, but she fretted over her own uselessness.

Then Jim came back from visiting Stephen. He said, 'She was reading! She forgot about Robbie! She went on reading for almost two hours. She only looked up when it was getting dusk and almost everybody had left the park. She told Stephen that.' He added bitterly, 'What a mother!'

It was four o'clock and they were having their afternoon tea and biscuits. Mabel sat back in her armchair. The room was swimming round; then it steadied. A spasm shot across her back. Ever since the first effects of the shock had worn off, she had been subject to these sudden spasms. It seemed to her so unnatural, no contact with Jean, treating Jean as if she were a convicted criminal. She did not know why this idea of Jean being treated as some kind of a criminal should have entered her head, but it had done, and once there, it stuck. She could not understand why her feelings on this point were so deep. After all, Jean had been very careless; no one could say less than that. But however much she argued with herself, there was no way in which she could bring herself to adopt the attitude of the two men. The thought of Robbie dead came to afflict her, but she held herself determinedly back.

Now she said in a faint voice, 'What do you mean, "what a mother"?'

'What mother doesn't put her children first?' Jim answered in a bitter tone. He had been bitter towards Jean right from the start. He held her wholly responsible for what had happened and would listen to no excuses. She had simply not done her duty and kept a proper eye on the child. 'Sitting there reading!' he added, in an even more bitter tone.

'When I saw Stephen, he told me it happened every day,' Mabel said, after a pause. 'These things happen every day,' had been his exact words. While she was repeating the words, she was thinking how peculiar they sounded.

'Well, he had to say that, didn't he?' Jim answered angrily. He looked at her as if she too were to blame.

'It's not easy keeping your eye and mind on a child *all* the time,' she ventured. '*I* know that.' He mind went back to when Stephen had been young and she had sat with him in the park.

'You managed it,' he said in the same angry voice.

Yes, she had managed it, but at a cost. She wondered if Jim had any idea of what it had cost her? Of course he had not. He had never been in her position.

In a softer tone, he went on, 'I'm not blaming the girl for having a read. She can't stare at a child all the time. I know that. But she went beyond what was reasonable. She told me herself she read for almost two hours without looking up. That's what I blame her for. Not caring about Robbie – burying her head in a book!'

Mabel could not believe what she had just heard. 'You saw Jean? You spoke to her?'

He nodded. And her son wouldn't even let her over the threshold. She felt stunned.

176

At last she managed to say, in a calm voice, 'How did she seem?'

Jim shrugged. 'Pale, of course. She was in bed. But quite sensible. Not hysterical. She told me what had happened. Then she offered me tea. She said Stephen would give me a cup.'

'It's shock!' Mabel said. The silly man surely didn't think she wasn't suffering?

'Yes. It could be that,' he agreed. He was nothing if not reasonable. 'I don't want to be unjust to her,' he added, almost apologetically. 'But she couldn't have cared all that much for Robbie, she'd have been more careful,' he insisted, repeating bitterly, 'Burying her head in a book!'

There was a long silence during which Jim's bitterness increased. He had looked forward to each Wednesday, when it was his turn to take Robbie out. He had travelled half across London and he had not minded the long journey. Now all that pleasure and happiness, all that interest in a budding life, was gone. He said, 'That's what comes of educating women! They get discontented. They don't know when to stop.'

At these words, Mabel experienced a sudden sense of outrage. She felt that she might be going to faint. She managed to get up. 'I'm going to lie down for a few moments,' she said in a low voice. 'I'll come down again later.'

'Yes, you do that,' Jim said, 'and try not to get too upset. We can't either of us alter it. The thing's done. We shall just have to face up to the fact that he's gone.'

Mabel went upstairs and lay down on her bed. Her back was hurting and she had a headache. She lay quiet for some ten minutes, then she realised that she was crying. She got up, sat at her dressing table and wiped her eyes. She sat quietly for a while, then she began to walk up and down the room. She stopped by the bed, stooped down and took off her shoes, then, in stockinged feet, she resumed her walking up and down. She did not want Jim to hear and come up to ask if she was all right.

'Yes. I'm all right,' she would say and he would tell her to lie down again and have a good rest. Then he would go back downstairs. That was always his way with her when she was upset, it had been his way with her from the beginning. And something within her resented the fact. She was not a child to be humoured.

With the resentment, there came back to her, with a sudden sharp pang of loss, that painful memory which she had thought

177

to have buried years ago – the memory of an impossible choice – a nursing career or Jim. For a moment she was transfixed. Then she turned her mind again to Jean.

She did not understand about Jean sitting reading for almost two hours – not once looking up to check what Robbie was doing. Apart from anything else, it did seem a very long time to concentrate without a break. She felt uncertain as to its absolute truth. Probably Jean had exaggerated from a sense of guilt. In any case she did not believe all that nonsense about Jean not caring for Robbie; those were nonsensical words.

Her thoughts were very disconnected. They chased from one incident to another. 'It's no use my arguing with Jim,' she said aloud. 'He wouldn't listen.' He would probably answer her words with silence. She was suffering from a keen sense of humiliation. It seemed that neither husband nor son was prepared to treat her seriously. At this thought, her long-suppressed resentment burst through the bounds which she had set it. Finally she allowed herself to think about her life with Jim.

They had started out as equals; she as a trainee nurse, he as a trainee maintenance engineer. After ups and downs which had looked at times like splitting them apart, they had finally married. After that, gradually everything had changed, until at last Jim had come to occupy a dominant position in their relationship, which he had maintained ever since. She had been left behind, feeling very inferior indeed. She had not practised clear thought for so long that attempting it now gave her quite a turn, but she persevered, pushed on from behind by a force which was the stronger for having been suppressed for so many years.

Thinking about Jim as a young man courting her, made her feel very kindly towards him. Those early days had been happy days! When Jim had sustained an injury at the hospital and she had nursed him, they had formed a kind of relationship. He had been a bit cheeky, nothing too much though, and she had enjoyed his mild flirtations because he had always been so nice, never forward like some of the men. Then, when he went back to his work, he had sought her out and they had gone to dances together. By the time his work moved elsewhere, they had established a steady relationship and went on meeting in the evenings and later at weekends also. He had told her that he hoped to become a fully qualified maintenance engineer, more for the interest of the job than for the financial rewards, but for that too. He had a very down-to-earth attitude to life. She had told him that even when she was still a child, she had set her heart on nursing; she was studying for her first exam and intended to go on until she became a Ward Sister. She remembered saying to him, 'It's hard work, both physical and mental, but I love it. It's my life.'

Over the next couple of years they had become very fond of each other, until finally he had asked her to marry him. In those days, if you married that was the end of your career. So Mabel had said 'No!' The decision had not been an easy one, for by that time she liked Jim a lot, but she could not bear the thought of giving up her nursing ambitions. They had parted. As his farewell gift, Jim had given her a small silver cup and she had given him a leather wallet. The little silver cup was on the bedside table. Now she picked it up and turned it round in her hands. It had figures of birds chiselled on it and was very pretty, with a handle like a thin woven cord. She had never seen another like it.

She had kept it near her all these years. She counted them up – there were over forty.

But fate had not left her alone. Only nine months later, she had met Jim again, quite by chance; they had renewed their acquaintance, he had again asked her to marry him, pressing her hard, and after lengthy agonising she had given way. Did she regret it? She did not know. At the time it had been a trauma. Looking back now, she saw clearly that the choice had always been an impossible one. Whichever choice she had made, she would have regretted the other.

She recalled how this very subject had come up between herself and Jim about a year ago when, as elderly couples do, they had filled in a blank afternoon with reminiscences, and she had recalled how much she had wanted a nursing career.

'Well, you made a different life for yourself,' Jim had said. 'You've enjoyed it, haven't you?'

'I suppose so,' she had said, not knowing whether or not she was telling the truth.

'Of course you have!' he had replied in his 'I'm telling you!' voice. She had stayed silent, not knowing what to answer, but aware of a faint resentment at his easy dismissal of what had cost her so much pain. Then she recalled how resentful she had been at Jim's encouragement of Jean's career ambitions when

179

Jean had first visited them. Now she saw that she had taken his words much too seriously. He had really only meant that Jean should go on with her career until the children came. He had taken it for granted, as he had made clear only a short while before, that as a mother she would put her children first. Here Mabel's thinking became confused. Who should come first then, if not the child? Should the husband come first? And what about Jean? Where should Jean come then?

'I'm all mixed up!' she told herself.

She recalled how very much she had wanted to do some nursing work until the first child came, which would not be for some years, when Jim was earning a better salary – perhaps in a private nursing home where state regulations did not apply – but he had told her he could never face his relatives, their thinking he could not keep a wife. His pride had come first, that was easy to work out. Of course things were a great deal different now. Many men wouldn't be able to maintain a home at any reasonable standard unless the woman was bringing in money. Still, by giving in, she had allowed Jim to stamp the mark of his authority on their relationship, and it had shown clearly during the war when she had submitted to his dictate that she should leave Stephen and return to look after him. She saw that now. Of course she'd had to do some work, but he'd put a stop to that once the peace came.

During the first few months of her married life, when Jim had gone to work, she had wept and wept – pretending cheerfulness when he had come home in the evenings. After a time she had become resigned. When she had shown distress, Jim had said, 'You'll be all right when you have a baby.' So she had put everything out of her mind except the home, her husband and her child; they had become her whole life. She had adopted the attitude, 'If you can't do anything about it, forget it. Don't think about it!' This was the first time since Stephen's birth that she had made any serious effort to look back at her life and try to be honest with herself.

Now, when she tried to think, she got all confused. It had not been like that at the start and for some years afterwards. She had enjoyed a good argument and had often started one up with Jim, if only to relieve the boredom of the day. But as time went on, she had given up this practice, which had at first afforded her real pleasure, because she had discovered that Jim's tongue had a sarcastic edge to it, and also, to her surprise and mortification, that on the whole he held a rather poor opinion of women's minds.

'They never keep to the point,' he would say. 'If you're getting the better of them, they start talking about something else.' He sometimes added, 'They all talk at once – they don't know how to listen.'

The television had later become a source of silent misery to her. All those silly girls – no one could deny they were silly. Their inane smiles and simpering ways and the free manner in which the male comperes kissed and pawed the women – and got away with it. In fact the women had seemed to like it. When Jim had commented adversely, she had been forced to agree. 'I don't know how they can act like that – degrading their own sex,' he would occasionally comment. He was seeing it from a different point of view to Mabel. He held rather strict, almost puritanical views. But she felt his censure all the same.

She would agree, 'I don't either.' So, gradually, she had seemed to pass over into the other camp. She found herself more and more agreeing with her husband. After all, it was a fact that all the great names were male. She did not want to think that way, but as the years had gone by she had more and more fallen into the habit of denigrating her own sex. For one thing, it made life a lot easier. You accepted that men and women were different and if that really meant that women were inferior, well, you didn't think about it. You shut it out and concentrated on what was yours by acknowledged right – your home, your child, your husband.

On the whole, so far as she could tell, she had not lived unhappily doing this. She had the consolation of knowing that she had done it very well. She had had a satisfied husband and a child who was a credit to them both. Never a complaint or a rude word from either of them. She had done her duty by both and they by her. Well, what was amiss with her then, she asked herself, taking another, more composed turn around the room, still very quietly. She decided that it was because her son had shut her out and her husband talked her down, and there was nothing she could do about either.

It was so very many years since she had stuck up for herself, done more than disagree silently. All her self-confidence had ebbed imperceptibly but surely, with the passing of time, until now there was hardly a shallow pool remaining.

'Then if I'm used to it, why have I suddenly got myself into a fuss?' she asked aloud. It was all this condemnation of Jean. It wasn't fair. She couldn't explain the reason – she knew Jim would beat her down if she tried – but deep inside her she knew that it was unfair and she resented it deeply. She wondered if Stephen was treating Jean in the same manner that he was treating her; coldly, distantly – sitting in judgment.

'I've got to do something about it,' she said, again aloud. But what? She did not know. She did not even know the true position, how matters stood between Jean and Stephen, but she felt that Jean was beleaguered by men and that she must go to her aid.

'I won't have it!' she said in a loud voice, unlike the low tones in which she had until then been speaking. 'It's not fair! I won't have it!' And the sound of the firm tone startled and then comforted her. It was strengthening to hear her own voice, even if it only spoke to an empty room. It was so long since she had heard it speak at all.

On that thought, she dried her eyes, powdered her face, put on a trace of lipstick, combed her thinning hair, adjusted her dress and necklace and went down the stairs mentally as if she were about to start a crusade.

'Is your tea as you like it, dear?' she asked mildly, handing her husband a plate of sandwiches.

'It's a bit on the weak side, but it doesn't matter,' Jim replied. 'Had a good rest?'

'Yes,' she answered. 'I did have a good rest. I feel a lot better now.' And then she fell away again: it was like her to be unsteady. Going down the stairs, she had been so full of resolution, even lighthearted, but when she was seated opposite Jim and started to make the effort, she found her voice would not come. She could not have a row, defy her husband and earn the resentment of her son. She collapsed into moral chaos, despising herself, but unable to get moving, The weeks passed. Then the months. Then she learned that her son and daughter-in-law had separated. This finally reactivated her sense of purpose. She decided that she must, and would, go to see Jean. The thought then occurred to her that before she could do this she would have to know Jean's new address and the only person who could tell her was Stephen. She wasn't even sure that he knew, but she would need to ask and that meant explaining the reason. She knew that Jim would disapprove, but the idea of defying her son was a greater problem to her. From the start she had wanted to go to Jean, but her son had forbidden it. She could not put his attitude in any other way. She had thought his reason nonsense, but had stood in too much awe of him as a grown man to defy him when it came to his wishes concerning his own wife.

She had idolised him, put him on a pedestal, so that it was doubly difficult for her to consider taking any action which might imply a criticism. She worried over this for several days, then decided to tackle Jim first. His reaction was decided.

'You shouldn't meddle!' he told her. 'Stephen wouldn't like it.'

'They're separated, dear.'

'Still, it's interfering in his life.'

Finally, one Sunday when Stephen came to lunch, she plucked up courage. Together in the kitchen, she washing up, he drying, helped her to make a start. She said in as casual a tone as she could manage, a little off-hand, 'By the way, dear, I'd like to look in on Jean. She must be feeling lonely. I haven't seen her for a long while, you know, and she's still my daughter. Write down her address for me, will you, before you leave.'

'I don't know her address,' he answered coldly and in a surprised, displeased tone. He corrected himself, 'That is, she may have moved. Only my solicitor would know that. Is it really necessary, Mother?' he asked.

'Yes, dear,' she said, in a gentle voice. Then an inspiration came to her. 'I know it's different for men,' she told him, 'But we women are brought up to be caring. I daresay you men think us emotional, but we can't help how we're made. It's natural for us to want to comfort.'

In her anxiety at displeasing him, she had rambled on further than she had meant to go. When he answered, in an abrupt tone, 'I'm glad to learn women are caring, Mother,' she thought that her inspiration must have been in some way lacking. He gave her the address of his solicitor, handing it to her without a word or a look. She felt dreadful. Did he think her callous towards him? She dared not ask. He had withdrawn himself so completely from her, right from the start. Had she known it, his attitude was not due to any hostility on his part, but simply that neither his pride nor his hurt would tolerate sympathy and he was sure his mother would start being sympathetic.

Mabel dropped a few lines to Jean once she had got her address from the solicitor and, while waiting hopefully for an answer, decided to visit Jean's parents. She had maintained a loose contact with Jean's mother while Robbie had been alive. Now she decided she would call one Saturday morning, about her own coffee time, around ten-thirty, and stay just a short while. Although she had written a letter of condolence she had received no reply. She had not seen Mary to speak to her since the tragedy.

She could not even remotely have guessed at the true situation. Mary and Bill fell out so violently that the child's death became almost incidental to their rage against each other.

'Well, now we see whose side of the family she's on,' Mary had thrown at Bill, jeeringly. 'Clever, was she? Took after your mum, did she? Not my side, oh no! Too clever for my side! Well, she has been clever, hasn't she? Keeping her head stuck in a book while her own flesh and blood drowned. That's clever, all right!' She went on and on, hurling insults at her husband's family, taking full advantage of the chance to get her own back for all the years of humiliation she had had to put up with. Then, when she was alone, she broke down and wept.

Bill bore his wife's taunts as well as he could, getting out of the room as soon as he was able without too obvious a humiliation, often not answering her. He could think of no replies to her taunts, except, 'It's the way you brought her up, you silly cow. You'd spoil a virgin, you would!'

'You have to bring your dirty mind into it!' she retorted.

And so they went on until the subject became exhausted between them. They were not able to comfort each other.

Bill's feelings against Jean were, if anything, more violent than those of his wife. He grieved at Robbie's death, but he felt it above all as a personal humiliation. He had never really bothered with either of his children. He had spoilt them with toys when they were very young, taken the easy way out. He had always put football, the pub, his cronies, first, but his pride was there all the time. Now that pride had taken a fatal knock. His clever girl, the daughter he had always seen as so like his own mother, who had passed all those difficult exams and hooked a well-educated man who was going to be a teacher and rise in the world – she had turned out to be just a silly bitch, like her mother. He blamed his wife. He couldn't have said exactly in what way she was to blame, but he knew she was, and gradually, in his thoughts, he shifted Jean over to his wife's side

184

of the family and forgot all his former boastings. She became 'like her mother'.

Into this atmosphere, all unknowing, Mabel walked one Saturday morning at about ten-thirty. 'I was up this way so I thought I'd call in for just a few minutes,' she said, when Mary opened the door. She put on a bold face as if certain of a welcome.

'Well, I'm going out soon, but you can come in, if you want,' Mary answered grudgingly.

So she sat down in the living room and Mary became a bit more gracious and put the kettle on to make tea. It had occurred to her that here was an opportunity to unload her feelings. She forgot all about having said that she was going out. Pouring the tea and offering Mabel biscuits, she sat down opposite her at the table and began, 'Sorry I didn't answer your letter, but I'm not one for writing.'

'I didn't expect an answer,' Mabel said in a kind voice. 'I knew you'd be too upset.'

'Upset? I should say I was upset!' Mary answered, her lips tightening and her whole face going sour. 'I've had to bear the brunt of it ever since, I can tell you.'

Mabel didn't understand. 'The brunt?' she queried, thinking Mary was referring to her husband's grief.

'Yes! The brunt. My husband blames me!' Seeing Mabel's puzzled look, she went on, 'Says it's because of me – my side of the family. When it was all glory and bright lights, it was his side of the family. Now it's all laziness and stupidity, it's my side.' She gave her disdainful sniff.

Seeing the distressed look on Mabel's face, Mary added, 'Oh, I'm sorry for your son, of course. I'm very sorry. But it's our daughter that did it.'

'Did what?' Mabel asked, feeling that she was being stupid.

'Neglected her duty, of course,' Mary answered, in an annoyed voice, and she threw Mabel a hostile glance. 'Kept her head stuck in a book while her own flesh and blood drowned! What's that if not neglecting her duty?' She uttered these words with an angry fervour, thinking of how she herself had always done her duty and under conditions that this well-dressed, snotty-looking woman opposite could have no idea of. She knew something of Stephen's background, had delivered Robbie back there after visits. A nice, cosy set up; an easy life

185

that woman had had, sitting at the table sipping tea in that put-on, daisy manner.

'There was probably a reason why Jean didn't notice Robbie wasn't any longer with the other children,' Mabel said tentatively. She knew the reply did not fit in with the facts as told by Jean and was glad that Jim was not there, but in her state of general ignorance, she could do no better.

Then she heard Mary's voice again '... and she was darn lucky, the silly bitch. If it had been my man he wouldn't half have taken the belt to her.' Gazing at Mabel, Mary thought, 'What would she know of all that?'

Mabel felt that she had entered another world, a world she had occasionally read about in the Sunday newspapers, but which had always remained unreal to her. 'Take the belt to her?' she echoed in a half voice. 'But she must have been suffering...' She broke off and fell silent. Did Mary really think her daughter should have been physically assaulted by Stephen when he heard Robbie was dead? The idea horrified her. It stood her on the edge of a very dark pit.

'Suffering?' Mary took up the word with bitterness. 'Suffering!' she repeated. 'A nice house, with nice furniture, a husband with money, nice clothes, only one kid... She got out and about didn't she? Holidays? She didn't know she was born!'

There was a long silence. Then, in a calmer tone, Mary asked, 'Don't you think she deserved a beating then? Reading a book while her own child drowned?'

'I read myself,' Mabel said, then at once felt that it was an unsuitable remark.

'Oh!' Mary gave a sniff of disdain.

For some seconds there was a silence between the two women. Then Mary said, 'Of course, it's my husband's pride. It's hurt his pride.'

'His pride?' Mabel echoed.

'Yes.'

Mabel experienced a sensation like blood pressure. It frightened her. She got up. As she did so, her head swam. Then the room steadied. 'I shall have to get along,' she said hastily.

At the door, Mary said, 'If you see her tell her to keep well away from here – if my husband sees her, her age won't save her. And I won't come to her rescue.'

186

Mabel did not answer. She walked along the street feeling faint. She could not go straight home to face Jim. She turned into a small café in a side street, sat down at a table away from the window and tried to console herself in her usual way, a nice hot cup of tea. But this time even the tea was beaten.

She was thinking, 'Yes, Jean did have something to answer for – not keeping a close eye on Robbie, not noticing that time was passing, becoming so abstracted from what was going on around her.' In view of the terrible result, one could not brush it aside, treat it lightly. She felt her heart contract for Robbie. Still, there might be reasons which were not obvious that would lessen the offence, or, at least, lead one to understand why it had happened... Why did everyone keep on about Jean reading? Would her action have been less heinous if she had fallen asleep or been chatting? Everybody kept talking about Jean reading a book. What book? Did anyone know what book? There was no crime in reading a book. Jim was always reading books. Stephen had always been reading books when he was at home. You couldn't get him away from them at meal times – she'd had to shout into his ear.

She didn't want to condone, but she did want to understand. It seemed she was the only one who did. 'I shall keep an open mind,' she told herself finally, rising from the table and making for the door. 'I owe that much to them all, Robbie as well.'

At the end of the week there came a brief reply from Jean. Mabel could call one evening after seven o'clock. No warmth, no caring either way. Mabel wrote back with a date. Then she started to worry. Should she take fruit or flowers? Or nothing at all? Would it look cold if she did not – or formal if she did? In the end she decided against taking anything, but she worried over the question for hours.

'I'm going to see Jean tomorrow evening, dear. I hope you won't be lonely,' she told Jim. What a silly remark! As if he would be lonely so long as he had a book.

Jim looked across at her, startled, 'To see Jean?'

'Yes, dear,' she answered mildly.

With a rush of anger, he said, 'You're not to go!'

'Well, dear, Jean is a human being and I am her mother, even if it's only a mother-in-law, and, as far as I can see, she needs a mother, so really no one has the right to tell us we may not meet.' She spoke very quietly, but very firmly. She was aware that it was quite a little speech for her.

'You're not to go!' he repeated angrily.

Still very quietly, she replied, 'You've had your way all these years, Jim, and now I'm having mine.' She was a little frightened at her own defiance but she stuck.

Into his angry silence, she spoke again, 'You've always said how sentimental we women are, always fussing around people. Well, we can't help our nature, dear. God made us like that! That's why I've looked after you and Stephen all these years.' She added hastily, 'And enjoyed doing it.' She repeated, 'We can't help our nature, dear,' smiling at him and without a hint of sarcasm in her tone. 'Women feel pity. They want to help.' She had enjoyed her second little speech that evening. Suddenly she was aware of feeling very strong. It was one of her strong moments. She was conscious of having got him on his own ground, the ground he had placed her on all those years ago – the caring ground. He could not win over her there.

She could see he was stumped and she paused a moment to enjoy her victory. She had got the better of him at last. Then she said, as if it were an afterthought, 'Stephen gave me the address. Otherwise I wouldn't know where to go.'

She saw the surprised look on his face. 'Oh well! That's all right then,' was his only further remark.

Mabel went to bed in a state of slight exhilaration. She had won a victory and that was so unusual that she could not help enjoying the sensation.

CHAPTER SEVENTEEN

IT was late March: six months after Robbie's death. Jean was living in the flat found for her by Stephen and working as a typist in an estate agent's office. When she got Mabel's letter, she thought, 'She can come and I'll get it over,' but when the agreed evening arrived, she found herself unnerved by a dream of the night before. Shortly after Robbie's death she had been violently upset by a nightmare in which an accusing voice had uttered terrible words. Last night the dream had recurred – the voice and the words. 'It's Mabel's visit,' she thought. But she was nonetheless shaken. Going to work had provided a relief, but now that she was home the dream came back with a vividness that threatened to break her down. There was no possibility of putting off her mother-in-law so Jean forced herself to become calm: to put out the cups and saucers, the spoons, the sugar, serviettes, a cake stand with four slices of cake and an assortment of biscuits, and take a last look round the room to make certain that everything was in good order. Finally she took a bath and put on a pair of clean jeans and a fresh blouse. The root of all her preparations was her shrinking from Mabel. She did not like her; she expected from her only condemnation and impertinent questionings. 'Get it over! Get it over!' she kept repeating to encourage herself.

Afterwards she lay down on the settee, closing her eyes and trying not to think. When the door bell rang some ten minutes later, she had to make herself get up and answer it.

To Mabel, she seemed thinner, paler, a little older, but otherwise calm and self-possessed. The usual greetings over, Jean took Mabel inside and they sat down facing each other, Jean on the settee, Mabel in the one armchair. Neither had so far shown any emotion. They might have been meeting for a casual half-hour chat.

Mabel sat very stiff, her hands folded on her lap; very much the well-dressed, self-possessed, elderly matron, but inwardly praying for inspiration. She was feeling absolutely tongue-tied, facing that still, silent figure on the settee, so obviously waiting for her to say what she had come for. All the opening ideas she had thought up had flown out of her head and she could think of nothing except trivialities. 'You look better than I thought you would, dear,' she said. 'How awful! What a beginning!' she said to herself.

'Yes. Most people say that,' Jean answered, uttering the first words that came into her head. She was not going to give Mabel any help.

'Are you working now, dear?' Mabel asked. She hated the 'dear', it sounded so patronising, but without it her remark seemed heartless, mere curiosity.

'I'm working as a typist in an estate agent's office,' Jean said. This information surprised Mabel. She had taken it for granted that Jean would have gone back to her library work. For a woman with Jean's qualifications and active mind, typing in an estate agent's office struck her as a most unrewarding sort of a job. Wasn't she finding it awfully boring? Mabel was about to say, then she turned away from the question.

Instead she asked, 'Is it well paid? Everything is so expensive these days.' She had dropped the 'dear'.

'Yes. It's quite well paid,' Jean said.

And so they went on for some minutes more. Then Jean got up and said, 'I've got a tiny kitchenette through that door.' She pointed to a half-open door at the side of the room opposite to the window. She added, 'It's very convenient. I'll get us some tea.'

She went into the kitchenette, leaving the door wide open. Mabel could see her filling the kettle, putting it on the gas ring and lighting the gas. She looked round the room and noted how the table had been set out with considerable care. The room was very tidy, almost as if nobody lived in it, and no dust. She guessed that Jean had prepared with thoroughness for her visit.

'That's how she sums me up,' Mabel thought. And she felt hopeless. When she had set out, she had been reasonably full of confidence. She had rehearsed various openings to the main topic, but now they seemed equally inadequate. When it came to it, words were useless, she decided.

Jean came back into the room and fussed round the table, making remarks about the cake and biscuits, her own tastes and Mabel's tastes, but inside her she was feeling terribly on edge. From being silent, she became full of words. While the kettle was heating up, she got positively loquacious, informing Mabel of all the minute details of her daily existence and the most trivial incidents from her life at the office.

Mabel listened, mostly in silence, with a sense of despair. She was going to depart as she had come, knowing nothing. She wanted so desperately to be of help.

The kettle began singing. 'I'll just make the tea; won't be a minute,' Jean said. She had fallen into an easy style of speaking, as if she and Mabel were old friends. This was her guard, Mabel thought, this calm, friendly, talkative, off-hand manner. She had settled down to it and there was nothing Mabel could do about it. After all, what had she expected? That Jean would throw herself into her arms?

'Words are no good,' she said to herself for the umpteenth time. She had never been able to explain anything to Jim by talking to him. And then she had an inspiration. She got up and stood in the kitchen doorway. Jean was standing with her back

190

to her. She had just poured the hot water into the tea pot and put the kettle back on the stove. She had picked up a milk jug. Mabel took a deep breath. Then she stole up behind Jean, just as she was about to pick up the milk bottle, put her arms round her waist and hugged her tightly to herself. She hugged her so tightly that she was finding it difficult to breathe. She did not utter a word. She felt Jean resist, but she held on.

Jean had never in her entire life been pressed to another woman as she was being pressed now – certainly not by her mother. She realised with a shock of total surprise that Mabel was telling her that she understood her grief, that she felt for her and that she cared about her. This silent outflow of sympathy broke through the barrier of her protective reserve; it broke her rigidity, her self-control, it acted almost like a form of magic. She dropped the milk jug onto the floor, where it smashed into pieces. She stopped resisting Mabel's pressure, instead she twisted her body around and clung to Mabel. She burst into violent sobbing.

Mabel held fast to her inspiration and uttered not a word – only kept her arms so tightly around Jean that after a little they began to ache. She held on until the paroxysm of grief had spent itself, then she gently coaxed Jean into the living room and into the armchair where she relaxed limply, closing her eyes and lying quite still. Mabel then sat down herself, folded her hands in her lap and waited patiently.

Her inspiration would not leave her now. She thought of it as such, but really it was only an understanding which she had not known she possessed. It had been born out of her life experience, but she had never before been called upon to make use of it so she was unaware that she possessed it.

After some time, during which the tea went cold and Mabel found herself wondering if Jean had gone to sleep, Jean opened her eyes, saying, 'I had a terrible dream last night. A voice accused me...' She broke off.

'You'd better tell me about it,' Mabel said quietly.

There was a long pause, then Jean said, 'You wouldn't want to have anything to do with me if you knew.'

'I'm quite sure I should,' Mabel said cheerfully, but she knew she must not press for a confidence which Jean might later regret. Now was not the moment. Putting on a brisk voice, she said, 'Oh dear! The tea must have gone cold. I'll make us some more.' She went into the kitchen to refill the kettle and light the gas. She picked up the broken pieces of milk jug, wrapped them in an old newspaper and put them into the bin. 'There!' she said, pouring out two cups.

Gradually normality returned. No further reference was made to the dream. Mabel left soon afterwards, promising to write and visit again. At the door, she said, 'You must tell me if I'm a nuisance. I don't want to be a nuisance.' Jean did not answer, but she shook her head as if in denial.

When Mabel got home, Jim asked, 'Well! What did she say?'

Mabel looked at Jim as if she did not understand.

'Yes! What had she to say to try and justify herself?'

'Say?' Mabel repeated. 'Oh! She didn't *say* anything.'

'No! I should think not,' he retorted. 'There's nothing she *can* say.'

'No, dear,' Mabel agreed calmly. 'There isn't anything she can say.'

CHAPTER EIGHTEEN

ALTHOUGH Mabel and Jean did not see much of each other, they kept in touch and a friendship grew up between them. With the warmer weather, Mabel suggested a week by the sea – it would do them both good. Jim would no longer go away; he was content with his golf and with occasional day outings. Mabel had never left Jim before, but she told herself boldly that there was a first time for everything. Phoning Jean in her lunch hour at work she broached the idea.

'Think about it. Don't say "Yes" if the real answer is "No",' she told her. Rather to Mabel's surprise, Jean agreed at once so long as they did not choose a quiet place. This surprised Mabel again. She knew Jean had always liked solitude. However she sat down at once and booked up for a week in August in a small boarding house in Brighton to which she had been recommended. When she asked Jim if he would mind, all he said was, 'You go! I can look after myself.' But when the day came, he asked, 'What have you left me?' She showed him the larder, full of tins as if for a month's siege, the inside of the fridge the shelves stacked with meat puddings and a variety of sweet dishes. It had taken her almost a week to achieve all this and she thought she would need a holiday to recover. All Jim said, was, 'That's all right.' Before she finally departed, she wrote out a menu for each main meal and high tea for each day of the week and left the sheet of paper sellotaped down on the kitchen table in case it blew off and he didn't see it.

In the train, she told Jean, 'I've booked two single rooms. I didn't think we'd want to be together all the time; besides, I snore!'

When they got to Brighton and Jean saw the huge hotels and Front without trees, she felt that she would be able to settle down there for a week. It was so totally unlike anywhere she and Stephen would have chosen. The boarding house was small, with only four separate tables in the dining room; clean and in a quiet road. They both felt they would be at home there and when the landlady said she could fit in a table for two by the window their satisfaction was complete.

Before she went down to breakfast the next morning, Mabel spent quite a while making up her face and deciding what to wear. Not that she had brought all that number of changes with her, or owned them, but she was always a little nervous when meeting people for the first time. She looked out of the window. She could just glimpse the sea through a gap between the houses – stormy with white horses, the sky more cloud than blue, a chilly feel. She decided on her dark blue crimplene suit with the light blue blouse which she kept to wear with it, surveying herself in the long mirror which the landlady had thoughtfully provided in the bedrooms and touching her recently permed hair so that it lay in neat waves. The landlady was a dear, Mabel thought, remembering the table for two in the window alcove.

She was happy. She always felt most at ease with herself when she was acting in the role of a supporter. She had made up her mind to this holiday entirely for Jean's sake, to give her a break and so she was free to enjoy herself without any feeling of guilt at having left Jim. She took one last look at herself in the mirror, picked up her handbag and went downstairs.

There were already three couples in the breakfast room, all middle-aged; then an elderly lady about her own age, Mabel guessed, followed by an elderly couple; then another woman on her own. With herself and Jean that made twelve. Jean came in a few moments later and the tally was complete.

'Not very warm today,' one of the women ventured. Everybody then agreed, either by word or nod, that indeed it was not at all warm.

'I think it may rain,' Mabel commented, gazing out of the window. Soon everybody had been drawn into the conversation. Then the warm milk for the cornflakes arrived, followed by tea, bacon and eggs, and the talk fell away. Mabel was at her ease now that she had placed herself inside the group by her few words.

Jean hadn't spoken. She was dressed, like Mabel, in a crimplene suit, a dusty pink with a white blouse and tie-over collar which gave a soft look; her brown hair had been well brushed and shone. Mabel looked at her approvingly. She was thankful that Jean took care with her appearance. She would have felt very embarrassed going about with someone who was unkempt.

'I always feel like a walk after a meal,' Mabel said. 'It's no weather for sitting anyway and I don't suppose you'd want to at your age.' She felt she must take the initiative and get them going. Jean agreed at once so they put on their outdoor things and sallied forth.

It certainly was below the normal temperature for the middle of August; that is, if one could say such a thing as normal when dealing with the English climate, Mabel commented, as they walked briskly along the Front. Jean said she thought there wasn't anything normal about the British climate.

They walked along in silence. Mabel felt she had done her bit and turned her eyes to the surroundings. They rewarded attention. The huge hotels, some ornate, some with Edwardian exteriors, others very functional and modern, were all standing straight and in a line, like soldiers at a victory parade; they gave Mabel a sense of order and security which she was enjoying more and more, the further they walked along. She had never been to Brighton before; Jim preferred smaller places.

'I like it here,' Jean said suddenly, breaking her long silence.

They spent all the morning walking along the Front, reaching Hove. Here the houses appealed greatly to Mabel – white and clean, some with bow windows. The surroundings were white and clean too, everything in sight beautifully proportioned. They sat for a while in one of the garden squares, until the cool breeze drove them towards a place to eat.

In the afternoon, they walked back the way they had come, and then in the opposite direction, beyond the pier. As they made their way to the hotel for dinner, Mabel said, 'Well, we certainly don't need much to make us happy!' Jean agreed.

The next day passed much as the first had done, except that the weather being still very blustery and cool, they deserted the Front to investigate the famous Lanes. To Mabel's surprise, Jean did not seem keen. 'I thought this would be just what you would like,' she said, when Jean showed a lack of interest. Jean did not answer.

They wandered along the narrow lanes, stopping to look into the windows of the numerous craft shops, gazing up at the sloping roofs and jutting upper storeys of the old houses and threading a slow path through the throngs of people. Mabel was attracted to a shop displaying old coins. What a different world it is, she was thinking, as they strolled along. They drank coffee in a rather dark, old-fashioned cafe.

'What about going a coach ride this afternoon?' Mabel suggested, 'It would make a nice change. There are many fine old country houses not far away.' But Jean thought she would prefer to take a look at the precinct.

'All right, dear, if you'd prefer that,' Mabel said, but she did not fancy walking round a shopping precinct after a morning spent in the Lanes. She could do that at home. Then Jean said it would be too tiring for Mabel after the morning's jaunt and they had better go on the pier. They could find a sheltered spot and after all had come to the sea. Mabel was disappointed, she had a liking for big gardens and old houses, but she made no objection.

In a shelter on the pier, with the wind whistling around her knees and her shoulders hunched to try and keep warm, for the first time Mabel began to feel sorry for herself instead of for Jean. 'It's certainly no weather for lying about,' she commented, trying to make her voice sound cheerful.

She would have been sorry could she have known what her words did to Jean, haunted as she was by memories. She had chosen a large, conventional seaside resort because nestling in her heart was Yarmouth harbour; its sailing yachts, its silvery light, its evening waters, still as a pool. Here the sea was the open sea – no tiny pier with white shell beach, no narrow cement walk alongside a sea wall, no sweeping curve of violet bay or spit of land with red brick tower, no pale blue luminous sky of the West Wight, no great white chalk cliffs, with rocky beaches far below, no downs, sloping gently, no running free as

195

the wind down the long slope to Freshwater Bay. Instead she chose big hotels, a Front without trees, while at the back, no cows and rough grass, no meadow with hummocks, but a large, busy, noisy shopping centre. From the first she had tried hard not to think of the past, but in spite of all her efforts, it would intrude – remembrance of the blister on her heel, Stephen carrying her so tenderly up the slope and back to their hotel, lying under the tree, in the field, Stephen asleep and she tracing his outline on the grass, putting her little finger under his little finger, raising it and letting go so that it dropped back slack onto his chest, and how he had opened one eye and asked drowsily, 'What are you doing, darling?' and she had answered 'Nothing!' She thought she could smell the hot scent of the cow dung. She could feel his arm around her waist. He had always known when she was tired. Once the tears had come into her eyes and she had turned her head hastily lest Mabel should notice her distress.

'The garden at the hotel is very pretty,' she had said, to cover up her emotion. She liked the garden; it was small, prim, well-tended. It bore no similarity to the spring garden of their honeymoon with its winding, untidy paths, its flaxen grasses, its tiny blue irises and wild roses, its tangled undergrowth and bird song. Instead it had a smooth lawn with trim edges, and soil without weeds planted with staked flowers.

She liked the big, crowded shopping precinct, but she had not liked the Lanes with their historical and architectural interest. It was a place where Stephen might be found, however unlikely. She had thought once that she had seen him. While Mabel was staring at coins in a window, she had noticed a man standing some yards off at a corner, his face turned half away, but with a look of Stephen in the outline of his features, and her heart had given a sudden, painful thump. Then as he turned and she saw him full face, the likeness was gone.

She was grateful to the weather for being indifferent. The sky hesitated between sun and sudden showers, the sea often had a wind-driven look, misty green and grey. She gave silent thanks to the stormy, open sea – no crystal clear waves breaking softly on the beach with a thin edging of white foam spreading outward and losing itself among white pebbles. Her spirit could rest on that stormy sea. The rough, brown pebbles of the beach could only hurt her feet, not her heart.

Now Mabel had said, 'It's certainly no weather for lying

about,' and at once all her efforts had been wasted. She had been seized up and transported back to that other place where there was no sand but the scent of warm clover, the smell of cows, the midges, the shade of trees and grass to lie on.

After that she was silent for what seemed to Mabel an age; she was getting chilled and dangerously near to boredom. 'I think I'll take a walk round the pier,' she announced. Jean could go on sitting there, staring out to sea if she wanted, but Jean sprang to her feet at once, just as if someone had stuck a pin into her, Mabel thought, and they walked together round the pier head. Jean wrenched her mind free and forced herself to answer Mabel's remarks in a sensible, ordinary way. She was conscious of having treated Mabel badly. The sun peeped out for a short while. Jean began to chat. She was either silent or very voluble, Mabel was thinking, listening to her. Now she would find some-thing to say for the next twenty minutes. They went into a cafe for a cup of tea.

Jean knew that Mabel was having a poor time with her as companion and she really did make a great effort for the rest of the day. Mabel began to feel hopeful that perhaps things might be improving, but Jean went to bed very tired from her efforts. For, try as she might to escape, she was always hearing Stephen's voice speaking to her. It said, 'Unfit ... not normal,' over and over again. She could hear his voice clearly, every inflection, every intonation, the deliberate, precise words which expressed exactly his scornful conviction that that was what she was. Unfit. Not normal.

The more worried Mabel became about Jean, the more she ate. She chose fish and chips for lunch. She said to Jean, 'I read a story once about a man who woke up and found he had turned into a beetle. I think I shall wake up one morning and find I've turned into a plaice!' When Jean laughed, she was pleased.

She wondered how Jim was getting on, but it was a vague kind of wonder. She had sent him one funny postcard. 'I expect his head's in a book!' she had told herself and then forgotten all about him. It was so grand not having to prepare or cook a meal before she ate it; so grand not to know beforehand what dish would be placed in front of her at dinner; so grand not to have to think out for the umpteenth time what to have for their main dish, every blessed seven days of every blessed week. Some of the guests grumbled about the meals – they thought they had too many cold dishes for after, but Mabel was satisfied so long as she didn't have to do the thinking.

They had been at Brighton three days before Stephen's name came up by chance because Mabel was off her guard. They had been on a ride along the Front in an open bus and were walking back. The day was milder so they were able to sit down when they felt like it on one of the many seats looking out to sea which was calmer now and more blue.

'The weather's improved, Mum,' Jean said. It was an expression she did not often use, but it came out now and then and Mabel had accepted it with a certain pleasure. Secretly she had always wanted a daughter and had been very disappointed when no other children had followed Stephen. But now she disliked the term. It dragged her back from her present position of grand independence.

She said, 'Oh, goodness! Don't call me Mum. Jim calls me Mum. Stephen calls me Mum. I'm fed up with being Mum!' She spoke almost irritably. And then she remembered.

There was a long silence as they sat on the bench looking out to sea. The word 'Stephen' hung in the air. Its utterance seemed to have struck both women dumb. Mabel could not think of anything to add to what she had said and sat on in a state of horrible mental discomfort.

Jean got up abruptly and walked on, leaving Mabel to follow her. They passed a Punch and Judy show on the sands. Mabel thought Jean would walk on, but she showed a desire to go down, so they listened to the show along with a large crowd of children and some grown-ups. Then they climbed the steps back to the Front.

As they walked along, Mabel found herself thinking that their footsteps would be making imprints on the cement by the time the week had come to an end. As if guessing her thoughts, Jean asked, 'Why don't you go some coach outings by yourself, Mabel? You must want to.'

'I have enough of going about on my own at home,' Mabel retorted, a little tartly. 'It's a lovely change to have another woman with me.' And she thought how nice it was, in spite of everything, not to have a man with them, but to just walk and talk in a friendly way.

They must have walked another mile at least, before they sat down again. Mabel was a good walker and liked the exercise. They sat on an empty seat close to the promenade railings. It was like being on the deck of a liner, Mabel was thinking. At last the sun had come out to stay and she felt warm. She relaxed and closed her eyes, inclined to a short nap. She was missing her afternoon snooze. She did doze off for a few minutes. Then she became aware of Jean's voice and came wide awake. Jean was saying, 'I couldn't speak, you see. I tried to, but he didn't understand. So I stopped trying. I kept quiet. I suppose you think it was silly of me.'

Mabel wondered what she had missed in her less than half-awake state. Was Jean talking about Stephen? In a fluster, she spoke without prior thought, with a spontaneous emphasis, 'Oh, goodness, no, dear! I've kept quiet for years. Women do, you know!' After those few words, she was silent. Jean did not comment. So she found herself struggling on, 'You see,' she said apologetically, 'I'm a great coward! I hate being laughed at. I'd do almost anything to avoid that. I dread being made to look stupid.' She hoped Jean would say something, but she went on being silent.

Mabel began to feel that once again she must have said something silly. Then she rallied. She went on to tell Jean about her early life; how she and Jim had met, how they had parted, how they had met again, and the final resolution of her conflict in marriage. 'I stuck for months,' she said. 'I didn't seem able to choose.'

'No!' Jean said, speaking for the first time. The tone of her voice implied recognition.

Mabel felt sufficiently encouraged to go on. She told Jean how wretched she had been for a long time and how Jim had said she would be all right when the baby came. And when the baby did come, how he had said, 'I told you that you'd be all right then!' How slowly she had lost confidence in herself and come to feel very inadequate compared to Jim; even more when he had risen to a responsible position in his job. She had felt left far behind. And how, when she had wanted to say something that was of importance to herself, Jim had been able to silence her with arguments she could not answer. 'I think I lost respect for my own sex,' she ventured. 'I don't know how it happened. I did try now and then to look back and find things out, how I'd got to where I was, but I always had to give it up. So I accepted my life as it was.' She added defensively, 'Well! No one likes a silence after they've said something that's important to them – as if what they've said is too silly to take notice of!'

Jean spoke again then. 'Yes,' she said. And she gave a slight nod.

Mabel said, 'Men are so sure of themselves, you see.'

'Oh, yes! They are!' Jean said.

There the subject dropped. Jean did not seem inclined to say anything more and Mabel was left with an uncomfortable feeling that she might have missed the most important part of what Jean had been saying while she was in her doze. She had an equally uncomfortable sense of having once again let herself be carried along on a stronger current of words than she had intended; given herself another jolt similar to when she had been upstairs with Jean on their first meeting. She seemed always to be giving herself jolts these days. Thoughts, even more feelings, needed to be kept under wrappings in a well secured parcel labelled 'APPROACH WITH CARE!

They gave the Thursday over to buying presents. 'I'd like to buy you something nice, Mabel,' Jean said.

Mabel was pleased. 'I'd love to have something from you,' she said, 'and to give you something,' she added. So immediately after breakfast they set out on the quest. Mabel was wondering what she could buy Jim. She remembered the slippers she had chosen for him at the end of her day in London, but she did not mention this memory to Jean because she had been celebrating Robbie's birth. Then she had experienced a slight sense of guilt at leaving him on his own for a whole day. Now, to her surprise, she felt no guilt at leaving him alone for a week.

Jim was rather particular about what he was given for presents; he liked to choose his own books, so that was out. He wanted something useful. Mabel eventually decided on a thick, woollen scarf for the winter – angora, rather expensive. Jean admired it. Then Mabel asked Jean what she would like and Jean chose a print of Brighton Front with a long row of regency houses. Mabel chose a sea shell, the kind which makes a murmuring sound when held up to the ear. 'I like anything like that,' she said. 'I'm quite childish really.' But when Jean asked the price, Mabel was shocked and said to Jean afterwards that the shop was taking advantage. Then Jean laughed, saying they always do and not to worry. 'It's worth it, if it's what you want.' Then they went on to buy other presents and altogether did a good morning's shopping. They returned to the boarding house loaded and wondering how they were going to get everything packed.

After lunch, they decided they would go on the pier. The weather had turned cool and blustery again, the sea wore a sombre look with more than a hint of rain. It was the sort of stormy sea, with white horses, which both liked. But Mabel did not like the cold.

'There's one thing about August,' Jean commented as they walked along the pier. 'It's never cold.' Mabel thought that depended on one's age, but she did not say so.

There were not a lot of people on the pier, 'Too chilly,' Mabel thought. They went below to watch the fishermen. There was quite a cluster of them. The waves banging against the piles and swishing by under her feet made Mabel nervous and she was glad when they went back up. There was hardly anyone about except themselves, but the windows of the restaurant a short distance further down the pier showed a brisk trade. Mabel looked forward to joining the customers, but Jean seemed determined to sit it out, saying it was too early for tea, the clouds were thinning and the sun would show in a short while. Mabel sat down with Jean inside the shelter at the head of the pier. They chose the side facing the open sea.

'Fancy! France is over there,' Mabel commented. Her old desire to travel came over her.

'It's time you went abroad,' Jean told her. 'We'll go to Paris together.' With an inward thrill, Mabel said that Paris would suit her very well.

The sun had come out and gone in again; the difference in temperature was very marked. Mabel began to feel cool. This made her think of warming food. She found herself wondering how far Jim had progressed through the meat puddings and fruit pies which she had baked for him. Her thoughts idled for a while and then returned to Jean, sitting so quietly beside her – much too quietly for her age. The holiday would soon be over and she was as far as ever from understanding what was going on in Jean's mind. 'I was wondering, dear,' she said hesitantly, 'why you don't get a different job. With your qualifications, isn't typing a bit boring?' She hoped she had not gone too far. In her nervousness, she had reverted to the 'dear'.

There was a long silence, then Jean answered, 'Yes. Very!' There was another long silence. Mabel did not speak. Finally Jean added, 'But I can't, you see.' She seemed to think this remark self-explanatory.

'Why not, dear?' Mabel ventured, when it was clear that Jean meant to say nothing further.

'Oh! If I told you, you wouldn't want to have anything more to do with me,' she said, in a matter-of-fact voice.

'I should think that very unlikely,' Mabel replied gently.

'That's because you don't know.'

'Well, tell me, dear,' Mabel said.

This time the silence was so long that Mabel largely lost hope. Then Jean said, 'It's a dream I had.'

Mabel remembered. The dream! She had quite forgotten about the dream. She had puzzled over it for a time, but since there was no answer, she had let it sink. Now she recalled vividly Jean's distress.

Firmly, she remarked, 'I think you had better tell me and take a chance.' She experienced a sudden sense of misgiving. She waited.

At last, in a low controlled tone, Jean said, 'It spoke into my ear – the voice I mean.' She had turned her head half away from Mabel and was staring out to sea. 'I was standing in a black hole – the kind they say exists in space.' She hesitated, then went on, 'That's the only way I can describe it – a black hole, dense and packed with violence. The violence was all around me, but where I was standing it was...' She broke off, searching for words, '*absolutely still*'. Silent – the kind of silence you would only experience if you were suffering sensory deprivation.' She stopped speaking. Mabel stayed quiet. Jean spoke again. 'In spite of the stillness, the violence was worst where I was standing – absolute violence and absolute stillness together. That was what was so unnerving – the stillness of death *inside* the awful violence.' She gave a sigh, as if the mere recollection had drained her of energy.

'What a dreadful nightmare,' Mabel said.

'Oh, I didn't mind that,' she retorted shortly, as if Mabel had missed the point. 'It was unnerving at the time, but later I could have forgotten. It was the voice.'

'Oh, the voice!' Mabel repeated, trying not to appear dense.

'Yes. The voice. It spoke into my ear, you see. It didn't utter a sound and yet I heard every syllable. It said...' she broke off, then forced herself to go on, her voice taking on a higher pitch. 'It said,' 'You're glad he's dead! You know you are. You're glad he's dead!" And I kept shouting back, "I'm not! I'm not! I'm not!" and the voice kept on answering me, "You

202

are! You *know* you are.'" She stopped speaking. There was a long pause.

Then Mabel said, 'It was simply the awful strain and shock, dear. Isn't it obvious?'

Jean turned towards Mabel, looking her full in the face. 'No!' she said with emphasis and in a steady voice, 'It wasn't the strain or the shock. You see, the voice was speaking the truth. That's why I denied it so vehemently. I *was* glad.'

Mabel was shocked. During her worst moments of irritation and boredom, she had never wished Stephen dead. It was unthinkable. Something of this showed in her face. Jean saw the expression.

'You've been good to me,' she said. 'I didn't want you to go on liking me under false pretences. I told you when you first came to see me, if you remember, that if you knew me you wouldn't want to have anything to do with me.'

There was a silence between them then. Many months ago, Mabel had come to a decision. She would not pass judgment. Stephen and Jim could judge if they wanted.

'They can get on with it,' she had said to herself. 'I shan't!' She had kept to that resolution. Now it was facing its hardest test. She was horrified at what Jean had said, but even more horrified by Jean's insistence on her own interpretation. She had to struggle with herself for some moments, during which the silence continued, but in the end her resolution won out against the odds. She rallied.

'Bosh!' she said. She flung the word at Jean with a passion quite unusual for her. It really expressed her feeling that the thing was utterly beyond her. The word seemed the right one, for it clearly comforted Jean, who was thinking she had lost Mabel.

'Yes,' she said in her normal tones. 'That's what I can't understand. How could I want Robbie dead? I loved him dearly. And yet I must have. I knew the voice was speaking the truth.' She hesitated, then finally came out with, 'It was – *authentic*.'

This was quite awful. Mabel felt its awfulness. Then Jean gave a sudden convulsive spasm and a dreadful sob was forced out of her. She started shivering. The shivers were going right through her body; she put her arms round her body and shrank herself together to try to stop them. Mabel sat still and upright, her hands folded on her lap just as she had done on the former occasion when Jean had lain exhausted in the armchair. All she could give now by way of aid was her self-control, her lack of emotionalism.

'So now you see,' Jean said at last, the shivering having subsided into a series of mild tremors.

'No! I don't see,' Mabel retorted, with emphasis. And to herself she added, 'I wish I did.' She saw absolutely nothing except that Jean had gone through an awful experience and was not clear of it yet.

'If I could only understand,' Jean said, 'I might be able to forgive myself.'

'There must be a key to understanding the dream,' Mabel said. 'Perhaps you're not looking for it in the right place.' The words had been uttered more for something to say than because they meant anything much to the speaker and they fell to the ground.

There was a long silence during which Jean turned away from Mabel back to the sea and Mabel sat staring ahead of her. During the silence the subject hung in the air between them, beyond the power of either woman to bring it within the grasp of comprehension. Then Jean said, 'I can't forgive myself. I keep thinking I forgot him on purpose.'

This was too dreadful. Mabel got up hastily, saying abruptly, 'It's raining. We're wet. We'll catch our deaths. Come on – tea!' and she almost pulled Jean to her feet. It had been spotting for some time and the wind had been driving the rain into the shelter. Their faces were quite wet and when Mabel put a hand to her hair it was damp.

They walked hurriedly towards the restaurant. Mabel was thinking, 'Tea!' Was there no other solution to the world's problems? It seemed there was not. 'I'm going to the toilet first,' she told Jean. She felt a wreck. She was not going into the restaurant looking like that, not even for Jean. She washed her face in warm water, then ran the tap and soaked her hands. She felt the comforting heat softening her stiff muscles. 'Oh, that's lovely!' she sighed, drying her hands on a paper towel. She combed out her damp, straggled hair before a mirror. She was relieved to see that Jean was doing the same. They both looked fit for inspection now. She imagined everyone would be looking at them when in fact no one took any notice of them when they sat down at a table in the middle of the room. Mabel had no desire to look out at the sea. She was thinking it would be a long time before she would want again to sit at the end of a pier.

They had chosen the more posh of the two pier restaurants; the other, further down towards the shore, was self-service. The order came – fresh scones and strawberry jam, plenty of it, along with a large teapot full of very hot tea and a jug of cold milk. Mabel gave a sigh of relief at the sight.

Afterwards, they went straight back to the boarding house and luckily they were both able to soak themselves in a steaming bath. Over dinner Jean said, 'I've been very selfish, Mabel. I know you wanted to go on some coach rides. I felt I couldn't face doing anything Stephen would have enjoyed. Forgive me.'

'Grief is selfish, dear,' Mabel said.

'You're always honest,' Jean said. 'You don't say I wasn't selfish.'

'Well, you were! I got frozen,' she retorted cheerfully.

It was easier to be honest about Jean's emotions than her own.

The following day was Friday, their last full day. After breakfast, they went down to the coach station and booked places on a coach which was going for a full day's outing to two large houses with famous gardens. The weather was still cool, but beginning to warm up and in the afternoon it got quite hot with the sun out and away from the sea breezes. Mabel took off her coat and revelled in the heat. They went over both old houses admiring the paintings, the crystals, the porcelain, the enamels, the carpets; they wandered all round the large gardens and explored the greenhouses with their exotic plants. Jean forgot to think about herself and afterwards realised with surprise that she had enjoyed the day. It was a cheerful, warm interlude which Mabel long remembered with pleasure.

Since the journey was a short one, Mabel decided to have a hair shampoo before taking the train home. Jean went for a walk and met her coming out of the hairdresser with her hair tightly set. Jean thought she had preferred it when it had been more natural, but she did not say so. 'Now I feel fit to meet the neighbours,' Mabel remarked.

In the train, Jean said, 'You're the only one who hasn't sat in judgment on me, Mabel. Thank you.' She added, 'And to think I was once afraid of you.'

'Of *me*?' Mabel exclaimed.

On the London platform, at the top end where their ways

parted, they stood a moment. 'You've helped me feel more normal,' Jean told her. 'Thank you,' she said again. Then she turned and made off before Mabel could reply.

In the tube Mabel thought that in spite of the serious parts, she had enjoyed being in the company of another woman. She arrived home with a chill, which showed up on the third day and put her to bed. 'I must have got it when we were sitting at the end of the pier in the rain,' she said to Jim, incautiously.

'Well!' he retorted sarcastically, 'If that's how women go on when they've no man with them, they'd be better off staying at home.' She felt too off-colour to think of an answer – and in any case, he was having to go up and down the stairs for her, so she thought it better to keep quiet.

CHAPTER NINETEEN

O N the day of their final parting, when Stephen had closed the door of the flat behind him leaving Jean inside alone, he vowed to himself: 'Never again!' He walked to where he had parked his car a little further down the street. He got into the car and sat, unmoving. He wanted to turn the key and start up the engine, but it was a few minutes before he could bring himself to do so. It seemed that in leaving Jean he was about to do something unnatural, but he could not stay where he was not wanted.

He drove back to the flat he had found for himself, not far from school. Contracts for the sale of their home had been exchanged some weeks ago. Jean had shown no interest at all and in the end he had had to see to everything himself. She had, however, insisted that she wished to take with her as few possessions as possible. So he had furnished her flat sparsely, but adequately. But when he came to sort out the books, her former indifference vanished. 'I don't want any of the books,' she had said. This had surprised and at the same time annoyed him. He had seen no sense in it. What was he to do with her books then, he had asked her. He could not take them all – his flat, like hers, was small. 'Sell them,' she had replied. She did not waste words on him. Some time later he sent her a cheque.

He noticed that a photo of Robbie at two years and one of himself and Jean taken during their Isle of Wight holiday were missing. He made no comment. He took the other photos and the snapshots off the sideboard, put them into a large envelope and took them with him. They went into the back of a drawer in his flat. She would not have any of their wall prints so he disposed of them as well, but he could not bring himself to let go the print of an English country lane in summer, which had hung over the mantlepiece – their first buy, full of sunshine. He did not hang it up, but put it in a corner, face to the wall. He told himself he would part with it when he felt more settled. Later he let it go to a friend whose young daughter was furnishing her first flat and was looking for a cheerful, inexpensive print for her living room. When she said the quality was too good for her to accept without paying him something, he had replied, 'No! I like to think it's going to someone who will get real pleasure from looking at it.'

The kitchen utensils created a problem; he did his best to divide them fairly. When he asked Jean if she had preferences, she did not answer. The rocking chair he put into a sale without asking her. At the finish the two flats looked strangely different from the home they had shared together; neither had any real personality. This suited Stephen. He certainly did not wish to be surrounded by reminders of his failed marriage.

For he knew that his marriage had failed utterly. Failure was a new experience. Until then he had been greatly favoured – a stable and loving home environment, a sharp awareness of his importance as a boy, good looks and a good intelligence and, as he grew older, the knowledge that girls admired him and sought his company.

By early manhood he was facing life with the conviction that he could successfully cope with any problem. Reserved by nature, his home had given him a sense of civilised manners so that he did everything with a certain outward modesty, but he had a fine idea of himself. Going about with Jean had done nothing to lessen that idea. Then he had met an incomprehensible defeat. She had said, 'I hate you!' She had uttered the three words in such a tone and with such a look that he could harbour no illusions as to the truth of it.

If it had been due to a moment of hysteria, a shock reaction, he could have understood, but it was not. The words had been preceded by a lengthy period of unmistakable cooling, ending

207

with a final unbending coldness and sexual withdrawal. She had ceased to want him, so that he had felt he was raping her. She had shut him out body and spirit. Finally she had come to hate him. He was beginning to develop an obsession with those words 'I hate you' and the need to find a reason for them.

When he was in his flat on his own, he tried to think through the problem in a logical, consistent way. He went back over their life together – his part in that life. He was looking for a clue much as scientists look for clues in the natural world. He examined with care everything that might possibly provide it. She had wanted a child; he had not forced the decision on her. He recalled querying her first, hesitant suggestion, pointing out how very much her work meant to her, mentioning her ambitions for the future. He had thought she was on the pill. Then she had announced that she was pregnant. It could only have been on purpose, even if subconsciously so. He did not deny that he had been glad, he had wanted children. But he had not anticipated her entire devotion. Then she had seemed to tire of Robbie. She had even been unkind to him, pushing him away from her so that he had run crying to his father calling out, 'She's nasty! She's nasty!'

He thought of how he had taken on himself all the responsibilities of caring for the family. Money did not walk in through the front door. He had worked hard, very hard, for everything they had. He had provided all the comforts, the security Jean and his son had enjoyed. The worry had been all his.

He had not been a slacker in the home either. He had helped in every way he could, often when he was tired. What could she have known about the responsibilities he had shouldered, he thought resentfully. All she had to do was to look after one child and spend the money he had provided for them both. She could go out and about. Hadn't he even encouraged her to do this? She even had a neighbour who was willing to look after Robbie.

He had not beaten her, he had not ill treated her, he had not behaved as her father behaved toward her mother. The thought of doing anything of the kind would have been abhorrent to him, but nevertheless, it came into his head that she should have been grateful to him that he had not. He had not been miserly, he had not even been ungenerous. He had been considerate in bed. He had helped her when she had been feeling off colour. He had never pestered her. He had never flown into a temper, never shouted at her. He had never been unfaithful, never even interested himself in another woman. He had not left her alone in the house in the evenings like many men did. He had taken her on holiday.

When he had gone through this list, the result produced in him a quiet glow of satisfaction at his own worthy conduct. He felt anger and resentment, because Jean had withheld recognition of his virtues. He found himself sitting in judgment on her yet again. He had told her that he would forgive her. If only she had shown a sign of remorse, but she had not. She would not. He had felt her utter refusal through her silence. His resentment rose in him like a flood of dark, very bitter waters. For a while he almost forgot Robbie. It was her unjust treatment of himself that filled his mind and spirit with anger.

Then he said to himself, 'She's not worth thinking about!' and turned to correct the homework which he brought back to the flat almost every evening. He spent more time on it than he need have done. He was finding his best solace in his work, and had even volunteered for extra duties. Had his school not faced him with daily problems, he doubted whether he could have preserved his equilibrium. As it was, he managed to push his worries to the back of his mind for the greater part of each day. The weekends were the most difficult, but he read a lot – mostly books connected in some way with education. All through this troubled period he never lost completely his interest in his job.

Nevertheless he was finding that it was easier to say, 'She's not worth thinking about,' than to obey his own injunction. Jean was not alone in being haunted by the past. His lack of will-power in this respect came as an unpleasant surprise to Stephen. In believing that he could place the past firmly and finally behind him he had reckoned without a side of himself rather at odds with his capacity for cool thought. It was an imaginative quality capable of being stirred and influenced by sudden, odd impressions. It had been at work during his early relationship with Jean, it had led him on. Now it led him back and worked against his peace of mind. Against his will it took him back to that moment when she had come up close to him and said, 'I hate you!' It kept returning him to the look in her eyes, the look on her face, the tone of her voice, the hatred flowering in her like a sudden, unnatural growth. And beneath that clear image, like two photographs superimposed one upon the other, he saw another image, familiar and cherished, the

209

look which had first taken hold of his imagination and which he had thought of ever since as 'that beautiful look'. This contradiction in his idea of her caused him suffering. He chided himself, made efforts to escape, but could not.

The desire to comprehend was a strong ever-present urge. But as the months went by without any possibility of solving the problem, so the urgency slowly weakened. Still, there were moments, alone in his flat after a hard day at school if he was feeling more than usually tired and depressed, when the need to understand would return stronger than ever. Then he wanted to rush out, to find her, to force the truth out of her. He wanted to shout at her, 'What have you got against me that you wouldn't even speak to me? I did everything for you.' How shy she had been when they had first gone out together, she had been almost without a friend, and he had shown her London, taken her everywhere, indulged her cultural interests, taken her out and about when she had no one else – brought her out, in fact. He could not stop himself thinking, 'She was lucky to have got me!' His pride said to him that he could have had almost any girl he had fancied. He wanted to tell her angrily, 'I always put you first! Everything else in my life was of secondary importance except Robbie.' He believed that this had been the case although his work had always meant a great deal to him and his ambition was still very much alive.

He imagined her at work in a library – taking examinations, making her steady way up the career ladder until she stood where she had always planned to be. Then he recalled his parting words and longed again to meet her so that he could repeat them, 'You've got what you wanted!'

His orderly upbringing now stood him in good stead. He kept his flat clean; he shopped and cooked for himself. He did everything in a methodical manner. It became his habit to shop for the week on Friday night. On a Saturday morning he vacuumed the flat and took his dirty clothes to the launderette. In the afternoon he did his ironing. Once a month he went home for Sunday lunch and on his way back visited one of his friends who had gone to live in Camden Town. The neatness and order native to his childhood had imprinted itself upon his personality, and he experienced a sense of gratitude towards his parents for this help in his present trouble.

After two years, he told himself he had got over it. Jim thought so too. Mabel had her doubts. But in spite of what

Stephen told himself, he had not got free of Jean – sometimes he saw her in the softened glow of memories, and sometimes in the harsh light of judgment, and the two images remained apart and unreconciled. It simply never occurred to him that somewhere along the line he might have failed badly.

He intended to put his past life firmly behind him, to make himself feel, except perhaps at odd moments, as if it had never really happened. He resolved that later, when he had time to see to it, he would get a divorce. Then all ties between them would be severed. About one thing he was quite clear. He would never marry again, never again be a father.

It was some two and a half years after the parting that quite by chance Stephen and Dick met. They had not seen each other since the separation. Stephen had been visiting his parents and was standing at the stop for the bus to Camden Town when there was a tap on his shoulder and a voice in his ear said cheerily and in a surprised tone, 'Well! If it isn't Stephen! How goes it?' The voice sounded faintly familiar. He turned, then with a sense of sudden shock, found himself looking into a pair of hazel eyes belonging to a youngish man with light brown hair, fair complexion and a few large freckles on his nose and forehead.

'You remember me, don't you?' the voice enquired in a friendly tone.

'Yes, of course.' Stephen answered. To his surprise, he found that his voice had taken on a note of pleasure. The eyes had not the same expression, but their colouring and the colour of his hair was the same.

'I've been doing the old duty,' Dick announced. It turned out that this was the first time for two years that he had gone to see his parents.

'Not surprising we haven't met before then,' Stephen said, a little dryly.

'That's right!' Dick agreed, unabashed. The bus came and they got in. 'Come and see us,' Dick invited after he had given Stephen his news.

'I'm awfully busy at weekends,' Stephen said, attempting to excuse himself. 'Correcting homework,' he added in explanation.

'Of course, you teach,' Dick said, remembering. 'Oh dear, what a job! Couldn't wait to leave school myself – never learnt a thing!' He made this remark with a certain pride. Finally, Stephen had to write down his address and Dick did the same.

'See you!' Dick said, as he got off the bus. Stephen was glad that Dick went to see his parents so seldom, he did not want to bump into him again. Then two days later there came a few friendly lines from Betty with an invitation to call whenever he felt like it – Sunday week would be a good time, she was going with Tina to visit her friend in their former home, so Dick would be on his own and most likely bored. He'd be doing a favour. Stephen was surprised and mildly interested to learn that they had left their communal set-up and were now living on their own. He thought, 'I shan't go,' but when the Sunday arrived he changed his mind, putting the change down to the fact that he did not know what to do with himself. He would not admit that he was drawn towards Dick because he was Jean's brother and reminded him of her.

He easily found the street where the couple were living; like his own place, it was in a rather run-down area. The street was full of children playing which made Stephen feel at home at once. For an instant he wanted to go away. Then he took himself in hand and pressed the bell. An unreasoning fear lest the door should be opened by Jean had entered his mind. When the door did open, he met Dick's cheery gaze.

'Hello! Come on in.' Dick led the way up the stairs at the top of which was a safety gate, tied back. 'To keep Tina from falling down the stairs,' Dick commented, 'I don't know what good it is now.' Actually Betty had been trying to get him to take it off its hinges for years. On principle she refused to do the job herself. It was his job and he should do it. The trouble with no set tasks, she had discovered, was that everything could easily fall on one pair of shoulders, unless that person was firm.

Stephen sat down and looked round the small living-room. It was in a mess – items of daily living scattered about, signs of dust everywhere, but no actual dirt. He liked the atmosphere. Clearly people were living here; not like his own room, neat and ordered, but somehow with an empty feeling. He suddenly became depressed. Perhaps his looks betrayed him, or else it was Dick's normal hospitable behaviour, for he asked, 'Have a drink? We've got beer, sherry, cider. Betty likes cider, I like beer.'

'I'll have a beer,' Stephen said. In the ordinary way, he never drank. Drinking by oneself had no taste to it.

'It's light ale,' Dick commented as he poured out two half-pint glasses. 'I have to be careful, Betty won't stand heavy

212

drinking – and she isn't keen on the smell of beer, so it's rather hard on a chap. Cheers!' He took a long pull.

'What are you doing now?' Stephen asked.

'I'm a qualified electrician,' Dick replied with pride. He sat down. 'Not posh, like you, of course,' he added naively. 'You and Jean are a pair.' Then he said quickly, 'Oh, sorry! I forgot,' but he was not unduly embarrassed by his gaff. He went on to ask in his usual easy manner, 'We heard you two had split up. What happened?'

'Oh that! We didn't understand each other any more,' Stephen said in an off-hand tone.

This explanation seemed to satisfy Dick. 'You don't mind my mentioning her, then?' he asked.

'No.' After all what had he come for, if not for that?

Dick seemed to regard this reply as a licence to indulge. He plunged in. 'Well, she was always the clever one, you see. Dad used to rave about how clever she was; said she took after his Mum, always had her head in a book – deep books, he called them. I was nowhere with Dad; he once told me I was slow next to Jean. But I reckon I've proved I'm not slow.' The word had clearly rankled with him and still did. He went on, 'What I say is, where would all these clever people be without electricians? They'd have to read their clever books by candlelight. I bet they wouldn't care for that!'

'No,' Stephen agreed. 'I shouldn't care for that either.' He could not see what Dick was on about. Everybody knew craftsmen were necessary, labourers too, if it came to that.

'Anyway,' Dick said, getting up and refilling his glass, 'I showed them when I went into a commune.' He took it as proof of original thinking.

'Want your glass filled up?' he asked. Stephen shook his head. His glass was still half full. 'No thanks. I don't often drink.'

'Oh dear!' Dick commented. 'Half the pleasure of living gone.'

He sat down again. The train of his thought had gone. 'What about the commune?' Stephen enquired, curious at last. 'Why did you two leave? We thought you were well settled.' Unconsciously he had made use of the word 'we'.

'Oh, yes. We were,' Dick said in a decided tone of voice. He added jovially and in a satisfied tone, 'Jean was struck all of a heap when I told her. I showed her she wasn't the only one who

213

could do some thinking!' He looked very proud of himself when he said this. He took another long pull at his beer. Then his look of satisfaction faded and he became a little crestfallen. 'Only it didn't work as far as I was concerned.' He paused, then since Stephen said nothing, he went on in a serious tone, 'I really did think about it before I went in – it wasn't done for a lark. I don't know what Jean told you about our home, but it was bloody awful! All the time we were growing up Mum was being beaten. We had the police in, but nothing happened. Mum had to accuse him in Court, and meanwhile he could go on living with her, so it's understandable why she didn't, isn't it? He paused, then said, 'Pretty rotten set up, when you think about it.'

'Jean did tell me,' Stephen said.

'She was very decent to me,' Dick said. 'Don't know if she told you that?'

'No,'Stephen said.

'Well she was! Often! Stood between me and Dad. Saved me from many a thrashing. Dad never touched her, you see. The apple of his eye, you see. She could get the better of him because of it. He did once try to strike her and she turned on him, quite fearless, and said, "I thought you said I was like your mother?" He stopped then. Dropped his hand. Funny, really,' he added, 'people you're allowed to hit and people you aren't.'

'You've never told me why you first went into the commune,' Stephen said. He wanted to get away from Jean this, Jean that.

Dick looked surprised. 'I told you,' he said. Then seeing that Stephen had not got the point, 'Power! I wanted to get away from power – the cock and hen situation. I agreed with Jean.'

It always seemed to come back to Jean. Stephen could not stop himself asking, 'Agreed with Jean about what?' The word Jean sounded strange on his tongue. It was so long since he had uttered her name.

'Agreed with Jean that it was wrong for one person to have power over another like Dad had over our Mum. Betty thinks that too. She was living in a commune when I first met her. Seems she had difficulties at home as well; she called it claustrophobic'. He became suddenly enthusiastic about Betty, rather to Stephen's relief. 'She's a great girl, you know! Great fun to go about with; very sporty and doesn't nag a fellow – at least, not often. She taught me to skate. A jolly fine dancer as well. Lots of fun.' Then he added, 'But sharp, you know! Not a

214

nagger, but sharp. All over in half a minute, but she can give a fellow a bee sting.'

Stephen was amused at this description of Betty. He could imagine her stinging. Dick picked up the two empty glasses and returned them to the sideboard. He sat down again. 'I'm boring you,' he said. 'Tell me about yourself. How do you like being single again?'

'Oh, it's all right; got quite used to it by now,' Stephen said in an off-hand tone.

'Got another girl?' Dick enquired with interest.

'No.' Dick's look implied that he thought this a pity.

Stephen wanted to ask Dick if he ever heard from Jean, but he could not bring himself to put the question. Dick answered the unspoken words.

'I haven't seen Jean for ages,' he told him, leaving the precise amount of time vague. 'She sends us birthday and Christmas cards, that sort of thing; oh, and she's been to Brighton because she sent us a card from there – some while back. But you know that, of course. Betty was surprised that she and your Mum had become so close.'

Stephen was stunned; Jean and his mother at Brighton together, yet he was never told! and then he recalled that he had as much as forbidden his mother to mention Jean. He had made it clear that he wished her to act as if Jean had never existed. He felt betrayed. He expected his mother to be loyal to him however he himself behaved. To change the subject, he said, 'You still haven't told me why you left the commune.'

'Oh, that's a long story,' Dick replied vaguely. Then, 'Well, to cut it short, it didn't turn out the way I'd expected. I didn't get away from the power game at all. I found I just hated other fellows getting on close terms with Betty and chatting her up. Betty said they didn't, it was me, I was being jealous and they were only being friendly, and that that was the whole point of the exercise, to learn to live in a friendly way outside a tiny group. What she called the nuclear family. But I think they did chat her up.' An annoyed look came on his face. 'I still *felt* the same, you see. I thought I wouldn't, but I did. I hated her being friendly with other men, and I couldn't change that feeling in me.' The annoyed look stayed on his face. 'And then Betty's a very *modern* sort of a person.' He stressed the word 'modern' in an aggrieved tone, as if the injury lay there. 'She's very forward – she takes the initiative most of the time.' There was a long pause, then he added in an embarrassed tone, 'Even in bed, and I don't like that. I get upset. I think that's the man's part.' He ended , rather lamely, 'I do still agree with all her ideas; about not being possessive and being equal, I mean; but the trouble was, I couldn't change how I felt. I went on *feeling* jealous and resentful. So, in the end, I said either we get out, or I get out. Only I wasn't going to leave Tina behind. We quarrelled over that as well. I'm very fond of Tina. After all she is my daughter.' In a tone of resentment, he added, 'I didn't like her calling other men Uncle; I thought, the next thing, she won't know who her real father is.'

Stephen wanted to laugh at this tale of woe, but he managed a sympathetic nod instead. 'I should think it might be difficult,' he commented.

'Do you think it would suit you?' Dick asked, hoping for support. He looked pleased when Stephen uttered a firm, 'No!'

Stephen would have liked to talk as freely about himself and Jean as Dick had talked about himself and Betty. Perhaps another person could shed some light, but his own temperament, and Dick's easy-going manner, stopped him. Dick was less introvert, could talk more easily about his problems. But apart from this difference between them, there was another obstacle in his path. He felt that if he started, he might end up emotional. Conditioned as he was, he was incapable of asking for, or accepting, support from another man. He missed having a woman to turn to. Jean had always lent a sympathetic ear to all his problems. 'I envy you,' he said suddenly, before he was aware of what he was going to say. 'You and Betty have been through difficulties and you're still together.' He felt suddenly horribly envious.

Dick looked surprised. 'Betty can be very sharp,' he began, and for a moment Stephen thought he was about to say something more, something important. Then he went all vague. 'We have our problems,' he ventured. 'Betty was all for staying. I had to insist.' But this was not what had been on the tip of his tongue. He wondered for an instant whether he should enlighten Stephen. Then he thought 'No', nothing was finally settled.

The two men chatted on for a while. Then Stephen said he must be going, and Dick saw him out, saying, 'Come again,' adding, 'make it a Sunday. Betty visits her commune friend then, says it's good experience for Tina – one of her ideas, you

216

know.' He spoke as if Betty was full of ideas. At the same time his voice expressed a certain scorn.

Back in his own room, Stephen found himself regretting his visit. He did not wish to think about his past life, and being with Dick had revived memories – a certain turn of the head, the colour of eyes and hair, inflections of the voice. Again Jean's face rose before him as he had first seen it, with that far off, beautiful gaze, then as he had seen it last, like stone, in that final, silent parting – and in between the look of hatred. Impatient with himself, he thought, 'This is sheer weakness! She'll drive me mad if I let her.' He had a sense of persecution; as if she were deliberately haunting him out of some obscure revenge.

He turned his thoughts to Dick. Clearly intellectual dislike of power over others was not enough. Poor Dick! He was interested in what he had to say about power, and he could not help being amused. He was certain of one thing – he had never, at any time, exercised any power over Jean. On principle, he had left her absolutely free.

Then he found himself wondering about Betty. How had Dick managed to persuade Betty to leave the commune against her own desire? Even from the little he knew of them both he had felt that Betty was much the stronger character. Finally he gave it up. It was wasted effort trying to understand anyone else.

CHAPTER TWENTY

THREE months were to pass before Stephen thought of paying another visit to Dick. He told himself it was merely to fill in an otherwise blank Sunday afternoon, but when Betty opened the door to him he wished he had not come. His face must have shown it for after telling him that Dick had taken Tina to the Zoo, she added with a smile, 'I don't bite! Come on in.' On the stairs, she said over her shoulder, in a slightly amused voice, 'I do live here, you know.'

She led the way into the living-room where there was an ironing board with an upturned iron at one end and, in the middle, a pyjama top spread out; on a chair close by was a pile of clean washing.

Betty pointed Stephen to a fireside chair. 'You can talk to me while I get on with this boring job,' she told him. She set to with vigour, humming to herself as if Stephen were not there.

He did not know what to say. Instead he let his eyes follow the outline of her arm as it moved along the ironing board. Her arms still retained the honey colour he had so much admired years ago.

As he did not speak, after a few moments Betty asked how long it was since they had seen each other. He could not remember.

'Oh, four or five years,' he answered vaguely. 'Good Lord! As long as that?' Betty glanced up at him with her steady, uninhibited gaze. The bold attractiveness he had noted at the registry office was still there; the almost black hair, worn shoulder length, the aquiline nose and somewhat large reddish lips, the warm glow of the skin which gave to her face a natural sun-tan look, the slim figure which carried itself upright. His memory of her proved to be very accurate; his only surprise was that she was not wearing a red blouse with red slacks and white canvas shoes with red laces, which was how he had always pictured her in his mind's eye, but instead was clad in dark green slacks and a green blouse patterned all over with bright orange, diamond-shaped stars, which admirably suited her dark hair and warm complexion. When she had spoken to him at the door, her voice had sounded the clear, almost bell-like quality of earlier years. She had not altered at all, he decided.

While he was thinking this, Betty was thinking, 'He's broadened out, but otherwise he's the same. Dick's right about his having style – he knows it too!' She gave an inward smile. People who took themselves seriously always amused her, but while she was smiling, at the same time she was feeling sorry for him. His face looked sadder. She guessed that he probably felt lonely. He was proud; too proud to confide in anyone. In this way she summed him up. Nevertheless she would make an effort, if only to find out why he had come.

'I haven't seen Jean for ages,' she said, in her clear tones. 'I did write and invite her over, but I only got a card, from Brighton. That's more than two years ago. She does send birthday cards, though, and presents for Tina, but my little girl hardly knows her. Seems a shame.'

218

She waited for Stephen to say something, but all he said was, 'We're not in touch.'

Seeing the closed look on his face, Betty gave it up for the present. 'The room's in rather a mess,' she commented, looking round as she folded up the pyjama top, laid it on a finished pile and reached for a shirt. It certainly was in a mess, Stephen silently agreed. The large table was almost covered over with small mantlepiece-type articles, a pile of crockery, another pile of blankets, and an assortment of knives, forks and spoons. 'We're sorting out things,' Betty said, following Stephen's eyes as he noted the collection of objects. 'I suppose Dick told you we're going our separate ways.' The words were half statement, half question; knowing Dick, she doubted if he had come clean.

This piece of unexpected information startled Stephen sufficiently to shake him out of his silent patience with a situation he had got himself into and from which he could not for the moment extricate himself. 'No,' he said, 'he didn't mention anything of the sort.'

'He wouldn't,' Betty commented, without any obvious surprise. 'If he can manage it, he much prefers to slide past unpleasant facts.' There was a slight sarcasm, but no animosity in her voice.

She folded the ironed shirt, laid it on top of the finished pile and started on a blouse. 'We aren't close any longer,' she said, speaking in a casual tone, as though she were discussing someone else's problem. 'I don't mean we dislike each other – we don't. Dick rather admires me. I'm very fond of Dick.' She hesitated, then went on in the tone of a person confessing to a weakness, 'I gave in to him about leaving our shared house hoping that would keep us together.' She added, 'The trouble is, if one person cares and the other person doesn't, or at least doesn't care as much, the one who cares most must always lose out. I cared the most. I still do.'

This was a revelation to Stephen. He felt a shift taking place in his idea of Betty. 'I'm comfortable with him,' she continued, 'and that seems a lot to me. He's generous, he's kind – he's lazy too, but then most men are when it comes to around the house. He can enjoy the moment without trying to lasso it. He has a great sense of fun; above all, he doesn't cling, he's not a limpet.' She repeated, with some emphasis, 'That means a lot to me, his not clinging.'

'Then why part?' Stephen answered, thinking them both a bit silly. They ought to have had his problems.

Instead of answering him, Betty asked, 'Were your parents possessive?'

'I don't know,' Stephen answered. The question had never occurred to him.

'My mother was very possessive,' Betty said. 'It was fear. I didn't realise it at the time, but that's what it was. I made up my mind never to let Tina get into that sort of a mess, not ever, whatever it might cost me.'

Stephen did not find any of this in the least illuminating. What had Tina to do with it? He was not quick at following muddled expressions of thought. He liked clear sign writing.

Betty finished the ironing without making any further conversation. She thought Stephen rude, making so little effort to talk. She almost asked him why he had come if only to sit. She folded up the ironing board and disposed of it in the kitchen, came back and set out two small occasional tables, one for Stephen and one for herself. She went back into the kitchen and put on the kettle. She called to Stephen, 'Come and look at our garden.'

What she called 'the garden' was a balcony which ran the entire length of the second floor flat and was reached by a door leading out of the kitchen. It contained a large number of green and flowering plants, obviously well cared for.

'I shall miss it,' Betty said. 'I bought most of these plants and I'm the one who waters them. But I'm leaving them. Susan will have to water them. We've got a garden at our house.'

'Who's Susan?' Stephen asked, gazing at the rows of plants.

'The girl Dick is going to marry,' Betty said. 'You know we're not married. Dick and Susan prefer a conventional set-up.' She added, 'Susan is seven years younger than Dick, but then, Dick is young for his age.'

Stephen had not known that Betty and Dick were not married. If Jean had known and told him, which he doubted, he had forgotten. 'I wish you'd speak in some logical order,' he told Betty irritably. 'I can't follow you.'

Betty poured the hot water into the teapot. 'I hope you like your tea strong,' she said. 'I've put in three heaped up spoons. But there's lots of hot water. Here! Take it in. I'll bring the rest.'

'Where do I put the teapot?' he called from the room.

220

'Anywhere!' she called back, with what sounded like a laugh. He put it in the hearth. She came in with the loaded tray.

"Well, don't just stand!' she ordered, 'make a space on the table.' He hastened to remove the pile of blankets.

Betty offered Stephen biscuits. They sipped the hot tea in silence. Then Stephen said, 'Go on about you and Dick.' Marital difficulties held an interest for him now.

She started off at a tangent again. 'I daresay you think me short, sharp, abrupt even,' she began, as if she was wanting to excuse some defect in herself and at the same time to challenge his idea of her. 'People often do, I understand. They think I lack feeling. The reason is that I can't stand anyone becoming emotional – it kills me right off. Stone dead! And I can't stand a lying relationship; pretending, faking feelings. Emotional false-hoods! That's what I grew up alongside and swore then that I'd never ever submit a child of mine to a similar fate.' She repeated, with emphasis, 'Never ever!'

'I don't think you lack feeling,' Stephen said, surprised. He added, 'I like you the way you are. You're the sort of person I could talk to.' He had no sooner uttered the words than he was amazed at what he had said. He was even more amazed by the knowledge that he had spoken the truth. There was something about Betty's cool manner which was totally reassuring. Yet only a short while ago he had sat in silent embarrassment, not knowing how to make conversation, wishing he had not come.

She was surprised and pleased at his remark; her pleasure showed in her face. Again Stephen felt a slight shift in his idea of her. 'I'll stack these few things in the sink, she said, 'then we can talk.' She was back in a few moments and sat down in the fireside chair opposite. There was a brief silence, then she said, 'Dick wanted us to stay together for Tina's sake. But that's what happened to me and I know it doesn't work.' She went on to tell Stephen about her childhood, finishing with,'It was such a waste on their part, all that effort; I can't remember a time in my life, even my very earliest memories, when I didn't know – know, I mean, that something was being hidden from me. It gave me an awful sense of insecurity as if I was walking in a fog and might stumble over something appalling any second. Just imagine a child growing up with that kind of feeling inside her. Then, when I was older, the falsity became clear to me. They used to kiss morning and night and I knew it was put on for me. Don't ask me how I knew – I just did. I came to feel I was acting out a

221

part in a play; when I entered a room and they were together there, it was just as if my entrance was some sort of a cue. I could see their expressions, the way they were talking and behaving towards each other, change. It was weird! I always knew when there had been a row by the way Mum stood or sat.' She added, 'And, of course, I used to listen on the landing when I was supposed to be in bed. That was another kind of play altogether!' She went on a bit, then said, 'I made up my mind when I was old enough to think about it, that I'd never put a child of mine through *that*.'

She finished, 'I should have been so much happier if they had separated and I had gone to live with one parent and been kept in touch with the other. Upsetting, but you know then where you are. The one thing a child can't take is being kept away from the truth. It can't breathe freely; it's a kind of half-strangulation.'

Stephen did his best to imagine what it must have been like, but it was too far removed from any experience of his own to have real meaning for him. 'But you and Dick are much more relaxed together,' he demurred.

Betty nodded. 'Because I make Dick come clean. That's my whole point. Tina would know at once if we started acting. She knows now we are splitting up and it worries her, but she can cling round us and cry about it and be angry with us because of it and we can talk to her together – me and Dick. She may not understand, but she knows Mummy and Daddy still like each other. And, above all, she knows she's not left out.' She thought there was nothing worse for children than being brought up by parents who put on a show of false emotions for their sakes. It destroyed all their faith in the sincerity of adults.

'I agree with that,' Stephen said. He did not think there could be anything worse.

'The truth is, I'm not right for Dick,' Betty confided sadly. 'He needs a different sort of woman. He always did. I attracted him, we had jolly times together, living in a communal house was a bit of a lark. He had 'a thing' about Jean, he wanted to show he could do something startling even if he wasn't 'bright'. Now he's more mature he wants to settle down and Susan is just his kind of a woman; very domesticated and what is called home-loving. I'm too independent for him – he thinks me abrasive.' There was a long silence. Stephen would have liked to say something comforting, but he did not go in for sentimental reassurances. Besides, he knew Betty would hate it and rather despise him for the falsity, so he said nothing.

'It's funny about Dick,' Betty said. 'His nicest side makes him weak. He doesn't like hurting people; he simply wants his own way and to be told it's all right!' She laughed. It struck her as funny. 'He doesn't want to hurt either me or Tina and at the same time he'd like to marry Susan. Even Dick can't manage all that – and he's pretty good at getting his own way without a scene. If we do have a row, he's upset until we've made it up – on his terms, of course!'

'Anyway, you've got a sense of humour,' Stephen said.

'Rather! You can't get through life without that.'

So they had decided to part. Tina would go with Betty, and Dick would see her and take her out whenever he wanted. 'He knows he can trust me,' Betty said.

'Is he fond of Tina? Stephen asked. He was feeling envious.

'Very! Very fond. He even offered to give up Susan, but there was a lot of pretence in what he suggested.' She added, 'To me the blood relationship comes very much second. It's the caring for a child that matters – by caring I'm not meaning domestic chores, the meals, although those may be a part of it – I mean a loving, sincere, non-possessive relationship. That's what makes a real mother – or father, for that matter.'

Stephen found what she was saying strange. He could not think of a blood relationship as secondary. To him it seemed the basis for all other relationships. He thought it callous of Dick not to want to know how Jean was getting on and strange that Jean should not care whether or not she saw her brother. He would have liked to have had brothers and sisters.

'I'm taking Tina back with me to our old home,' Betty told him. Dick doesn't approve, but I have the final say there.'

Remembering what Dick had told him, Stephen was about to ask Betty for details of life in their shared house when the front door slammed and voices were heard.

'That's Tina now,' Betty said, getting up and going to open the door. She greeted her husband and daughter on the threshold. 'How are the tigers? Here's Stephen,' she said in the same breath. Tina stared across at Stephen, then began to rattle on about the zoo while Dick patted her on the head.

'This is my girl!' he told Stephen proudly. She had a look of her mother about her, but with her father's smile and chin. She had his freckles as well.

'Hello,' she said, going across to Stephen without a trace of shyness. 'Who are you?' She was a lively child, full of a natural, uncurbed curiosity. She gave the impression of not having a care in the world, but, as Betty would have said, you can never tell with children.'

'I've told Stephen we're going our own ways,' Betty said in front of Tina, who looked enquiringly at her mother and then at her father. After she had had some milk and an apple, she went off to bed without complaining. When she was in bed, Dick went up to tell her a story. After some twenty minutes, he came back and they all sat down to supper. Over the meal, the two parents talked to Stephen and to each other very amicably. If either of them was upset at the thought of parting, it did not show. They would remain friends, there was no animosity. They simply recognised that they had never been suited to each other. Dick would like Betty better when he no longer had to put up with her independent ways.

At the front door, Betty said, 'I'd like to look in on Jean some time. I didn't want to seem to be intruding. Any objections?'

'None,' Stephen said.

'Any hope of you two getting back together?' After her own frankness, she thought she could ask him that.

'No chance at all!' he answered with emphasis.

'Well, come and see me in our house. I'll be going back in about six weeks, when someone moves out.' She told him the address and he said he could remember it.

'I'll be seeing you then?'

'Yes.' And he raised his hand in a parting gesture of friendship.

Walking along slowly, for he never hurried to get home now, he found himself pondering over Betty. He admired her very much. He was missing a woman to confide in and when he had said to her that she was the sort of person he could talk to, he had spoken the truth. But in spite of his remark and the admiration he felt for her, he had not brought himself to the point of confiding. Instead, he had taken refuge in listening. While she was speaking he had felt safe from his urge towards confession.

He thought about Betty and Dick's approaching separation. He did not understand how this parting could happen with such apparent ease or how they could meet in the future as mere friends.

CHAPTER TWENTY-ONE

O N the third anniversary of Robbie's death, Jean was still living in the flat which Stephen had found for her. She had no idea whether he knew this, since all contact between them had ceased once she had written to his solicitor to inform him that she no longer needed financial assistance. She knew that he was alive and well only because she was certain that Mabel would have told her had it been otherwise. The friendship between the two women which had been born during their week at Brighton had not died. They spoke over the phone at more or less regular intervals and met now and then for a day out. But it did not escape Jean's notice that she was not invited to Mabel's home. She guessed that this was due to Jim's objections. While she wondered at Mabel's subservience to her husband, she did not hold it against her.

When Stephen had parted from Jean with the words, 'You've got what you wanted,' she had been in a state of mental and physical exhaustion. To get up from the chair would have been an effort beyond her. She heard the front door close without any emotion. Seated in the chair, she had dropped off to sleep. When she awoke it was dark. She had groped her way to the settee and fallen across it, too exhausted to get to the bedroom. Fully dressed, she slept through the night. In the morning she was stiff and cold. She made herself get up off the settee and light the gas fire. Then she went into the kitchen for a hot drink. On opening the refrigerator she found it stacked to the roof; meat and fruit pies, butter, cheese, vegetables, a pound of steak and seven pints of milk. With his usual thoroughness, Stephen had provided her with more than a week's food supply. On the top of the fridge, there was a large cut brown loaf and biscuits. There also he had left a list of the addresses which she was most likely to need: supermarket, post office, nearest doctor's surgery and so on, with detailed directions as to how to get there. On the mantlepiece in the living room, she later found a short note from him giving his own address and telling her to contact him or his solicitor if she was short of anything. She need not worry about the rent; he had paid it for six months ahead. He would continue to send her an allowance until she wrote that she no longer needed it. He would send it on the first day of each month. Meanwhile he was leaving her fifty pounds.

She found the money and a stamped, addressed envelope for her possible use next to the note.

She made herself some tea, drank it as hot as she could bear, ate a slice of brown bread without butter and returned to lying on the settee. At lunch time she got up again and drank some milk. Then she went into the small bedroom and lay on the bed, eyes shut. In this manner she lived for days. She slept, she ate; she slept again, she ate again. When she was awake, she lay thinking of the contents of his letter. He had written, 'You needn't hurry to get a job. Get well first.' How strange that he could be so caring and yet at the same time so cruel.

Stephen's absence was an immense relief, but she found that being alone in a room was a terrifying experience. She knew that outside the room there was a street with people, shops, cars, buses, but it did not help. All that activity could have been at the other side of the world. She felt as isolated as if she had been on an ice floe in the frozen north. There was no one to whom she could turn – neither mother, nor father, nor brother, certainly not her husband. It made her knees go weak when she thought of her situation.

Apart from these moments of terror, she did not feel in any sense real and when, after some ten days, she was forced to leave the flat to go to the shops, the people in the streets and in the shops seemed equally strange. Her interest in life was dead. It was as if the world and herself had ceased to exist.

Weeks passed. Her interest in life did not revive, but its place was taken by a determination to rid herself at the earliest possible moment of any dependence on Stephen. When she thought of Stephen, she thought vindictively. When she took hold of a bank note and remembered that it was from him, she wanted to burn it. She took one pound note and indulged herself. She watched it flare up; when it was in flames, she imagined that it was Stephen burning. To free herself from this dependency became her sole reason for living. This determination took her to a doctor.

'How soon do you think it will be before I am able to work?' she asked anxiously.

'Not yet,' he answered firmly. 'You're much too thin.' He made out a prescription for medicine and pills and gave her advice on how to help her recovery. She listened to all he said and carried out his advice with scrupulous care. She went to bed early with a sleeping pill, got plenty of fresh air and exercise, made herself eat nourishing foods, drank plenty of milk and made a point of once a week taking a change – a meal out, a coach ride, or a bus ride through a different locality. She thought only of the aim she had set herself. Slowly she put on weight, her cheeks recovering some of their normal colour. But although she forced herself to take a good half hour's walk each day, she never went near the local park, instead she wandered around the streets and shops. Nor did she make use of the local library. She seldom read. Instead she hired a television set and sat looking at programmes which formerly had held no interest for her.

She pondered over job possibilities. She knew for certain only one thing – she must never again take up her old career, or touch work in any way related to it. Stephen's parting words, 'You've got what you wanted!' and the words of the dream, 'You're glad he's dead! You know you are!' combined to bar her way more effectively than any mere physical barrier could have done. Whatever work she undertook, it must not give her mental satisfaction, nor make use of her trained abilities, nor give her a sense of achievement. That would be to benefit from Robbie's death. That would be to confirm her guilt.

One day she recalled the fact that she had taken a typing course to aid her in her work. She knew then that she had only to recover her strength and she could stop the monthly payments. This realisation drove her on more effectively than a powerful engine. She followed her daily routine with unvarying care. Gradually a sense of reality began to return. She did not feel real in the sense of giving expression to herself, but she no longer felt as if she did not exist, and the people she saw in the streets and shops became ordinary beings such as she had always known, people to whom she could speak a few words if they spoke to her.

Six months after she and Stephen had parted, she got a job as a typist in a local estate agent's office. The same day that she started work she wrote to Stephen's solicitor informing him that no further payments would be necessary. When she had posted the letter, she experienced a sense of immense relief. An intolerable humiliation had been taken out of her life.

She had been at work for a few weeks when Mabel paid her a visit. She felt that there must be something worthwhile about her after all, if she was valued so much by a friend that she came half across London to see her, and that friend not just anybody, but Stephen's mother and Robbie's grandmother, a person who might have been expected to despise her.

Coming up to the third anniversary of Robbie's death, Jean became aware of a healing process going on inside her. It took the form of a reborn joy in simple things. She had been able for some weeks now to leave off her nerve pills. Then, one morning, as she was drawing back the curtains, she became aware of the sky for the first time for a long while. The risen sun was shining at the centre of a sea of light and beating their wings across this luminous space moved the dark shapes of four birds – high up and far off, yet clearly visible against the brightness. She found herself thinking how beautiful the sight was. From that moment her senses were awakened, and responded again to the simple, everyday experiences of life; the sky and birds flying, the sun on a warm red brick wall, leaves moving in the breeze, light and shade through foliage, flowers and fruit on a street stall, the colours of umbrellas in the rain and later, when she ventured into the park for the first time, old men playing bowls, young men and women at tennis, children sucking ice cream, cricket and football on the grass, and later still, a walk down a street of shop windows, a meal out, a chat over the phone, a visit to the cinema. She was slowly returning to normal.

With the third anniversary of Robbie's death, she was able to say, 'So long as I don't have to suffer again, I'm content. That's all I ask of life.' To be able to sit with quiet nerves seemed to her the greatest of all blessings. But the desire that nothing should happen to disturb her new-found peace made Jean feel and act in a manner much older than her years. It caused her to shun interests which she and Stephen had shared and places which they had visited together. She never went to the opera or ballet or exhibitions or art galleries, nor did she stroll at week-ends along the Embankment. She shunned the Festival Hall and Covent Garden.

As the months passed, she began to feel that she had been widowed and was just starting to get used to a single life again. But she did not make friends as widowed persons usually do after a while. On the whole the office staff had different interests and although no one was unkind to her, she was aware of being regarded as, in some senses, an outsider. She spoke very little, got on with her work, and rarely joined in the chatter. Some of the girls went out together after hours. She was not asked. For this she was grateful. She lived very quietly. The activity natural to her age was wanting.

Then it came into Jean's mind that she ought to do something about Rita, who had tried with considerable loyalty to contact her, but who had only been able to speak to Stephen and whose letters Jean had left unanswered. Finally Rita had said to Richard, 'She obviously wants to be left alone. She knows where I am if she feels differently later on.' The 'later on' had turned out to be all of three years, but when Jean did phone, Rita greeted her as if they had been in contact only last week.

'Richard will stay in to see you if you come on a Saturday,' Rita said. 'He's listening to what I'm saying.'

When the day came, Jean was sorry she had taken the step. Everything she did still required a nervous effort. She was getting used to this resistance and to combating it, but she took extra care with her appearance.

As she came out of the tube, she was met by Richard with the car. He looked healthy and tanned. 'Rita's getting the lunch,' he said. 'I'm going to take you for a blow on the Common.' The two children were with their maternal grandmother for the weekend. Jean asked after Rita's mother.

'Not too well,' Richard told her. 'She's getting arthritis in two of her fingers. You know her trade is dressmaking. She worries, which doesn't help. The children cheer her up, she loves having them.'

'Of course, you've got a son now,' Jean said bravely. 'Who does he take after?'

'Everybody says Ian is like me. Sarah looks more like her mother now.'

'It's supposed to be the other way round,' Jean said.

They got out of the car on the edge of the Common and walked. It was a cool, windy day and Jean welcomed the freshness after the tube. She asked if they both liked Ruislip as a place to live. Richard said it was pleasant but too modern for his own taste. 'I prefer places with more atmosphere.' His main interest was in old houses. 'You can tell from the materials used and the type of buildings how the people lived and saw themselves.' This interested Jean and made the walk enjoyable. Back at the car Richard said, 'You could do with a drink, I expect. I know a nice little cafe.'

They sat down at a table for two in a small alcove. 'Is Rita working full time now?' Jean asked. Somehow she thought Rita might be, she put very little beyond her.

'Of course she isn't working full time,' Richard said. His voice sounded annoyed. 'She's got two children.'

'Oh,' Jean said, feeling foolish.

'She teaches part-time at the local polytechnic. We have a woman come in. And we entertain a fair amount.'

'I expect you know a lot of people through your work.' Jean tried to sound sensible.

'Yes.'

'Personal friends?'

'Quite often. Business friends and personal friends tend to overlap – common interests, you know.'

'Yes. Of course,' Jean said, trying to sound as if a combination of business and personal friendships was quite within her own area of experience.

In the car Richard said, 'Rita manages to fit in most things very well.'

Rita gave them an Indian style meal. 'I'm a splendid cook now,' she told Jean. 'Whoever Richard brings home, I know exactly what to give them.'

Jean was thinking that Rita looked older. She was as vivacious as ever, but decidedly plumper and Jean could imagine how she would be in middle-age. Richard too was slightly changed, less athletic in his stride, although his hand-clasp still made her wince. She was surprised that she could take note of such small changes. The knowledge cheered her. It proved to herself that she was recovering her grip on everyday life.

'I'd like to ask you to stay overnight,' Rita said, 'but I'm so busy at the weekends now. I hardly have a minute.'

'What about your Help?' Jean asked.

'She's a gift, the real old-style. I've had her four years and there's nothing she won't do. The children love her. I'm very lucky, but she can't do everything. There's always jobs left over, and I do a fair amount of baking for the week ahead. I have to fit things in.'

Jean asked to see snaps of the children and they pored over albums. Then Rita said, in her raspy tone, 'That was your mistake, Jean. You should have married a man with money. As things are, women have to buy their way out.' Those few words were the only reference Rita made either to Robbie's death or the separation.

230

Later that evening, Richard commented, 'Jean's less attractive.'

'Well, she's older,' Rita suggested.

'No, it's not only that. She's lost her vitality.'

On her way home, Jean thought about Rita's few words on her choice of a partner. She had said nothing in reply, but they had made a cutting impression on her. Once again, she had felt judged. Still, she looked back on her afternoon with pleasure. She had enjoyed Richard's company, she had enjoyed seeing Rita again after so long, but a question hung over her thoughts. It seemed that Rita had acquired a new discipline called 'fitting things in' – this was now her special subject. Jean found herself wondering if fitting things in was all the future held for women – to fit things in would women always need money, always have to make use of the labour of other women? And by fitting things in would women ever be able to make independent lives for themselves?

The next day, Jean had two unexpected visitors. On answering the ring at the bell, she found Betty standing outside with another woman who was a stranger to her. 'Hello.' Betty greeted her with a smile and an easy manner, as if they had met only recently. 'We thought we'd look you up. This is my friend, Lydia.' Jean looked at Lydia and saw a woman of about the same age as Betty, rather mousy looking and quietly dressed in grey anorak and jeans; when she spoke, it was in a quiet, soft voice.

Jean was surprised and upset when Betty told her of the impending separation. Afterwards, she realised that it had been silly of her to be upset since she had never considered the two suited from the start. She cheered up when Betty said, 'There's no need to be sorry about it. Dick and I were not made for each other.' She told Jean about Susan. 'You'll like her; she's just right for him. She'll make him a cosy home and she's a good cook.' Jean had to smile at this summing up of Dick's priorities.

'You think they'll stay together?' Jean asked.

'Sure of it,' Betty replied with conviction. 'You can judge for yourself when you meet Susan.' As she was speaking, she was casting her eyes over the room.

Jean asked about Tina and Betty said Tina would be all right, Dick and she were not enemies. Jean offered them both tea, but they said they had only looked in on their way to an art exhibition at the National Gallery to see if she would like to join them. Jean said she was expecting her friend.

'Another time, perhaps?' Betty queried. Jean nodded.

'What job are you doing now? Betty asked. She was never backward in putting questions. She expected Jean to say library work. When she said that she was typing in an estate agent's office, Betty was surprised, but said nothing.

'I've left my own office,' she told Jean. 'I found I preferred a job where I could move about and see people. I'm behind the cold meat counter at a Co-op supermarket. I enjoy the work and it's worthwhile.

'Have you seen my parents recently?' Jean asked. 'I can't go, you know. They don't want to see me. I was wondering about my mother.'

'Dick sees her when he takes Tina,' Betty said. 'I don't think you need worry about your mum. Dick seems to think she's getting much better treatment since she's been bringing in money. And she can stick up for herself better. It's wonderful what a little financial independence does for a woman.'

'I used to be Dad's favourite,' Jean said. 'Now he doesn't want to have anything to do with me.'

As they got up to go, Betty said, 'Visit us. We'd like that. But give us a date beforehand. We're often out.' She included Lydia in a manner that implied they were close friends and went about together. Jean said she would like to call and would let them know.

Outside in the street, the two friends walked on in silence for some minutes. Boarding a bus for the National Gallery, they sat down. 'Did you notice there were no books in the room?' Betty asked.

'There were books,' Lydia corrected her. 'Two on the small table by the window.'

'Yes, but not what you would expect,' Betty said. She added, 'Of course, I forgot, you didn't see her when she and Stephen were together. Their living-room had books everywhere, you fell over them unless you were careful. They were even on the floor. There were books too in the bedroom. I say I read a lot, but not like she used to do.'

'That's certainly odd,' Lydia agreed.

'It *is* odd,' Betty said. She went on, 'And there's another weird thing. Why should she choose to be a typist? There can't be a spark of interest in it for her.'

'Repetitive work can be helpful if you can't concentrate,' Lydia suggested.

'She's been at it too long,' Betty said. The question nagged at her.

They spent two hours at the National Gallery enjoying their favourite paintings and looking at two new purchases, then they went downstairs to the self-service counter where they were careful to limit themselves to tea and biscuits.

'Look at those gateaux!' Lydia exclaimed. 'What a price!'

'Yes,' Betty agreed, regretfully.

'Treat yourself, if you feel like it,' Lydia said.

'Don't tempt me,' Betty said, shaking her head. 'I always feel like it!'

Over their tea, Betty commented, 'I don't think Jean was expecting anyone. I think she just didn't want to come here. It's got something to do with Stephen.'

Lydia asked sympathetically, 'Do you think we could help her in any way?'

'Where angels fear to tread...?'

'Perhaps so,' Lydia said. After a pause, she added in her quiet, rather soft voice, 'We could call on her now and then. Let her know we're here if she needs us. Just be good friends.'

'Yes. We could,' Betty agreed.

The two friends had been right in deciding that Jean was not expecting anyone. She simply could not face the National Gallery.

In spite of relapses, Jean's recovery was slowly reaching a stage where her days in the office were becoming dull, but she did not think of changing her job and did not recognise a possible danger in her boredom.

CHAPTER TWENTY-TWO

FIVE months went by before Stephen took up Betty's invitation to visit her in her old home. Then one Saturday afternoon a desire to renew their acquaintance, together with a curiosity to find out more about her way of life, took him to see her.

As he was going up the stairs he passed a smartly dressed, middle-aged woman going down; rather petite, with flaxen hair under her small brimmed brown hat and a manner of walking which made him think of her as a lady. He knocked on Betty's door and heard her call, 'Come in'. She was standing at the window, waving to someone below in the street. She turned to greet him with a welcoming smile.

'Did you pass my mother on the stairs?' she asked.

'Your mother? he echoed, surprised. 'She looked very smart!' For some reason, he did not think Betty's mother would look like that.

'Oh, she is smart – always!' Betty said, with emphasis. She added, in a pleased voice, 'She's looking a lot younger now she's happier.' She beckoned him to a seat.

'What does she think about your being here?' Stephen asked, sitting down.

'She'd like me to marry and settle down in the usual way. In spite of her own marriage being such an unmitigated disaster, she still thinks that's the only proper way to live.' She hesitated, then said, 'She came to ask if they could keep Tina for another few days. They want to take her to the big toy shop, you know, in Oxford Street. They both spoil her, Dad more than Mum.'

It seemed that she was having her usual effect on Stephen. He sat gazing at her without speaking. This amused her.

'I did want a quick bath,' she told him. 'I was just going when you came. We have our regular times here. I'll only be ten minutes. Then I'll show you over the place and introduce you to anyone who's in. Do you mind? There are books over there.' She pointed to two shelves. Stephen said he did not mind. She collected her bath towel and toilet accessories and made off. All her movements were quick and lively. Stephen got up and viewed the titles of the books. Betty seemed to read a lot of autobiographies. The room was large with adequate space for two people. There was a full-sized divan pushed up against one wall and a small divan in an alcove with a curtain which could be drawn across. The arrangement reminded him of Robbie's early days. The thought of Tina asleep behind the curtain moved him. He turned his thoughts elsewhere. He gazed round the room; the carpet, curtains and furniture were all in cheerful, warm bright colours. Stephen thought he could feel at home in such a room. The orange and green colouring was very typical of Betty. He did not tell himself that there was no logical reason why he should not make his own room just as warm and comfortable. He connected it all up in his mind with Betty; the atmosphere was hers.

Coming back just under the ten minutes, Betty asked, 'Admiring my colour scheme?' She was glowing from her bath and smelling of lavender. Her face was shining. She had changed out of a pair of very worn jeans and a dark blue jersey into a silky emerald green trouser suit with an almost black blouse. Stephen thought she looked stunning.

'It's cheerful,' he answered her.

He watched her with pleasure as she spread her bath towel over the back of an upright chair, hanging the toilet bag over the end of the same chair, saying that she would see to all that later; living in one room had its drawbacks, clutter was one of them. Then she sat down at a small chest of drawers and began to comb out her hair in front of the mirror fixed to its back. Stephen could not help himself; he felt an attraction. At the same time, he was thinking that there could not be a greater difference to Jean. He followed her movements as she energetically rubbed at the long black strands of her damp hair. He admired the shape of her neck and her round, firm arms with their warm colouring. As she lifted her arms to rub the thick hair on her head, Betty knew that he was admiring her. She was pleased at this. She had no desire to make love to him, but she liked his recognition of her attractiveness. If Dick could let her go with such apparent ease there were other men who would feel very differently. She had no wish to lead a celibate life. A long-term relationship was a different matter. Men demanded so much. It was a problem she doubted she would ever be able to solve. She could not change her independent nature. Meanwhile Stephen's admiration was welcome.

'Come on,' she said, getting up briskly. 'I'll take you round.' She led him from the room with her purposeful step. It was one of those large old-fashioned, dilapidated Edwardian houses with big rooms, high ceilings and windows, which necessitated standing on the top rung of a five runged ladder in order to clean the glass, or to put up or take down the curtains. At the back there was a big garden, with plenty of playing space and a vegetable area. There were two swings hanging from apple trees and a climbing frame. Bats and balls lay about. There was a wooden horse on which a child was riding backwards and forwards with vigour. Two small children were chasing each other, screaming with excitement. Betty introduced him to two young women digging among the vegetables.

'We take turns in the garden,' Betty said. 'We take turns at everything; in the kitchen, cleaning the landings, catering. We work on a rota basis. A couple of us go each week in a van to the wholesale market. But we clean our own rooms.' She gave a laugh. 'Clean – not tidy!' As they went round, she introduced Stephen to such of the residents who were in the house.

Then they went back upstairs and Betty knocked on the door opposite her own room. 'Lydia's my best friend,' she said. Lydia opened the door. She smiled at Stephen and invited them both in. As it was getting on in the afternoon, she made tea and they sat and chatted for a while. Stephen noted that Lydia moved and spoke very quietly, with none of Betty's outward exuberance. She was on the small side, with short, smooth, brown hair and a pale complexion. She was dressed in dark jeans and a grey jersey and would have gone unnoticed in a crowd. Her room was cosy, but all the colours were subdued; greys, pale pinks and browns. Stephen thought their friendship must be the attraction of opposites.

Back in her own room, Betty said, 'Lydia's a carpenter.' Seeing Stephen's surprise, she added, 'She was one of the first women to take the training course.'

'She doesn't look like a carpenter,' Stephen commented.

Betty looked at him. 'Don't be so old-fashioned,' she said tartly.

She had put him down and he looked and felt angry. Undisturbed, Betty opened a drawer, took out a box of chocolates and offered him one. She was thinking he could probably be sharp and a little of his own medicine wouldn't do him any harm. She was curious about him and Jean, but she knew better than to ask outright. Instead she turned the conversation to her mother.

'I'm glad you had a glimpse of Mother,' she told him, making her tone friendly to put him at his ease again. 'She's much happier now, you know.' Stephen did not know, but he was too huffed to ask a question.

'It all came out accidentally,' Betty went on, not at all put out by his attitude of indifference. 'When I told them I was leaving Dick, Mum started on about Tina. I mustn't because of Tina. So I told her the truth – how I'd always known about their not getting on and what misery their deceit had caused me and how

236

much happier I would have been if I had known the truth. I tried to make her understand that I knew it all along. Dad understood at once. Poor Mum! She went into hysterics. She said I was being cruel and after all she'd done for me.'

In spite of himself, Stephen showed interest. 'What happened then?' he asked. 'Oh, in the end it all came right. Much better than I'd expected. It turned out that Mum had had that kind of upbringing where you had to earn love. Naughty girls aren't loved! She was afraid of losing my respect if I came to think of her as less than perfect. You couldn't give Mum a present or congratulate her on anything she had done. It upset her. I could never understand. All the time I was growing up, she was like that. I once bought her a replica of a plate she had admired and instead of being glad she told me I shouldn't have spent money on her.' Betty laughed. 'I burst into tears!'

She went on, 'You know what she told me recently? She said, "I felt I had to apologise for being on the earth." Imagine that! She said, "I'm not a nice person." I just gave her a tight hug and said, "You're a nice person to me!" I keep on having to reassure her she's lovable.'

'Don't you find that trying?' Stephen asked, thinking of her hatred of emotionalism.

Betty gave a shrug of her shoulders. 'Well, I can't desert her, can I? Besides, she did her best for me, according to her lights, when I was young. I've caused her to suffer since I've gone my own way.'

'You're not as hard bitten as you like to make out,' Stephen commented. He had forgiven her.

Betty turned a thoughtful gaze on him. 'The ideas we give people!' She pointed to a large brown paper parcel on a side table. 'Mum's just left that for me. It's odd pieces of material and felts; I stuff dolls and make toys for her Church bazaars. We've got that in common. We're both good with our hands.' She gave a grin. 'She likes me doing it – she thinks it helps me to be a good girl!'

They chatted on for a while, Betty insisting on making Stephen another cup of tea and finally succeeding in putting him so much at his ease that he went away thinking all the afternoon had been pleasant and quite forgetting his ticking off.

At the front door, she said, 'Don't wait so long next time!' He promised that he would not.

Going back upstairs, she thought, 'He's a bit old-fashioned, but I like him.' She remembered that he had said she was the sort of person he could talk to. She wondered how long it would be before he could bring himself to mention Jean. For she felt sure he came for that.

It was not to be at the next visit, nor the visit after that, but some six weeks later he asked after Dick.

'He's getting married quite soon,' Betty said. 'He and Susan take Tina out.'

Stephen remembered that Dick had been uneasy about Tina not knowing who was her real father. Betty laughed. 'That's nonsense!' she said. 'We don't use the term 'Uncle' here. One shouldn't tell a child someone is her uncle if he is not. We all use first names. But it's true Dick never overcame his jealousies. He hated other men being friendly with either me or Tina. He couldn't stand my speaking well of other men.'

'I should think there would be problems,' Stephen suggested.

'You tell me what kind of living together is without its problems,' Betty retorted.

Stephen was silent.

'Dick got too much out of his mother's spoiling,' Betty said, rather brusquely. 'He wanted to carry it with him into his adult life. I think he really just wanted to show that he could do his own thing – and he admired me.' Rather wistfully, she added, 'We had jolly times.' She gave a sudden, loud laugh, 'Susan will spoil Dick the same as his mother. And he knows it! You have to work at changing yourself. Dick likes himself as he is!' This seemed to amuse her a great deal.

More seriously, she told Stephen, 'I know the ultimate answer is a caring society – *our* children, not my child, but meanwhile I feel we're keeping a flame burning, showing that there can be another, more mutually concerned way of living. I just hope the problems my daughter meets with here will be more fruitful than the problems I met with in my own home – at the least make her think, not stifle her.' With honesty, she confessed, 'We're very ambivalent here sometimes, especially when children come or couples decide to marry. Outside attitudes keep forcing their way in and weakening our solidarity.'

'Well, at least you try.' Stephen remarked. He admired that side of Betty.

She nodded. 'Yes! We do try. And one thing I'm convinced of – whatever the final answer turns out to be, if there is such a thing, it won't be living in tiny groups, inward-growing. That

238

will never produce the kind of adults the world needs. Do you know what I call it?' she asked. He shook his head.

'Blood apartheid,' she said.

He thought a moment. 'That's rather a good definition,' he told her.

At that the subject dropped. They went on to talk of other things. They got round to education and Stephen found himself discussing his educational theories with some enthusiasm. Betty listened with interest.

'So you're going to be a Headmaster,' she said, smiling at him.

'If any school will have me.'

She smiled again, 'That's false modesty. You know they will!' She had put him down a second time, but in spite of this by the end of the afternoon they were both conscious of a new bond between them. They would never be dull together, never bore each other, there would always be something of mutual interest to talk about. This was a sufficiently unusual relationship for each to feel grateful to the other.

The next time Stephen visited, Tina was with her mother. At once she ran up to him. 'I know you,' she said gaily. 'You came to our other home. What's your name?' He told her.

'Well, come on, Stephen,' she said, in an imperious tone, seizing his hand. 'I want you to play ball with me in the garden.' She gave his hand a tug. Betty laughed. Stephen laughed too, for he could see the likeness to her mother in Tina's decided tones. He thought he had better comply and went not too reluctantly. They returned in about an hour, Tina very satisfied with Stephen. Betty looked at his face and thought, 'That man likes children.' Tina ran up to Betty and began to hug her, her head against her mother. Betty stroked the child's hair tenderly.

'I just hope this house will teach her that there is a choice in the way one lives,' she said, looking at Stephen over Tina's head, a note of earnestness in her voice,' *How* she chooses is up to her. I was taught there was only one way.' She bent and gave her daughter a kiss.

'Well, you're doing your best,' he said feelingly. He himself could hardly claim success in family matters. It was no use applying to him for advice. He sat brooding over this. Betty, looking at his down expression, thought to herself that somehow she would have to help him up to the starting post otherwise he

239

was never going to get there. But now she said nothing. His visits, although not close together, had become regular. She could wait confident that sooner or later he would turn up again.

When he was leaving, Tina gave him a hug and told him to come back soon and he went away reluctantly. At the first sight of her, his sorrow had awakened, but playing with her in the garden he had felt an attachment which made him think with pleasure of seeing her again.

It was only after he had been visiting for some few months more that he talked about Jean and then, as she had guessed, Betty had to help him to it. It was a Sunday and Tina was out with the other children. After he had sat for a little while, Betty made up her mind to plunge straight in.

'I went to see Jean,' she said, in her usual tone of voice, firm and clear. 'You said you didn't mind. Do you remember?' He did remember. 'She didn't mention you.' She had added this so that he should not think they had been discussing him, but it proved a perfect opening.

'Oh, she wouldn't!' Stephen answered bitterly. 'I don't exist for her.'

Betty did not know what to make of that remark, so she remained silent. She sat down opposite him, her elbow resting on the arm of her chair; cupping her chin in her hand and fixing on his face her calm gaze, she made it clear that she was willing to give him her serious, undivided attention. She was telling him that she was settled to listen and that she did not wish him to draw back. Nor did he wish to draw back. In her quiet, unattached, attentive manner, he had found the listener he had for so long needed; a listener capable of standing off, offering him a genuine, yet reticent sympathy.

Feeling safe, he started. He had made the same remarks to himself many times before and the only result had been to increase his bitterness. Now to utter them aloud to another human being gave him a sense of immense relief.

'She wouldn't speak to me,' he said. 'She wouldn't even look at me. You don't know what that is like.'

Betty looked surprised. The little she knew of Jean did not incline her to think her capable of that kind of remorselessness. It seemed to imply a serious estrangement. But as to its possible cause, she could not even hazard a guess. She knew neither of them well enough for that. With few words, she managed to convey to him a thoughtful sympathy which encouraged him to go on.

He spoke with some passion of his devotion to his wife and his son. He told her of all the help he had willingly given in the house and with Robbie. Silently Betty compared his behaviour to that of Dick. The cause could not lie in any insufficiency there.

With some difficulty, he uttered the words, 'She told me that she hated me.'

'Then she can't be indifferent to you,' Betty pointed out quietly.

This thought had never occurred to him. He held on to it for a moment.

Then, 'It wasn't just at the end. She cooled towards me months before. She didn't want me.' This was the nearest he came to saying that Jean had rejected him sexually. The bitterness of his tone told Betty much.

She felt the need to say something. 'People often don't know what impression they are giving,' she said quietly, eyeing him steadily while he sat gazing at the floor. She had a clear picture of two people very close, and then one moving away, very far away. 'Take Mother and me, now. Mum was taught that it was natural for a child to love its parents; especially its mother. She accepted the teaching. She went on accepting it as a truth when life must have told her that it was not always so. When I came along, she demanded the same *natural* affection from me. When we had it all out, I said to her, "If only you wouldn't demand my love as a right, Mum." And do you know what she said? "Do I?" She was surprised. You wouldn't believe it – she didn't know!'

'I should think it's true that a mother has a natural love for her child,' he retorted, with an increase of bitterness.

Betty hesitated, but only for a moment. No! She would not step onto that roundabout. They would finish where they had begun and she would have lost him. She stayed silent.

He went on, 'Can you imagine a mother sitting for two hours reading, not bothering to look up to see what her own child was doing? At three and a half years of age? Two hours!' Betty objected that Jean had probably exaggerated the length of the time from a sense of guilt. That was very understandable.

'No! She was very certain of the time,' he retorted. She had looked at her watch before she started to read, again when she had stopped reading.

241

'She told you that?' Betty asked, interested and with a measure of disbelief. Like Mabel, she felt it was altogether too long a time to be reading without some sort of a break.

'Yes! Exactly as I'm stating it to you.' He concluded with conviction in his tone, 'She didn't care about either of us any more. That's the simple truth. We were just burdens she had to carry. She resented that fact, you see.'

Betty didn't see, any more than Mabel had seen on an earlier occasion. Her silence encouraged him. He felt he had proved his point. 'She's unfeeling,' he said. This was not at all Betty's idea of Jean. All the same she felt at a loss. 'And after Robbie's death, she wouldn't speak to you?' she asked, to make quite sure of the facts.

'Not at once. She told me what had happened. Then she said she hated me. Then she stopped speaking to me.'

Without consciously intending it, he had omitted to mention his own reaction to the news of his son's death – the words he had then uttered. While she lay on the bed, he had said to her, 'I'm sorry I said what I did. I didn't mean it.' She had closed her eyes and stayed like that as long as he was at her side. He had thought his apology adequate in view of the consequences of her neglect. He had forgotten the words, they had sunk beneath the weight of his grief, of his resentment at her earlier treatment of himself and Robbie. But he remembered clearly Robbie's cries of distress when he was thrust from her and his words, 'She's nasty! She's nasty!' These were the words that lodged and echoed in his mind.

'She used to thrust Robbie away from her,' he told Betty. 'He used to run to me in tears. She's unfeeling!' He repeated his earlier statement with a bitter resentment. This time Betty felt the need to give him a jolt.

'If she's so unfeeling,' she asked quietly, 'why is she punishing herself?'

'Punishing herself?' he echoed, surprised.

'Yes. Don't you know she's working as a typist in an estate agent's office?'

He had not known that and he was astounded. In an instant, Betty had shot to pieces his firm idea of how Jean was living. He had unquestioningly assumed that she had gone back to her former work as a library assistant. He had a clear recollection of her early ambitions and he had taken for granted that she was steadily rising in status and responsibility, studying, taking examinations, pursuing her chosen career path. Now all his certainties lay in pieces, without shape or meaning.

Pushing her advantage, Betty added, 'There can't be a spark of interest in it for her.'

There was a long silence. Betty felt sorry for him. He looked as if he had received a shock. In her quiet tone, she suggested, 'Mothers can get angry, that doesn't mean they don't care.'

He resisted then. 'They don't push a child away – or forget its existence,' he retorted angrily. 'She chose to have a child. She didn't expect me to stay at home to look after him, did she?'

Betty stayed quiet.

'I did more about the house than most men would think of doing,' he went on resentfully, conscious of a certain lack of sympathy. 'I even used to bath the baby.'

Betty wanted to smile. Instead, she said kindly, 'I don't think it's a question of blame. When you're alone, try to think back. Perhaps something will come to you.'

She saw the dissatisfied expression on his face. From his point of view, she was turning out to be an unsatisfactory confidante. She was sorry for his sake, for she liked him, but there was no further aid she could offer – only insincerities and that she would not do, nor would he desire.

She made tea and he sat and drank, looking unhappy. She waited for his further remarks, but he stayed silent. Into the silence, she said, 'We all get ideas as to how normal people feel and behave. We all dread being thought of as not normal. But really no two of us are alike. It's a mistake to compare.' He did not answer. She added, 'My mother has lived most of her life in the shadow, the fear of judgment. She told me it was like being made to stand up against a wall and be measured to see if she had grown to the extent she ought. Her parents were cruel to her without meaning to be. We can be cruel to people without meaning to be, especially if they feel we are judging them.'

By the merest chance, and without being in the least aware of the fact, Betty had said just the right thing to awaken in Stephen a chord of memory. He suddenly recalled having used the words 'not normal' to Jean. In his anger and grief, he had said to her, 'You're not a normal woman, Jean.' He had apologised and then forgotten. Now he remembered that it was after these words that she had said to him, 'I hate you.'

Abruptly and somewhat to Betty's surprise, he got up, saying, 'I must be going.' To conceal his discomfort, he added,

'People are strange! That's all there is to it really.' And he gave a dismissive shrug of his shoulders.

After he had gone, Betty wondered if she had said too much, or, in some way not clear to her, had gone too far and whether he would stop coming. She hoped not for she valued his friendship.

Stephen returned to his flat in a state of unease. He could not have said exactly in what the unease consisted, but he was conscious of its presence. It had first stirred in him when Betty was speaking of her mother; the extraordinary suggestion that filial affection was not always natural. He had a natural affection for his own parents; especially for his mother, but also for his father. He could not see how it could be otherwise, except, of course, in circumstances of battering or drunkenness. He could not see how Betty's mother could fail to feel affection for her parents, even if they had been over-strict. He thought her image of being put up against a wall and measured very exaggerated. Yet the fact that Betty, such a sane, balanced, down-to-earth sort of a person should accept this image, worried him. He did not know why it should since the matter seemed not to relate to any happening in his own life.

Later he found himself thinking about what Betty had let drop concerning cruelty. He was the sort of man who would not knowingly act with cruelty; the thought of doing any such thing would disgust him. She had said, 'We can be cruel to people without meaning to be, especially if they feel we are judging them.' He did not believe he had ever been cruel to Jean. For one thing, he had acted scrupulously to avoid any exercise of power over her; that sort of relationship was for their parents' generation, not for themselves. He had left her absolutely free, on principle. He placed a high value on principles. It was true that he had told her she was not normal, but he had uttered the words under severe provocation and afterwards had said he was sorry. Even as he was thinking this, he felt the half-hearted nature of that apology. He had not been able to help that – it was exactly how he had seen her. Nor could he now hide from himself that it was how he saw her still. She had not behaved like a normal woman either to himself or to Robbie. She had been unkind to her own child and indifferent to him.

Betty had said, 'Think back. Perhaps something will come to you.' She had thought neither of them to blame. Well, he did think back. He thought back for most of the rest of the evening, but for the life of him he could not uncover any reason why she should have turned against him. He remembered that almost at the end she had seemed to be acting normally again. She had stopped forgetting. She had gone back to looking after himself and Robbie as well as at the first. Then had come this inexplicable neglect of Robbie in the park. He could make nothing of her behaviour. Its source remained as great a mystery as ever.

Still, he did not feel comfortable in himself. He did not feel the same confidence in the rightness of his conduct. He had lost his earlier sense of absolute virtue. The root cause of his unease lay in his having been proved wrong in his most basic certainty – he had been so sure that he knew what Jean was doing. It proved him to have been quite mistaken in his summing up of Jean's intentions, so what else could he have been wrong about?

He turned his thoughts to Betty. He had been disappointed at the way in which she had attempted to hold the scales even, yet he respected her for it. She had measured up to his idea of her character. He was right to have felt safe with her. There was something fearless in her nature which he admired. Yet he knew that she was not the sort of woman with whom he could ever be happy. She lacked tenderness; at least, that was how he put it to himself. How very unlike Jean she was. He suffered a sharp pang of loss. Betty had said that people could be cruel without meaning to be, 'especially if they feel we are judging them'. Had Jean seen him as a judge then?

He experienced a sudden, strong reversal of feeling. He got angry with himself and angry with Betty for putting such uncertainties into his clear head. He had treated Jean with more consideration than she had shown to him. On that certainty he rested for what remained of the evening.

But that night he had a dream in which they were reunited. When he awoke, his disappointment was intense. He was glad to get up. He ate his usual one slice of toast and drank his usual one cup of tea. As he left the house for work he made a fresh resolve to forget her.

CHAPTER TWENTY-THREE

IN Jean's office was a man whose official title was Chief Clerk, but who was actually much more than that. Harold had entered the firm on leaving school at fourteen. He was now almost forty. He had steadily worked his way up over the years until he had come to occupy his present position. By now he knew the business backwards. His duty was to supervise the rest of the staff. He was very strict in matters of timekeeping and was absolutely trustworthy. He did not work in the main office, but in a small room with his name on the door. He had a pleasant, quiet personality, very persuasive without being pushy. Once entrusted with the task of showing prospective buyers over houses for sale, he soon proved that he could do the job with considerable success. His manners were almost old-fashioned in their courtesy. Clients mostly took to him. Over the years he had become a valuable asset to the firm.

In spite of his privileged position, Harold was not disliked by any of the staff – although the younger women found him un-interesting and on those rare occasions when he made an attempt to chat them up, irritating. They sometimes laughed at him among themselves, but in a gently contemptuous manner rather than with malice. They found it amusing that he was a bachelor. Although he was strict, he was, in some curious way, almost invisible. This was partly due to his equitable tempera-ment, but also because he was the kind of very ordinary-looking chap who melted into his surroundings; of medium build, with brown hair and eyes, conventionally dressed, always in the same kind of grey suit with brown shoes and a grey overcoat. A kind smile gave a certain attractiveness to his face. When anyone was in low spirits or in need of a sympathetic ear, he or she could be seen talking to Harold. He lent a patient ear to any tale of woe and did not gossip afterwards about what he had been told. Jean had summed him up early on as a nice, ordinary sort of human being.

Harold had taken a liking to Jean. He thought her very attractive. He appreciated the way she lost no time in getting down to work and did not gossip like the younger girls who were always breaking off to chat to each other. She was nearer his own age than the young ones and he felt more at home with her quieter, more polite ways, but she was so withdrawn in her manner that he did not think of making any approach. From her behaviour and the way she spoke, he thought her well educated – a cut above. When applying for the job, Jean had managed to conceal quite a few of her qualifications, but even so, after reading her record, he felt a little puzzled as to why she had chosen this particular work. He thought she could do much better for herself than copy-typing. He noticed that she seemed rather on her own and he felt sorry for her.

Two years were to pass before Harold tried to interest Jean in himself. During the lunch hour most of the girls ate sandwiches and made tea in the office, then went out to shop or for a walk. Jean often stayed in for the whole break or, if she went out, came back well before the others. Then one lunch hour, Harold found her with a book. This was unusual. He pondered over the new development for some weeks, then decided to try to engage her in conversation. For some months he did not get very far. Jean was amused by this sudden attention and thought of him as 'that funny little man'. Harold could not puzzle her out. She often looked sad. Was she sad, or simply serious by nature? He could not decide. He thought her very withdrawn, but interesting. She was different from any of the other young women with whom he had come in contact. He could not satisfy himself as to why – but then, his experience of women was very limited.

'Do you read a lot?' he asked her one lunch hour, when he found her again with a book.

She hesitated a moment, then answered, 'Not all that much. Do you?'

'I'm not a bookworm,' he reassured her. 'But, yes. I often take a book out of the library. It passes the evening. Can't always be looking at the telly. Lot of rubbish often.' Jean agreed and looked down again at her book. He stood in front of her for a moment, then, as she did not look up, he retreated to his own room.

One lunch time he came back holding a paper bag with four meringues in it. He offered Jean a meringue. 'Try one,' he said, adding encouragingly, 'They're made with pure cane sugar.'

'I've just eaten my sandwiches,' Jean told him, trying to refuse so that he did not feel rebuffed.

'That's all right,' he said. 'Take one home with you.' As she hesitated, 'Go on!' he insisted, holding the open paper bag almost under her nose. 'Take two! They will do you good.' He added, 'My mum, when she was alive, always used pure ingredients. That's why I enjoy good health. I don't suffer from indigestion either. Do you?'

'No,' Jean assured him, choking back a laugh. 'Thank you,' she said, giving way to his insistence and taking one meringue. He really was a funny little man. But he was kind. She thought she liked him. When he was in the main office, she took to watching him with a mild interest. She noticed that he treated the girls considerately and was never impatient, still less rude. He dealt with all the normal squalls of office life in an equitable manner. Even when he showed annoyance, which was seldom, his voice did not alter its mild tone. She wondered why he had not become a partner. She thought of Richard – she was certain that one day he would be a partner. Perhaps it needed money.

She was to discover that the funny little man had his own peculiar brand of perseverence. It consisted in never taking 'No' for an answer. Defeated, he always returned for another attack. One lunch hour he enquired whether she did not find her routine wearying – eating sandwiches, making herself tea, reading, always on her own. Wouldn't she like a variation? He would, he told her. But there was no fun in lunching out alone. He had enough of being on his own, in the evenings. Was she on her own in the evenings? Well, not always, Jean told him. Yes, she was often. No, she did not go out a lot. On her own? Not every time – of course not. Jean was not a good liar. Harold was adept at popping in the sudden, unexpected question which took her off guard. On its own, each answer gave little away; added up, they painted a clear picture of the way she lived. She was not aware of this. Many years of dealing with clients had produced in Harold the ability to ferret out what he wanted to know without seeming to be doing so.

But at the end of all his efforts, Jean still firmly refused him. He acknowledged his defeat without letting it make any difference to his friendliness. Jean thought she had heard the last of his suggestions, but some weeks later he varied it. He had never eaten at a Chinese restaurant and he fancied trying the one that had recently opened just up the road. But, again, he did not care for eating out on his own... Jean showed her annoyance. He was not in the least abashed. Instead he gave her a little lecture.

'You shouldn't let habit rule you,' he told her in a disapproving tone. 'You should always be prepared to try something new.'

248

He had conceived the idea that Jean was lonely. He worked away at this idea. He kept on dropping hints as to how much more pleasant it was to go out occasionally with another person. After some months, his perseverance paid off. Jean had suffered an even more boring morning than was usual. She had spent three hours typing out bills. Harold chose that lunch time to renew his invitation to the Chinese restaurant. Jean hesitated. Caution advised against, but the need for a break from monotony proved the stronger. With a slight reluctance in her tone, she agreed. It felt strange leaving the office in the company of another person.

The restaurant was above a shop; a large, rather dark room, lit with wall lamps, the tables laid with white cloths and bright cutlery. There were only a few customers. They sat down near the window. Jean glanced about her and felt alarmed. She had not anticipated a posh place. She was used to a business person's Chinese cafe – glass table tops and set menus. She had omitted to tell Harold that she wished to pay for herself, but let him pay for her, she would not. He was annoyed.

'I brought you here especially to treat you,' he told her in a rather injured tone. When she told him it was a matter of principle with her, he ceased to object. Jean rose a whole point in his esteem. He fretted about what she would have to pay, but relaxed when Jean said she was not a pauper.

'I hope you'll let me treat you sometime,' he said. Jean's heart sank. He was going to take the meal as a precedent. Still, she did enjoy it, even the chat. Nor was it as expensive as she had feared. Thinking about it afterwards, it made her realise how very much alone she was. Going out with Harold was quite different from going out with Stephen – the one man did not make her think of the other. Harold's interest in food amused her. He had told her, 'I like my food cooked by a good chef and nicely set out.' Stephen had never minded what he ate.

Jean had enjoyed the change from the office just as Harold had suggested to her that she would, but when he renewed the idea she shook her head and firmly declined. He did not seem put out. Another time, he told her. She was determined that he should not think she was willing to make a habit of eating out with him. Of course the fact that the two had gone out together became an office talking point.

Here their relationship stuck for some time. When Harold varied his attack and suggested an evening out, she at once declined. She seemed to herself always to be saying 'No'. Had she known, Harold was simply making use of his business experience – the knowledge that people could be worn down. He kept on finding different reasons for her refusals.

'I don't mind if you want to pay for yourself,' he told her. Jokingly, he added, 'I don't mind if you want to pay for me!' She was surprised at his quiet persistence, but sure she would not give way. However, in the long run, to soften the blows she was always giving to his aspirations, she did agree to go to lunch again. This was what he had aimed for and he was delighted.

They tried an Indian restaurant, which was a little more expensive, but very good. Again Jean enjoyed the meal and the chat. The occasional outing became once every three weeks, then once a fortnight, finally every Wednesday. Jean began to look forward to the Wednesday – a midweek respite from endless boredom. But she still maintained her refusal to go out with Harold in the evenings. He pressed her, but she remained firm. She would not go to a theatre or concert.

One lunch hour he said, over their coffee at the Indian restaurant, 'You won't let me treat you out. I wonder if you'll let me treat you at my flat? I can cook. I'd love to give you a meal.' She shook her head without answering. He was silent for a few minutes, then he leant towards her and said in a low voice, 'I'm trustworthy, you know.' He gave her a solemn look.

It was the look more than the words which affected Jean. She burst out laughing. He was very offended. Ashamed of her laughter, and anxious to make amends, Jean hastened to say, 'Of course I'll come.'

The dinner was not good. The gravy was thin, the joint could have done with twenty minutes longer in the oven, the roast potatoes lacked crispness, but, worst of all, the whole was not much more than lukewarm. Harold apologised, saying that he had been so anxious to have everything ready on time that he had misjudged. The rice pudding was stodgy white and not much improved by tinned plums, but Jean ate what was put before her and laughingly told him not to worry, she had not expected the Savoy. Had she but known it, the whole effort had fallen under the heading of Harold's simple but very effective cunning. He knew very well that he was not a good cook. He thought all women were endowed by nature with a special cooking ability lacking in the male genes – except, of course, in the case of top chefs at top hotels. He was hoping that the meal

250

would convince Jean of the necessity to give him a helping hand. He was not lazy and very willing to learn, but the thought of trying his hand had never entered his head while his mother was alive to answer all his needs.

'I should like to improve my cooking,' he told Jean with frankness.

'Was your mother a good cook?' she asked him, to avoid the necessity for a direct answer.

He talked about his mother for a good ten minutes. He was still living with her when she had died some three years before. He still missed her a great deal. He gazed round the room as if he expected she might suddenly materialise.

'When you've been close to a person it's very hard getting used to living without them,' he said in a rather pathetic voice.

'Yes,' Jean said, 'I know it is.'

'Do you still miss your husband?' he asked. Jean told him that her husband was still alive, but she was anticipating that any time now he would seek a divorce. Harold was surprised at this information.

'I thought you were a widow,' he said. When Jean shook her head, he did not try to probe. She liked him for that. An unspoken, mutual sympathy was born at that moment.

'I should think you were a good son,' she told him. He said he hoped he had been.

'Was your mother ill for a long time?' she asked.

'About a year,' he said. 'She was incontinent and I could have had her put in a home. But of course I wouldn't do a thing like that. I was given some nursing help during the day and the remainder of the time I managed.' He said this without self-pity or any lingering on the unpleasantness. Jean felt an added respect for him.

After the meal, he insisted on doing the washing up himself and made her sit in an armchair, got a stool for her feet, draped a shawl around her shoulders as he said there was a draught, and generally fussed over her. 'I don't want you to get a cold,' he said. When she tried to laugh him away, he insisted on her keeping the shawl. Then he went into the kitchen to make the coffee.

'I respect women,' he told her over the coffee. It was the sort of remark he was apt to come out with. He brought out photographs of his mother to show her. Then he put on some records of favourite classics. Afterwards he asked her if she was interested in different kinds of fish. Jean said she did not know much about it, but she thought she could be.

'I've done a lot of fishing,' he told her. 'I belong to an angling club. I've done all kinds – from a boat and on the bank.' It turned out that he had quite a small library on the subject and could talk about different kinds of fish so as to interest a lay person. Jean was quite fascinated.

'I've got a number of hobbies,' Harold said, not without a touch of vanity, 'but angling is my chief hobby.' He got out his different kinds of rods and explained the purposes for which each was used. 'Mum used to dress the fish when I was in luck,' he said, with a note of regret in his voice. 'She knew what sauce went with what fish.' Jean was amused at this, but was careful not to smile.

She stayed for an early cup of tea before saying firmly she really must go. 'I shall be out the next two Sundays,' she told him as she was leaving. This was not true, but she did not want him to think she might be lonely at the weekends and so encourage him to aim for a closer relationship than had already seemingly developed on its own. She added, 'If you're free in three weeks' time, I'll cook you a lunch at my place. You can learn from that.' He thanked her with obvious pleasure.

After she had gone, there formed in his mind a vague idea that perhaps he might have met someone who was in a similar situation to himself and that there might exist a common solution to a common problem.

Meanwhile Jean had arrived home, taken off her outdoor things and settled down in front of the television. She hoped that she had not given Harold the impression that she was friendless. This latter would in any case not have been strictly true since she went up to London with Mabel, to a cinema or theatre matinee about once every three months and she visited Betty and Lydia or they visited her about every six weeks. To her surprise they seemed to have taken a liking to her. But she felt, not without reason, that this was little enough to live on.

She forgot for quite a while to turn on the set. Instead she sat musing over her day out. There was no denying she had enjoyed herself. She thought, 'He's very nice! He really is.' She liked the way he had helped her on and off with her coat and opened the doors for her. She liked his concern lest she should catch a cold and his fussing ways. Only she did not think of his ways as fussing, but as considerate. She had found it pleasant to

252

be the centre of so much attention. It had made her feel she mattered.

During the next three weeks, mostly at work, Jean filled in quite an amount of time thinking what to give Harold for his promised dinner. Her work had long become automatic. Often she did not know what it was she was typing and could not have said had she been asked afterwards. She had very little else to think about – she lived such a very limited life.

When the Sunday finally arrived, she discovered that she was quite nervous. She had decided on a typical English Sunday dinner, but cooking had never been her strong point and she seemed to have forgotten most of what she had learnt with such effort in her housekeeping days. She had a feeling that Harold, in spite of his good nature, could be critical. About five minutes before he was expected, she got into a flap thinking she had burnt the greens and the room would smell of them, but luckily she had rescued them just in time.

Harold arrived to the minute. She hastened to offer him a drink. He ate everything she put in front of him and praised her cooking fulsomely. 'Almost as good as my mother's,' he told her, with just a hint of condescension as he accepted a second helping of Yorkshire pudding. When it came to the apple charlotte, he gave as his opinion that it was very nice, not too sweet, but went on to say that his mother usually added lemon juice.

This remark annoyed Jean. 'Well, your mother didn't cook this dinner,' she retorted, rather tartly.

Harold was full of apologies. 'I didn't mean to offend you,' he told her. He went on apologising until Jean wished she had kept quiet. He insisted on washing up.

After that he came every other Sunday for cooking lessons. He took the lessons seriously and after some weeks was able to dish up a good meal for them both. As his birthday came about then, Jean bought him a cookery book which he studied and used. He applied himself to the art of cookery as seriously as he had earlier applied himself to the study of the estate agent business. Jean found his earnest approach amusing, but she took care not to show it. She had discovered that he could not take a joke at his own expense. Instead she congratulated him profusely – he was like a little boy who had to be praised before he could do his best. Still, when he said to her, as he did from time to time, 'You cook almost as well as Mum did,' she experienced a glow of pleasure. She knew there was no higher praise and it made her feel of value.

When Harold, in his turn, put in front of her a meal which had cost him time and effort, she felt herself a person of importance.

Once, when Harold was at her flat, he noticed a discarded electric fire in a corner of the room. Jean told him it was not working any longer, she intended taking it down to the local authority dump. He took a look at it.

'It only needs a new part,' he said. He would get the part and fix it when he came again.

Jean was surprised. 'I didn't know I could buy a spare part – I don't know anything about electricity,' she confessed. He gave her an elementary lesson which she found interesting.

He got the part during the week and fitted it the next Sunday. The appliance lit as soon as he tested it.

'You've saved me a lot of money,' she told him, pleased. He was gratified.

'I'll do anything that needs doing,' he said, 'Just let me know.'

After he had gone, Jean found herself thinking how useful it was to have a man to turn to again. Harold's friendship had acquired value in her eyes – for it never occurred to her to think of him in any other way than as a friend. Gradually she came to feel sure of him. It had taken her much longer to feel sure of Stephen because she had been in love with him. This sense of security made it easier for her to say 'No' when he made suggestions which for reasons of her own she did not wish to agree to.

'I like to walk along the Embankment and look at the river traffic. Why don't you want to go?' he asked her. When Jean merely shook her head, he thought her unreasonable and decided that it was because she was a woman. He had had little close contact with women, but he knew that with the sole exception of his mother they were all unreasonable. His only other 'young lady' had been equally assertive – only not when it came to paying for herself. That was before she had cooled off – he still bore the scars of that jilting.

When, in spite of her refusals, Harold remained his constant self, making her feel important and necessary to him, Jean took him even more for granted. When he grumbled, she tended to laugh. There was a certain casualness about her manner of which she herself was unaware.

One day Harold asked, 'Why can't we have a firm date – say every other Sunday, like we had when you were teaching me to cook? I never know when you're going to see me and when you're not.'

'I never know what I'm doing,' she answered. When she said she was going out, she never told him where or with whom.

'You're a slippery eel,' he retorted, peeved.

She laughed at the fishing metaphor. When he looked annoyed, she gave him a date, but she maintained her resistance to any closer tie. One week she offered him a Saturday, the next week a Sunday, then she had no spare day for two weeks. The more he tried to lasso her, the more determinedly she evaded him. And Harold, always conscious of his dignity, felt insulted. But Jean went on thinking of him as a natural bachelor – it did not occur to her that he might harbour other ideas. The fact that the office staff tittered about them did not disturb her. He was like a safe father who took away a part of her loneliness without in any way disturbing her emotional peace. She never allowed herself to consider the future. That would have involved making plans. She wanted only to carry on indefinitely as she was doing. In a vague but certain way Harold was part of that indefinite future. He would be there.

And then, suddenly and without warning, he was not there any more. He was seriously ill and was rushed off to hospital for a major operation. His removal was like a wide crack opening across the entire width of a hitherto safe road. The smooth movement of her day to day existence was stopped. She had nothing to look forward to – nothing to think about to lessen the boredom at work. She missed the Wednesday lunch outings. The weekends became empty and long. Even those habits of Harold which had irritated her, she now missed, especially his fussing persistence. Suddenly nobody asked her what she was doing at the weekend, or felt bothered if the answer was 'Nothing'. Nobody asked for her company during the week. The office staff went their usual ways without regard to her. She was solitary among them as before Harold had started to take an interest.

Only when she learned that Harold was out of danger did she breathe freely again. Even then she worried. Every visiting period when she was not at work, saw her at his bedside. She came always with a gift of fruit or flowers. He only had to mention his liking for a particular fruit drink and she was sure to produce it at the next visit. She wanted to know everything that the doctors had said. When he told her, 'The doctors say I've got to be careful what I eat,' she hastened to reassure him, 'Don't worry about that. I'll see to whatever is necessary.' Her anxiety was obvious. To the other patients, when she had gone, Harold referred to her as 'my girl'.

On discharge day, Jean got leave of absence and called for him in a taxi. At his flat, she made him put his feet up and fussed round him. She had prepared a meal according to the hospital diet sheet. She undertook all the shopping, cooking and general chores during the months he was convalescent. She did all his washing and ironing. There seemed nothing she would not do for him. He had only to express a wish and she rushed to make it come true. To Harold it was as if his mother had come back from the dead to look after him.

When finally he was discharged from hospital care, all this expenditure of effort on Jean's part should have stopped, but it did not, although Harold was decent enought to insist on seeing to his own meals. Jean continued to keep an eye on his welfare and went on doing his shopping and washing and ironing. Harold's illness had given her a good fright and she became suddenly amenable to all his suggestions.

Harold seized his opportunity very much as he would have done had a previously resistant client begun to show signs of wobbling. He pressed his advantage with professional caution. First he suggested that they resume their Wednesday lunches – she at once agreed. Encouraged, he suggested that they go to the theatre one evening – she agreed. He went a little further. He suggested that they make an evening out a weekly event, it would help him recover his zest for life. She agreed without hesitation. Finally he suggested that they make Sunday a firm date. Without any sign of hesitation, she agreed.

Her continued anxiety about his health flattered his vanity. He savoured the pleasure of revenge. He became aware that she was afraid of losing him and this knowledge made him bold. One evening he dared to kiss her. He never attempted to go further because he considered sex before marriage as a sign of moral laxity. When Jean responded in a half-hearted manner, he was satisfied. But he had become ambitious. He had long felt a justified pride in the fact that he had made such a success of his working life without any of the advantages enjoyed by so many. Jean was a well-educated, attractive young woman. He

256

was aware that the young girls in the office tittered among themselves about his bachelorhood. Well, he would show them! He was not entirely self-centred. Marriage would be a good thing for Jean as well. Of course there was the divorce, but she had been separated for some years so the obstacle was slight. She must have gone through a lot – he would make her happy.

Had Jean been less on her own, the separation might have given her an opportunity to stand back and take a serious look at the quality of the relationship into which she had allowed herself to drift. Instead the opposite happened. The bonds were drawn tighter.

When one Sunday, during dinner at her flat, he leaned over the table towards her and said, 'When you get this divorce, what about you and me getting together?' she knew what he meant and found herself giving an ambivalent, almost acquiescent, answer.

'We'll discuss it when the time comes,' she told him.

'That suits me!' he answered with emphasis. His triumphant tone told her that he was taking her reply as an assent. In his thoughts, they were now unofficially engaged. Her knowledge of how he had understood her words caused her some discomfort, but she could not bring herself to raise any doubts. She was too afraid of losing him.

After he had left, she even found herself giving his hopes serious consideration. There was a lot to be said for a partnership which protected her from loneliness within a cocoon of appreciation and need – without any of the harassment and pain of a passionate relationship.

CHAPTER TWENTY-FOUR

ONE Saturday morning, while Jean was cleaning her flat, a ring came at the doorbell. She was both surprised and pleased to see Dick. 'Hello!' she exclaimed with warmth in her voice. 'Nice to see you again after all this time.' She had retained her soft spot for her brother. Now he sat himself in the only arm-chair, stretching his legs out and gazing round with a proprietary air.

'Not a bad pad,' he said approvingly.

Now in his thirties, Jean thought her brother looked quite a bit older. He had broadened out and had an altogether more settled air. 'How many years is it?' Jean asked incautiously.

'You should know!' Dick retorted. 'You've been living like a hermit.' His voice had a sarcastic edge. The old roughness between himself and his sister was still there.

There was a short silence between them, while each viewed the other. Dick was thinking that Jean had lost some of her youthful attractiveness. He almost said so, but remembered in time that women were sensitive to that sort of remark. It was true that Betty had never shown any such sensitiveness, but he did not question the usual ideas on the subject.

Jean poured him out a glass of sherry.

'I suppose you know Betty and I have gone our separate ways?' he asked.

Jean nodded.

'We're not enemies,' Dick assured her.

Jean smiled. 'Of course not!' Dick would never summon up the energy needed to hate anyone – besides, he was not vindictive. She knew Betty still cared for him, but not so keenly as to make hatred on her part likely. 'How are you and Susan getting on?' she asked. 'I hear Betty has moved back to her old place.'

Dick nodded. 'Yes. She's taken Tina with her. I don't approve of that. I think Tina should have been left with me. Susan could have looked after her and Betty could have seen her whenever she wanted. I think it was selfish of her.'

Jean looked at him in silence.

Dick went on, 'Susan and I will be getting wed in a few weeks time. That's why I came – to let you know.' He added, in a satisfied tone, 'Susan's just right for me. Betty never was.'

'I know,' Jean said. This annoyed Dick, as, too late, she realised it would do.

'I don't see how you could know,' he answered shortly, 'but, of course, you always do know, don't you!' He had the decency not to mention Jean's own marriage, although the thought did enter his mind. In a defensive tone, he went on, 'Betty was awfully self-willed, you know. And I was very young. I would never have done it otherwise. Still it was an experience. I don't regret it. Only I'd rather Tina had a proper upbringing in a

258

proper home.' He chose to forget all that he had previously said about possessiveness and power.

'You gave me a real surprise that time,' Jean said. She could see that he was pleased.

His tone became more genial, less defensive. 'A sowing of wild oats, I suppose! Anyway, now I want a proper set-up.' Jean thought he was saying he wanted stability. He had never had it as a child, nor, it seemed, with Betty.

'Susan won't live with me until we are married,' he told Jean. 'I don't mind, if that's what she wants.' Jean was surprised. She wondered what difference a marriage ceremony could possibly make to the quality of a relationship – it certainly had not helped Stephen and herself.

Dick spoke of Susan's attitude with pride. 'She doesn't play hard to get,' he assured Jean. 'She likes me and she's loyal. But you'll see for yourself.' And he went on to deliver a greeting from Susan with a warm wish to meet her future sister-in-law. Jean was delighted.

'You can see Susan at my flat,' Dick said. 'She comes over – she's getting things ship-shape. Betty was never very good at that side of things, you know.' Jean thought of Betty's room with its warm, bright colours. Her brother had never had more to complain of than muddle.

Dick drank a second glass of sherry, enquired how Jean was getting on, and was satisfied with her formal answers. 'I saw Stephen some time ago,' he said, in a tone as if he was referring to a rather distant mutual relation. 'I met him by accident and asked him home. I was surprised when he visited. He's seen Betty a few times since. He seems to like her.'

'I know,' Jean said. She did not ask any questions about the visit.

'Betty never could keep anything to herself,' he objected. At the same time he was thinking, 'She's just as superior in her attitude as she always was.' He had imagined that the failure of Jean's marriage would have humbled her a little. He always mistook his sister's reticence for pride. His own nature being simple and straightforward, when he met people who did not open up as easily as he did, he put them down as toffee-nosed.

'How is Mum?' Jean asked. Dick told her that both their parents were well and that they both spoiled Tina.

'I'd like to see them,' Jean said. Dick shook his head vigorously. 'I wouldn't try! They're both very nasty about you.'

He added, 'There's no need to worry about Mum.' Now she was working full time, bringing in quite a lot of money, she was able to look after herself.

'She always did have spirit,' Jean said. It had been the independence money brings which was lacking.

A date for Jean and Susan to meet was fixed and Dick got up to go. 'I'll be out when you come,' he said at the door, adding condescendingly, 'You won't need me to natter.'

While she was finishing her cleaning, Jean thought about her brother. He had left his home without any difficulty. He had survived his time with Betty unscathed, and Betty would not try to get her revenge. From the little she had learned about Susan she was hopeful that Dick would be happy at this second attempt. Life had been kind to him – no wonder he looked in good health, relaxed and self-satisfied.

As for Dick, he was not indifferent to his sister's happiness, nor careless of what she might have been through, but he felt himself unable to understand the complexities of her marriage and its failure. Jean was like that – always had been – took life too seriously. The point was to learn to live it. He put her trouble down to too much education. He himself was proof that one could get on very well in life without all that book learning.

That same afternoon Lydia called. Jean greeted her with genuine warmth. At school she had only had Rita for an intimate. She had never felt able to ask anyone to the house and so, when she received an invitation, she had always found an excuse not to accept. By the time she reached the polytechnic she had become very reserved. Then, when she met Stephen, their relationship had quickly cut out anyone else. She was beginning to enjoy her new women friends with whom she felt she had much more in common than with Rita.

'I've come to ask if you'd like to join me at a witches' weekend,' Lydia said, laughing. She was going to a course at one of those country houses set in large grounds which are used for educational purposes. She had chosen *Witches in English History*.

'It's a subject that interests Betty and myself,' she said, adding that Betty could not come. Jean hesitated, but the temptation proved too strong. Before she could change her mind, she broke her taboo – Yes! she would go. Then she remembered there was a problem – Harold. She had never cancelled their agreed Sunday date before. She explained this to Lydia showing her disappointment on her face.

'Surely he won't mind if you say how much you'd like to go?' Lydia queried. Jean thought of Harold's kindness – of course he wouldn't mind.

'He won't mind,' she said. 'He's very kind.'

Lydia had known vaguely that there was a man in Jean's life, but never having met Harold he had remained a dim figure, not of much significance. Now she was curious and was pleased when Jean said that he was coming to take her to the cinema and, if Lydia liked to stay, she could introduce them to each other.

They had tea and chatted. Harold arrived about six o'clock. He thought of it as 'taking Jean out' and Jean herself had come to think of it in that way, in spite of the fact that she always paid for herself.

Jean introduced her friends to each other. They shook hands. Harold looked embarrassed. He was a bit put out to find Lydia there. He took it for granted that Jean would be on her own, waiting for him, when she knew he was coming, but he concealed his annoyance under an amiable manner, making an effort to be gentlemanly towards Lydia.

'I wish I'd known you were going to be here,' he said. 'I'd have brought some chocolates for the three of us.' Lydia thought that very quaint.

Lydia was surprised that Jean took such a long time coming to the point. She got the impression that Jean did not know how to tell Harold that she would be away for a weekend. When she did, it was almost as if she was asking his permission. 'I hope you won't mind,' she said, in an apologetic tone. 'It's a chance, Lydia's going, and the subject interests me.'

'What? Witches!' Harold was incredulous. He could not see anything interesting in witches. He thought it a silly subject. He nearly said so, but stopped himself just in time. 'I don't mind if you're so keen,' he told her, trying for a friendly tone, but his voice sounded as if he had made an effort. Jean ought not to go off on a Sunday.

They chatted on for a little while, then Lydia said she must be going. 'I'll book up then?' she asked, as she was leaving.

'Yes,' Jean answered. Lydia thought she looked a bit uncomfortable. When she got back she looked in on Betty and told her the result of her visit. 'Jean said he was kind, but he didn't like her going off without him. He tried hard to conceal the fact, but it showed.' She added, 'He's got quite a polite gentlemanly kind of style, but I think he's probably possessive and expects to be put first.'

'Is she serious, do you think?' Betty asked.

'She may be – she certainly found it difficult telling him.' Thoughtfully Lydia added, 'I can't see him as right for her. It's a bit of a puzzle.'

'*She's* a bit of a puzzle,' Betty commented.

The afternoon arrived for Jean to visit Susan. She had an idea that Susan might be the sort of person who took note of how people dressed and she wanted to be liked so she put on one of her better frocks, dusty pink in a silky material with a graceful line. She thought the colour suited her and would make her look less peaky.

She took care not to arrive before three-thirty, as agreed. While she was waiting on the doorstep, she found herself wondering whether her own idea of Susan would square with that of Dick and Betty. She had a shrewd idea of Dick's expectations and Betty had said that Susan was a 'nice, kind, home-loving sort of a girl – Dick's sort'.

Then the door opened to reveal Susan. She was in her late twenties, a few years younger than Dick, slightly on the short side, plumpish, with brown hair and brown eyes. When she smiled, her eyes as well as her mouth smiled and her face took on a very pleasant expression. She was the sort of young woman who would not be remembered for any outstanding feature, but who would be at once recognised when she smiled. She was dressed in a well-worn pair of brown slacks and a loose-fitting red jersey.

'Hello,' she said cheerily. 'Come on in.' As Jean followed her in, she was thinking that if first impressions held true, then here was the type of partner she had always imagined for Dick.

Inside the living room, Susan said, 'You've got the same nose as Dick, and there's a similarity about the right side of your face – not the left.' Jean felt slightly embarrassed beneath such a scrutinising gaze.

'Which side do you like best?' she enquired, laughing. Susan laughed herself then.

'Sorry!' she apologised. 'I didn't mean to be rude. I suppose I'm interested, you being Dick's sister.'

Jean felt the words as a kind of welcome. She took off her coat, feeling a bit silly in her best frock, and Susan whisked her coat away, hanging it up on a hook in the hall and returning to the room in a trice.

Looking at her on the doorstep Jean had summed her up as a placid, very comfortable personality, perhaps a little indolent, but now that she had suffered Susan's close scrutiny and witnessed her coat carried off with a brisk step, she saw that her first impression would have to be modified. Susan might enjoy an equitable temperament, but she was also observant. Nevertheless the comfortable, kindly side was very real. She showed it in the warmth of her welcome and her attention to Jean's comforts.

'I guess you're thirsty after your journey,' she said, and she went at once to put on the kettle for a cup of tea. Whereas Mabel carried off the duties of hostess with a too obvious expenditure of nervous energy, all Susan's movements were relaxed.

Although Jean had only met Susan about ten minutes ago, she was already at her ease with her. Over the tea, she asked Susan about herself – she thought there had probably not been anything very painful in her life, and because of this she would be able to talk about herself without becoming tense or embarrassed. She was right in the second supposition, but quite wrong in the first, as Susan quickly made clear.

'My parents were killed in a road accident when I was very young,' she told Jean. She had been six years old, and the only child. There were no relatives, so she had been brought up in a children's home. Susan did not tell her story with any emotional overtones; she spoke about her childhood in the rather forbidding charity home in a tone which implied that what had happened to her was not unusual. Had she been unhappy? Susan said she thought she had not been especially unhappy, but not very happy either. On the whole she would have preferred foster parents, but fostering was not so much accepted then as now. She said this without any kind of self-pity. She went on to tell Jean that she was working in a light engineering factory. She liked her work – it was repetitive, but she could chat to the other women. The factory was light and airy, the work clean and the canteen food had improved a lot since there had been a strike and a new cook had taken over.

'We have two choices now,' she said, referring to the meals. She and Dick had met on a dance floor.

'Like our Dad and Mum,' Jean told her. 'They both loved

dancing when they were young.' It struck her as odd talking about her parents in this familiar manner and yet not being free to visit them. She did not mention this to Susan. Instead she asked, 'Is that why you're so keen on a home and family of your own?' In the course of their conversation, Dick had said, 'Susan wants two children. And she's very keen on having a nice home.' Jean had rather resented that last remark, suspecting an implied criticism of Betty.

'I'd like a couple of kids, yes,' Susan agreed, 'and I want to make a cosy home for Dick.' Jean said she could understand.

'I wanted that even before I met Dick – children, I mean,' Susan said. 'But no rules or regulations – I've had my fill of those.' That was the only critical remark she made of the Home. She went on, 'Oh, I know Dick's probably lazy about the house, but I don't mind that. Most men are lazy at home. As long as he brings in the money, I'll see to the rest. I think he's patient and kind, you see.' She added, with a laugh, 'I like decorating anyway!'

Jean's idea of Susan took on an added dimension. She had certainly sorted Dick out and she knew how to plan ahead. As if reading her thoughts, Susan said, 'I know I don't easily get upset, but I have my priorities. I feel it's a great responsibility bringing up children. I can't understand those women who want to rush off to work and leave their children – not unless they need the money, of course. I say, why have children in the first place?' As Jean made no comment, she went on, 'I hope to be able to help out at home. I've been to craft classes for some years now. I'm rather good at patchwork. I've sold quite a few cushions and I want to try a small bed quilt – perhaps for a child.'

Jean said she admired people who were good with their hands.

'Oh, it's not the hands,' Susan corrected her. 'That's the least of it! I find the sewing part very relaxing. I usually listen to music. No, the problem is deciding on the pattern and blending in the colours. That partly depends on what you've got, of course. I enjoy collecting. I buy from jumbles, and remnants, ends of rolls, and so on, in shops. I lay the pieces out on a small table and look at them each time I go by. Then, one day, perhaps after weeks, I get an idea for a pattern and the shading. I mark it out on the material. The sewing is easy.'

Jean said she thought so far as she was concerned, the sewing

264

would be prison work. Susan found the remark amusing. 'I shall have to take you to some craft exhibitions,' she told Jean. It was clear that her new sister-in-law had ignored some of the great pleasures of life and needed educating.

In not seeking to probe into Jean's past life, Susan showed another nice side of her nature. She knew from Dick that Jean had been through the trauma of a failed marriage. It never entered her head to be critical.

She let Jean know she was concerned about Tina. Jean did her best to reassure her. One could never tell with children, but she thought Tina would be all right. Dick and Betty were not nasty to each other and Tina had always known a sense of security. 'I think she'll be able to absorb this particular jolt,' she told Susan. 'In a way, if it had to happen, she's rather lucky, you know. She'll have what amounts to two mothers.'

Later they had a full tea. Susan enjoyed being hospitable. She cut Jean a large slice of her own home-made coconut cake. 'I like cooking,' she told Jean. 'Do you?'

Jean gazed at the beautifully risen cake. She told Susan she only cooked from necessity. Susan seemed to find this surprising – much as Dick had found it surprising when Stephen had said he did not like beer. 'Oh, what a pity!' she said, 'Cooking is a large part of the pleasure of life for me.' Jean commented that Dick was very lucky. He liked his food, especially sweet things. She thought of the time when he had eaten up all his birthday cakes before finally leaving home without a word to his mother.

'I'm so glad Tina isn't a tug-of-war child,' Susan commented.

'Dick doesn't row,' Jean told her. Susan took this as a compliment, although it had not been meant that way.

Hesitatingly, Susan suggested, 'I think Betty overwhelmed him.' She did not make this remark with malice. She had only met Betty on two occasions, but that had been her impression. Jean also thought this, but she made no comment. She would have liked to say to Susan that Dick had been lucky in Betty and did not appreciate his luck. She had not borne him malice when he had ceased to care for her, nor tried to create hostility between father and child – both of which sometimes happened. But she said nothing because she did not want to distress Susan. As for why Dick retained such a hold on Betty's affections – well, she would have to know a lot more than she did about Betty's own life experiences to understand that. But she

265

admired her fortitude and was sad that she seemed the only one who did.

They continued to chat after the tea things had been cleared away. Susan's undemanding, easy manners made time pass quickly. 'I think there's nothing more important than giving children a happy childhood,' Susan said, going back to what was at present her main interest. 'It sets them up for whatever they may have to face later in life.'

'I didn't know you were a philosopher,' Jean said, smiling. Like so many articulate people, she often made the mistake of confusing silence with lack of thought.

Perhaps something of this attitude came across to Susan, for she said in a defensive voice, 'Oh, you mustn't think I haven't got a serious side. I have – Dick has too. He's quite a philosopher, as you call it.'

This statement surprised Jean. She did not know this other side of her brother, who had early contracted a habit of shutting up in front of his sister. Susan went on, 'He doesn't say much and gives the impression he's not thinking. But he's really quite thoughtful. He told me all about his time in the commune and why he wanted to leave. He's very interesting when he gets going. He talks to me a lot, about all kinds of things. He says he's never been able to talk to any girl the way he can talk to me. That's nice, isn't it?'

'Very!' Jean answered, suddenly envious of Dick's good fortune.

Hesitatingly, Susan said, 'I don't slap him down, you see. I listen to what he has to say.' With a sudden boldness in her tone, she added, 'I take him seriously. You don't have to be well educated to hold sensible opinions, and be worth listening to – and learning from!'

Jean felt rebuked. She thought it unfair of her brother to have talked about her to Susan. He ought not to have given her preconceived ideas. But she remained silent.

Instead she asked, 'Will you stay on at the factory after you're married?'

'I'll have to for a time,' Susan answered. 'We've talked it out. We want to modernise the flat before we start a family. That will take money – even do-it-yourself is not cheap.' She looked round the room. 'And I do want my own colour scheme.' Jean followed Susan's eyes. How strange to be in Betty's room without Betty. How different it would look after its transformation.

She wondered if she would feel so much at home in it when it was all neat and newly painted.

'Dick is going to see to the ceilings and the kitchen – we'll need new cupboards, the present ones have woodworm,' Susan told her. The idea of Dick decorating did not come easily to Jean.

'I shall paint the walls,' Susan was saying. And then, as if penetrating Jean's thoughts, 'Dick isn't lazy when he's interested, you know. I think he'll be quite proud of his home when it's all finished.' Jean had a vision of her brother in the process of transformation.

At the door, Susan suddenly threw her arms round Jean, kissed her warmly, and said, 'You'll come to visit us quite often, won't you? We shall expect you. You don't have to wait until I leave work. Weekends are free – we shan't be working on the flat all the time. And remember, when the children come, you'll be their aunt, their only aunt, so they'll want you to take them out.'

At the corner of the road, Jean turned and looked back. Susan was still standing on the doorstep, looking after her. Jean waved and Susan waved back. Jean turned the corner. She sat on the bus in thought. Dick would prove a good provider – he was not lazy at work. Jean thought how lucky Susan was. She was cut out exactly right for the role society demanded of her. There was no doubt that she was happy and that her happiness gave a glow to her personality.

She forgave Susan her lack of understanding for women who felt differently, and whose needs were different, and who yet desired a husband and family just as much as men desired a wife and children. She knew from her own life that, for a person who was fulfilled and content, there was nothing more difficult than to enter into the feelings of another person who appeared to insist on being perversely unhappy.

CHAPTER TWENTY-FIVE

JEAN prepared for her study weekend with a keen sense of pleasure – it was so long since she had enjoyed any mental stimulus. Also she was drawn to Lydia's quiet voice and manner. She did not know that it was Lydia who had suggested to Betty that they call now and then so as to be on hand if needed. Had she known, she would have thought it typical of her. Without admitting it to herself, she was glad of the break from Harold. The fact that her companion was a woman gave her an added and welcome feeling of relief from pressure.

Five minutes before time she stood on the pavement outside her flat, suitcase in hand. Lydia arrived at the wheel of a small van which she and Betty had clubbed together to purchase.

'Hop in,' she said cheerily.

The weather was more like April than early May; showery, with thin light clouds and glints of sun. Until the London traffic was left behind, they were silent. Then they began to talk. Jean did not think Lydia would mind if she asked a few personal questions – she liked her sufficiently to want to know more about her.

'Totally uninteresting!' Lydia told her, with a laugh. 'No drama – solid middle class background, both my parents are doctors.' She had trained for social work. 'Until they started talking about "inadequates" and getting people "to accept reality". Then I thought, "That's it! Out!"' She had been interested in carpentry at school, envied the boys, so had gone to a training centre. 'I don't know if I'd have done it if I'd known what I was letting myself in for – from the men, I mean – but now I'm glad I stuck it. When I pass a block of flats and think, "Part of *my* work is in there," I feel really good.'

Jean wanted to know if it was very difficult being the only woman on a job normally done by men. Were the men hostile?

'Some are,' Lydia said. 'They like to play tricks, like handing you a cup of tea with a huge black spider floating on top. But the decent ones are more of a trial – you feel you mustn't be nasty to them. They offer to show you how to do jobs you did successfully in your trainee days. Qualifications don't count because the men won't believe that you can do the work as well as they can. You have to prove yourself. But you get your reward. I worked once on a large council housing estate and I had women come up to me and say, "Good for you! It's great seeing women in this kind of job." That used to make my day.'

Lydia turned into a side lane. They were well away from the built-up areas now. 'Let's get some air,' she said. They got out and walked up and down, breathing the diesel-free atmosphere.

'I wonder why I choose to live in a town,' Jean said. 'It's so fresh and quiet here.' Lydia said she'd soon get tired of it.

They arrived in time for lunch. The drive up to the Georgian-style country mansion, standing in large grounds, was lined with tall bushes of white rhododendrons. Having disposed of the car, the two made for the front entrance. Inside the hall was a notice board with information sheets pinned up. They got the key to their room from the reception desk and went upstairs to the second floor. In their room, they found a middle-aged woman with a tanned face, busy unpacking. It turned out that she was from Norfolk and worked a farm with her husband. 'All sorts come,' she told them.

From that moment it seemed to Jean that time took wing. She could not believe any weekend could pass so swiftly. There were lectures, group discussions, chats at the bar, at meals and during strolls in the open air. Then there was the excitement of getting to know students from varied backgrounds, of all ages and many different occupations, with sometimes unexpected points of view.

On the Sunday Jean woke early, dressed quietly so as not to disturb her bed-mates, and went for a walk in the grounds. They spread some way and she had not seen the parts furthest from the house. The air was cool, real English weather – light clouds and shafts of sun with now and then drops of rain. It was pleasant to walk very fast and to feel the rapid beat of her heart and a slight breathlessness. She felt better. Perhaps one day she would be well again.

Suddenly she came on a lake. It was the first time she had gone near a lake since the day Robbie had drowned. Now she stood at the edge and looked down into the water – deep, clear and still. As she stood, two drakes flew over, wings beating, long necks outstretched. She turned and retraced her steps. She was ready for breakfast.

On the way back Lydia asked, 'Did you think it worthwhile? Did you enjoy yourself?'

Jean answered with enthusiasm. It was a long time since she had met so many different people and listened to such interesting conversations. Her only criticism was, 'It was over too soon!' She had not realised that witch hunts were a part of the social control of women.

'Rather!' Lydia said. 'You and I would have been 'for it' in those days. We're everything we ought not to be – we're

269

enjoying ourselves without men, daring to have our own ideas, going about on our own, living on our own – altogether too independent.' Jean was silent. Her imagination felt the heat.

Again Lydia stopped the car in a country lane and they got out for a stroll. 'You're not in a hurry to get back are you?' she asked. Jean thought of Harold. She felt certain he was waiting for her in her flat; she had lent him the key. She hesitated. Lydia took her silence for consent. They passed a solitary farmhouse and Jean wondered how it would feel to live in that lonely spot. On the way out she had been attracted to the quiet, but now she wanted people.

'It's not lonely to them,' Lydia said. 'It's full of living creatures, from cattle to birds and even insects. They'd feel lonely where *we* live.' Glancing at Jean she went on, 'You look a lot better than when you came. Much more *alive.*'

Jean was not pleased. She flushed. 'I don't go about dead!' she retorted. She was piqued, but she knew Lydia had spoken the truth – more alive was exactly how she did feel. She also felt that in two days she had become younger. Had she looked back, she would have recognised this sense of renewed youth. She had experienced it on the afternoon that Robbie had drowned. Nevertheless, she said resentfully, 'I don't know why you should say such a thing.'

But Lydia would not draw back. She had waited for such an opportunity. 'You often behave a lot older than your age,' she commented. 'As if you lacked energy. Yet back there you were full of energy – you were walking in the grounds while I was still in bed!'

A bitterness rose in Jean. 'It's easy for you to talk,' she told Lydia. 'You're used to living on your own. I'm not. It takes a long time.'

To her surprise, Lydia burst out laughing. This was unusual with her, she more often gave a quiet chuckle. 'Thanks!' she said, 'I was married for over five years.' Jean was stunned. All her ideas of Lydia fell into disarray.

'You never said!'

'Well, you're not exactly communicative about your own marriage!'

Lydia waited for Jean to speak, but she walked on in silence.

'It's no secret,' Lydia said. 'David and I got a divorce by mutual consent.'

'Oh!'

The tone of the exclamation told Lydia that Jean took the divorce to mean that the marriage had failed.

'If it's not life-long, people always think that, but it can be good while it lasts. It doesn't have to go on until one of the partners dies. We were very happy together – but I grew out of the relationship.'

Jean could not help showing her curiosity. Marriages held a poignant interest for her.

'I think we should turn back,' Lydia suggested. 'We've walked quite a way.' They turned about.

'Go on!' Jean said. Her tone was demanding, but Lydia did not mind.

'I met David on a return flight from Greece,' she said. 'I'd been hiking across the country – I knew just enough Greek to get by. It was my present to myself before my first carpentry job. He sat next to me in the aeroplane and we got talking. He was an aerospace engineer, intelligent and keen on his work, very articulate, but not handsome, a snub nose and a peculiar twist of the mouth – odd-looking until you got used to it. He was much taken by my hiking on my own all over Greece – he thought it bold of me. And my carpentry job struck him in the same way. A bit naive, really. He said it was 'great' to meet a woman who 'did her own thing'. He asked if he could see me again and we were married six months later.'

'Quite romantic!' Jean commented.

'I'm afraid the romance wore off once we were behind our own front door,' Lydia answered wryly. 'He hadn't thought that part out. He'd taken so much for granted, and I hadn't seen it. I thought it was understood I could go on having a life of my own as well as a life with him – and he would do the same. At first he didn't say anything when I went out of an evening with a friend, or to a class, or simply because I wanted to be on my own – he could understand that least of all. Then he began to complain. First it was, "What! Going out again?" Then after a bit, "What about my dinner?" If he got in before me from work and peeled the potatoes, he'd make a point of telling me, he'd say, "I've peeled your potatoes" and expect me to feel grateful. In the end I got fed up with it and I said, "Why *my* potatoes? Aren't *you* having any?" He didn't like that. Then on another occasion, he complained that the sheets needed changing. So I said, "Why do *I* always have to see to the sheets? We *both* lie on them?" Do you know what he said then? – "I'm not a woman!" He used

271

to boast that he did a lot more for me than most men would do.'

'Oh!' Jean said.

'Let's face it,' Lydia said resignedly, 'If there is one thing men can't tolerate it's an independent woman. Oh, they *say* they can. David said "Great!"' She had thought at first that she might have been unlucky, but later she had got to know quite a few women married to husbands who considered themselves progressive, and it was no different. They didn't expect to have to make out grocery lists, wash or iron clothes, think about what to have for the main meal, or cook it, or keep an eye on when the bread was nearly finished, when to clean inside the fridge, when to take down the curtains, when to clean the windows – that list of endlessly recurring items that women carry about inside their heads. 'They think like David, "I'm not a woman!"'

'They'll help,' Jean said, recalling the past.

'Oh, yes! If you ask them! What they won't do is take on domestic *responsibilities* – that's the woman's job.'

Back in the car, Jean asked, 'What's David doing now, do you know? Is he on his own, like you?' Lydia shook her head.

'He married again – nine months after the divorce. I was upset – so quick – illogically, I know. But it was just as if our happy times hadn't meant anything to him. Whilst I treasure my memories. It was only that I couldn't go on being mother to a grown man.' She put the car into gear and they drove off. 'I have to be independent in the way a man is independent,' she said. 'Most men don't want that kind of woman. I don't think my problem has a solution – or at least, not yet.'

Jean wanted to answer Lydia's confidences with her own – but she did not know how. She still felt as if she had been to a part of the world where no one had ever been before and that having found her way back it was impossible to tell anyone at home what it was like 'out there'. And there was the sense of guilt always silencing her. She was grateful to Lydia because she did not make any attempt to probe her personal life, but accepted the withholding of confidence without resentment.

Neither spoke much during the return journey. Lydia put Jean down at her front door. 'Thank you,' Jean said. 'I did enjoy myself.' She had got out of the car and with this short farewell was about to close the door when Lydia put out a hand and leaned towards her, as she stood in the road.

272

In her quiet tones, she said, 'Forgive me for interfering, but I think it's dangerous for you to be so bored.' Jean did not answer. She shut the door and turned away. Lydia drove off.

Indoors, as she had anticipated, Jean found Harold waiting for her. He told her in a voice which he tried to make pleasant, but which, in spite of his effort had a note of disgruntlement, that he had been waiting for some time. She was an hour later than she had said she would be. Still, he added, with a touch of graciousness in his tone, he did not mind.

'I'm sorry,' Jean said, without thinking. She had not intended to apologise. Then, to her own distaste, she found herself lying. 'We were held up,' she said. She took off her coat and hurried to make tea. Harold sat drinking with a rather glum expression and without asking how the weekend had gone. Jean thought that if he did not ask she would not say. They sat in awkward silence.

At last Harold enquired, 'Well! Did you learn about witches?' He put the question in a rather jeering tone.

Jean felt riled. 'Yes. I did,' she said. 'I met some interesting people and I enjoyed being with Lydia.' She could not have said anything that would have annoyed him more.

'More than my company, I suppose?' he asked jealously.

'Of course not,' Jean found herself answering. 'It's different. She's a woman. It's nice being with one's own sex now and then.'

There was a long pause. Harold did not enquire further. Jean sat drinking her second cup of tea. Harold did not want a second cup. Jean's thoughts drifted back to the weekend. She scarcely realised yet that she was home – still less, that Harold was sitting opposite. Her mind and feelings were fully occupied. Suddenly, into her dreaming, his words dropped, 'I've been thinking while you've been away. It's silly our paying the rent for two flats. What about you getting on with that divorce you're expecting any week, but which never comes. You could apply for a divorce yourself.'

At his words, Jean felt as if a pistol shot had suddenly gone off close to her ear drum. She gave a violent start. Her start annoyed Harold. 'A divorce?' She repeated the word as if she did not understand its meaning.

'Yes! A divorce!' he answered her, clearly angry at her response. 'Once the application is in, we could think about fixing a date.'

'A date?' Jean's voice held alarm.

'Yes! A date! You said, "Yes" when I asked you if you'd marry me.'

'I said I'd consider it,' Jean told him, annoyed that he had misquoted her – at the same time flustered because she was not sure what exactly she had said.

'Well, it's the same thing,' he insisted stubbornly. Then, when she kept silent, he added sulkily, 'It seems I don't come first any more.' When she still remained silent, he went on, 'I thought I came first.'

'You often do,' she answered. It was a truthful answer, but she felt it was not what she wanted to say.

'I suppose you didn't think what *I* was going to do while you were away?'

She ignored his question. Then she said suddenly, 'I don't want children.'

He brightened up. 'Oh, if that's all it is!' he said. 'No trouble there. I'm past bothering with kids now.' In a tone as if he were doing her a favour, he continued, 'I don't mind at all.'

Jean was finding out that there were things he did not mind at all and things he minded very much – being put second was one of the latter.

'I'm beginning to wonder if I come first at all,' he persisted. He was going to go on until she answered him.

At that moment, following straight on after her weekend, she was stronger than was usual with her. She would have liked to be frank with him – to tell him that she wanted more, not less freedom for herself in their relationship. She did not want to be bound to him so closely. She certainly did not want a formal bond. She tried for the courage and almost found it, but not quite. She could not rid herself of her awful fear of once again being alone – of once again having no one to turn to but herself. And this fear proved too strong for her – the fear that he might stop seeing her altogether.

In response to his repeated question, she gave him a false reassurance. And when he said, in a pathetic voice, 'I need you, you know! I can't get on without you,' she felt he had made a claim on her pity which it would be cruel of her to turn down.

274

CHAPTER TWENTY-SIX

ONE Saturday evening, Jean arrived at Harold's flat with a book. She had come from the library. After the usual greeting, she sat down and began to leaf through the pages. Harold had not seen Jean read except in the office lunch hour. He reacted with annoyance.

'What's that book?' he asked, and when she told him, 'Oh, still on about witches! Your new friend has made you silly.' He said this in a sneering tone.

Jean knew he was jealous, but she did not feel like treating him as a baby. This idea of Harold as a baby had not entered her mind before. He switched on the television and sat staring at the picture in a huff.

A tiny flame of defiance lit within her. She said, in a casual tone, 'I don't much care for what is on tonight. You look, I'll read.' It was the first time she had made such a remark. Harold took it as criticism of his taste.

'Well! That's a new one!' he said, in an injured tone. Indeed it was. Until that moment, she had never voiced any preferences. Harold had thought she approved of his choices. He could not know that her acquiescence was because she did not care. She had found it soothing to sit gazing at the screen knowing that all she had to do was to keep quiet. There were occasions when she had been interested, but mostly she was not. Either way, it had not mattered to her. The screen had shut out all else – that was what she had wanted. Afterwards they had chatted and Harold had made their drinks and her favourite sandwiches. Jean had liked being waited on. This unexciting regime had fully contented her. She watched as old people watch – satisfied so long as nothing was being demanded of her. But suddenly she was no longer content. Passivity had given way to interest – an interest of sufficient strength to arouse her to an act of defiance.

Harold felt his supremacy under threat. First there had been these female friends, then the weekend away, now this new fad of reading. He was beginning to sense exclusion. He got up and turned off the television. As he had hoped, Jean looked up.

'Why did you do that?' she asked, surprised. 'I thought you liked that programme.'

'I thought you did,' he retorted in a sulky tone. It was a

comedy series. Jean shut the book, feeling guilty. 'Turn it on,' she said. 'I'll watch.'

'Oh, don't do me a favour,' he answered in what he intended to be a lofty tone. 'I was evidently under a misapprehension. I thought you were enjoying the episodes. Otherwise I wouldn't have inflicted them on you.'

She did not bring a book with her a second time. Harold told himself that he had nipped that nonsense in the bud. It never occurred to him that his attitude might be considered egotistic. He had been the most important person in his mother's life. He had never experienced any other kind of relationship and could not imagine it. He had had a girl friend for a very short time and she had certainly made sure she came first. He thought it had to be one or the other.

He made this very clear in a variety of ways, all of which were acutely embarrassing to Jean. She did not often go out on her own. When she did, it was to visit Lydia and Betty, or Susan and her brother who were now married. Yet each time she told him he took it in the spirit of a minor tragedy. He showed his disfavour by a mild sulk. His sulks never lasted for long, but equally they were unfailing and they began to get on Jean's nerves. She dreaded having to tell him, but she was not willing to give up her new friends. Except for Rita, she had never had women friends before, only acquaintances, and in their company she was experiencing what could not be given her by any man – a keenly enjoyable sense of shared experience. She made an effort to explain this to Harold.

'Men and women don't live the same sort of lives,' she told him. 'I get a different thing from friendship with a man than with a woman.' She hoped he might understand this, but he made it very clear that he not only had no intention of trying to understand what she meant, but that he resented her words as a kind of challenge to his own position. She could not see why and gave up the attempt. She decided that one simply could not hope to explain certain things to a man.

Unexpected visitors, although not a frequent event, were a source of unease. When it happened Harold made his displeasure very evident; he would put on an air of surprise. If this device failed to shift the offending person, as usually happened, he would get up and take his leave with an ostentatious flourish which, although absurd, made his meaning clear. This was exceedingly embarrassing for Jean. When the visitor was Lydia, even more Betty, she felt humiliated at their seeing how completely unable she was to control Harold's behaviour. To an increasing extent the possibility of a caller got on Jean's nerves.

'You ought to be glad that I've got friends. You don't want me to be friendless and alone, do you?' He took umbrage at this.

'I didn't think you were alone,' he told her.

She started to think of him as selfish – a thought which earlier had never entered her mind. Until now she had considered him self-effacing. How had she come to enter such a close relationship? When she tried to look back and mark out its path, she found she could not do so. It had just happened – or so it seemed to her. She especially regretted having tied herself every Sunday. An appetite for change had been activated in her by her weekend with Lydia. The more bored she became at work, the more she longed for interesting activities in her spare time. Until now she had found this interest in very small events – a meal out, a visit to a cinema, playing dominoes and cards with Harold, even tiddly-winks. Television thrillers and cowboy films had given her a taste of adventure. She had not minded that Harold's interests were not the ones she would formerly have chosen. The fact that he was there, that she could count on his being there, that for him she came first, had sufficed to make all else of small account. This made her objection to his possessiveness illogical and unfair. She was honest enough to admit this to herself, but it did not help towards a solution. For she had also to acknowledge that the limpet-like association which formerly had warmed and sustained her was now starting to take on a stifling feel. Yet when she thought of life without Harold, her heart sank. She found it difficult to get to sleep. She had harrassing dreams.

She saw clearly the absurdity of her dilemma – she could not face life without Harold. At the same time she knew that they were not and never had been suited. She was forced to recognise in herself a powerful need to feel needed – to be given reassurance through little acts of consideration and praise of the kind which Harold was so good at, and which seemed to come so naturally to him. It was as if without such constant reassurances she did not fully exist – and she dreaded that most of all.

Now and then she thought about Stephen and their early days together before Robbie had been born. Had she felt then the

277

kind of need she felt now? She did not think she had. She thought than then she had felt fully alive. She had known that she existed – that she was real. She would have liked to trace those days in her memory, hoping they would provide a clue to her present state, but here she came up against an obstacle. As soon as she started to think about Stephen, she found, to her distress, that she was wishing him ill, she hoped that he was suffering. She struggled to overcome these vindictive feelings, but she could not – they were too strong. The only way to escape from them was to stop thinking about Stephen, so she put him resolutely out of her mind.

Eventually her emotions became so contradictory as to reduce her to a state of bewilderment. About one fact only was she clear, she was ruled by fear – fear that she would be left on her own and would have only herself to rely on. This fear rode her, deciding for her what she should do and how she should behave, quite regardless of any wishes of her own. She longed for the fear to go away so that she could see what it was that her real self wanted her to do. In the end this desire became so strong that she was driven to seek outside aid.

As confidante she had only two choices – Betty or Lydia. She hesitated between them. Betty would not be sentimental and that was something she needed. A soft sympathy would shut her up at once. On the other hand, Betty was apt to talk a lot. She had a preference for telling all. Jean was sure she would not be able to tell all. Betty might try to get it out of her under the mistaken belief that clarity would reveal a solution. She was a great believer in every problem having a solution if only one could find it. She would sit listening, waiting for an opportunity to pounce and to be helpful. Jean thought that would tighten her up. Lydia, on the other hand, was much less helpful when it came to suggestions. She had once said to Jean, 'I don't believe in playing god in the machine.' She was modest and this modesty made her a very good listener. So she chose Lydia. It would be easier to confess frankly, 'Thanks for coming, but I don't really know what it is I want to say.'

Those were the very words she used when Lydia came to her flat a week later. It was a Saturday morning. Harold did his weekly shopping then. Jean had wanted to be quite sure that he would not call. At Jean's opening remark, Lydia gave a slight, friendly smile, but made no reply. She had brought Jean a jar of her own home-made strawberry jam. Now she was seated on the new fireside chair, added to Jean's furniture since she had started 'entertaining'. Lydia did not break the silence – she waited. The two women knew each other well enough by now not to be embarrassed.

At last Jean said, 'I've got a problem with Harold. I wondered if you might have any ideas. I like him a lot, but he's terribly possessive. He seems to think he owns me. I don't want to hurt him, you see, but I do want a much looser relationship.' She hesitated, then repeated, 'I don't want to hurt him. That's what's so awkward. How to go about it without hurting him.' She went on to give an outline of their relationship from the beginning. She finished, 'We've been very close for quite a long time, you see.'

'Yes,' Lydia said, with quiet emphasis. 'I do.'

She understood that Jean had got herself into a tight relationship from which she now sought freedom, but that for some reason she could not bring herself to take the necessary steps. She did not think the problem existed for the reason Jean had given, although it might be a part. The main reason was somewhere else.

'He'd be very lonely if I gave him up,' Jean said. 'I know he would. Unfortunately he doesn't know how to share a person. He wants me to himself all the time.' She added, 'He's rather pathetic, you know.'

Lydia was surprised at this statement. Harold had not struck her as pathetic.

'He knows how to make people feel uncomfortable,' she said, with a smile. She was thinking of the reception she and Betty had received on their last visit. Jean went red and apologised for Harold. It was a bachelor trait, she told Lydia. He was not at his ease with women. For some minutes, she went on excusing Harold, then praising him, and finally pitying him once again. When she had finished, Lydia said she thought the only fair thing was to be frank – let Harold know that her feelings had changed. Jean said she thought he did know.

'He said he can't live without me,' she told Lydia. 'He's said it more than once.'

Lydia sat and considered. Then she asked, 'Suppose you were to die?' The question took Jean aback. This thought had never entered her head. A little lamely, she answered that she supposed in that event Harold would have to live without her.

'The next time he says he can't live without you, ask, "Would you kill yourself if I were to die?"' Lydia suggested quietly. Jean was silent.

Lydia asked suddenly, 'Suppose Harold were to die? Could you live without him?' When Jean did not answer, she repeated the question. When Jean still did not answer, she added, 'Isn't that really the problem?'

'Honestly, I don't know,' Jean said, feeling ashamed of her weakness. 'If he said tomorrow it was all over, part of me would welcome it. But another part would be frightened and feel sick.' That Jean found this admission hard did not surprise Lydia. She hastened to let her friend know that she understood. Jean was not to think that her decision to leave David had been easy; still less, to stick to it and carry it out. 'It was quite hellish for a time,' she confided. 'Yes, I know I said I'd grown out of the relationship – I had – but I hadn't grown *into* anything else. I had to go through the breaking off first, before I could grow any more.'

Encouraged by Lydia's understanding attitude, Jean confessed, 'He's very kind, you see. He's always thanking me and saying how much my coming into his life has meant to him.'

'And you like his saying that?'

Jean nodded. 'Yes! It makes me feel I'm needed.' She added, 'I suppose that sounds silly to you?'

Lydia shook her head. 'Goodness – no! It took me years getting past that one. Women are conditioned to respond to that kind of appeal.' She gave a laugh. 'We're computerised for automatic sympathetic responses! Seriously though, have you noticed how often men re-marry quite soon after their wives have died?'

'That's very cynical.'

'Not really. I'm not suggesting they don't feel the loss. I'm only saying they need a woman. After all, think what we do for them!'

Jean said she supposed Harold had not felt the need for another woman while his mother was alive. He had gone about with a girl for a short while until she jilted him. He had told her that although he had not used the term jilted.

'She stood him up?' Lydia asked.

'I suppose so.'

'And he didn't cut his throat, or take an overdose, or throw himself under a tube train?' Lydia asked, with just the trace of a smile. Jean said she supposed he could not have done. Then suddenly she too smiled.

280

'That's better!' Lydia said.

After that, it was less difficult for Jean to admit to her irrational fear. She could not understand its roots. 'I don't seem able to face life without someone to lean on,' she said. 'It's a mystery to me. I can't make it out. I'm not a coward.'

Lydia said she did not think it had anything to do with cowardice. Once a woman lost confidence in herself as a person, she lost confidence in living. 'Why don't you try what a more interesting job would do for you?' she suggested. She had never understood why Jean did not make use of her qualifications.

There was a lengthy silence. Lydia could sense that they had got deeper. Then Jean spoke. 'I can't!' she said. 'The last words my husband said to me when we parted were, "You've got what you wanted."'

'Wanted what?' Lydia asked.

'He thought I wanted to be free of our child. He thought that wish was behind my carelessness. I was careless. I was reading a book in the park, my son ran off, fell into the lake. He drowned.' She hesitated, then added, 'I was the cause of my son's death.'

She half expected Lydia to say something silly, like, 'Oh, I'm sure you were not the cause.' When Lydia did not, she was grateful. Here was someone who was taking her seriously.

'I was reading a book in the park,' she repeated. 'I forgot all about Robbie. He was only three and a half. I ought not to have forgotten. It was such a relief – reading the book, I mean – I never realised how time was passing. It seemed to have gone in a flash – the two hours, I mean.' She asked, 'Have you noticed how strange time is? There are occasions when it just vanishes – it isn't there any more, it's gone – and other occasions when it doesn't move at all? When I was in the house, some mornings time never moved at all.' As she said these last words, her voice took on an odd note.

For an instant Lydia had the impression that Jean was about to say something more – something important. Then she drew back. Her drawing back was obvious from the change in her manner. She had been very tense – suddenly she was all brisk and practical. Lydia must be longing for a cup of tea. She was being an awful hostess.

In the kitchen, she thought, 'Over coffee, I'll tell Lydia about my dream – and the voice.' But she did not.

Lydia was thinking, 'It can't do any harm and it might do some good.' So over her cup of tea she told Jean about the women's group to which she belonged. 'We call it consciousness raising,' she said.

'I shouldn't like it,' Jean told her. 'I could never talk about my personal life to strangers.'

'You don't have to talk, you can just listen,' Lydia assured her. 'I think you might find that your experiences aren't as unusual as you think – your feelings too. It's my guess that many women have similar feelings.' She was not quite sure what Jean's feelings were, but from what Jean had allowed her to know she could make a near guess.

All Jean answered was, 'I hope not!'

Lydia did not try to persuade her. She let the subject drop. But when she said goodbye, she kissed Jean in an undemonstrative manner.

In spite of its inconclusive nature, the talk with Lydia had done Jean good. When, some days later, Harold put on a sulk because she was going out for the evening without him, she found the courage for quite a sharp retort, 'I can't limit my friendships in the way you want. You must take me as I am, or not at all.' The last few words were out before she was aware that she was saying them. They gave her a mild shock. She had actually brought herself to the point of risking his leaving her. But he did not leave her. On the contrary, her dressing down seemed to have done him good. He became less demanding and now she had the right in practice, if not formally acknowledged, to go out on her own, or with friends, whenever she might choose. He showed his displeasure still, but in a more muted way. He no longer got up and left when a friend visited, but sat on for a while. He still sometimes sulked, but Jean received a distinct impression that she had reined him in. He ceased to harrass her about a possible divorce. It seemed that he had become aware of treading on fragile ground and did not want to take a risk. Their positions were being slowly reversed. This small victory over her fear gave Jean a sense of self-confidence which for years had been almost totally lacking.

Some months later she made the decision to go with Lydia to her women's group. She did not do this because she believed any good to herself would come out of it, but because she wanted to please a friend who had shown her so much kindness,

282

been so willing to listen without censuring. Had Lydia continued to press her, she would not have gone.

On her first evening Lydia introduced her simply as 'Jean'. The group was comprised of seven women; the youngest twenty-eight, the eldest fifty-three. They met in the small front room of a semi-detached house belonging to one of the members; it was a bit of a squash, but they managed to be comfortable. Jean thought they must have something important in common to over-ride such a wide disparity in their ages.

For some months the answer did not become clear to her. The women talked, Jean sat and listened. She did not feel as embarrassed as she had anticipated. She noticed another woman who scarcely ever spoke and nobody seemed to mind, or to think her silence something upon which to comment, nor was any attempt made to draw her into the conversation. Lydia herself spoke little. This was something new in Jean's experience of groups. At the polytechnic everyone was expected to make a contribution to whatever subject was under discussion. Here there seemed to exist an acceptance of people as they were. She relaxed and began to make mental notes, which later, in her flat, she jotted down. In a few weeks, she had a short list, which lengthened as time went on. The list included – How Women See Themselves, Mothers, Fathers, Guilt, Responsibility to Ourselves, Children, Different Ways of Seeing Sons and Daughters, Feelings Around Depression, Doctors, Periods, Childbirth Experiences, Cultural Repression, Ridicule, Feelings of Worthlessness. For some months, her reaction to these discussions was that, although interesting, she could have gained as much from books.

It was only after almost six months that the real difference became clear to her. It took so long because she was experiencing something entirely new. Although she had her headings, they did not express the essential content of what was happening. At first she had been conscious of muddle and confusion. She had wished the speaker would keep more to the point. She took for granted that there must be a point. She looked for an objective analysis of whatever was being discussed. It did not occur to her that life was not like that. Life was not experienced under neat headings, nor was it possible to analyse these experiences objectively – and experience was what the group was all about. Eventually it struck her that her inability to pin the whole thing down was because it came under the heading of subjectivity – a dreadfully suspect and despised word in certain quarters, especially among male academics. Finally she came to realise that what the women were talking about was not what they thought, but how they felt – what it actually *felt* like to be inside a given situation. The muddled expressions, the emotions, the strayings from one point to another, the statements which appeared to contradict each other, the apparent lack of logic – all this was due entirely to what should have been from the start a simple, obvious fact, that life was like that – real life, not text-book life. And Jean began to feel at home in the group, even to the extent of not minding when Lydia could not come.

She had been going for nine months before she did at last speak. She tried to give expression to her feelings during those two and a half years after Robbie's first birthday. She longed to make a clear statement – something she and others could grasp and comprehend. But guilt still clung to her like mud at the bottom of a river and she actually felt, while speaking, as if she was stifling, her breath coming in gasps. Her words were one muddled, shapeless heap. She sat down with a sense of despair.

In spite of the difficulty with which she had spoken, to one woman at least her fragmented speech had conveyed strong meaning, for after the group had broken up and the members were putting on their coats, this woman came up to Jean, touching her on the arm timidly and speaking quietly into her ear. She was one of the older women, in the mid-forties, neatly dressed and looking every inch a conventional suburban housewife.

'I must have a word with you,' she said. 'I want to thank you. You said just what I've always felt. But I can't put it into words. I don't know if you've noticed, but I don't say much.'

'I don't usually say anything at all,' Jean answered, 'and now I wish I'd kept quiet.'

'Oh, you mustn't wish that!' the woman replied, almost passionately. 'What I wanted to tell you – your experience in the park – well, I understand. While you were speaking, I was thinking, "Oh! The park! The park! I know just what she means about another species."' Jean turned and for a moment the two gazed at each other. Then the woman moved away. To Jean it was as if someone had touched her hand and said, 'Yes! I know! I was there too!'

As she was walking down the street, another member of the

group, a woman in her late thirties, caught up with her and said, 'What you told us about your husband reminded me of mine. I tried to explain to him how I felt tied to the children, and he told me I was suffering from an early menopause. I was only thirty-four!'

When she got back to her flat, Jean sat down and thought about her experience. She sat for a long while assimilating her new knowledge which reduced itself to one simple, all-significant fact – for so long now she had felt herself to be a person who had returned from a part of the earth where no other had been before and that having come back it was impossible to tell those who had remained at home what it was like 'out there'. This feeling had been so absolute that she had not been able to get beyond it to utter a single word – not until that evening. Now she knew that this uninhabited part of the earth from which she had returned had not be uninhabited then, nor was it now. It was simply that she had not met the inhabitants, or, more likely, going by her own experience at the group, had not recognised them when she *had* met them. She understood at that moment what was meant by saying that words heal. Her experiences were not unique – she was not, as she had imagined, alone in the world.

She went into work the next morning looking tired, but cheerful.

However, her final cure did not come about until after more months of listening to women telling other women how it felt inside the married set-up. Incredible though it seemed to her afterwards, this was all that had been necessary to free her from the crippling belief in her own guilt.

When the insight did come it came without searching, unexpectedly, so that to Jean it took on the aspect of a miracle – although later she realised that the suddenness had been the outcome of a long process of seeking. She had not been thinking about her sense of guilt. She was sitting on the edge of her divan tying up her shoe lace. And it came into her head that she had not been looking in the right direction. She had always concentrated on the voice in her dream. The words, 'You're glad he's dead! You are! You *know* you are!' had shocked her so much, yet she had been unable to deny their truth. To stand in a black hole packed with violence and to sense absolute still-ness had been very unnerving. But one got all kinds of weird sensations in nightmares. Afterwards, on cool reflection, they left behind no more than very unpleasant memories which faded with time. Deep as the impression had been, she could have got over that particular memory fairly easily. The voice was an altogether different matter. It was authentic. So she had concentrated on the words and found in them a confirmation of Stephen's own accusation, 'You've got what you wanted!' If she had not wanted to be rid of Robbie what had happened would not have happened. Her carelessness had been deliberate – the fact that she had not known this made no difference – it proved Stephen right when he had said, 'You're not a normal woman... You were never fit to be a mother.' She had gone about for years accepting his judgment. Now, suddenly, she knew that she was completely normal.

The truth came to her at the same moment that she realised she had been looking in the wrong place for the key to the mystery of how it was possible for her to feel a normal woman when she was not. But there was no mystery – there never had been. The evidence had been there all the time in the still centre of the black hole. Mabel had been right when she had suggested to her on Brighton pier that perhaps the solution lay elsewhere. Sitting on the divan in the act of bending down to tie her shoe lace, it entered her mind that the violence, with its still centre, was an exact expression in dream terms of what had been going on inside her for two and a half years – a struggle between two powerful forces of her nature ending in the extreme, violent repression of one of those two forces, of half her essential needs as a human being. It was not and never had been true that she had desired Robbie's death – she had loved him too much for that. It was knowing this that had caused her such bewilderment. The case against her could not be true and yet the facts of her unkindness, her final neglect, had seemed to prove it true. Stephen had believed it to be true. Now she knew that the truth was quite otherwise and very simple. The way she was forced to live had faced her with the necessity of choosing between the two essential needs of her nature and this had produced the only possible outcome – she had been unable to choose and so in a very real sense she had ceased to exist. This was the still centre of her dream. She had been locked into a state of paralysis, as if by an arm lock. Then the arm lock had been taken off. She herself, without realising, had done this. In the park, with the book on her lap, turning its pages, she had given a chance of life to her suppressed half. The degree of its

286

strength had been equal to the degree of its suppression. It had simply taken her over. She recalled how time had ceased to exist, and how finally looking up from her book after what seemed a few minutes, she had felt as if a strong wind from off the downs had been blowing through her mind so that all the mental fatigue which she had been enduring for so long had gone. Her mind had been clear, fresh and bright. She had felt young again.

The entire meaning of the words had lain in a simple sigh of relief that the intolerable tension of an impossible dilemma was at an end.

All this passed through her mind in a flash of revelation. She put a hand to her forehead. 'Ah!' she exclaimed, as if suffering the pain of a heart attack. She rolled over onto the bed and lay on her stomach. She gave a single sob. Then she lay still. Tears came from under her closed eyelids. After a while, she went to sleep. When she woke up, she was well.

She lay on her back and thought about her good luck. For in the end she had been lucky. No mere intellectual understanding could have sufficed to rid her of her sense of guilt. Only an actual experience of the power of her repressed need could achieve that, and this the dream had supplied. Only she had not been able to interpret the dream correctly. Why the realisation had come when it did, she would never know.

For a time she could not fully trust her luck. She might have gone through the remainder of her life without the knowledge that had come to her in a seeming flash. But time did in the end convince her that she had hit on the truth. She no longer felt the dreadful compulsion to keep on going over and over the same old ground. She stopped thinking about the past altogether. She was cured of her obsession.

She was conscious of no longer feeling the former vindictiveness towards Stephen. It had evaporated like the early morning mist when the sun gets up and makes all clear. She could think of him without wishing him ill. This was a great relief to her. It was as if by forgiving herself she could forgive him also.

After a couple of weeks, she went to see Betty and Lydia.

'I'm so glad for you,' Betty told her. She added, smiling, 'She isn't going to need us any more now.'

Jean knew Betty was teasing her, but she said earnestly, 'I shan't need you except as good friends, but I shall always need you as that.' She felt their friendship as something tremendous in her life – something rock-like.

'Now you're free to leave that boring job,' Lydia said.

'Yes,' Jean answered. 'Now I'm free!

CHAPTER TWENTY-SEVEN

'DO I have to go on seeing Jean outside my own home until I die? Mabel asked Jim, over breakfast. She was getting very tired of meeting in trattorias.

Jim hesitated, then grudgingly replied, 'She can come if you want. I don't have to see her.'

'No, dear,' Mabel retorted stoutly. 'I won't have that, she's not a leper, although you treat her as if she were.'

They had an argument. Finally Jim gave in. 'And you'll be nice to her?' Mabel persisted.

'I shan't bring up the past, if that's what you mean,' he retorted.

'I said be *nice* to her.'

'Oh, all right – only don't keep on!'

'Thank you dear,' she said, in an apologetic voice. On those rare occasions when she got her own way, she always felt a little guilty.

Later that same evening, Mabel penned a letter of welcome. They had not met since Jean had gone back to her old library some four months ago. There would be so much to talk about. Jim could just say a friendly 'hello' then take himself off to the back room with a book. Of course it would be a bit of an ordeal for Jean, but quickly over, and for the best. Anyway Jim never did like listening to women 'nattering' as he called it.

During those four months life had altered radically for Jean. At first the effort required for change had seemed almost too much, she had got so used to passivity, but once she had taken the first step, every next step was easier, until finally it had come to seem natural to make decisions and be responsible for what she did with her own life.

Reactions of friends sometimes surprised, even annoyed her. Rita especially irritated her. She adopted an all-knowing attitude. 'You did yourself harm when you took a job like that,' she told Jean over the phone. 'It wasn't for you.' It was clear that she and Richard had been discussing her. Jean wondered what Rita could know about a life so very different from her own, but when Rita went on to say that she and Richard would be lunching in the West End the following week on Jean's free afternoon, and what about their getting together for a chat, she readily agreed. Nevertheless she felt a certain resentment for it had not occurred to her that her friends might be talking about her. At the time her action had appeared the only possible one and she had felt that everyone must know the reason, even though her mind could have told her that this was unlikely.

Still, she was pleased, while at the same time surprised and again a little annoyed when, some days after their meeting, Rita phoned, saying, 'I thought you'd like to know Richard thinks you're your old self again – he says you've got back your vitality.' When Jean expressed mild surprise, Rita retorted, 'My dear! You look ten years younger at least!'

A fortnight later, she phoned again. Jean could tell by her excited tone that something important had happened. 'Richard has got a partnership!'

'Oh, I'm so glad,' Jean answered. 'But isn't it a bit sooner than you expected?'

'Yes, it is – although Richard's put in a lot of hard work. He's been able to put some money into the firm just when they needed extra capital. We had a legacy from a distant relative about sixteen months ago – at least Richard did – he didn't know the chap even remembered him – he'd emigrated – apparently he didn't marry or have a family. Bit of luck, eh?'

'Yes,' Jean said, to whom all this was news. 'Goodness!' she exclaimed.

'*Thank* goodness, you can say! That's the end of our financial worries – we've had plenty!' Jean must come over one weekend soon. 'But don't make it next weekend – I shall be rushed off my feet! My woman's away. Illness in the family – nothing serious. Meanwhile it keeps me busy.'

'It must,' Jean said.

'Well, I certainly hope she'll be back soon. I'm dependent on her.' Saying she couldn't stop to chat, she rang off abruptly. Jean smiled as she put down the phone. She stood for a moment thoughtful. She was conscious of Rita moving steadily further and further from her – soon visiting her would be like a trip abroad.

Jean was working out her notice at the office and looking forward to her last day as eagerly as if she was in the final weeks of a long sentence. At first she had not minded – she had been too stupefied and there had been the tremendous relief of financial independence. The repetitive nature of the work had even soothed her nerves. But as time passed, other needs had surfaced. Finally she had come to think that if there really was a hell, its essence must lie in boredom.

However there was one ordeal which must be faced before her release. She had to have it out with Harold. She was feeling to blame and hoping to salvage something for him from the wreck of his hopes. 'Because I'm leaving,' she told him, 'it doesn't mean the end of our friendship. I want us to go on seeing each other and being friends.' She had gradually been prising herself free. They no longer spent every Sunday together, but only when arranged. They still went to lunch each Wednesday and now and then to a theatre or cinema. But the old regularity had gone. Harold had not liked it: her leaving the firm was the last straw. He was indignant. He took it as some kind of a slur on his profession. 'Oh, you needn't bother,' he told her, with a very ill grace. 'I don't want that kind of friendship thank you very much. It's all or nothing.' He added, with some vigour, 'Nobody makes a mug out of me!'

During the remainder of her notice Jean sought to placate him by being extra nice, but he gave her little chance. His attitude was like that of a small hurt boy. Jean was sorry for him. He had been wounded in his pride. But he would not respond to her overtures. He insisted on aloofness, only speaking to her when absolutely necessary. Their mid-week lunch outing ceased. So did their evenings and occasional Sundays. If she suggested an outing, he said he was busy. In the end, she gave it up. She was conscious of a certain sense of guilt – she had not been honest with him when her own feelings had started to change, she had not contradicted his expectations. But she did not agonise. She had learnt how to cope with guilt. She admitted to herself that his rejection of her was a relief.

Jean was given a farewell party and the next day left with gifts and good wishes. They spoke about her for a few days, then they forgot about her. When Jean woke in the mornings she felt for some weeks that she must be going to the office – it took quite a while before she realised fully that it was over.

There were times when she wondered about Stephen. She

was surprised that he had not asked for a divorce. It never entered her mind to take that step herself. For one thing, she was quite certain that she would not remarry. She never even considered a reconciliation – his words, 'You were never fit to be a mother ... you are not a normal woman,' stood between them, an insurmountable barrier.

She never asked herself if she was happy – happiness did not seem important. What mattered was to wake in the mornings with the knowledge that during the day her mental faculties would be active. She would not have cared had she been forced to exist on a saltless diet so long as her mind could live. She had learnt this the hard way, not something she had read in a book.

She supposed it just possible that one day she might again have a close relationship with a man, if she should come across a man with whom she could share interests and companionship – but she would not go in for the conventional relationship, she would not cook and clean for him. Meanwhile she was happy knowing that she had the support and friendship of other women – Lydia, Betty, women in her consciousness-raising group, women whom she might meet in the future. If the land became dry, they would always be a life-giving stream.

She had altogether lost her fear of being on her own – the need for an emotional crutch. She realised now that her relationship with Harold had been just such a crutch. Her response to this declared need of her had really been a rationalisation of her own inner weakness. She had once in the past confessed to herself, 'I *need* to feel needed.' Now she no longer felt this need. She no longer cared whether or not she was appreciated. She had acquired an identity of her own. All the same she was conscious of real pleasure when one day Susan phoned her and said, 'You are to become an aunt! Does that please you?'

'Oh, yes! I shall like that very much,' Jean answered.

When Jean made her visit to the house, Mabel greeted her with warmth. She had grown very fond of Jean over the years, secretly thinking of her as the daughter for whom she had longed, but she took great care not to make this obvious. She did not want Jean to feel in any way tied. That would spoil their relationship. As she had a natural instinct to be possessive, she had to keep warning herself off. She was especially careful on leave-taking not to ask Jean when she would be seeing her again. She left that to Jean.

The meeting with Jim was awkward – more for Mabel than for Jean, who took calmly Jim's brusque manner and abrupt departure from the room. Mabel felt herself going hot.

Anxious to put Mabel at her ease, Jean gazed round the room, commenting, 'It looks just the same – as if I'd been here yesterday.'

'Well, we don't need anything new,' Mabel said, trying to cover up her discomfort. 'At our age, it's not sensible to buy new things. We've all we need.'

'You're not old,' Jean objected.

'Time passes, dear. I'm seventy-four!'

'Well, you don't look like it,' Jean retorted, giving Mabel a kiss.

'I don't know about me,' Mabel said, gazing at Jean with a surprised pleasure, 'but you certainly look younger even than you are.' Jean had a youthful, alive air which had been missing for a long time. She had more colour in her face too. Mabel was glad of that because she had secretly feared that Jean might be anaemic.

'You look much less tired, dear,' she said.

'Oh, I feel a lot less tired!' Jean told her, taking off her coat.

It was three o'clock. They sat and chatted. They were still talking at five o'clock when Mabel said she must get Jim some tea, or he'd wonder what was happening.

When she came back into the room with tea and cakes on a tray, she said, 'He didn't realise the time. He's having a good read. Talk about not being missed!' She sounded relieved.

During the two hours the women had gone over a great deal of ground. Mabel had not known about Harold so Jean did not need to go into that, but Mabel was delighted to learn all about the new job.

'That's much more in your line, dear,' she said, with enthusiasm. She added, 'I always knew there was a simple explanation to that voice.'

'But you were shocked at the time,' Jean reminded her.

'Yes, I was shocked,' Mabel admitted frankly. 'At first, but afterwards, when I went over what you had said, well, I told myself it was just something that I couldn't grasp. And, after all...' she broke off, hesitating. Then, in a sudden burst of honesty, 'Don't all we mothers, at times ...?' She broke off again.

292

The silence that followed was satisfactory to both women. Mabel poured out a second cup of tea for them both. 'Have another bun?' She offered Jean the cake stand. Jean shook her head. 'I will,' Mabel said, helping herself to her third coconut bun.

She wanted to ask Jean about Stephen. Did she still harbour any feeling for him? Did she have any idea if he harboured any feeling for her? Had they any contact at all? Was all hope of a reconciliation lost? But she would not violate the quality of their relationship by such questions. Above all, she wanted Jean to feel safe with her. So instead of what was uppermost in her mind, she asked for more details about Jean's new job and was interested when Jean told her about her plans for the future and her research.

'Will you write a book on the subject?' Mabel asked. Jean said she was hoping to do so.

'You know what you want,' Mabel said, with an encouraging smile. She was thinking, 'Like me, when I was young!' Aloud she said, 'My two men always knew what they wanted. Once they'd made up their minds, an earthquake wouldn't have shifted them!' She thought, 'Nobody reproached either of them.' On the contrary, people had spoken as if in their case ambition was a virtue.

She asked, 'Are you happy, dear?' Now that they knew each other so well she could use the term 'dear' without fearing that it might sound a bit condescending. Jean would know that it was just a natural warmth of feeling.

'Happy?' Jean repeated the word as if it had a strange sound. 'I don't know,' she answered with honesty, 'I never think about happiness. I feel fulfilled. If that's happiness, then certainly I am happy.'

A little later, Mabel commented, 'Well, to think that you've become so bold! Picketing Miss World – I should never dare!'

'I'm glad you don't find it silly,' Jean said. 'Many people do.'

'Silly?' Mabel said. 'No. I can't see anything silly about it.' Then she thought of Jim. It was just possible that he might find it amusing, but she did not say this to Jean. Instead she said, 'It's funny how things turn out. When you first came here with Stephen I took quite a dislike to you.' She did not enlarge.

Jean said, 'You frightened me! I felt I would never be able to live up to you.' Both women laughed at the recollection.

When Jean got up to go Mabel started a confused apology for Jim.

'Don't worry!' Jean said in a reassuring tone,' I don't mind and Jim will get used to me. 'You're past the age when you can be expected to meet people outside. I shall come here.' She added, with emphasis, 'And you can say *anything you like* to me, you know that.' She put her arms round Mabel and kissed her. Mabel felt the tears come into her eyes.

Jean bent down to button up her coat. She asked, 'Do you think Stephen would understand – about the voice, I mean?'

At that moment Mabel would have given a great deal to be able to answer in the affirmative, but she would not lie to Jean. She answered in a quiet voice, 'I don't think he would, dear.'

No more was said. The two women kissed again.

Mabel shut the front door behind Jean. She felt that for a short while she had been in another world and was now back in her own. Her anger returned. Jim had promised her that he'd be nice. Instead he'd been abrupt and frosty, then made off as if he didn't want to be in the same room. She'd asked especially – this time she'd let him know. She started towards the door, then checked herself. He'd most likely give her a short answer, or worse, none at all – but she had to go in, or he'd guess she was upset. She put her head round the door. He was fast asleep in the armchair, legs stretched out. She gave a sigh of relief. She would not have to pretend friendly feelings.

How quiet the front room was – she stood for a moment. What a change in Jean! 'She doesn't need me any longer,' she thought, conscious of a pang of regret alongside a glow of self satisfaction at her own part in Jean's recovery. When her son had left home she had felt that the most useful part of her life was over. Things had turned out quite the opposite. She had been a rock to a shipwrecked human being. She had helped to bring her ashore. Her imagination liked to toy with dramatic metaphors. She recalled that Jean and her mother had never been close – perhaps that was one reason why she had responded, on that first memorable evening to her hug of sympathy. She walked to the window and looked out – Jean had long disappeared up the road. She thought, 'What a lot has been added to my life by the discovery that women can enjoy each other, can be fun together, without men.' She supposed she had known this when she was a girl, but she had forgotten once she had married. It had always been, 'If Jim isn't taking me out,' until at last she had lost her friends. Now, suddenly, she was sorry. Then she comforted herself with knowledge of her monthly outings to the West End. She would tell Jean she wanted those to go on. 'I always feel like a dog off a lead,' she told herself, smiling. 'If I could, I believe I'd start to bark!' Being with the young – for to her Jean was very young – was delightful, but it did make her realise the difference. She had always kept herself spruce, had always had a certain dread of being labelled 'that old woman.' Now Jean had noticed her tiredness at the end of their outings. Why hadn't Jim noticed her tiredness when she got home? She felt a sudden slight dizziness. She retreated from the window hastily and almost fell into her armchair.

She was feeling humiliated – whenever that happened she seemed to have an attack of dizziness. Now she was thinking, 'Why am I such a moral coward?' She was ashamed of the fact. She'd been like that all her life – afraid of ridicule – but especially after the early stages of her marriage. She had suppressed her resentments rather than risk Jim's dismissive remarks – or those silences which left her feeling ignored and inadequate. She hadn't been able to bear being treated like a child.

She felt really depressed for a while. 'Why can't I ever get angry?' she thought. 'I wouldn't get this blood pressure then.' It frightened her. Surely she didn't need to go to the extent of being *extra nice* to Jim when he made her resentful? But she often did – she fussed round him, made him a drink, drew the little table up to his armchair, asked if he was comfortable. 'I'm mad!' she said aloud, and didn't know whether to hit herself or have a good laugh. In the end she saw the funny side and laughed. She relaxed in her armchair, and her dizziness went.

She thought consolingly, 'There's Jean!' Jean had said, 'You can say anything you like to me, you know that.' She imagined all the things she would say. She would tell her that she thought men were selfish – not stubborn, as she had used to say, a word which when applied to men somehow had an almost admirable ring about it. She would say, 'Men are arrogant, you know Jean. They like to make women feel they know nothing while *they* know everything. They like to make us feel stupid. Then we keep quiet. Jim's like that.' She would say, 'When *I'm* off colour, Jim simply says, "Why don't you go to bed?", but when *he's* the same, he expects hot lemon juice and coddling!' She would tell Jean, 'Men like to think everything is really women's fault. That's why they say "son of a bitch!" as a final insult. Jim wouldn't ever, but he *thinks* like that.' Jean wouldn't despise her if she confessed, 'I always feel guilty if I'm not well and Jim gets me a meal. I feel I must get better quickly. Yet I get him a meal every day.' How wonderful it would be to say out loud – '*I don't think any of that is fair!*'

Then she thought, 'Jean said, "Age doesn't matter," but it does!' She didn't want to upset Jim. Nobody could live with a person the number of years she had lived with Jim and not care about them. She did mind if he was sick, or upset, or worried. She did want to console and aid him. It was only that she would have liked a bit more of the same for herself. Then there were all their memories. Only the other day they had been going over some of the happy ones. When she came to consider it, she'd had plenty of times worth cherishing. It was only that so much of herself had lacked a means of expression – and when she had sought an outlet, she had been silenced. But you had to make allowances – most men were like children in many ways. She sat and stared at her double vision. Then there was loneliness – Jean wouldn't understand about that – she was too young – she could pick herself up and go on. Imagine living in the house on her own! At the thought, she felt a swarm of fears and insecurities. Jean had gone away to live her own life. The room was very quiet and very empty. There was a dead feeling about it. She was suddenly very frightened. She got up hastily and went to wake Jim.

Had Jean known Mabel's thoughts concerning herself, she would have been very happy – her feelings for her friend ran deep. She felt towards her an immense gratitude – she had come to her aid when aid had been needed most. She wanted to help by lending an understanding ear. Her own experience had taught her that the deeper the feeling the less a person was willing to expose it to ridicule. She knew that Mabel would always remain silent when she most desired to speak – well, she could speak to her.

That same evening, when Jean got home from her visit, she hastened to take off her outdoor things and prepare the supper, for she was expecting Betty. She picked three letters up off the doormat and put them down on the living room table while she went into the kitchen, not bothering to glance at the handwritings. She took out of the refrigerator bacon, eggs and mushrooms, with two tomatoes. In a short while she had everything prepared and had laid the table in the living room. Then she sat down with her letters. There were two foolscap envelopes and in between them a white envelope. Immediately she glanced at it she knew the writing for Stephen's. So it had come at last. Anticipated for so long, it was still a shock.

She slit open the envelope, but she did not take out the sheet of paper – she did not want to read what was written on it. She put the envelope on the table and went into the kitchen to cook. While she was cooking, she kept thinking about the letter. She kept on making excuses to herself – Betty would arrive any moment, she must have the meal ready. The air smelt of bacon and cooked mushrooms. She found quite a number of items that needed her attention, but still Betty did not come. Finally she put the meal to keep warm and sat down to read the letter. The sight of the familiar handwriting affected her. He would be asking for a divorce – well, it had to come one day.

But he was not. Instead he wrote that he had not been able to forget her and would like a reconciliation, although he thought it very likely she would not. In that case, he would apply for a divorce, but first he asked her to grant him a meeting. He wrote, 'I can't say a final goodbye without first understanding the reasons for your turning against me – why you came to hate me.' He went on to write that he felt he had been to blame in his treatment of her immediately after Robbie's death. He thought he had been cruel, but he had not intended it. He could only ask her to forgive him. If she felt she could speak to him now, after all these years, then would she do so. He did not find it tolerable to part from her in silence. He finished by leaving it to her to name a time and place of meeting. He reiterated his hope that she would not refuse.

This was not at all what she had expected. She did not in the least wish to see him. The thought filled her with a horrible uncertainty. She would not know what to say to him that he would find meaningful – and the humble tone of the letter unnerved her. She knew he was a proud man.

Over the meal Betty asked, 'Do you still care for him – sufficiently, I mean, to make this effort worth while?'

Jean shook her head. 'I don't know,' she said, with honesty. 'I wish I did.'

'If you didn't care for him at all, you'd know,' Betty commented. Jean did not answer.

'He hasn't been to see us for a long while,' Betty said.

Stephen's visits had never been a subject for discussion between them. Now was no exception. A silence ensued.

Then Jean said, 'I owe a lot to you and Lydia. Between you, you saved me from making a terrible mistake.'

Betty took it that she was referring to Harold. 'Oh, you'd never have married him,' she retorted, laughing. 'You saved yourself.'

'I was nearer than you know,' Jean answered. She added earnestly, 'I couldn't have done it alone – escaped, I mean.' But they could not help her now. This she had to face on her own.

They talked about other matters for the rest of the evening.

Putting on her coat, Betty said, 'If I were you, I'd try to find out how I feel.'

'I can't!' Jean answered. 'Not until I see him. I'll know then.'

Jean did not reply to Stephen for a week. Then she wrote a brief note agreeing to meet him at her flat and naming a date and time: Saturday afternoon, in fourteen days. She could not face him sooner.

CHAPTER TWENTY-EIGHT

STEPHEN too was glad of the respite. On the day of the silent parting he had driven away determined to put his past life behind him – but, as it had turned out, he had not succeeded in forgetting Jean nor in reconciling himself to the final failure of his marriage.

Alone in his flat he had made great efforts to reach some kind of understanding. With scrupulous thoroughness, he had gone through his behaviour pattern and had found it satisfactory. He had never acted as if he had a god-given right to be treated as head of the family. He had paid attention always to Jean's wishes – even at the very end he had respected her idiosyncratic desire regarding the disposal of her books and the furnishing of her flat. Some marriages failed because the wife resented her husband's demands for sex or for children – he had always been reasonable about sex, he would have liked a child, but he had left Jean free. She had decided that she wanted a child – he had accepted the duties of father and husband. This was all there had been to it until she had turned peculiar. He could understand her later behaviour only in the light of a quirk in her personality – that had been the kindest attitude to take.

He had brought himself round to this way of thinking only after a struggle. He really thought her behaviour entitled him to label her abnormal. 'Unfeeling' he had said to Betty, but he had thought abnormal the truer word. He also had to put up a fight against his sense of grievance that she had withheld recognition of his worth. He had been used to people recognising in him a slight superiority – especially women. Where he understood, his feelings were strong, his loyalties the same. If he was also egocentric, he was not aware of it. He did sometimes dimly realise that he often stood back from people and judged them. Until very recently he had seen nothing amiss in that; it had linked up with a certain moral fervour which was a part of his nature – a firm idea of the right way to live. Then Betty had uttered the word cruelty and a cloud of doubt had settled over the clear light of his good behaviour. He recalled his words, 'You're not a normal woman. A normal woman wouldn't sit reading while her child drowned. You were always unfit to be a mother.' Yes, they had been harsh words. He ought not to have uttered them while she was grieving – for he did now allow her that sentiment. He did not tell himself that what he had said was untrue, only that he should not have given voice to the truth at that particular moment. It had been his duty to console her. He ought to have comforted her and he had not. He had let her down and in so doing he had failed himself as well. Along with his remorse there was a strong sense of humiliation. Significantly he thought in terms of duty. Underneath all his theorising he had a very clear idea of how a man ought to behave towards a woman who was in any sort of trouble.

He pondered the mystery of her job. He had been so sure that he knew her intentions and he had been quite wrong. What else had he perhaps been wrong about? He recalled with a certain unease that he had parted from her with the words, 'You've got what you wanted now'. She had clearly not got what she wanted. He could not in the least understand why.

Ambivalence streaked right through his feelings about Jean. He felt remorse, he felt humiliation. Sometimes the one was the stronger, sometimes the other. He could not reconcile himself to the thought that he had acted with a measure of cruelty. Cruelty was repugnant to him. He ceased to excuse that part of his behaviour, but he always came back to the central mystery – her rejection of himself and of her son long before the final tragedy. That had been the climax of days, weeks, months of indifference and latent hostility. He had said, 'What have you got against me that you won't even speak to me?' Her constant unkindness must weigh heavier than his lapse under stress. But he missed her. He was often lonely. His work never lost its interest for him, it was the great stabilising factor in his life, but it was not a whole life he was living. For a whole life he needed a woman as well as work – without both, it was a crippled life.

Often he considered a divorce, but on every occasion that he pondered this, he found himself unable to make a decisive move. Jean had still too firm a grip on him. He was that sort of a man. His feelings, once attached, did not loosen easily, so his ambivalence continued, his remorse and reawakened tenderness went on struggling with the old, bitter resentments.

It was during one of those times when his tender feelings were well in the ascendant and the sense of a crippled life most strongly felt, that he made his decision to seek a reconciliation. If that was impossible, then he would get a divorce. Perhaps one day he might marry again. He did not want to go on indefinitely as he was now.

Of course he had no sooner posted the letter and so made the step irretrievable than he wanted to take it back. He was angry that Jean had not written first. Still he comforted himself that at last the matter would be resolved one way or the other. When the reply came, he did not know whether he was glad or sorry. He only knew that he was not able to face with indifference the thought of their meeting. He would see her and she would speak to him. This last came as an immense relief. Only he knew what her silence had done to him.

It was with this mixture of feelings, tender and resentful, that he got ready to meet Jean at her flat. He had a bath and put on a neat, dark suit. He groomed his hair and polished his shoes. He went on polishing his shoes until they shone. He paid extra attention to everything he did. He was conscious of a need to look his best. He arrived on time. The note on the bell told him to go on up. As he mounted the stairs he recalled that day, now so long ago, when he had gone down those same stairs repeating to himself the words, 'Never again!' The memory was still vivid. He wondered why he had come. He could only think of her as hostile to him.

He halted before the shut door. Its blank face seemed to be saying to him, 'Go away!' He stood hesitant. He did not want to go in. Then, impatient at his own weakness, he gave a sharp rap on the tiny knocker, waited a moment, and turned the knob. He felt the door yield. He pushed it open and went in. He closed it behind him and stood for a second, before, with an effort, he raised his eyes and looked across the room.

Jean was standing by the mantlepiece as if awaiting guests. This impression of waiting came from a certain stillness in her posture. To greet him in this distant manner, rather than close up at the door, was due to her insecurity at meeting him at all. Since there was no escape, except an escape which would leave her always uncertain of her own strength, she had decided to let him come, but to keep a space between them – as wide a space as possible. They stood in silence gazing at each other.

It was the moment each had been secretly dreading. For five years, they had not seen each other. At their time of life, five years was a long span. Each would see a change in the other, but that was not a point which caused either of them any real concern. Their concern was lest they should find themselves capable of meeting with indifference – *that* would be unbearable.

Jean's heart gave a painful thump. Had she but known it, Stephen's heart did the same. He had come exactly on time. This well known trait brought with it a reassuring sense of familiarity. She smiled. 'You're on time,' she said.

'Yes,' he answered. He was moved by the sound of her voice. He came a few paces into the room.

'You look well, Stephen,' she said, not relinquishing her position by the mantlepiece. He did not look thin or worn.

'You look well too, Jean,' he said. She was not thin or pale.

And illogically each felt a grievance against the other.

He added, 'You haven't altered.'

Jean gave another smile. 'I think I have,' she said, with a slight emphasis. She meant it in more ways than her youth.

She motioned him to a chair by the window and sat down herself in a wicker seat close to where she had been standing. There was a space still between them. She had arranged the room that way. A silence ensued during which a current of reawakened emotion stirred in each, reaching out to the other. In both the full glow of youth, its clear brightness, was gone. But to neither did it seem to matter. One question at least had been answered. They might part, but they knew now that neither was capable of indifference at sight of the other.

Like Stephen, Jean had felt the need to look her best. She had put on the dusty pink dress which suited her so well, washed her hair that morning so that it shone, while her hazel eyes were as fine as ever – the antagonism and indifference had gone out of their gaze. This lack of anticipated hostility made Stephen feel at a loss. There was no outward sign of embarrassment either. She was giving him a frank, uninhibited look, as if they had parted friends.

It was not apparent to him that she was meeting her ordeal with high courage. He pulled himself together. He made an effort to think clearly. He had, after all, come for a purpose. He referred to the contents of the letter. He had thought everything over with great care and for a long period before he had come to his decision to seek a reconciliation. He made a point of his not having acted lightly.

'Of course!' she responded gravely. As if he would undertake any action lightly. She saw that he was finding it difficult to continue. He had stuck. She sat quietly, giving him all the time he might need. She was feeling courageous.

'I owe you an apology, Jean,' he started. How formal that sounded. How cold. He wished he had not said it.

At last he came out with, 'I failed you when Robbie died. I ought to have realised that you were suffering. I ought to have comforted you. I did not. I regret that now.' He hesitated, then, with an obvious effort, 'I was cruel to you.'

'Yes!' she agreed quietly. 'You were cruel to me.' He meant at the time of Robbie's death. She meant more than that. She saw him wince at her instant acceptance of his self-criticism. He was feeling his cruelty as a reflection on himself.

She went on, 'I forgive you. I've forgiven you for a long time now. It was only that you didn't understand.'

She had uttered the words that he had wanted to hear – the forgiveness for which he had asked in his letter. Now that he had it, he did not like it. If there was any forgiving to be done then he was the one who should do the forgiving. He made an exception of his conduct towards her at the time of Robbie's death and now he chose to take her forgiveness as applying to that period of their relationship only. The truth was his feelings towards her were too ambivalent for him to accept easily anything she might say.

302

Following this humble admission of his failing, he expected her to respond by a similar admission of her own, but she did not. She had from the start been very cool and detached in her manner – very composed. She had said she forgave him, but without any real warmth in her tone. He found this cool attitude very off-putting. He could not guess at the difference between her behaviour and her feelings. Now she was sitting very quiet, very calm, and he was conscious of a renewed dread of her silences. He would have felt at ease if he could have taken her in his arms, stroked her hair, kissed her cheeks and neck and told her that he still loved her, that the past was the past, that he forgave her everything and that they would start again, but her manner told him that she was not willing for him to do that. He sat uncertain how to proceed.

She broke the silence by enquiring, 'Do you still look on me as not fit to be a mother? As not a normal woman?' He felt himself blushing.

'No! Of course not!' he answered with emphasis. The emphasis was very strong, almost violent. He wished he had sounded less emphatic.

Immediately she asked, 'Why not?' When he did not reply, she added, 'It's a logical question, isn't it?' If he had altered his mind about her there must be a reason.

'It was the shock,' he answered, after a slight pause. He had thought she understood this when she had said she forgave him.

But she was still feeling courageous. 'Didn't you think that of me before the shock?' she asked. She knew that there were times when he had.

In the face of what he felt to be an unjust, unrelenting pressure, he became resentful. This made him burst out with, 'If you had only been prepared to listen! We could have straightened it all out then. We need not have parted.' With sudden self-pity, he added, 'You don't know what it feels like, trying to make some-one you care for understand and they won't listen.'

'Oh!' she said.

He got the point of her exclamation. But what he saw as her unjustified off-hand manner towards him, not any longer hostile, but worse, indifferent and self-righteous, had the effect on him of freeing his suppressed sense of resentment, his sense of undeserved ill-treatment at her hands when he had taken the

303

first step towards a reconciliation. 'I did listen,' he retorted, anger in his tone. 'We often talked about how you were placed.'

'Yes,' she acknowledged. 'We did talk. But you always knew what I *ought* to be feeling. You took that for granted and so you never really listened. You knew how a normal woman would act and feel. That, and not the shock, was why you spoke as you did. The shock merely enabled you to utter what until then you had left unspoken.'

She had pinned him down to the truth. He had indeed seen her behaviour towards himself and their son in just that way. But he was still held back from a frank expression of his resentments by his sense of shame at what he saw as his failure at the time of Robbie's death.

To get it out of the way finally, he said, 'I do know I failed you when you needed me most. I've admitted it, haven't I?' He spoke in a low, humble tone, again confessing his fault and this time hoping for her final absolution. He wanted to forget about it once and for all.

'Oh!' she answered in an abrupt voice. 'I lost hope in you long before that!' Her words were like a hard blow full in the face of his humility. She knew that she was not being fair to him. She was not meeting him half way as he had a right to expect after his confession. She was conscious of offending against her sense of natural justice, which was always keen. He had made the effort, she ought to do the same, but she was faced with the old problem – the problem she had all along dreaded. She did not know what to say that would have real meaning for him. How could she enable him to enter into an experience which looked so very different to those viewing it from the outside? He had not the remotest idea of what she had been through. She needed an image which would correspond exactly to the strength of her feelings during those two and a half years – from the time of Robbie's first birthday until the end. She could not think of any such image. Words, explanations, on their own, were useless.

She saw his face alter at the harshness of her reply, but he would never understand if she syphoned off the harsh truth. She had to save them both from a shallow reconciliation. For she knew exactly what he wanted – he wanted an emotional reunion. He wanted her absolution first – after that he had made up his mind to forgive her. But she was not willing to be forgiven. She clung on hard to her courage.

He said resentfully, 'I never dictated to you– I never tried to exercise any power over you.'

She would not let that pass. 'The power you exercised over me seemed to you *natural*,' she said. 'That's why you never saw it as power.'

She felt that something important had been achieved when his sense of injury, of injustice, broke cover at last. With a sudden fierceness of tone, he exclaimed, 'I did everything for you and Robbie.' And he went through the whole long list of his efforts on their behalf. It made a weighty package. 'You can't deny my care for you both,' he finished.

'I don't deny it,' she answered, glad of his anger and humble in her turn. 'I took all you did for me and Robbie for granted – I should not have done that.' At that moment she realised for the first time exactly how very much she had taken for granted.

He was conscious of a deep sense of relief. He had humbled her. She had at last acknowledged his worth. Now he felt free to ask those questions which had, for so long, lain on him like a physical burden. 'Just what did I do that you should hate me? Do you know, have you any idea, how you looked at me? How you spoke? The tone of your voice? If I'd been the worst criminal on earth you couldn't have looked at me, spoken to me, with more hatred in your eyes, in your voice.' He broke off, waiting for her to answer, but she sat without speaking. It was like her to be silent, he thought bitterly.

'You talk about my cruelty,' he said. 'You can be cruel too.'

'I know! she answered.

'You turned against me long before Robbie's death. You can't deny it! If I touched you, you shrank from me. You didn't want me any more.' He spoke emotionally now, his hurt pride showing clearly. 'Didn't you ever think what it cost me lying beside you, keeping my hands off you, because you couldn't stand my touch?' She was going to speak then, but he rushed on, 'And you treated Robbie harshly. You own son! Not like a mother! Don't you remember how he used to come running to me, crying, "She's nasty! She's nasty!" If I said you were not natural, it was because of that.'

He had hurt her now. Reminded her of what she would have liked to forget, but could not. There was a long pause. At last he had said all that for so many years he had wanted to say. He thought she was going back to one of her inexplicable silences. He was almost on the point of deciding to make a final end, to get up and leave, when, in a tone which it had taken her all those moments to make quiet and controlled, she said, 'I never turned against you! All my pain was because I loved you.' There was a further long pause. Then she went on in the same quiet, controlled tone, 'When I was suffering and you asked me with such scorn whether I expected you to stay at home with the child while I went out to work – after that, I couldn't say anything. You'd silenced me. I felt then that you looked on me as belonging to another species – that what would have been intolerable to you ought to be tolerable to me. After that, I couldn't speak.'

He was listening to her now. She could see him bending the whole force of his intellect to the task of grasping her meaning, but she knew that it was not his intellect that would bring him within hailing distance of her. Only his imagination could do that, but his imagination could not reach her if its path was blocked by false conceptions of how a normal woman ought to act and feel.

She had halted in her explanation, but now it was his turn to remain silent. At last, she continued, 'I did hate you then! I hated you again when you told me I was unnatural – when you put your thoughts into words. After we'd parted I went on hating you for a very long time. I couldn't bear accepting money from you. The day I was able to end that position of dependence, I felt as if a continual pain had suddenly ceased.' She paused for a second, then finished, 'I horrified myself – I wished you so much ill.'

They looked at each other – then they looked away. There was a silence.

Jean went on, 'It was only later, much later, after something had happened to enlighten me, that I realised the truth. I realised that I'd hated you for so long and so much not only, not even mainly, because of your cruel words and behaviour, but because of my own sense of guilt – it was the belief in my own guilt that was tormenting me. That was the reason why I couldn't take up any work that would give me satisfaction – I felt that would be benefiting from Robbie's death. I accepted that I had been an unloving wife, an uncaring mother, selfish, not like other women, unnatural. Once I understood that was not the case, I lost my vindictive feelings towards you – I lost my hatred. I realised that I had judged myself by your standards, through your eyes, allowed myself to believe that your idea of me was the true idea, that I really was as you had said. That was why your words hit me so hard. All my actions after Robbie's death arose out of my own sense of guilt.'

She looked across at him. She said in a gentle voice, 'I don't reproach you. I've no right to blame you – still less, to accuse you. I was just the same! We entered on our life together with such fine ideas, but our feelings were quite different.'

He looked back at her then and for the first time her love for him came through in the expression of her face. He saw it clearly – the old look.

'Don't be sad,' she said. 'It's a very simple mistake. People are making it all the time.'

Her words, but even more her look, encouraged him. 'I love you, Jean!' he said. She felt that he considered this short statement adequate to cover everything – but she was determined, having come so far and at such cost, not to surrender now.

'I love you too,' she responded quietly, 'but love isn't enough! Haven't we proved that? I want you to understand.' She said thoughtfully, 'I think I could have borne even your hating me – at times I think you did hate me a little. What I couldn't bear was your sitting in judgment on me from your privileged position.' She added, 'And it wasn't that I didn't want you any more, but you demanded what I could only give freely. When my feelings became alienated I couldn't reach you any longer. Then you raped me.'

'Are you accusing me of being a rapist?' he asked. She had outraged him now. She shook her head. 'No! Of course not! All I mean is that this is what actually happens when a man becomes alienated from a woman's true feelings.'

'You're very harsh,' he said, with emotion.

'If I speak half truths, you won't understand, dearest,' she answered gently. It was her first endearment.

Then she drew back again. She reminded him of his parting words, 'You've got what you wanted!' and of how those words had stood as an absolute bar in the way of her taking up any work which would give her mental satisfaction.

Other words had stood in her way as well – words not spoken by him. But her courage did not reach to mentioning these. 'Did you wonder about my job?' she asked. He said he had wondered, that this was what had first set him thinking that he might have been at fault in his understanding.

'I know there were times when I was unkind to Robbie,' she

307

said. 'No one could have felt more self-reproachful than I did – but they were few next to the times when I was kind to him. You noticed only when I was unkind. You took the other times for granted – it was natural for a mother to be kind to her child.'

He told her that he had not meant the words on which they had parted, 'You've got what you wanted now!' They had come out of the bitterness of his heart. He had long regretted them.

'But you spoke the truth,' she replied, with firmness. Her courage was still high. She saw that he did not understand.

'There was another part of me that...' she began. And then, suddenly, as if shot, her courage fell right out of the sky and lay on the ground, dead. She could not go on. She could not say to him, 'There was a part of me that was glad when Robbie was dead.' Something of her faltering, her distress, showed on her face.

Anxious to reassure her, he said, 'I understand about the unkindness, dearest.' He felt sufficiently encouraged to use an endearing term himself. 'Mothers often get depressed and shout at their children. When you said once that you wished you had never had him, that was only because you were over-tired. It's my fault that you felt this sense of guilt. Of course you loved our son. You were his mother.'

'His mother!' She repeated the words in a sharpened, edgy tone.

'Yes, of course! His mother!' he repeated after her, as if those two words made any further explanation unnecessary. He added, 'You needed to get out and about more.' He had clearly forgotten how much she had got out and about – how, in order not to seem to be scorning his advice, she had worn herself down getting out and about. She understood that he had solved the problem in his own way – the conventional way.

He saw her distress without remotely guessing its cause. He became even more remorseful, seeking to reassure her about doubts which he considered arose out of his own unfeeling words. He did not ask her about the park. She thought that at any moment he would enquire about her sitting reading while Robbie had drowned, but he did not. He had faded it out of his memory. He wanted her back. She knew that he had done this to ease both their passages.

'You were just a normal mother,' he repeated, with added emphasis on the word normal. In his mind he was turning her into one of those women in a sociological tract – mothers got

308

over-tired, mothers shouted at their children, mothers got depressed, absent-minded, neglected their babies, battered them... Listening to him assuring her that she had been a normal, loving mother, she felt herself being lowered into a huge pit of undifferentiated, loving feelings – a kind of primaeval warm soup, labelled 'Mothers'.

'Actually,' he was going on, 'you were a very normal mother. Even when you were being unkind, underneath you were always a very caring mother.' And she wished that the word mother could be blotted out of the dictionary and never ever be uttered again – the word and all it stood for.

He went on to talk a lot about how he had let her down when she had needed him most. She was afraid of his emphasis on this side of the matter. It was becoming clear to her that he had been made uneasy by this idea of his having failed her, of his having been cruel. Well, it was true, but he had not succeeded in identifying correctly the real nature of either his cruelty or his failure. Instead he was supplying her with an alibi for those times when even he could see that Robbie had not come first.

He told her that he wanted her to come back to him. He spoke with an emotion and passion unusual with him. He said, 'Let's start again!' She wanted to respond to his urging, to answer, Yes, she would come back to him. They would start afresh. Her heart began to beat with a painful longing. While he, on his side, was ready to forgive her everything – for he still thought in terms of forgiveness – and to face the future to-gether, find a way to solace each other for what could not be altered. He was ready to take her in his arms. Had she made a single motion towards him this is what he would have done and the truth would have remained for the rest of their lives a mute-ness between them.

But she took a grip on her courage and made no movement towards him, for she understood that he had made a diversion for himself from the real road of truth. He had not worked things through. He did not want to. He simply wanted her back and to this end he was prepared to forgive what he could not understand. His insight began and ended on this one note – forgiveness. She would not take him back on those terms.

Her mind was clear. She would not surrender now – not now, because of his physical nearness – not after all she had passed through and won for herself. She saw that he was waiting, anxious for her answer, hoping, and she thought how strange it was that now she was the cool, logical one and he was the emotional, unclear one in this duel between them – a duel in which he fought to keep his original idea of her and she fought to give him a new idea.

'You know I've gone back to my old job at the library,' she said, and she went on to tell him of her plans for the future. She finished, 'I'm not the same person. I've changed.' He held so many false ideas blurring her true image.

But he denied the change. 'I do understand the need for you to use your mind,' he said.

She wanted to answer, 'Yes! But you took it for granted that I had made a choice – a choice you were not called upon to make.' He had not allowed for that when he had judged her.

Instead, she said, 'I'd like us to visit Robbie's grave together. I've never been, you know.' The feeling had come suddenly to her that when she stood by Robbie's grave she would not again be able to retreat as she had done earlier that afternoon when her courage had fallen out of the sky. She could not have said why she felt this, but the feeling was very strong that there she would keep her courage. There she would find the way.

He agreed at once. He knew where the grave was in the cemetery. He had been quite a few times since the funeral. She had a vision of him standing by the grave alone and she felt a sharp pang of pity for him. They fixed a date – the next weekend.

After tea, Jean walked with him to the bus stop. 'I won't cross the main road,' she said, 'I'll wait here. A bus should come any minute.'

He did not offer her his hand. He had not walked close to her. He was standing off. He would not put pressure on her. She was grateful to him for that. There was a small park a little way from the cemetery gates, he told her. There was a bench just inside. They could meet there. So it was agreed. She stood on the pavement watching him cross the road and walk the few paces to the bus stop. She had longed to reach out and console him for she had seen in his face that he was leaving her unhappy and doubtful as to her intentions, but she had held her impulse in check. Life had taught her the danger of pity in women. Culture was full of forgiving, self-sacrificing women – women seen through the wish-fulfilling eyes of men. Women moulded by men into the shapes desired by them. She had been taught

310

the hard way that this kind of relationship was not healthy for either the woman or the man – often fatal to both.

Gazing back across the road to where Jean stood, Stephen wanted to feel that what had passed between them that afternoon was a new beginning, but recalling her words, 'I've changed!' and the tone in which she had uttered them, he feared lest it might be the end. Each time the traffic blotted her out from his view, he expected, when the road cleared, to find her missing, but each time she was still there, waiting. The bus came. He looked for the last time across the road and saw her lift a hand in his direction – a gesture of recognition to which he responded with a wave and a kind of hope.

Jean walked slowly away. As she walked, she was thinking, 'Yes! I still love him.' That particular doubt had been finally cleared up. She was conscious of a sense of achievement. It seemed no small thing to have managed that, in spite of so much. He had suffered. You forgave people if they had suffered – but forgiveness and a relationship were two entirely different matters. Forgiveness was only the starting point. Her task stared her dauntingly in the face. If she could tell him that alongside her grief there had existed a not insignificant part of herself that had been glad Robbie was dead. If she could trust him with that truth, trust him not to turn away from it in horror, not to dilute it or explain it away, but to accept it just as she stated it, in its entirety, then, and only then, could she believe him capable of coming sufficiently close to her in understanding for a new relationship to be forged – a true, honest relationship which could survive through the years.

She had little faith in the effect on him of mere words – statements of how she had felt. She needed something beyond that, more vivid, capable of gripping his imagination – an image which would mirror for him the exact extent and power of those needs against which she had fought so hopeless a battle, and which he could accept because it would be within his conditioning.

Her hope of his winning through, in so far as she had any hope, rested entirely on her knowledge of that side of his personality which he himself respected least and found on occasions embarrassing – his ability to be moved and held by strong impressions. This had first brought them together and it had been the cause of his recent unease. There were many men to whom she could have said, 'I hate you!' in that particular way and who would have been capable of shrugging it off. It had not proved so with him. He had shown himself a man imaginatively capable of taking the full force of the hatred directed straight at him in look and in tone. He had tried to get away – oh yes, he had tried! But it had not proved possible. The truth of that lay in his having been there that afternoon.

But she would not offer to him a patterned truth, a truth neatly cut round to fit the socially made garment of his assumptions about her desires and needs as a woman. If he were not to have a true comprehension of her inner needs than the quality of their relationship would always be anaemic, not worth struggling for. The relationship she sought was one in which she would be able to give voice to her authentic feelings without fear of rejection or ridicule. She would settle for nothing less. If she could not have it like that, she would do without.

To help him to it, she needed an image. Was such an image possible? She did not know, but she did know that it would not make its appearance as a result of mental effort. Either it would not surface at all or it would rise spontaneously out of the depths of her feelings – and the odd thought came to her that she would recognise it as surely as a murderer recognises the ghost of his victim.

The day came that she was to meet Stephen inside the park gates, close to the cemetery. Still no image had come to her rescue.

CHAPTER TWENTY-NINE

JEAN had arrived early not because she was impatient, but because she felt a need to sit quietly for a while before what she anticipated as an ordeal. It was not winter and snowing as it had been the first time she had waited for Stephen, but a mild autumn day similar to the one when she had been with Robbie in another park. She could not help remembering.

She sat down on the empty bench just inside the gates. It was a quarter to three. He was not due until on the hour. She gazed about her. The sun was already misting over, the tops of the sycamore trees dissolving into a white haze. The park was

312

small, but managed to contain a sand pit, a children's play-ground with swings and roundabouts and a paddling pool. There were late roses in the rose garden where a few couples were sitting, and blue hydrangeas in the flower bed close to the bench. She wanted to think up an opening sentence for what she needed to say, but the words would not come. At least she succeeded in stilling her emotions. She sat on.

Then she saw him. He was coming through the open gates with his usual purposeful step. Her heart sank a little, but she at once got to her feet to greet him. She gave a cheery smile. Before he could speak, she found herself saying, 'Shall we take a walk before we go in?' adding quickly, 'We could circle the park in ten minutes. It's quite small.' He agreed at once. They started on their tour of the park, walking very slowly. They were to take much longer than ten minutes.

'There aren't any tennis courts,' Stephen commented. 'I think this park is meant mostly for children and the elderly.' They had turned to the right in the direction of the sand pit and the swings, a half-circle would take them back to the entrance.

In the sandpit very young children were playing; women, probably mothers, sitting on benches close by. The sight did not give Jean a happy memory, but with her distress came the voice of the woman at the group, 'The park! Oh, the park!' As they passed, she looked along the row of seated women – knitting, chatting, or simply gazing ahead. Had she really been so odd in what she had felt? She no longer believed so.

They were walking so slowly that they seemed almost to be pacing it out. They passed the groups of children sporting themselves on the swings and roundabouts – Jean recalled that now far-off afternoon when she had thrown snowballs at Stephen while children were enjoying themselves on the climbing frame. They came to the rose garden. She suggested that they sit for a few minutes. On a bench opposite were an elderly couple, on another bench a little way off two middle-aged women, each on her own, a space between.

'I wonder what they're thinking,' Jean commented. Each woman was staring vaguely ahead. It was as if both had become suddenly weary.

'Probably not thinking at all,' Stephen answered, uninterested.

Most of the roses had dried off and hung from limp stems, but there were a few late yellows and one salmon-coloured. There

313

was no particular reason why they should be sitting there in the pleasant, autumn warmth. They had not reached the age when a rest was welcome – but neither of them wished to hurry. Jean had pushed resolutely out of her mind what was soon to come. She wanted the happiness of Stephen's presence beside her to go on for as long as possible – that special kind of happiness which had been absent during the years he had not been with her. She wished she felt otherwise – indifferent, peaceful – but she had not learnt to be honest with herself in order now to deny her true feelings. She was glad to linger in the park before getting up to walk to the cemetery and meet that moment which might part them for ever.

Stephen did not linger because he anticipated any moment of crisis. He was not entirely free from doubt – he had experienced that doubt most strongly at the bus stop, gazing across to where Jean was standing, expecting that at any instant she would turn and be gone – but later, in his own flat, confidence had returned. They would not part after their visit to the cemetery – the visit would be the start of a renewed relationship. Like Jean, he was happy. For a while after their separation, he had wanted only to forget. But time had shown him that on his own he could lead only a crippled life. Without work, his life would lack purpose, lack dignity – without a woman he felt emotionally deprived. Only both could make him a complete human being. He did not say to himself that this was true for all men. He knew only that it was true for himself. He knew also that he could not hope to change himself – in certain ways he was fixed.

Following up the train of his thoughts, he said, 'Tina's a nice child.'

'Very!' Jean answered, surprised. She did not tell Stephen that she scarcely knew Tina, that she had purposely kept away from her. He might think her unnatural towards her own niece. The word 'unnatural' still clung to her memory, if no longer to her image of herself. 'I'm soon to be an aunt,' she told him. He expressed his pleasure. They fell silent again.

Then, out of the blue, as it were, Jean asked, 'Did I bore you sometimes? I mean after Robbie's birth.' She added, 'And later.'

'Of course not!' he retorted. When he spoke in that manner, with a short, sharp emphasis, she always knew that he was lying. He had seen her early on as subject to sudden flowerings;

then, later, she had seemed to become like a plant of a dull green colour, without glint or shading, always the same look. Had he spoken this truth, she would have asked him why he thought she had changed in that particular way, and what he thought had been the quality of their relationship after Robbie's birth, when she was no longer at work – but she could not, because he had lied.

She got to her feet with an abrupt movement. 'Let's go!' she said. He was surprised, but he made no comment. They walked towards the entrance, passing under a short avenue of lime trees, their leaves fading to pale yellows and light greens. At the entrance they stopped to admire the bed of blue hydrangeas which had caught Jean's eye earlier on. She was thinking, 'I shall remember this hour!' She had forgotten that special kind of happiness which comes only when in the presence of someone very close and dear.

The big, iron gates of the cemetery stood wide open revealing a broad gravel path. Compared to the park, the grounds seemed enormous. The grass was cut short, its edges trimmed, the grave stones were all upright with a white, scrubbed look – there were no leaning stones, moss or weeds. Fresh flowers lay on some of the graves, on others withered tokens of affection, yet others were bare. They passed the small chapel where services for the dead were held. They walked on and on. Gravel paths ran in many directions. It was a continent of the dead.

At last they came to Robbie's grave. It was a small grave – a child's grave. It was covered with smooth, short grass, edged with white pebbles. A tablet was set into the grass. Inscribed on it were the dates of Robbie's birth and death, no verse. The stark simplicity made the grave all the more touching – it gave nothing away.

In silence they stood side by side and looked down. A deep sadness came over Jean, but the former anguish was stilled. She hoped it was so with Stephen. She remembered how dear Robbie had been to her, and it was at that moment, standing beside the grave in the silence of the cemetery, Stephen silent beside her, that her hope was at last realised – the image which she had need of, for which she had searched so long in vain, stole up to her quietly, entering her mind without any conscious effort on her part, an image exactly true to her feelings during those two and a half years and of a nature which Stephen's conditioning could find meaningful. It was the image of a second child.

She felt her heart start to pound, but she looked down at the grave and her courage held. She could not look at him, but her voice was steady as she spoke. 'There is something I must say'. She paused. 'Listen!'

He responded to the appeal in her voice. 'I'm listening.'

'At the flat,' she went on, 'I reminded you of the words you spoke when we parted, "You've got what you wanted now". You told me the words had come out of the bitterness of your heart. You regretted them. They were not true.'

'Yes?' he asked enquiringly.

'And I answered, "But you spoke the truth".'

'I remember,' he said, 'I told you it was my fault that you felt so much guilt.'

'But before that,' she said, 'before you said that about guilt... I wanted to go on, complete the sentence... don't you remember? I started to say, "there was another part of me that..." and I stopped. Didn't you wonder why I stopped?'

He shook his head. He was puzzled at her bringing all this up again. He had thought they had dealt with it, got it finally out of the way.

'I lost my courage!' she said. She lifted her face and turned it towards him, for the first time looking into his eyes. There was something very determined in her look. There was no longer hatred there, but still it reminded him – and he was conscious of a moment of unreasoning fear lest she should be about to utter words better left unsaid.

She spoke in a just audible, but distinct tone. 'I want to tell you,' she said, 'that there was a part of me that did want Robbie dead – that was glad when he was dead.'

She saw the look of incredulity on his face. It hastened her words, before he had a chance to speak. 'I had a dream, a nightmare,' she went on in a kind of rushed rapidity. 'There was this voice speaking into my ear, "You're glad he's dead! You know you are! You know you are!" And I kept shouting back, "I'm not! I'm not!". But even while I was shouting, I knew I was glad. I knew I was glad he was dead.'

She stopped speaking. She experienced a sense of immense relief as if a crushing burden had been lifted off her. She had finally done it.

316

He reacted as Mabel had reacted. He said, 'It was the strain, dear. Nothing more! It was the strain.'

She gave a slow shake of her head. 'No! It wasn't the strain. When I woke, I knew the words were the truth. They were how a part of me felt. They were authentic!' She emphasised the final word.

And, like Mabel, he was silent.

She broke the silence with, 'I loved Robbie!' What more was there to say, except those few words.

He spoke then. 'That's logic for you!' His voice was very bitter. Her words had released in him memories he had determined to suppress. 'Was that why you sat reading for two hours?' he enquired, speaking in a distant, cold voice, as if to a stranger.

'No! she answered. Adding, 'I'll try to help you to understand, but you must *listen*.' Then she tried to tell him. First about her love for Robbie – how, for the first year, it had possessed her so that no other side of herself had seemed to exist. Then how gradually with the passing of time the other side of herself had come alive again – like a second birth, a second child – until finally she had seemed to have not one child, but two.

'I knew the second child was a part of me,' she said. 'I could *feel* it.' She hesitated, then went on, 'Try to imagine a mother asked to choose between her two children – one to go on living, the other to die. Try to realise the impossibility of that choice. Try to think of my mental faculties as one of those two children. Like any human child, it needed food to live – not occasional crumbs, but daily feeding. My child was a long time dying. I felt it fading away – but always I was trying to nourish it, trying to give it warmth, trying to keep it alive. And I couldn't! I had nothing on which to nourish it in the way it needed nourishing – consistently, day by day. All I could give it were scraps! I knew it was struggling to live and I knew it was slowly dying. Finally I couldn't bear its struggles any longer. I killed it. I killed it the only way it could be killed – by killing myself. That was when I seemed to you to act so strangely, indifferently. Like the child, I too ceased to exist. In the end I didn't know who I was any more.'

She was silent. He was silent too. In his long silence she felt a kind of hope. Then he spoke. 'You must have known what was involved in caring for a child.'

Like her courage earlier, now it was her hope that fell to the ground. She could not do anything better for him than that image. But she rallied. 'No! she answered him. 'You can't know before you've been through it.' And she saw clearly what his problem was. He had not been through it – he was not expected to go through it.

She felt very calm all of a sudden. She had succeeded in what she had wanted to do. She had given him an image which exactly corresponded to her feelings during those years.

He did not seem to know what else to say. He stood looking ahead, staring in the direction of the distant cemetery gates. Then he looked down again at the grave. 'You couldn't really have been glad he was dead,' he said.

That was not what she had said. She corrected him. 'A part of me was glad.' She would leave it at that. It was the part of her that had been glad her son was dead that he had to accept, not the part that had not. 'I lost myself for a while,' she said. 'I was so absorbed in the baby. The rest of me lay quiet. I forgot it was there. Then it woke up – just like a baby wakes up and demands attention. It started crying. I tried to anaesthetise it, but it wouldn't go to sleep again. It was too strong for me.'

'That afternoon in the park,' she said. 'It took me over.' She added, 'And I forgot. I forgot Robbie. I forgot until it was too late.' Remembering his suffering then, she said, 'I'm sorry!'

She knew that he was facing a problem outside his experience. She tried to introduce a lighter note into the silence.

'Honestly now!' she said, 'weren't you rather bored with me at times? All those magazines! All those cookery books!' When he did not answer, she said that she thought he had been.

This time he did not deny her statement.

'It was hard on you,' she said, 'I know that! But mental faculties aren't a tap to be turned on and off by an act of will. Not with me, anyway – trying exhausted me. I had to turn them off permanently – go dry. That was why I stopped reading – stopped thinking. That was my method of surviving. I failed! All that resulted was that you were bored with me.' Again he did not deny her statement.

She looked down at Robbie's grave. 'I shall always love him,' she said, 'but if it were possible for me to bring him back – bring him back, I mean, at the age he was when he died – and for me to be placed again where I was then – well, I wouldn't do it.'

She had not intended the words. Having uttered them, she

went cold. She must have lost him now. There was a long silence.

At last he spoke, repeating her words, 'You wouldn't do it?' His voice expressed disbelief. She could see by the look on his face, how shocked he was. To him it was a kind of second murder.

'I couldn't!' she said. She added, in a low voice, 'I wouldn't be able to stand it.'

There was another long silence. 'You wouldn't bring him back? Do you mean that?' he persisted. So she had not repented.

She meant him to understand that she thought she had nothing of which to repent.

'I would not,' she answered. She meant to close to him any possible sentimental avenue of escape.

'You've not been listening! I killed my mental abilities. If you kill your mental abilities, you kill yourself. I killed myself – my possibilities. It was a form of suicide – a murder! I had no right to kill myself.' With a quiet emphasis, she repeated the words, *'No right!'* What a journey she had gone to arrive at that simple truth.

Again she looked down at Robbie's grave. It seemed that when either of them was stuck this was the inevitable thing to do. For her it had meant salvation – she had found the courage to tell the whole truth. It was the whole truth that was so difficult to tell. It was easy to tell a maimed truth. If he went on thinking of her as a rejecting mother, she could not help that.

They had been standing by the grave a long while. It was almost dusk. Now that her task was done, she moved away. After a brief glance down at the little grave, he followed her. They walked side by side up the gravel path towards the gates. There was no one about. If mourners had come and gone, they had not noticed them. Now for the first time she put out a hand to take his hand, but he would not. They walked in silence, past the many graves, past the small chapel, towards the cemetery entrance. He did not turn his head to look at her.

Outside the gates, their ways parted. He stood irresolute. It was clear to Jean that he did not know what to say, what to do. What had happened had not been what he expected. He had expected a reconciliation scene.

'Think about it,' she said, as they stood on the pavement outside the gates before she turned from him to the bus stop.

'Don't hurry. There's plenty of time. I can wait. I shan't fall in love again!' Then, with a sudden pleading, 'Try to understand – it's only what you're asking for yourself – not to lead a crippled life!'

Unknowing, she had hit on the one word which was exactly right. He understood what was meant by a crippled life. It stirred in him the sense of a glimmer of light, uncertainly glimpsed, at the far end of a long, dark tunnel. 'I'll try!' he said, in an abrupt tone. 'I'll think about it.' He gave her the only promise which he could give with honesty.

She knew he was very upset. She did not turn at once towards the bus stop as she had intended, but instead she stood and watched him cross the road and walk away from her up the street. She wanted to run after him, to catch up with him, to fling her arms round his neck, to put her face up to his, to kiss him, to tell him that she knew she had shocked him, that she had hurt him, that he was bitterly hurt and disappointed in his hopes, that if he broke down and wept, if she saw him break down and weep, it didn't matter, that with her he was free to show emotion – their chances of understanding would be so much greater. She remembered the time when he had come into the bedroom and taken her red hat down from off the hook and wept over it. The sight of his weeping had seemed to her then unnatural, but now she no longer felt that way. Now it seemed natural to her that men should weep. Tears were not only for women – his tears were held back by that belief. Yet her heart told her that this was not the sole reason for his walking away from her with that cold, proud, distant look which in the past she had dreaded as much as he had dreaded her silence. He was deeply shocked.

He disappeared from sight among a crowd of shoppers. The street was very noisy after the stillness of the cemetery. She turned at last and walked towards her own bus stop. She was resting all her hopes on his ability sometimes, when stirred, to feel outside of what he had been taught to consider sensible and proper – she knew he was not incapable of that. He would certainly find it strange that a woman should feel so strongly about the full use of her mental abilities as to equate the strength of this need with the strength of the need to have a child, but at least it would make sense to him. She had given him a powerful image – his imagination would look at it. There was just a chance that he might come to understand her

320

paralysis when faced with an impossible choice – comprehend what she had meant by being taken over, even why, if it were within her power, she could not resurrect Robbie from the dead. Yet she doubted. For if she had learned one thing above all else during her long journey since their parting, it was that there existed a huge gulf between thoughts and feelings – a gulf so wide that the eye simply passed over it as if it were not there. She recalled the first occasion of their sleeping together and the problem that they had faced then, and how his tender, caring concern and her desire to please him had acted together to overcome an obstacle which had held a threat to their happiness – after which triumph they had neither of them been able to imagine any difficulty beyond their joint power to overcome. They had not been aware then of that other divide which was so much more difficult to avoid – which had set them apart as belonging to two different species.

In the bus, she thought, 'I feel different!' Her body felt lighter, her spirits almost gay. How strange! Then she thought, 'It's because I've won through!'

Her flat seemed silent and empty. She missed Stephen's presence, but she had learned that there was a worse loneliness – it came when two people who cared for each other and were together could not comprehend each other's needs.

She went into the kitchen and put on the kettle. This made her think of Mabel. She smiled. Mabel had once said that tea was the only remedy capable of dealing with all life's problems. She took the tea into the living room and sat down, pouring out a cup. She thought sadly of her mother whom she could not visit. Then she thought how powerless both her mother and Mabel were when it came to the men they lived with. Yet it was not lack of courage that made them put up with so much. What then? She knew the answer now for it had happened to her also. She had allowed Stephen to tell her who she was.

She thought, 'I've got Lydia and Betty – other women I'll meet in the future – but in the end I've got to rely on myself. I've got to respect and to trust myself.' She recalled Lydia's words, 'I need to be independent in the way a man is independent.' The need was the same for both sexes.

That night she found it very difficult to settle to anything. She took up a book and tried to read, but her thoughts kept returning to Stephen. Was he thinking of her? Almost certainly he was. What were his thoughts? Was he trying to bridge that wide gap between the intellect and the emotions? It was asking a great deal of him – was it asking too much? She knew now that emancipation was not just about ideas – it was about changes at the deep level of personality and feelings. Ideas had to be lived – had to be *felt* ideas. She had been lucky. She had been aided by the dream experience. Her intellect alone could never have reached that far. For Stephen there was no such help.

She gave up all effort to read. What a tremendous fight she had put up to save Stephen for herself. She was amazed that he meant that much to her. Yet she knew that she had been right to reject false compromise – the essential thing for them both now was to face their emotions honestly. Her one fatal error had been her attempt at forcing her feelings along a path they could not take. The result had been simply her finishing up by not knowing who on this earth she was.

Because she was determined to be honest she admitted to herself then that even if Stephen proved capable of comprehending and coming close to her, this would not give them a smooth path. Harmony in human relationships did not come from good intentions – Stephen had had plenty of those – it came from justice. She must be strong. Men would never understand if women were weak.

She sat without thinking – it was restful like that. Then her mind switched back to the past. She saw herself sitting at the kitchen table. She saw herself taking a knife and making a small cut across the palm of her left hand. She saw herself looking at the blood – needing the blood to tell her that she existed. 'Who am I?' she had asked, in anguish. She had not been able to answer the question.

Now she knew. She would not risk that knowledge again. She could live with loss – she could not live without herself. She had learnt that the hard way.

She was calm now, aware of an inner strength – a strength she could rely on because it had been born and tested in struggle. Her mind held the one vital fact crystal clear and steady – she must never again allow herself to get into a situation where she woke up in the mornings and did not know who she was. The pain apart, it would mean that she had given up her right to be fully human. She would not a second time surrender that right.

More Sheba fiction

Loneliness and other Lovers, Ann Oosthuizen
Alternative best seller, now reprinted.
This compelling story of an older woman's discovery of feminism blows away the doubts of women who might have heard women's liberation used as a term of abuse. Far from losing her female-ness. Jean explores and enriches her sexuality, her politics and her future options. Discarded by her husband for a younger woman, she moves out of the suffocating security of an oppressive marriage into a fuller, more challenging life.

'The women's movement stands in this novel in the position reserved for the hero in another kind of romance: strong and perfect, but also dangerous and exciting.' *Spare Rib*
'For a woman new to (or nervous of) the implications of feminism it should provide a reassuring and encouraging introduction.' *City Limits*

Second Edition 1982 £2.75 USA $6.95 164 pp 198 × 129 mm

Everyday Matters, New Short Stories by Women
In 1982 Sheba advertised for women to send us short stories for a new collection of women's writing. This book is our selection from those sent to us. The stories describe and dissect our relationships with mothers, lovers, husbands and friends – or with the state itself.

'If the conventional women's magazine stories offer a diet that's oversweet, then this collection provides an antidote that includes a sharp dash of bitters… daily life is closely inspected, turned inside out and well shaken as part of the feminist process of telling the unconventional and often uncomfortable truth.' *Michele Roberts, City Limits*

November 1982 £3.50 USA $7.95 160 pp 198 × 129 mm
ISBN 0 907179 14 2

Come come, Jo Jones
A razor-sharp portrayal of the interactions of friendship between women and lesbian love. This intriguing, tragic, but also humorous first novel shocks us towards new insights into the links between childhood, language and our adult emotions. It is an imaginative, erotic novel; a book you will want to keep – and can't forget.

'Disconcerting, witty, sensitive and crammed with intelligence, *Come Come* is very interesting indeed.' *Hilary Bailey, The Guardian*

October 1983 £3.95 206 pp 198 × 129 mm ISBN 0-907179-17-7

Zami: A New Spelling of My Name, Audre Lorde
'In *Zami* we travel with Audre Lorde, the character and narrator, across many physical and mental landscapes. From the Harlem of her girlhood and excursions across 145th Street to trade comic books, to the Greenwich Village haunts frequented by "gay-girls" in the 1950s; from a hiatus to a Connecticut factory town, where she meets her first woman lover, to a sojourn in Mexico, where she learns to feel visible "among dark people who said *negro* meant something beautiful", and where she discovers more about making love to women than she ever imagined – "passing beyond childhood, a woman connecting with other women in an intricate, complex and ever-widening network of exchanging strengths."' *Lisa Jones, City Limits*

'Like Lorde's poetry, *Zami* is filled with finely distilled reflection, as sage and resonant as ancient wisdom literature.' *Susan McHenry, Ms Magazine*

June 1984 £3.50 264 pp 198 × 129 mm ISBN 0 907179 26 6

Everyday Matters 2, More Short Stories by Women
'This collection of stories by new women writers is a powerful redress to the anodyne (if compelling) magnets of romantic fiction. Here are women from a range of backgrounds, black, Asian, white working class, giving insights into the under-represented aspects of many women's lives. Unrequited love (lesbian), preparation for an arranged marriage, the pain of being on the edge of madness; the forms are varied – third person narrative, stream of consciousness, diaries, letters, first-person narrative... they are all honest, close to the bedrock of an alternative view of personal and emotional life.' *Michelene Wandor, The Listener*

June 1984 £3.50 $7.95 164 pp 198 × 129 mm ISBN 0 907179 21 5

Marge, Kitty Fitzgerald
What is it about the woman who lives opposite her that obsesses Marge? And why does she seek revenge for her own wrecked life? *Marge* is a new thriller form which combines suspense with different insights into the effect on women of family life, psychiatric hospitals, social workers, and loneliness. This is a rare book and a compelling read.

'A tale of obsession and the obsessed, the violated and violating – a psychic thriller fit for our times, all too believable. Kitty Fitzgerald's indignation is muted by compassion and understanding. A serious book.' *Fay Weldon.*

November 1984 £3.75 USA $8.95 152 pp 198 × 129 mm ISBN 0 907179 23 1